A TEST of WILLS

Charles Todd

BANTAM BOOKS

New York Toronto London Sydney Auckland

This edition contains the complete text
of the original hardcover edition.
NOT ONE WORD HAS BEEN OMITTED.

A TEST OF WILLS

A Bantam Book / Published by arrangement with St. Martin's Press.

PUBLISHING HISTORY
St. Martin's Press hardcover edition published 1996
Bantam paperback edition / July 1998

ISBN 0-553-57759-X

Published simultaneously in the United States and Canada

Bantam Books are published by Bantam Books, a division of
Bantam Doubleday Dell Publishing Group, Inc. Its trademark,
consisting of the words "Bantam Books" and the portrayal of
a rooster, is Registered in U.S. Patent and Trademark Office
and in other countries. Marca Registrada. Bantam Books,
1540 Broadway, New York, New York 10036.

PRINTED IN THE UNITED STATES OF AMERICA

OPM   16   15   14   13   12   11   10   9   8   7

A
TEST
of
WILLS

RAVES FOR CHARLES TODD'S
A TEST OF WILLS

"Most 'Golden Age' detective novelists wrote as if the First World War hadn't happened. In *A Test of Wills* Charles Todd gives us a Golden Age crime story in its proper historical setting. This is an intelligent, controlled, and well-organized first novel, rich with promise of a bright future. I look forward to the next."

—Reginald Hill, author of *The Wood Beyond*

"Psychologically sophisticated, tautly written and craftily plotted . . . It should prove a pleasure to follow this series."

—*San Jose Mercury News*

"War-wounded Britain in 1919 is beautifully conveyed in an intricately plotted mystery. With this remarkable debut, Charles Todd breaks new ground in the historical crime novel."

—Peter Lovesey, author of *Bloodhounds*

"Strong, elegant prose; detailed surroundings; and sound plotting characterize this debut. . . . Highly recommended."

—*Library Journal*

"The debut of Charles Todd's Inspector Ian Rutledge is an auspicious one. In a novel full of complex and believable characters, perhaps the most complex of all is the Great War itself, which backlights this mystery with its monumental horrors."

—Gaylord Dold, author of *Schedule Two*

1

In this quiet part of Warwickshire death came as frequently as it did anywhere else in England, no stranger to the inhabitants of towns, villages, or countryside. Sons and fathers had died in the Great War; the terrible influenza epidemic had scythed the county—man, woman, and child—just as it had cut down much of Europe; and murder was not unheard of even here in Upper Streetham.

But one fine June morning, as the early mists rose lazily in the warm sunlight like wraiths in no hurry to be gone, Colonel Harris was killed in cold blood in a meadow fringed with buttercups and cowslips, and his last coherent thought was anger. Savage, wild, black fury ripped through him in one stark instant of realization before oblivion swept it all away, and his body, rigid with it, survived the shotgun blast long enough to dig spurs into the mare's flanks while his hands clenched the reins in a muscular spasm as strong as iron.

He died hard, unwilling, railing at God, and his ragged cry raised echoes in the quiet woods and sent the rooks flying even as the gun roared.

•   •   •

In London, where rain dripped from eaves and ran black in the gutters, a man named Bowles, who had never heard of Colonel Harris, came into possession of a piece of information that was the reward of very determined and quite secret probing into the history of a fellow policeman at Scotland Yard.

He sat at his desk in the grim old brick building and stared at the letter on his blotter. It was written on cheap stationery in heavy ink by a rounded, rather childish hand, but he was almost afraid to touch it. Its value to him was beyond price, and if he had begged whatever gods he believed in to give him the kind of weapon he craved, they couldn't have managed anything sweeter than this.

He smiled, delight spreading slowly across his fair-skinned face and narrowing the hard, amber-colored eyes.

If this was true—and he had every reason to believe it was—he had been absolutely right about Ian Rutledge. He, Bowles, was vindicated by six lines of unwittingly damaging girlish scrawl.

Reading the letter for the last time, he refolded it carefully and replaced it in its envelope, locking it in his desk drawer.

Now the question was how best to make use of this bit of knowledge without burning himself in the fire he wanted to raise.

If only those same gods had thought to provide a *way* . . .

But it seemed, after all, that they had.

Twenty-four hours later, the request for assistance arrived from Warwickshire, and Superintendent Bowles happened, by the merest chance, to be in the right place at the right time to make a simple, apparently constructive suggestion. The gods had been very generous indeed. Bowles was immensely grateful.

The request for Scotland Yard's help had arrived through the proper channels, couched in the usual terms. What lay behind the formal wording was sheer panic.

The local police force, stunned by Colonel Harris's vicious murder, had done their best to conduct the investigation quickly and efficiently. But when the statement of one particular witness was taken down and Inspector Forrest understood just where it was going to lead him, the Upper Streetham Constabulary collectively got cold feet.

At a circumspect conference with higher county authority, it was prudently decided to let Scotland Yard handle this situation—and to stay out of the Yard's way as much as humanly possible. Here was one occasion when metropolitan interference in local police affairs was heartily welcomed. With undisguised relief, Inspector Forrest forwarded his request to London.

The Yard in its turn faced a serious dilemma. Willy-nilly, they were saddled with a case where discretion, background, and experience were essential. At the same time, it was going to be a nasty one either way you looked at it, and someone's head was bound to roll. Therefore the man sent to Warwickshire must be considered expendable, however good he might be at his job.

And that was when Bowles had made his timely comments.

Inspector Rutledge had just returned to the Yard after covering himself with mud and glory in the trenches of France. Surely choosing him would be popular in Warwickshire, under the circumstances—

showed a certain sensitivity for county feelings, as it were. . . . As for experience, he'd handled a number of serious cases before the war, he'd left a brilliant record behind him, in fact. The word *scapegoat* wasn't mentioned, but Bowles delicately pointed out that it might be less disruptive to morale to lose—if indeed it should come to that—a man who'd just rejoined the force. Please God, of course, such a sacrifice wouldn't be *required*!

A half-hearted quibble was raised about Rutledge's state of health. Bowles brushed that aside. The doctors had pronounced him fit to resume his duties, hadn't they? And although he was still drawn and thin, he appeared to be much the same man who had left in 1914. Older and quieter naturally, but that was to be expected. A pity about the war. It had changed so many lives. . . .

The recommendation was approved, and an elated Bowles was sent to brief Rutledge. After tracking the Inspector to the small, drafty cubicle where he was reading through a stack of reports on current cases, Bowles stood in the passage for several minutes, steadying his breathing, willing himself to composure. Then he opened the door and walked in. The man behind the desk looked up, a smile transforming his thin, pale face, bringing life to the tired eyes.

"The war hasn't improved human nature, has it?" He flicked a finger across the open file on his blotter and added, "That's the fifth knifing in a pub brawl I've read this morning. But it seems the Army did manage to teach us something—exactly where to place the blade in the ribs for best results. None of the five survived. If we'd done as well in France, bayoneting Germans, we'd have been home by 1916."

His voice was pleasant, well modulated. It was

one of the things that Bowles, with his high-pitched, North Country accent, disliked most about the man. And the fact that his father had been a barrister, not a poor miner. Schooling had come easily to Rutledge. He hadn't had to plod, dragging each bit of knowledge into his brain by sheer effort of will, dreading examinations, knowing himself a mediocrity. It rubbed a man's pride to the bone to struggle so hard where others soared on the worldly coattails of London-bred fathers and grandfathers. Blood told. It always had. Bowles passionately resented it. If there'd been any justice, a German bayonet would have finished this soldier along with the rest of them!

"Yes, well, you can put those away, Michaelson's got something for you," Bowles announced, busily framing sentences in his mind that would convey the bare facts and leave out the nuances that might put Rutledge on his guard, or give him an opening to refuse to go to Warwickshire. "First month back, and you've landed this one. You'll have your picture in the bloody papers before it's done, mark my words." He sat down and began affably to outline the situation.

Rutledge left the outskirts of London behind and headed northwest. It was a dreary morning, rain sweeping in gusts across the windscreen from a morbidly gray sky draped like a dirty curtain from horizon to horizon, the tires throwing up rivers of water on either side of the car like black wings.

Hellish weather for June.

I should have taken the train, he thought as he settled down to a steady pace. But he knew he couldn't face the train yet. It was one thing to be shut up in a motorcar that you could stop at will and another to be enclosed in a train over which you had no control at all. Jammed in with a half dozen other people. The doors closed for hours on end, the compartment airless and overheated. The press of bodies crowding him, driving him to the brink of panic, voices dinning in his ears, the roar of the wheels like the sound of his own blood pounding through his heart. Just thinking about it sent a wave of terror through him.

Claustrophobia, the doctors had called it, a natural fear in a man who'd been buried alive in a frontline trench, suffocated by the clinging, slippery, unspeakable mud and the stinking corpses pinning him there.

Too soon, his sister Frances had said. It was much too soon to go back to work! But he knew that if he didn't, he'd lose what was left of his mind. Distraction was what he needed. And this murder in Warwickshire appeared to offer just that. He'd need his wits about him, he'd have to concentrate to recover the long forgotten skills he'd had to put behind him in 1914—and that would keep Hamish at bay.

"You're to turn right here."

The voice in his head was as clear as the patter of rain on the car's roof, a deep voice, with soft Scottish inflections. He was used to hearing it now. The doctors had told him that would happen, that it was not uncommon for the mind to accept something which it had created itself in order to conceal what it couldn't face any other way. Shell shock was an odd thing, it made its own rules, they'd said. Understand that and you could manage to keep your grip on reality. Fight it, and it would tear you apart. But he *had* fought it for a very long time—and they were right, it had nearly destroyed him.

He made the turn, glancing at the signs. Yes. The road to Banbury.

And Hamish, strangely enough, was a safer companion than Jean, who haunted him in another way. In God's blessed name, how did you uproot love? How did you tear it out of your flesh and bone?

He'd learned, in France, to face dying. He could learn, in time, how to face living. It was just getting through the desolation in between that seemed to be beyond him. Frances had shrugged her slim shoulders and said, "Darling, there are other women, in a year you'll wonder why you cared so much for *one*. Let go gracefully—after all, it isn't as if she's fallen in love with another man!"

He swerved to miss a dray pulling out into the road without warning from a muddy lane running between long, wet fields.

"Keep your mind on the driving, man, or we'll both be dead!"

"Sometimes I believe we'd both be better off," he answered aloud, not wanting to think about Jean, not able to think about anything else. Everywhere he turned, something brought her back to him, ten thousand memories waiting like enemies to ambush him. The car . . . the rain . . . She'd liked driving in the rain, the glass clouded with their warm breath, their laughter mingling with the swish of the tires, the car a private, intimate world of their own.

"Ah, but that's the coward's road, death is! You willna' escape so easily as that. You've got a *conscience*, man. It won't let you run out. And neither will I."

Rutledge laughed harshly. "The day may come when you have no choice." He kept his eyes pinned to the road, as always refusing to look over his shoulder, though the voice seemed to come from the rear seat, just behind him, almost near enough to touch him with its breath. The temptation to turn around was strong, nearly as strong as the desperate fear of what he might see if he did. He could, he had found, live with Hamish's voice. What he dreaded—dreaded more than anything—was seeing Hamish's face. And one day—one day he might. Hollow-eyed, empty of humanity in death. Or accusing, pleading in life—

Rutledge shuddered and forced his mind back to the road ahead. The day he saw Hamish, he'd end it. He had promised himself that. . . .

It was very late when he reached Upper Streetham, the rain still blowing in gusty showers, the streets of the town empty and silent and shiny with puddles as he made his way to the Inn on the High Street.

"Highland towns are like this on Saturday nights," Hamish said suddenly. "All the good Presbyterians asleep in their beds, mindful of the Sabbath on the morrow. And the Catholics back from Confession and feeling virtuous. Are you mindful of the state of your soul?"

"I haven't got one," Rutledge answered tiredly. "You tell me that often enough. I expect it's true." The black-and-white facade he was looking for loomed ahead, ghostly in another squall of rain, a rambling, ancient structure with a thatched roof that seemed to frown disparagingly over the faded inn sign swinging from its wrought-iron bar. The Shepherd's Crook, it read.

He turned in through a wisteria-hung arch, drove past the building into the Inn yard, and pulled the motorcar into an empty space between a small, barred shed and the Inn's rear door. Beyond the shed was what appeared in his headlamps to be a square lake with pagodas and islands just showing above the black water. No doubt the kitchen garden, with its early onions and cabbages.

Someone had heard him coming into the drive and was watching him from the back steps, a candle in his hand.

"Inspector Rutledge?" the man called.

"Yes, I'm Rutledge."

"I'm Barton Redfern, the landlord's nephew. He asked me to wait up for you." Rain swept through the yard again as he spoke, and he hastily stepped back inside, waiting to hold the door open as Rutledge dashed through the puddles, his bag in one hand, the other holding on to his hat. A minor tempest followed him across the threshold.

"My uncle said you were to have the room over the parlor, where it's quieter at night. It's this way. Would you like a cup of tea or something from the bar? You look like you could use a drink!"

"No, thanks." There was whiskey in his bag if he wanted it—if exhaustion wasn't enough. "What I need is sleep. It rained all the way, heavy at times. I had to stop beyond Stratford for an hour until the worst had passed. Any messages?"

"Just that Inspector Forrest will see you at breakfast, if you like. At nine?"

"Better make it eight."

They were climbing a flight of narrow, winding stairs, the back way to the second floor. Barton, who looked to be in his early twenties, was limping heavily. Turning to say something over his shoulder, he caught Rutledge's glance at his left foot and said instead, "Ypres, a shell fragment. The doctors say it'll be fine once the muscles have knit themselves back properly. But I don't know. They aren't always as smart as they think they are, doctors."

"No," Rutledge agreed bitterly. "They just do the best they can. And sometimes that isn't much."

Redfern led the way down a dark hall and opened the door to a wide, well-aired room under the eaves, with a lamp burning by the bed and brightly flowered curtains at the windows. Relieved not to find himself in a cramped, narrow chamber where sleep would be nearly impossible, Rutledge nodded his thanks and Redfern shut the door as he left, saying, "Eight it is, then. I'll see that you're called half an hour before."

Fifteen minutes later Rutledge was in the bed and asleep.

He never feared sleep. It was the one place where Hamish could not follow him.

Sergeant Davies was middle-aged, heavyset, with a placidity about him that spoke of even temper, a man at peace within himself. But there were signs of strain in his face also, as if he had been on edge for the past several days. He sat foursquare at Rutledge's table in the middle of the Inn's small, cheerful dining room, watching as Redfern poured a cup of black coffee for him and explaining why he was there in place of his superior.

"By rights, Inspector Forrest should be answering your questions, but he won't be back much before ten. There's been a runaway lorry in Lower Streetham and the driver was drunk. Two people were killed. A nasty business. So's this a nasty business. Colonel Harris was well respected, not the sort you'd expect to get himself murdered." He sighed. "A sorry death for a man who went through two wars unscathed. But London will have gone over that."

Rutledge had spread homemade jam on his toast. It was wild strawberry and looked as if it had been put up before the war, nearly as dark and thick as treacle. Poised to take a bite, he looked across at the Sergeant. "I'm not in London now. I'm here. Tell me how it happened."

Davies settled back in his chair, frowning as he marshaled his facts. Inspector Forrest had been very particular about how any account of events was to be given. The Sergeant was a man who took pride in being completely reliable.

"A shotgun. Blew his head to bits—from the chin up, just tatters. He'd gone out for his morning ride at seven sharp, just as he always did whenever he was at home, back by eight-thirty, breakfast waiting for him. That was every day except Sunday, rain or shine. But on Monday, when he wasn't back by ten, his man of business, Mr. Royston, went looking for him in the stables."

"Why?" Rutledge had taken out a pen and a small, finely tooled leather notebook. "On this day, particularly?"

"There was a meeting set for nine-thirty, and it wasn't like the Colonel to forget about it. When he got to the stables, Mr. Royston found the grooms in a blue panic because the Colonel's horse had just come galloping in without its rider, and there was blood all over the saddle and the horse's haunches. Men were sent out straightaway to look for him, and he was finally discovered in a meadow alongside the copse of trees at the top of his property."

Davies paused as the swift pen raced across the ruled page, allowing Rutledge a moment to catch up before continuing. "Mr. Royston sent for Inspector Forrest first thing, but he'd gone looking for the Barlowe child, who'd gotten herself lost. By the time I got the message and reached the scene, the ground was well trampled by stable lads and farmhands, all come to stare. So we aren't sure he was shot *just* there. But it couldn't have happened more than a matter of yards from where we found him."

"And no indication of who might have done it?"

The Sergeant shifted uneasily in his chair, his eyes straying to the squares of pale sunlight that dappled the polished floor as the last of the rain clouds thinned. "As to that, you must know that Captain Wilton—that's the Captain Mark Wilton who won the VC—quarreled with the Colonel the night before, shortly after dinner. He's to marry the Colonel's ward, you see, and some sort of misunderstanding arose over the wedding, or so the servants claim. In the middle of the quarrel, the Captain stalked out of the house in a temper, and was heard to say he'd see the Colonel in hell, first. The Colonel threw his brandy glass at the door just as the Captain slammed it, and shouted that that could be arranged."

This was certainly a more colorful version of the bald facts that Rutledge had been given in London. Breakfast forgotten, he continued to write, his mind leaping ahead of Davies' steady voice. "What does the ward have to say?"

"Miss Wood's in her room, under the doctor's care, seeing no one. Not even her fiancé. The Captain is staying with Mrs. Davenant. She's a second cousin on his mother's side. Inspector Forrest tried to question *him*, and he said he wasn't one to go around shooting people, no matter what he might have done in the war."

Rutledge put down his pen and finished his toast, then reached for his teacup. He didn't have to ask what the Captain had done in the war. His photograph had been in all the papers when he was decorated by the King—the Captain had not managed to bring down the Red Baron, but he seemed to have shot down every other German pilot whose path he had crossed in the skies above France. Rutledge had watched a vicious dogfight high in the clouds above his trench one July afternoon and had been told later who the English pilot was. If it was true, then Wilton was nothing short of a gifted flier.

Colonel Harris had been a relatively young man for his rank, serving in the Boer War as well as the Great War and making a name for himself as a skilled infantry tactician. Rutledge had actually met him once—a tall, vigorous, compassionate officer who had known how to handle tired, frightened men asked once too often to do the impossible.

Without warning, Hamish laughed harshly. "Aye, he knew how to stir men. There were those of us who'd have blown his head off there and then if we'd had the chance, after that third assault. It was suicide, and he knew it, and he sent us anyway. I can't say I'm sorry he's got his. Late is better than never."

Rutledge choked as his tea went down the wrong way. He knew—dear God, he knew!—that Hamish couldn't be heard by anyone else, and yet sometimes the voice was so clear he expected everyone around him to be staring at him in shock.

He waved Davies back to his chair as the Sergeant made to rise and slap him on his back. Still coughing, he managed to ask, "That's all you've done?"

"Yes, sir, then we were told to leave everything for the Yard and so we did just that."

"What about the shotgun? Have you at least checked on that?"

"The Captain says he used the weapons at the Colonel's house, if he wanted to go shooting. But none of them has been fired recently. We asked Mrs. Davenant if she had any guns, and she said she sold her late husband's Italian shotguns before the war." The Sergeant glanced over his shoulder, and Barton Redfern came across the parlor to refill his cup. When the young man had limped away again, the Sergeant added tentatively, "Because of that quarrel, of course, it *looks* as if the Captain might be the guilty party, but I've learned in this business that looks are deceiving."

Rutledge nodded. "And the murder was three days ago. After last night's rain, there'll be nothing to find in the meadow or anywhere else along the route the Colonel might have taken on his ride. Right, then, do you have a list of people to talk to? Besides the ward—Miss Wood—and Wilton. And this Mrs. Davenant."

"As to that, there aren't all that many. The servants and the lads who found the body. Laurence Royston. Miss Tarrant, of course—she was the lady that Captain Wilton had courted before the war, but she turned him down then and doesn't seem to mind that he's marrying Miss Wood now. Still, you never know, do you? She might be willing to throw a little light on how the two men got on together. And there's Mr. Haldane—he's the Squire's son. He was one of Miss Wood's suitors, as was the Vicar."

Davies grinned suddenly, a wholly unprofessional glint in his eyes. "Some say Mr. Carfield took holy orders because he saw the war coming, but actually had his heart set on the theater. He does preach a better sermon than old Reverend Mott did, I'll say that for him. We all learned more about the Apostle Paul under Mr. Mott than any of us ever cared to know, and I must admit Mr. Carfield's a welcomed change!" He recollected himself and went on more soberly, "The two Sommers ladies are new to the district and don't go about much. I doubt if they'd be helpful, except that they live near where the body was found and might have seen or heard something of use to us."

Rutledge nodded as Redfern returned with a fresh pot of tea, waiting until his cup had been filled before he commented, "Miss Wood seems to have been very popular."

"She's a very—attractive—young lady," Davies answered, hesitating over the word as if not certain that it was appropriate. "Then of course there's Mavers. He's a local man, a rabble-rouser by nature, always putting his nose in where it doesn't belong, stirring things up, making trouble for the sake of trouble. If anything untoward happens in Upper Streetham, the first person you think of is Mavers."

"That's not a likely motive for shooting Harris, in itself."

"In Mavers's case, it is. He's been annoying the Colonel since long before the war, nothing we've ever been able to *prove*, you understand, but there've been fires and dead livestock and the like, vindictive acts all of them. The last time, when one of the dogs was poisoned, the Colonel threatened to have Mavers committed if it happened again. He's got a very sound alibi—Inspector Forrest talked to him straightaway. All the same, I'd not put murder past him."

Rutledge heard the hope in Davies' voice, but said only, "I'll keep that in mind. All right, then, if that's the lot, we'll start with Miss Wood. She may be able to give us a better picture of this quarrel, what it was about and whether it might have had anything to do with her guardian's death. I'll want you there. Inspector Forrest can spare you?" He capped his pen, stowed the notebook in his pocket, and reached for his cup.

Davies looked stunned. "You didn't bring a Sergeant with you, then?"

"We're shorthanded at the Yard at the moment. You'll do."

"But—," Davies began, panic sweeping through him. Then he thought better of what he had been on the verge of saying. The man to speak to was Forrest, not this gaunt-faced stranger from London with his clipped voice and bleak eyes.

Then he bethought himself of the one fact he'd avoided so far, the one bit of evidence no one wanted to accept. He had been told to wait until Rutledge brought it up, but the man hadn't mentioned it. Because he discounted it? That would be too much to hope for! More than likely, the Inspector intended to rub the Sergeant's nose in it, now that he had his chance. But Davies knew it had to be dragged into the open, like it or not. You couldn't just ignore it, pretend it didn't exist—

He cleared his throat. "There's more, sir, though I don't know what it's worth. Surely they told you in London?" Staring at Rutledge, waiting for some indication that the man *knew*, that he didn't need to go into embarrassing detail, Sergeant Davies read only impatience in the face before him as the Inspector folded his napkin and laid it neatly beside his plate.

"A possible witness, sir. He claims he saw the Colonel on Monday morning." No, the man didn't know; it was hard to believe, but for some reason he hadn't been told! Davies hurried on. "In the lane that cuts between Seven Brothers Field and the orchard. And he saw Captain Wilton standing there beside the horse, holding on to the bridle and talking to the Colonel, who was shaking his head as if he didn't like what he was hearing. This must have been about seven-thirty, maybe even a quarter to eight. Then the Captain suddenly stepped back, his face very red, and the Colonel rode off, leaving the Captain standing there with his fists clenched."

Rutledge silently cursed London for ineptitude. He pulled out his notebook again and asked curtly, "How far is this place from where the Colonel was found dead? And why didn't you mention this witness sooner?"

The Sergeant's face flushed. "As to how far, sir, it's at *most* two miles east of the meadow," he answered stiffly. "And I was sure they'd have told you in London— You see, the problem is that the witness is unreliable, sir. He was drunk. He often is, these days."

"Even an habitual drunk has been known to tell the truth." Rutledge added another line, then looked up. "We can't discount what he says on those grounds alone."

"No, sir. But there's more, you see. He's—well, he's *shell-shocked*, sir, doesn't know where he is half the time, thinks he's still at the Front, hears voices, that kind of thing. Lost his nerve on the Somme and went to pieces. Lack of moral fiber, that's what it was. It seems a shame for a fine man like the Captain to be under suspicion of murder on the evidence of an acknowledged coward like Daniel Hickam, doesn't it? It isn't right, sir, is it?"

But London had said nothing—*Bowles* had said nothing.

In the far corners of his mind, behind the spinning turmoil of his own thoughts, Rutledge could hear the wild, derisive echoes of Hamish's laughter.

2

$\mathcal{M}$isunderstanding the horrified expression on Rutledge's face, Sergeant Davies nodded sympathetically. "Aye," he said, "it's hard to swallow, I know. You were in the war, then? My youngest brother was in the Balkans, lost both arms. Took it like a man. Not a shred of weakness in Tommy!"

He began to fiddle with his cup as he went on, as if to distract himself from the rest of what he had to say. "Of course we didn't know about Hickam at first, I just came across him that same morning, lying under a tree on the lane, sleeping one off. When I tried to wake him up and send him off home, he swore he was sober as a judge, and told me I could ask the Colonel and the Captain, they'd vouch for him. I thought he meant *generally*, you see."

The cup spun out of his fingers, clattering against the sugar bowl and almost tipping over the cream pitcher. Davies caught it, returned it to his saucer, then plowed on, trying to conceal the sense of guilt that was still plaguing him. "I didn't pay any heed to him at first, I was in a hurry to find

Inspector Forrest and tell him about the murder, but Hickam's place was on my way back to Upper Streetham and he was in no shape to get there on his own. By the time I'd reached his house, listening to him ramble all the way, it was beginning to sound a bit different from what I'd first thought. So Inspector Forrest went to talk to him that afternoon and got a little straighter version, and we couldn't just shrug it off, could we? Right or wrong, we had to take note of it, didn't we?"

It was an appeal for forgiveness, an admission of responsibility for what had plunged Warwickshire and London into this present predicament. If he'd left well enough alone, if he hadn't bothered to stop in the first place, no one would ever have thought to question the likes of Hickam about the Colonel or the Captain. There would have been no reason, no need.

Rutledge, still fighting his own battle for control, managed to keep his voice level, but the words came out harsh and cold, apparently without any sympathy for the Sergeant's moral dilemma. "What did Captain Wilton have to say about Hickam's story?"

"Well, nothing. That is, he says he wasn't in the lane that morning, he was walking in a different direction. He says he's seen Hickam from time to time in the mornings, reeling home or sleeping wherever he was or having one of his crazy spells, but not on that occasion."

"Which doesn't mean that Hickam didn't see *him*."

Sergeant Davies was appalled. "You're saying the *Captain's* lying, sir?"

"People do lie, Sergeant, even those who have earned the Victoria Cross. Besides, Hickam's description of what he saw is strangely complete, isn't it? The Captain holding the Colonel's bridle, the Captain's face turning red, the Captain stepping back with clenched fists. If it *didn't* happen that morning, if Hickam saw the two men together on another occasion, it could mean that their quarrel on the night before the murder had its roots in an earlier confrontation. That there was more animosity between the Colonel and his ward's fiancé than we know at this point."

Sergeant Davies was dubious. "Even so, Hickam might have misread what he saw, there might have been a perfectly reasonable explanation. What if the two men were in agreement instead of quarreling? What if they'd been angry at someone else, or about something that neither of them liked?"

"Then why would Wilton deny that he'd met Harris in the lane? If this encounter did have some perfectly innocent explanation? No, I think you're on the wrong track there."

"Well, what if Hickam confused what he saw with something that happened at the Front? He doesn't like officers—he might even have made mischief on *purpose*. You can't be really sure, can you? Hickam might be capable of anything!" The disgust in Davies' face was almost a tangible thing.

"I can't answer that until I've spoken to Hickam and the Captain." Hamish's laughter had faded, he was able to think clearly again. But his heart was still pounding hard with the shock.

"Shall we start with them, then? Instead of Miss Wood?"

"No, I want to see the Colonel's house and his ward first." The truth was, he wasn't prepared to face Hickam now. Not until he was certain he could do it without betraying himself.

Had anyone guessed in London? No, surely not! It was sheer coincidence, there were any number of shell-shocked veterans scattered across England. . . . Rutledge got to his feet. "My car is in the back. I'll meet you there in five minutes." He nodded to Barton Redfern as he walked out of the dining room, and the young man watched the two police-men until they were out of sight, then listened to Rutledge's feet beating a quick tattoo up the car-peted stairs while the Sergeant's heavy leather heels clicked steadily down the stone passage leading to the Inn yard.

Upstairs in his room, Rutledge stood with his hands flat on the low windowsill, leaning on them and looking down into the busy street below. He was still shaken. Only a half dozen people knew about his condition, and the doctors had promised to say nothing to the Yard, to give him a year to put his life back together first. The question was, had Bowles kept silent about Hickam because he hadn't thought it was something that mattered? Or because he had known it was and might embarrass Rutledge?

No, that was impossible. It had been an over-sight—or at most, Bowles had tried to make this murder investigation sound more attractive than it was. A kindness . . . ? He remembered Bowles from before the war, good at his job, with a reputa-tion for ruthless ambition and a cold detachment. Sergeant Fletcher, who'd died in the first gas attack on Ypres, used to claim that Bowles frightened the guilty into confessing.

"I've seen 'em! Shaking in their boots and more afraid of old Bowels than they were of the hang-man! Nasty piece of work, I've never liked dealing with him. Mind you, he did his job fair and square,

I'm not saying he didn't. But he wasn't above using any tool that came to hand. . . ."

Not kindness, then, not from a man like Bowles.

Still, what London had done didn't matter now.

Because here in his own room, away from Davies' watchful eyes and Redfern's hovering, Rutledge was able to think more clearly and recognize a very tricky problem. What if Hickam turned out to be right?

If it should come to an arrest—so far there was not enough evidence to look that far ahead, but assuming there was—how could the Crown go into a court of law with a Daniel Hickam as its prime witness against a man wearing the ribbon of the Victoria Cross? It would be ludicrous, the defense would tear the case to shreds. Warwickshire would be screaming for the Yard's blood, and the Yard for his.

He had wanted an investigation complex enough to distract him from his own dilemmas. Well, now he seemed to have got his wish in spades. The question remained, was he ready for it? Were his skills too rusty to handle something as difficult as the Harris murder successfully? Worse still, was he too personally involved? If so, he should back out now. This instant. Call the Yard and ask for a replacement to be sent at once.

But that would require explanations, excuses—lies. Or the truth.

He straightened, turned from the window, and reached for his coat. If he quit now, he was finished. Professionally and emotionally. It wasn't a question of choice but of survival. He would do his best, it was all anyone could do, and if in the days to come that wasn't enough, he must find the courage to admit it. Until then he was going to have to learn exactly where he stood, what he was made of.

The words *coward* and *weakling* had stung. But what rankled in his soul was that he had said nothing, not one single word, in Hickam's defense. In betraying Hickam, he felt he had betrayed himself.

Rutledge and Sergeant Davies arrived at Mallows, the Colonel's well-run estate on the Warwick road, half an hour later. The sky had cleared to a cerulean blue, the air clean and sweet with spring as the car turned in through the iron gates and went up the drive.

Completely hidden from the main road by banks of old trees, the house didn't emerge until they rounded the second bend and came out of the shadows into the sun. Then mellowed brick and tall windows, warmed to gold, reflected the early morning light. Setting them off was a wide sweep of lawn mown to crisp perfection, the flower beds sharply edged and the drive smoothly raked. One glance and you could tell that not only had pride gone into the upkeep of this house, but unabashed love as well.

To Rutledge's appreciative eye, a master's hand had created this marvelously graceful facade. For the stone cornices, quoins, and moldings around the windows enhanced rather than overwhelmed the effect of elegant simplicity that the designer had been striving for. He found himself wondering who the architect had been, for this was a small jewel. Where had such a gift taken the man after this?

But Davies couldn't say. "The Colonel, now, he would have told you, and if he wasn't too busy, he'd have taken out the old plans for you to see.

That was the kind of man he was, never a stickler for rank. He knew his place, and trusted you to know yours."

As Rutledge got out of the car, he found himself looking up at the windows above. One of the heavy drapes had twitched, he thought, the slight movement catching the corner of his eye. In France, where life itself depended on quick reflexes, you learned to see your enemy first or you died. It was as simple as that.

The staff had already placed a heavy black wreath on the broad wooden door, its streamers lifting gently in the light breeze. A butler answered the bell. He was a thin man of middle height, fifty-five or thereabouts, his face heavy with grief as if he mourned the Colonel personally. He informed Rutledge and Sergeant Davies in tones of polished regret that Miss Wood was not receiving anyone today.

Rutledge said only, "What is your name?"

"Johnston, sir." The words were polite, distant.

"You may tell your mistress, Johnston, that Inspector Rutledge is here on police business. You know Sergeant Davies, I think."

"Miss Wood is still unwell, Inspector." He cast an accusing glance at Davies, as if blaming him for Rutledge's ill-mannered persistence. "Her doctor has already informed Inspector Forrest—"

"Yes, I understand. We won't disturb her any longer than absolutely necessary." The voice was firm, that of an army officer giving instructions, brooking no further opposition. Certainly not the voice of a lowly policeman begging entrance.

"I'll enquire," the man replied, with a resignation that clearly indicated both personal and professional disapproval but just as clearly made no promises.

He left them standing in the hall before a handsome staircase that divided at the first-floor landing and continued upward in two graceful arcs. These met again on the second story, above the doorway, to form an oval frame for a ceiling painting of nymphs and clouds, with a Venus of great beauty in the center. From the hall she seemed to float in cloud-cushioned luxury, far beyond the reach of mere mortals, staring down at them with a smile that was as tantalizing as it was smug.

Johnston was gone for nearly fifteen minutes.

Hamish, growing restive as the tension of waiting mounted, said, "I've never been inside a house like this. Look at the floor, man, it's squares of marble, enough to pave the streets in my village. And that stair—what holds it up, then? It's a marvel! And worth a murder or two."

Rutledge ignored him and the uncomfortable stiffness of Sergeant Davies, who seemed to grow more wooden with every passing minute. The butler returned eventually and said with ill-concealed censure, "Miss Wood will receive you in her sitting room, but she asks that you will make your call brief."

He led the way up the staircase to the first floor and then turned left down a wide, carpeted corridor to a door near the end of it. The room beyond was quite spacious, uncluttered, and ordinarily, Rutledge thought, full of light from the long windows facing the drive. But the heavy rose velvet drapes had been drawn—was it these he had seen stir?—and only one lamp, on an inlaid table, made a feeble effort to penetrate the gloom.

Lettice Wood was tall and slim, with heavy dark hair that was pinned loosely on the top of her head, smooth wings from a central parting cupping her ears before being drawn up again. She was wearing unrelieved black, her skirts rustling slightly as she turned to watch them come toward her.

"Inspector Rutledge?" she said, as if she couldn't distinguish between the Upper Streetham sergeant and the representative of Scotland Yard. She did not ask them to be seated, though she herself sat on a brocade couch that faced the fireplace and there were two upholstered chairs on either side of it. A seventeenth-century desk stood between two windows, and against one wall was a rosewood cabinet filled with a collection of old silver, reflecting the single lamp like watching eyes from the jungle's edge. Sergeant Davies, behind Rutledge, stayed by the door and began to fumble in his pocket for his notebook.

For a moment the man from London and the woman in mourning considered each other in silence, each gauging temperament from the slender evidence of appearance. The lamplight reached Rutledge's face while hers was shadowed, but her voice when she spoke had been husky and strained, that of someone who had spent many hours crying. Her grief was very real—and yet something about it disturbed him. Something lurked in the dimness that he didn't want to identify.

"I'm sorry we must intrude, Miss Wood," he found himself saying with stiff formality. "And I offer our profoundest sympathy. But I'm sure you understand the urgency of finding the person or persons responsible for your guardian's death."

"My guardian." She said it flatly, as if it had no meaning for her. Then she added with painful vehemence, "I can't imagine how anyone could have done such a terrible thing to him. Or why. It was a senseless, savage—" She stopped, and he could see that she had swallowed hard to hold back angry tears. "It served no *purpose*," she added finally in a defeated voice.

"What has served no purpose?" Rutledge asked quietly. "His death? Or the manner of it?"

That jolted her, as if she had been talking to herself and not to him, and was surprised to find he'd read her thoughts.

She leaned forward slightly and he could see her face then, blotched with crying and sleeplessness. But most unusual nevertheless, with a high-bridged nose and a sensitive mouth and heavy-lidded eyes. He couldn't tell their color, but they were not dark. Sculpted cheekbones, a determined chin, a long, slender throat. And yet somehow she managed to convey an odd impression of warm sensuality. He remembered how the Sergeant had hesitated over the word "attractive," as if uncertain how to classify her. She was not, in the ordinary sense, beautiful. At the same time, she was far, very far, from plain.

"I don't see how you can separate them," she answered after a moment, a black-edged handkerchief twisting in her long, slim fingers. "He wasn't simply killed, was he? He was destroyed, blotted out. It was deliberate, vengeful. Even Scotland Yard can't change that. But the man who did this will be hanged. That's the only comfort I've got." There was a deeper note in her voice as she spoke of hanging, as if she relished the image of it in her mind.

"Then perhaps we ought to begin with last Monday morning. Did you see your guardian before he left the house?"

She hesitated, then said, "I didn't go riding that morning."

Before he could take her up on that stark reply,

she added, "Charles loved Mallows, loved the land. He said those rides made up, a little, for all the months he spent away. So he usually went out alone, and it was never a fixed route, you see, just wherever his list for that day took him—it might be inspecting a crop or a tenant's roof or the state of the hedges or livestock, anything. And he came back feeling—fulfilled, I suppose. It was a way of healing after all he'd been through."

"How many people knew what was on his list each day?"

"It wasn't written down, it was in his head. Laurence Royston might be aware that Charles was planning to look into a particular problem, if they'd discussed it. But for the most part it was Charles's own interests that guided him. I don't suppose you were a soldier, Inspector, but Charles once said that the greatest crime of the war was ruining the French countryside for a generation. Not the slaughter of armies, but the slaughter of the land." She leaned back, out of the light again, as if realizing that she was running on and had lost his attention.

I didn't go riding that morning—

Rutledge considered those words, ignoring the rest of what she had said. It was as if that one fact separated her entirely from what had happened. But in what way? He had heard soldiers offer the same excuse to avoid discussing what they had witnessed on the battlefield but had not been a part of: "I wasn't in that assault." I don't know and I don't want to know. . . .

A denial, then. But was it a washing of hands, or a means of telling the absolute but not the whole truth?

Her face was still, but she was watching him, waiting in the security of the darkness for him to ask his next question. Her grief appeared to be genuine, and yet she was doing nothing whatsoever to help him. He could feel her resistance like a physical barrier, as if they were adversaries, not joined in a mutual hunt for a murderer.

She in her turn was silently counting her heartbeats, willing them to a steady rhythm so that her breathing didn't betray her. In feeling lay disaster. Not for this London stranger with his chill, impersonal eyes was she going to lay out her most private emotions, and watch them probed and prodded for meaning! Let him do the job he had been sent to do. And why was it taking so bloody *long*? Charles had been gone for three *days*!

The silence lengthened. Sergeant Davies cleared his throat, as if made uneasy by undercurrents he couldn't understand.

For they were there, strong undercurrents, emotions so intense they were like ominous shadows in the room. Even Hamish was silent.

Changing his tactics abruptly, Rutledge asked, "What did your fiancé, Captain Wilton, and your guardian discuss after dinner on Sunday, the night before the Colonel's death?"

Her attention returned to him with a swift wariness. The heavy-lidded eyes opened wide for an instant, but she answered, "Surely you've spoken to Mark about that?"

"I'd prefer to hear what you have to say first. I understand that whatever it was led to a quarrel?"

"A quarrel?" Her voice was sharp now. "I went upstairs after dinner, I—didn't feel well. Charles and Mark were in the drawing room when I left them, talking about one of the guests invited to the wedding. Neither of them liked the man, but both felt they had to include him. An officer they'd served with, my guardian in the Boer War and Mark in France. I can't imagine them quarreling over that."

"Yet the servants told Inspector Forrest that there had been angry words between the two men, that, in fact, Captain Wilton had stormed out of the house in a rage, and that Colonel Harris flung his wineglass at the door the Captain had slammed behind him."

She was rigid, her attention fixed on him with fierce intensity. Even the handkerchief no longer unconsciously threaded itself through her fingers. He suddenly had the impression that this was news to her, that she had been unaware of what had happened in the hall. But she said only, "If they heard that much, they must have been able to tell you what it was all about."

"Unfortunately, they witnessed only the end of it."

"I see." As if distracted by some thought of her own, she said nothing for a time, and Rutledge waited, wishing he could know what was going on behind those long-lashed eyes. Then she roused herself and repeated, "Yes, that *is* unfortunate, isn't it? Still, you must know that neither Charles nor Mark is a hotheaded man."

"I'd hardly describe slamming a door in anger or breaking a crystal glass against it as coolheaded. But we'll have the answer to that in good time," Rutledge responded, noting with interest that she hadn't rushed to Captain Wilton's defense when she had been given the perfect opening to do just that. Yet she must have realized where such questions were leading?

Oddly enough, he thought she had. And discounted it. Or ignored it? Accustomed to reaching beyond words into emotional responses, he found her elusiveness puzzling. But he couldn't be sure whether that was his fault—or hers.

He took another tack, giving her a second opening but in a different direction. "Do you believe this man Mavers might have killed the Colonel? Apparently he's caused trouble for your guardian for a number of years."

She blinked, then said, "Mavers? He's been a troublemaker all his life. He seems to thrive on it. He sows dissent for the sheer, simple *pleasure* of it." Glancing at Sergeant Davies, she said, "But turning to murder? Risking the gallows? I can't see him going that far. Can you?" She frowned. "Unless, of course, it might be just what he wanted," she added thoughtfully.

"In what way?"

"He's been everything from a conscientious objector to a roaring Bolshevik—whatever might stir up people, make them angry. But everyone has more or less grown used to his ranting. Sometimes I even forget he's *there*. Laurence—Mr. Royston— always said it was the best way to take the wind out of his sails. But Charles felt that it might tip Mavers over the line, that being ignored was the one thing he dreaded. That it was anybody's guess what he might do then. Charles was a good judge of character, he knew Mavers better than the rest of us did. Still, if I were you I'd be wary of any confession Mavers made, unless it was backed up by indisputable proof."

Which was a decidedly puzzling remark. She had just been offered a ready-made scapegoat, and she had refused it. In his mind, Rutledge went back over what she'd just said, listening for nuances. Well, if she *was* trying to shift the direction of the enquiry, she had done it with an odd subtlety that was only just short of brilliant. Davies, out of her range of vision, was nodding as if he agreed with her about Mavers being the killer, and she'd said nothing of the sort.

If it hadn't occurred to her that the Captain needed defending, why had questions about the quarrel made her so wary? Had Harris been at fault there, and she was trying to preserve his good name, his reputation? Rutledge moved to the mantel, hoping that the change in angles might help him see her more clearly in the shadows. But her face was closed, her thoughts so withdrawn from him that he might as well try to read the engraving on the silver bowl at her elbow. The pallid light reached neither of them.

"Is there anyone else in the village to your knowledge with a reason to wish your guardian dead?"

"Charles had no enemies." She sighed. "There are those who might wish Mark dead, if you believe the gossips. But Charles? He was never here long enough to make enemies. He was a soldier, and leave was a rare thing, a time of respite, not for stirring up trouble."

"No land disputes, no boundary quarrels, no toes stepped on in the county?"

"I've not heard of them. But ask Laurence Royston, his agent. He can tell you about running the estate and whether there were disputes that might have festered. I can't help you there. I only came here to live near the end of the war, when I'd finished school. Before that, I was allowed to visit on school holidays when Charles had leave. Otherwise, I went home with one of my classmates."

Questioning her was like fencing with a will-o'-the-wisp. *I don't know, I can't help you there, I didn't go riding that morning*— And yet he had believed her when she said that hanging the murderer would bring her comfort. In his experience, the shock of sudden, violent death often aroused anger and a thirst for vengeance. But it seemed to be the only natural, anticipated reaction he'd gotten from her. Why did she keep drifting away from him?

He was reminded by a shifting of feet that Sergeant Davies was in the room, a witness to everything she said. A man who lived in Upper Streetham, who presumably had a wife and friends . . . was that the problem? He, Rutledge, was a private person himself; he understood the fierce need for privacy in others. And if that was the case, he was wasting his time now.

"How did you spend the morning? Before the news was brought to you?"

She was frowning, trying to remember as if that had been years ago, not a matter of days. "I bathed and dressed, came down to breakfast, the usual. Then I had a number of letters to write, and was just coming out of the library to see if Mr. Royston might take them into Warwick for me, when—" She stopped abruptly, then continued in a harsh voice. "I really don't recall what happened after that."

"You didn't leave the house, go to the stables?"

"Of course not, why on earth should I tell you I did one thing when I'd done another?"

Rutledge took his leave soon afterward. Davies seemed relieved to be on his way downstairs at the butler's heels, showing an almost indecent haste to be gone.

But Rutledge felt unsatisfied, as if somehow he had been neatly outmaneuvered in that darkened room. Thinking back over what the girl had said, he couldn't pinpoint any particular reason for disbelieving anything she'd told him, but doubt nagged at him. She couldn't be more than twenty-one or twenty-two, and yet she had shown a self-possession that was uncommon at that age—or any other. And he hadn't been able to break through to the person underneath. To the emotions that must be there. To the unspoken words he'd wanted to hear but that she had managed to hold back.

Her detachment, then. That was what disturbed him. As if she didn't connect the reality of violent death with the questions that the police were asking her. No passionate defense of her fiancé, no rush to push Mavers forward in his place, no speculation about the nature of the killer at all.

It was almost, he thought with one of those leaps of intuition that had served him so well in the past, as if she already knew who the killer was—and was planning her own private retribution. . . . *"I can't imagine how anyone could have done such a terrible thing to him,"* she'd said. Not *who*—how.

Then as he reached the foot of the stairs he remembered something else. Both Sergeant Davies and the butler had mentioned a doctor. Had the girl been given sedatives that left her in this sleep-walker's state, detached from grief and from reality too? He'd seen men in hospital talk quietly of unspeakable horrors when they'd been given drugs: stumbling to describe terrors they couldn't endure to think about until they were so heavily sedated that the pain and the frantic anxiety were finally dulled.

He himself had confessed to Hamish's presence only under the influence of such drugs. Nothing else would have dragged that out of him, and afterward he had tried to kill the doctor for tricking him. They'd had to pull him off the man, and he'd fought every inch of the way back to his room.

It might be a good idea, then, to speak to the family's doctor before deciding what to do about Lettice Wood.

Before the butler could see them safely out the door, Rutledge turned to him and asked, "What was your name again? Johnston?"

"Yes, sir."

"Can you show me the drawing room, please. Where the quarrel between the Captain and the Colonel took place?"

Johnston turned and walked silently across the polished marble to a door on his left. He opened it, showing them into a room of cool greens and gold, reflecting the morning light without absorbing it. "Miss Wood had coffee brought in here after dinner, and when the gentlemen joined her, she dismissed me. Soon afterward she went upstairs, sending for one of the maids and saying that she had a headache and would like a cool cloth for her head. That was around nine o'clock, perhaps a quarter past. At ten-fifteen I came here to take away the coffee tray and to see if anything else was needed before I locked up for the night."

"And you hadn't been into or near the drawing room between taking the tray in and coming to remove it?"

"No, sir."

"What happened then? At ten-fifteen?"

At Rutledge's prodding, Johnston stepped back into the hall again, pointed to a door in the shadows of the stairs, and went on reluctantly. "I came out of that door—it leads to the back of the house—and started toward the drawing room. At that moment, Mary was coming down the stairs."

"Who is Mary?"

"There's seven on the staff here, sir. Myself, the cook, her helper, and four maids. Before the war there were twelve of us, including footmen. Mary is one of the maids and has been here the longest, next to Mrs. Treacher and myself."

"Go on."

"Mary was coming down the stairs, and she said when I came into view that she was looking to see if the banisters and the marble floor needed polishing the next morning. If not, she was going to put Nancy to polishing the grates, now that we were no longer making up morning fires."

"And?"

"And at that moment," Johnston answered heavily, "the door of the drawing room opened, and the Captain came out. I didn't see his face—he was looking over his shoulder back into the room—but I heard him say quite distinctly and very loudly, 'I'll see you in hell, first!' Then he slammed the drawing-room door behind him and went out the front door, slamming that as well. I don't think he saw me here, or Mary on the stairs." He seemed to run out of words.

"Finish your story, man!" Rutledge said impatiently.

"Before the front door had slammed, I heard the Colonel shout, 'That can be arranged!' and the sound of glass shattering against this door."

His hand drew their eyes to the raw nick in the glossy paint of one panel, where the glass had struck with such force that a piece of it must have wedged in the wood.

"Do you think Captain Wilton heard the Colonel?"

In spite of himself, Johnston smiled. "The Colonel, sir, was accustomed to making himself heard on a parade ground and over the din of the battlefield. I would think that the Captain heard him as clearly as I did, and slammed the front door with added emphasis because of it."

"It was a glass that shattered, not a cup?"

"The Colonel usually had a glass of brandy with his coffee, and the Captain always joined him."

"When you cleaned this room the next morning, did you find that two glasses had been used?"

"Yes, sir," Johnston answered, perplexed. "Of course."

"Which means that the two men drank together and were still on comfortable terms at that point in the evening."

"I would venture to say so, yes."

"Had you ever heard a quarrel between them before this particular evening?"

"No, sir, they seemed to be on the best of terms."

"Had they drunk enough, do you think, to have become quarrelsome for no reason? Or over some petty issue?"

"With respect, sir," Johnston said indignantly, "the Colonel was not a man to become argumentative in his cups. He held his liquor like a gentleman, and so, to my knowledge, did the Captain. Besides," he added, rather spoiling the lofty effect he'd just created, "the level in the decanters showed no more than two drinks had been poured, one each."

"Do you feel, having witnessed the Captain's departure, that this was a disagreement that could have been smoothed over comfortably the next day?"

"He was very angry at the time. I can't say how Captain Wilton might have felt the next morning. But I can tell you that the Colonel seemed in no way unsettled when he came down for his morning ride. Very much himself, as far as I could see."

"And Miss Wood was in her bedroom through-out the quarrel? She didn't rejoin the men in the drawing room, to your knowledge?"

"No, sir. Mary looked in on her before she came down the stairs, to see if she needed anything more, and Miss Wood appeared to be asleep. So she didn't speak to her."

"What did the Colonel do after the Captain left?"

"I don't know, sir. I thought it best not to dis-turb him at that moment, and I came back twenty minutes later. By that time, he had gone up to bed himself, and I went about my nightly duties before turning in at eleven. Would you like to see Mary now, sir?"

"I'll talk to Mary and the rest of the staff later," Rutledge said, and walked to the door. There he turned to look back at the drawing room and then at the staircase. Under ordinary circumstances, Wilton would have noticed Johnston and the maid as soon as he came out of the drawing-room door. But if he had been looking back at Charles Harris instead, he might not have been aware of either servant, silent and unobtrusive behind him.

With a nod, Rutledge opened the front door be-fore Johnston could reach it to see him out, and with Sergeant Davies hurrying after him walked down the broad, shallow stone steps and across the drive to the car.

Hamish, growling irritably, said, "I don't like yon butler. I don't hold with the rich anyway, or their toadies."

"It's a better job than you ever held," Rutledge retorted, and then swore under his breath. But

Davies had been getting into the car and heard only the sound of his voice, not his words. He looked up to say, "I beg pardon, sir?"

The heavy drapes of the sitting room upstairs parted a little, and Lettice Wood watched Rutledge climb into the car and start the engine. When it had passed out of sight around the first bend of the drive, she let the velvet fall back into place and wandered aimlessly to the table where the lamp still burned. She flicked it off and stood there in the darkness.

If only she could think clearly! He would be back, she was certain of that, prying into everything, wanting to know about Charles, asking about Mark. And he wasn't like the elderly Forrest; there would be no deference or fatherly concern from him, not with those cold eyes. She must have her wits about her then! The problem was, what would Mark tell them? How was she to *know*?

She put her hands to her head, pressing cold fingers into her temples. He looked as if he'd been ill, this inspector from Scotland Yard. And such people were often difficult. Why had Forrest sent for him? Why had it been necessary to drag London into this business, awful enough already without strangers trampling about.

Why hadn't they left it to Inspector Forrest?

"Will we speak to Mavers now, sir?"

"No, Captain Wilton next, I think."

"He's staying with his cousin, Mrs. Davenant. She's a widow, has a house just on the outskirts of town, the other end of Upper Streetham from Mallows."

He gave Rutledge directions and then began to scan his notebook as if checking to make certain he had put down the salient points of the conversations with Lettice Wood and Johnston.

"I thought," Rutledge said, "that the servants claimed that the argument between the Colonel and the Captain concerned the wedding. Johnston said nothing about it."

"It was the maid, Mary Satterthwaite, who mentioned that, sir."

"Then why didn't you say so while we were there? I'd have spoken to her straightaway."

Davies flipped back through his notebook to a page near the beginning. "She said she went up to Miss Wood's room to bring a cold cloth for her head, and Miss Wood was telling her that she had left the gentlemen to discuss the marriage. But the way Miss Wood said it led Mary to think it wasn't going to be a friendly discussion."

"And then, having seen the end of the quarrel, the maid merely jumped to the conclusion that that was what they were still talking about?"

"Apparently so, sir."

Which was no evidence at all. "When is the wedding?"

Davies flipped several more pages. "On the twenty-second of September, sir. And Miss Wood and the Captain have been engaged for seven months."

Rutledge considered that. In an hour's time—from the moment that Lettice Wood left the pair together until Johnston had seen Wilton storming out of the house—the subject of conversation could have ranged far and wide. If there had been a discussion of the wedding at nine-fifteen, surely it would not have lasted an hour, and developed into a quarrel at this stage, the details having been ironed out seven months ago and the arrangements for September already well in hand. . . .

Without warning, he found himself thinking of Jean, of their own engagement in that hot, emotion-torn summer of 1914, a lifetime ago. Of the endless letters passing back and forth to France as they dreamed and planned. Of the acute longing that had kept him alive when nothing else had mattered. Of the wedding that had never taken place—

Of Jean's white face in his hospital room when he had offered her the chance to break off the engagement. She had smiled nervously and taken it, murmuring something about the war having changed both of them. While he sat there, still aching with love and his need for her, trying with every ounce of his being to hide it from her, she'd said, "I'm not the girl you remember in 1914. I loved you so madly—I think anything would have been possible then. But too much time has passed, too much has happened to both of us—we were apart so *long*. . . . I don't even know myself anymore. . . . Of course I still *care*, but—I don't think I should marry anyone just now—it wouldn't be fair to marry *anyone*. . . ."

Yet despite the quiet voice and the scrupulously chosen words that tried desperately to spare both of them pain, he could see the truth in her eyes.

It was fear.

She was deathly afraid of him. . . .

3

$\mathcal{M}$rs. Davenant lived in a Georgian brick house standing well back from the road. It was surrounded by an ivy-clad wall with ornate iron gates and set in a pleasant garden already bright with early color. Roses and larkspur drooped over the narrow brick walk, so heavy with rain from the night before that they left a speckled pattern of dampness on Rutledge's trousers as he brushed past them on his way to the door.

Surprisingly, Mrs. Davenant answered the bell herself. She was a slender, graceful woman in her thirties, her fair hair cut becomingly short around her face but drawn into a bun on the back of her neck. Tendrils escaping its rigorous pinning curled delicately against very fine skin, giving her a fragile quality like rare porcelain. Her eyes were dark blue with naturally dark lashes, making them appear deep set and almost violet.

She nodded a greeting to Sergeant Davies and then said to Rutledge, "You must be the man from London." Her eyes scanned his face and his height and his clothes with cool interest.

"Inspector Rutledge. I'd like to speak to you, if I may. And to Captain Wilton."

"Mark has gone for a walk. I don't think he slept well last night, and walking always soothes him. Please, come in."

She led them not into the drawing room but down a passage beyond the stairs to a comfortable sitting room that still had a masculine ambience, as if it had been her late husband's favorite part of the house. Paintings of hunting scenes hung above the fireplace and on two of the walls, while a collection of pipes in a low, glass-fronted cabinet stood beneath a small but exquisite Canaletto.

"This is a dreadful business," she was saying as Rutledge took the chair she offered him. Sergeant Davies went to stand by the hearth, as if her invitation to be seated had not included him. She accepted this without comment. "Simply dreadful! I can't imagine why anyone would have wanted to kill Charles Harris. He was a thoroughly nice man." There was a ring of sincerity in the words.

An elderly woman in a black dress and white apron came to the doorway, and after glancing toward her, Mrs. Davenant asked, "Would you care for coffee, Inspector? Sergeant?" When they declined, she nodded to the woman and said, "That will be all, then, Grace. And close the door behind you, please."

When the woman had gone, Rutledge said, "Do your servants live in, Mrs. Davenant?"

"No, Agnes and Grace come in daily to clean and to prepare meals. Agnes isn't here just now, her granddaughter is very ill. Ben is my groom-gardener. He lives over the stables." She lifted her eyebrows in a query, as if expecting Rutledge to explain his interest in her staff.

"Can you tell me what state of mind Captain

Wilton was in when he came home from Mallows the evening before the Colonel was killed?"

"His state of mind?" she repeated. "I don't know, I had already gone to bed. When he dined with Lettice and the Colonel, I didn't wait up for him."

"The next morning, then?"

"He seemed a little preoccupied over his breakfast, I suppose. But then I've grown used to that. Lettice and Mark are very much in love." She smiled. "Lettice has been good for him, you know. He was so *changed* when he came home from France. Dark—bitter. I think he hated flying then, which is sad, because before the war—before the killing—it had been his greatest passion. Now Lettice is everything to him. I don't think Charles could have stood in the way of this marriage if he'd wanted to!"

Rutledge could see that she was fond of her cousin—and from her unguarded comments he gathered that it hadn't yet occurred to her that Wilton might have killed Harris. It was interesting, he thought, that she spoke freely, warmly, and yet with an odd—detachment. Was that it? As if her own emotions were locked away and untouched by the ugliness of murder. Or as if she had held them in for so very long that it had become second nature to her. It was a response to widowhood in some women, but there could be many other reasons.

"Did Captain Wilton go for a walk on Monday morning?"

"Of course. He likes the exercise, and since the crash—you knew that he crashed just before the war ended?—since then riding has been difficult for him. His knee was badly smashed, and although it's hardly noticeable now when he walks, controlling a horse is another matter."

Rutledge studied her. An attractive woman, with the sort of fair English beauty that men were supposed to dream about in the trenches as they died for King and Country. She was dressed in a soft rose silk that in the light from the long windows gave her skin a warm blush. The same blush it might have when stirred by passion. He found himself wondering if Charles Harris had ever been drawn to her. A man sometimes carried a picture in his mind when he spent long years abroad—a tie with home, whether real or fancied.

"Where does Captain Wilton usually walk?"

She shrugged. "I can't tell you that. Where the spirit takes him, I daresay. One day as I came home from the village, I saw a farm cart dropping him off at our gate, and he told me he had walked to Lower Streetham and halfway to Bampton beyond! Along the way he'd picked a small posy of wildflowers for Lettice, but it had wilted by then. A pity."

"I understand that he had a quarrel with Charles Harris on Sunday evening after dinner. Do you have any idea what that was about?"

With a sigh of exasperation, she said, "Inspector Forrest asked me the same question, when he came about the shotguns. I can't imagine Charles and Mark quarreling. Oh, good-naturedly, about a horse or military tactics or the like, but not a *serious* argument. They got along famously, the two of them, ever since they met in France, on leave in Paris."

"I understand that the Captain had spent some time here before 1914. He and Colonel Harris weren't acquainted then?"

"Charles was in Egypt, I think, the summer my husband died. And Lettice of course was away at school."

"The wedding arrangements, then. They appeared to be progressing smoothly?"

"As far as I know. Lettice has ordered her gown, and next week she was to go to London for the first fitting. The invitations have been sent to the printer, flowers chosen for the wedding breakfast, plans for the wedding trip made—I doubt if Mark would have objected if Lettice had wished to go to the moon! And Charles doted on her, he wouldn't have begrudged her anything her heart desired. She only needed to ask. What was there to quarrel about?"

Mrs. Davenant made the marriage sound idyllic, such a piece of high romance that even death couldn't stand in its way. And yet in the three days since Charles Harris had been found murdered, Lettice had apparently not asked to see Wilton. Nor, as far as he, Rutledge, knew, had Wilton gone to Mallows.

He was about to pursue that line of thought when the sitting-room door opened and Captain Wilton walked across the threshold.

He was wearing country tweeds, and they became him as well as his uniform must have done, fitting his muscular body with an air of easy elegance. The newspaper photographs of him standing before the King had not done him justice. He was as fair as his cousin, his eyes as dark a blue, and he fit the popular conception of "war hero" to perfection.

"Wrap a bluidy bandage around his forehead, gie him a sword in one hand and a flag in the other, and he'd do for a recruitment poster," Hamish remarked sourly. "Only they bombed poor sods in the trenches, those fine airmen, and shot other pilots down in flames. I wonder now, is burning to death worse than smothering in the mud?"

Rutledge shivered involuntarily.

Wilton greeted Rutledge with a nod, making the

same comment that his cousin had made earlier. "You must be the man from London."

"Inspector Rutledge. I'd like to talk to you, if you don't mind." He glanced at Mrs. Davenant. "If you would excuse us?"

She rose with smiling grace and said, "I'll be in the garden if you want to see me again before you go." She gave her cousin a comfortable glance, and left the room, shutting the door gently behind her.

"I don't know what questions you may have," Wilton said at once, setting his walking stick in a stand by the door and taking the chair she had vacated. "But I can tell you that I wasn't the person who shot Charles Harris."

"Why should I think you were?" Rutledge asked.

"Because you aren't a fool, and I know how Forrest danced around his suspicions, hemming and hawing over my abrupt departure from Mallows on Sunday evening and wanting to know what Charles and I were discussing that next morning when that damned fool Hickam claims to have seen us in the lane."

"As a point of interest, did you and the Colonel meet on Monday morning? In the lane or anywhere else, for that matter?"

"No." The single word was unequivocal.

"What was your quarrel about after dinner on the night before the murder?"

"It was a personal matter, nothing to do with this enquiry. You may take my word for it."

"There are no personal matters when it comes to murder," Rutledge said. "I'll ask you again. What were you discussing that Sunday evening after Miss Wood went up to her room?"

"And I'll tell you again that it's none of your

business." Wilton was neither angry nor irritated, only impatient.

"Did it have anything to do with your marriage to Miss Wood?"

"We didn't discuss my marriage." Rutledge took note, however, of the change in wording. *My*, not *our*.

"Then did you discuss the settlement? Where you'd live after the wedding? How you'd live?"

Muscles around his mouth tightened, but he answered readily enough. "That had all been worked out months before. The settlement was never a problem. Lettice has her own money. We'd live in Somerset, where I have a house, and visit here as often as she liked." He hesitated, then added, "I'd expected, after the war, to go into aircraft design. Next to flying it's what I wanted most to do. Now—I'm not as sure as I was."

"Why not?" When Wilton didn't answer immediately, Rutledge continued, "For reasons of money?"

Wilton shook his head impatiently. "I'm tired of killing. I spent four years proving that the machines I flew were good at it. And that's all His Majesty's ministers want to hear about aeroplanes at the moment, how to make them deadlier. My mother's people are in banking; there are other choices open to me." But there was a bleakness in his voice.

Rutledge responded to it, recognizing it. He himself had debated the wisdom of returning to the Yard, coming back to the business of murder. Before the war it had been another facet of the law his father had given a lifetime to upholding. Now—he had seen too many dead bodies. . . . Yet it was what he knew best.

Then, bringing himself up sharply, he said more harshly than he had intended, "Have you seen Miss Wood since her guardian's death?"

Wilton seemed surprised that it should matter to Rutledge. "No, as a matter of fact, I haven't."

"She apparently has no other family. Under the circumstances, it would be natural for you to be at her side."

"And so I would be, if there was anything I might do for her!" he retorted stiffly. "Look, I went to Mallows as soon as I heard the news. Dr. Warren was already there, and he said she needed rest, that the shock had been severe. I sent up a message by Mary—one of the maids—but Lettice was already asleep. Warren warned me that it could be several days before she recovered sufficiently to see anyone. I've made an effort to respect his judgment. Under the circumstances, as you so aptly put it, there isn't much else I can do, as long as she's asleep in her bedroom."

But she hadn't been asleep when Rutledge called. . . .

"Dr. Warren has been sedating her, then?"

"What do you think? She was wild at first, she insisted that she be taken to Charles at once. Which of course Warren could hardly do! And then she collapsed. She lost both her parents when she was four, and I don't suppose she remembers them clearly. Charles has been the only family she's known."

Rutledge took the opening he'd been given. "Tell me what sort of person Charles Harris was."

Wilton's eyes darkened. "A fine officer. A firm friend. A loving guardian. A gentleman."

It sounded like an epitaph written by a besotted widow, something Queen Victoria might have said about Prince Albert in a fit of high-flown passion.

"Which tells me absolutely nothing." Rutledge's voice was quiet, but there was a crackle to it now. "Did he have a temper? Was he a man who carried a grudge? Did he make enemies easily, did he keep his friends? Was he a heavy drinker? Did he have affairs? Was he honest in his business dealings?"

Wilton frowned, his elbows on the chair arm, his fingers steepled before his face, half concealing it. "Yes, he had a temper, but he'd learned long ago to control it. I don't know if he carried grudges or not, but most of his friends were Army, men he'd served with for many years. I don't know if he had enemies—I never heard of any, unless you wish to include that idiot Mavers. As for his drinking, I've seen Charles drunk—we all got drunk in France, when we could—but he was a moderate drinker as a rule, and affairs with women must have been discreet. I've never heard him described as a womanizer. You'll have to ask Royston about business matters, I've no idea how they stand."

"You met Harris during the war?"

"In France just at the end of 1914. In spite of the differences in age and rank we became friends. A year ago, when he heard I was coming out of hospital, he brought me to Mallows for the weekend. That's when I met his ward. If he had secrets, he managed to keep them from me. I saw nothing vicious, mean, or unworthy in the man." The hands had come down, as if the need for them as a shield had passed.

This was a better epitaph, but still no help to Rutledge, who wanted the living flesh and blood and bone of the man.

"And yet he died violently in a quiet English meadow this past Monday morning, and while everyone tells me he was a good man, no one seems to be in any particular haste to find his killer. I find that rather curious."

"Of course we want the killer found!" Wilton responded, coloring angrily. "Whoever it is deserves to hang, and what I can do, I shall do. But I can't think of any reason why Charles should have been shot, and you damned well wouldn't thank me for muddying the waters for you with wild, useless conjectures!"

"Then we'll start with facts. When did you leave this house on Monday morning? Where did you go?"

"At half past seven." Wilton had gotten himself under control again, but his words were still clipped. "Exercise strengthens my knee. On Monday I followed the lane that runs just behind the church and up the hill beyond, skirting Mallows. I reached the crest of the ridge, went on toward the old mill ruins on the far side of it, which lie near the bridge over the Ware, then returned the same way."

This was not the lane where Hickam claimed to have seen the Colonel and the Captain having words. "Did you hear the shot that killed him? Or sounds of the search—men shouting or calling?"

"I heard no shooting at all. I ran into one of the farm people on my way home, and he told me what had happened. It was a shock." He stirred suddenly, as if reminded of it. "I couldn't really believe it. My first thought was for Lettice, and I went straight to Mallows."

"Did you meet anyone during your walk?"

"Two people. A farmer's child who had lost her doll and was sitting on a stump crying. I spoke to her, told her I'd keep an eye open for the doll, and asked if she knew her way home. She said she did, she often came that way to pick wildflowers for her mother. Later I saw Helena Sommers. She was on the ridge with her field glasses and didn't stop, just waved her hand."

"What about the Colonel's man of business, Royston? He went down to the stables looking for Harris and got there just as the horse came in without its rider. In time, in fact, to direct the search. Do you think he's honest? Or is there the possibility that the meeting he was expecting to have with the Colonel at nine-thirty might have been one he had reasons to prevent?"

"Do you mean, for example, that Royston may have been cheating Charles, embezzling or whatever, had been caught, and expected to be sacked at nine-thirty, when Charles came in?" He frowned again, considering the possibility. "I suppose he could have reached the meadow ahead of Charles, shot him, and made it home again before the horse arrived in the stable yard. Assuming he took the shortcut over the stile and the riderless horse stuck to the track. But you can't count on horses, can you? Not if they're frightened."

Rutledge thought, No one has mentioned a shortcut—

"But Charles never spoke to me about any trouble with Royston," Wilton continued, "and of course there's the shotgun. He hadn't taken one from Mallows. Forrest checked those straightaway."

"I've heard someone say that it would have been less surprising to hear you were the victim, not Harris." Across the room Rutledge saw Sergeant Davies stir as if to stop him from betraying Lettice Wood.

But Captain Wilton was laughing. "You mean Lettice's other suitors might have had it in for me? I can't see either Haldane or Carfield lying in wait to murder me. Can you, Sergeant?" The laughter died suddenly and a shadow passed over the

Captain's face. "That's foolishness," he added, but with less conviction.

Rutledge left the questioning there and took his leave.

Mark Wilton waited until he had heard the front door close behind the two policemen, then sat down again in his chair. He wondered if they had spoken to Lettice, and what she had said to them. What would she say to *him*, if he went to Mallows now? He couldn't bring himself to think about Charles Harris's death, only what difference it might make. He closed his eyes, head back against the chair. Oh, God, what a tangle! But if he kept his wits about him—if he was *patient*, and his love for Lettice didn't trip him up, it would all come right in the end. He had to believe that. . . .

As Rutledge and the Sergeant let themselves out, they saw Mrs. Davenant coming toward them with a basket of cut flowers, roses and peonies with such a rich, heavy scent that Rutledge was reminded of funerals.

"I'm sending these to Lettice, to cheer her a little. Have you talked with that man Mavers? I wouldn't put anything past him, not even murder! We'd be well rid of him, believe me. He was haranguing people in the market square on Monday morning. Nobody really paid any attention to him—they seldom do. Making a nuisance of himself, that's all he thinks of!"

Rutledge thanked her, and she went back to her flowers, humming a little under her breath in quiet satisfaction.

As the car pulled away from the gate, Hamish said unexpectedly, "The Captain's a right fool! And too handsome for his own good. If a husband didn't want him dead, a woman might."

Ignoring the voice, Rutledge turned to Davies and said, "Where can I find Daniel Hickam? We might as well talk to him and get it over with."

"I don't know, sir. He lives in his mother's cottage at the edge of the village—just ahead there, that ramshackle one beyond the straggling hedge." He pointed to a swaybacked cottage so old that it seemed to be collapsing of its own weight, a bit at a time, and leaving in doubt whether it would go first in the center or at the walls. "She's dead, and he's taken over the place, doing odd jobs where he can to earn his food."

They stopped by the hedge and went to knock at the door, but there was no answer. Davies lifted the latch and peered inside. The single room was dark and cluttered, but empty.

"He must be in town, then."

So they drove on into Upper Streetham, and saw Laurence Royston coming from the post office. Sergeant Davies pointed him out, and Rutledge looked him over.

He was in his late thirties or early forties, already graying at the temples, neither plain nor particularly attractive, but he carried himself well and had that appearance of solidity which people seem instinctively to trust, whether trust is justified or not. His face was square, with a straight nose, a stubborn chin and a well-defined jaw set above a heavy neck and broad shoulders.

Rutledge blew his horn and Royston turned at the sound, frowning at the unknown man in the unfamiliar vehicle. Then he noticed Sergeant Davies in the other seat and came over to them as the car pulled into a space between two wagons.

"Inspector Rutledge. I've taken over the Harris case, and I'd like to talk to you if I may."

Royston stuffed the mail he was carrying into his coat pocket and said, "Here?"

Rutledge suggested the bar at the Shepherd's Crook, half-empty at this time of day, where they ordered coffee from Redfern. When he'd gone, Royston said, "I've never had such a shock in my life as Charles's death. Even when I saw the grooms holding his horse, and blood all over the saddle, I thought he was hurt. Not dead. I thought—I don't know what I thought. My God, the man came through two wars with hardly a scratch! There's the Boer musket ball in his leg still, and a German sniper got him in the left shoulder in France, but even that wasn't particularly serious. I never imagined—" He shook his head. "It was horrible, a nightmare you can't accept as real."

"You were expecting to meet the Colonel that morning at nine-thirty?"

"Yes. For our regular discussion of the day's work. He liked to be involved when he could. My father told me once that he felt Colonel Harris had had a difficult time deciding between the traditional family career in the Army and staying at home to run Mallows. And you could see that it might be true. So when he was there I kept him informed of everything that was happening."

"Why did you go down to the stables?"

"It wasn't like Charles to be late, but we had a valuable mare in foal, and I thought he might have looked in on her and found she was in trouble. So I went to see. I needed to drive into Warwick, and if he was busy, I wanted to suggest that we put off our meeting until after lunch."

"There was nothing set for discussion that you were glad of an excuse to postpone?"

Royston looked up from his coffee with something like distaste on his face. "If anything, I'd have been glad to postpone going into Warwick. I had an appointment with my dentist."

Rutledge smiled, but made a mental note to check on that. "How long have you worked for the Colonel?"

"About twenty years, now. I took over when my father died of a heart attack. I didn't know what else to do; Charles was out in South Africa. When he got home, he liked the way I'd managed the estate and asked me to stay on. It was a rare opportunity at my age, I was only twenty. But I'd grown up at Mallows, you see, I knew as much about the place as anyone. Charles could have found a far more experienced man, but I think he was glad to have someone who actually cared. That was the way he did things. He looked after his land, the men serving under him, and of course Miss Wood, to the best of his ability."

"And you'll go on running the estate now?"

Royston's eyebrows shot up. "I don't know. God, I hadn't even thought about it. But surely Miss Wood will inherit Mallows? There's no family—"

"I haven't seen the Colonel's will. Is there a copy here, or must I send to his solicitors in London?"

"There's a copy in his strongbox. He left it there, in the event he was killed—with the Army, I mean. It's sealed, of course, I don't know what it says, but I see no reason why I shouldn't give it to you, if you think it will help."

"Why would anyone shoot Colonel Harris?"

Royston's face darkened. "Mavers might've. He's the kind of man who can't make anything of himself, so he tries to drag down his betters. He's run on about the Bolsheviks for nearly a year now, and how they shot the Czar and his family to clear the way for reforms. I wouldn't put it past the bastard to think that killing the Colonel might be the closest he could come to doing the same."

"But the Colonel isn't the primary landholder in Upper Streetham, is he?"

"No, the Haldanes are. The Davenants used to be just about as big, but Hugh Davenant was not the man his father was, and he lost most of his money in wild schemes, then had to sell off land to pay his debts. That's Mrs. Davenant's late husband I'm speaking of. She was lucky he died when he did. He hadn't learned a lesson as far as I could tell, and she'd have been penniless in the end. But he had no head for business, it was as simple as that."

"Who bought most of the Davenant land? Harris?"

"He bought several fields that ran along his own, but Haldane and Mrs. Crichton's agent took the lion's share. She lives in London, she's ninety now if she's a day, and hasn't set foot in Upper Streetham since the turn of the century."

"Which leaves us with Mavers wanting to shoot the Czar and a choice between Harris and the Haldanes."

"People like Mavers don't think the way you and I do. He had a running feud with Harris, and if he wanted to kill anyone, he'd probably choose the Colonel on principle. In fact, he once said as much when the Colonel threatened to put him away if he tried to poison the dogs again. He said, 'Dog and master, they deserve the same fate.'"

"When did this happen? Before the war or later on?"

"Yes, before, but you haven't met Mavers, have you?"

"He has witnesses who say he was here in the

village on Monday morning, making one of his speeches to people coming in to market."

Royston shrugged. "What if he was? Nobody pays any heed to his nonsense. He could have slipped away for a time and never be missed."

Rutledge considered that. It was a very interesting possibility, and Mrs. Davenant had made much the same comment. "Do you think Captain Wilton killed Harris?"

Royston firmly shook his head. "That's ridiculous! Whatever for?"

"Daniel Hickam claims he saw the Colonel and the Captain having words on Monday morning, shortly before the shooting. As if a quarrel the night before had carried over into the morning and suddenly turned violent."

"Hickam told you that?" Royston laughed shortly. "I'd as soon believe my cat as a drunken, half-mad coward."

Prepared for the reaction this time, Rutledge still flinched.

The words seemed to tear at his nerve endings like a physical pain. Through it he asked, "Did you see the body yourself, when word was brought that the Colonel had been found?"

"Yes." Royston shuddered. "They were babbling that the Colonel had been shot, and that there was blood everywhere, and my first question was, 'Has any one of you fools checked to see if he's still breathing?' And they looked at me as if I'd lost my wits. When I got there I knew why. I tell you, if I'd been the one who'd done it, I couldn't have gone back there. Not for anything. I couldn't believe it was Charles at first, even though I recognized his spurs, the jacket, the ring on his hand. It—the body—looked—I don't know, somehow obscene— like something inhuman."

• • •

When Royston had gone, Rutledge finished his coffee and said gloomily, "We've got ourselves a paragon of all virtues, a man no one had any reason to kill. If you don't count Mavers—who happens to have the best alibi of the lot—you're left with Wilton and that damned quarrel. Tell me, Sergeant. What was Harris really like?"

"Just that, sir," the Sergeant replied, addressing the question as if he thought it slightly idiotic. "A very nice man. Not at all the sort you'd expect to end up murdered!"

Very soon after that they found Daniel Hickam standing in the middle of the High Street, intent on directing traffic that no one else could see. Rutledge pulled over in front of a row of small shops and studied the man for a time. Most of the shell shock victims he'd seen in hospital had been docile, sitting with blank faces staring blindly into the abyss of their own terrors or pacing back and forth, hour after hour, as if bent on outdistancing the demons pursuing them.

The violent cases had been locked away, out of sight. But he had heard them raving at night, the corridors echoing with screams and obscenities and cries for help. That had brought back the trenches so vividly he had gone for nights without sleep and spent most of his days in an exhausted stupor that made him seem as docile and unreachable as the others around him.

And then his sister Frances had had him moved to a private clinic, where he had mercifully found peace from those nightmares at any rate, and been given a doctor who was interested enough in his case to find a way through his desolate wall of silence. Or perhaps the doctor had been one of Frances's lovers—oddly enough, all of them seemed to remain on very good terms with her when the affair ended and were always at her beck and call. But he had been too grateful for help to care.

Watching, it was easy to see that Hickam was used to vehicles coming from every direction, and he directed his invisible traffic with efficient skill, sorting out the tangle as if he stood at a busy intersection where long convoys were passing.

He sent a few one way, then turned his attention to the left, his hand vigorously signaling that they were to turn and turn *now*, while he shouted to someone to get those sodding horses moving or called for men to help dig the wheels of an artillery caisson out of the sodding mud. He snapped a smart salute at officers riding past—there was no mistaking his pantomime—then swiftly turned it into a rude gesture that would have pleased tired men slogging their way back from the bloody Front or the frightened men moving forward to take their place.

In France Rutledge had seen dozens of men stationed at junctions in the rain or the hot sun, keeping a moribund army moving in spite of itself, yelling directions, swearing at laggards, indicating with practiced movements exactly what they expected the chaos around them to do. Many had died where they stood, in the shelling or strafing and bombing, trying desperately to keep the flow of badly needed arms and men from bogging down completely.

But the carts, carriages, and handful of cars of Upper Streetham merely swerved a little to miss Hickam, used to him and leaving him standing where he was in the middle of the road as if he were something nasty that a passing horse had left behind. Some of the women on foot hesitated before crossing near him, drawing aside their skirts with nervous distaste and turning their faces in fear. Yet none of the village urchins mocked him, and Rutledge, noticing that, asked why.

"For one thing, he's been home nearly eleven months now, since the hospital let him go. For another, he took a stick to the ringleader, shouting at him in bastard French. Broke the boy's collarbone for him." He kept his eyes on Hickam as he swung around to face another direction, jerking his thumb at a line of convoy traffic, locked in a past that no one else could share.

"The lad's father told us the boy deserved what he got, but there were others who felt Hickam ought to be shut up before he harmed anyone else. People like Hickam—well, they're not normal, are they? But the Vicar wouldn't hear of an asylum, he said Hickam was an accursed soul, in need of prayer."

"God Almighty," Hamish said softly. "That's you in five years—only it won't be traffic, will it, that you remember? It'll be the trenches and the men, and the blood and the stink, and the shells falling hour after hour, until the brain splits apart with the din. And you'll be shouting for us to get over the top or take cover or hold the line while the nurses strap you down to the bed and nobody heeds your frenzied screams when Corporal Hamish—"

"I'll see us both dead first," Rutledge said between clenched teeth, "I swear—"

And Davies, startled, looked at him in confusion.

4

$\mathcal{Y}$ou can see he's half out of his head," Davies said again uneasily, as Rutledge sat there, rigidly staring at the disheveled figure in the middle of the sunlit, busy High Street. The Sergeant wasn't sure he'd understood the London man, and wondered if perhaps he had misquoted what the Captain had said to the Colonel: "I'll see you in hell first." Should he correct Rutledge then? Or pretend he hadn't noticed? He wasn't sure how to take this man—on the other hand, he hadn't seemed to be in haste to arrest Captain Wilton, and that counted for something.

"Out of his head? No, locked into it. Hickam must have been directing traffic when the shelling started, and stayed with it until one came too close. That's why he's behaving this way," Rutledge said, half to himself. "It's the last thing he remembers."

"I don't know about that, sir—"

"I do," Rutledge said curtly, recollecting where he was, and with whom.

"Yes, sir," Davies answered doubtfully. "But I can tell you there's no talking to him now. He won't hear you. He's in his own mad world. We'll have to come back later."

"Then we'll see the meadow where the body was found. But first I want to find the doctor. Dr. Warren."

"He's just down there, past the Inn. You can see his house from here."

It was a narrow stone-faced building that had been turned into a small surgery, and Dr. Warren was just preparing to leave when Rutledge came to his door and introduced himself.

"I want to ask you a few questions, if you don't mind."

"I do," Warren said testily. He was elderly, stooped and graying, but his blue eyes were sharp beneath heavy black brows. "I've got a very sick child on my hands and a woman in labor. It'll have to wait."

"Except for one of the questions. Are you prescribing sedatives for Miss Wood?"

"Of course I am. The girl was beside herself with grief, and I was afraid she'd make herself ill into the bargain. So I left powders with Mary Satterthwaite to be given three times a day and again at night, until she's able to deal with this business herself. No visitors, and that includes you."

"I've already seen her," Rutledge answered. "She seemed rather—abstracted. I wanted to know why."

"You'd be abstracted yourself on what I've given her. She wanted to see the Colonel's body— she thought he'd been shot neatly through the heart or some such. Well, his head had been blown off at nearly point-blank range, leaving a ragged stump of his neck. And I had to tell her that before she'd listen to me. Oh, not that bluntly, don't be a fool! But enough to deter her. That's when she fainted, and by the time we got her to bed, she was just coming out of it. So I gave her a powder in some water, and she drank it without knowing what it was. And now there's a baby that's going to be born while I stand here discussing sedatives with you. A first baby, and the husband's worthless, he'll probably faint too at the first sign of blood. So get out of my way."

He went brusquely past Rutledge and out toward the Inn, where he apparently left his car during surgery hours. Rutledge watched him go, then ran lightly down the steps to his own car, where Davies was still sitting.

Driving on down the High Street, Rutledge slowed as Davies pointed out the track that began behind the tree-shaded churchyard, the one that Wilton claimed he had taken. It climbed up through a neat quilt of plowed fields, mostly small-holdings according to the Sergeant, that ran to the crest of a low ridge, and then it made its way down the far side to a narrow stone bridge and the ruins of an old mill. A three-mile walk in all, give or take a little.

The church sat not on the High Street itself but just off it, at the end of a small close of magpie houses that faced one another on what Davies called Court Street. Rutledge thought these might be medieval almshouses, for they were of a similar size and design, all fourteen of them. He turned into the close and stopped at the far end, by the lych-gate in front of the church. Leaving the motor running, he walked to the rough wall that encircled the graveyard, hoping for a better look at the track. He wanted a feeling for how it went, and whether there might be places from which a plowman or a farm wife feeding chickens might overlook it. He needed witnesses, people who had seen Wilton out for his morning walk and climbing this hill with nothing in his hand except a walking stick. Or— had not seen him at all, which might be equally important . . .

The start of the track was empty except for a squabbling pair of ravens. The rest of it ran out of sight of the village for most of its length, for it followed the line of trees that bordered the cultivated fields, and their branches shaded it this time of year. He could see a cow tied out to graze, and that was all.

Returning to the car, he asked, "Can you reach the meadow where the body was found, from this track?"

"Aye, you can't see it from here, unless you know where to look, but there's a smaller track that branches off from this one, about two fields away from us. If you follow *that*, you'll come to the hedgerow that runs along the boundary of the Colonel's land. It's there that the smaller track connects with another one running up from Smithy Lane—I'll show you that, because it's where I found Hickam, drunk as a lord. Think of it as a rough H, sir, this track by the church and the other by Smithy Lane forming the legs and climbing to the ridge, whilst the bar of the H is the smaller one cutting across."

"Yes, I follow you. Once you've reached the hedgerow, what then?"

"Find a break in it and you'll be in the fields where the Colonel raises corn. Above them there's a patch of rough land that's put to hay, between the hedgerow and a copse of trees. On the far side of those trees lies the meadow. That's the scene of the murder."

Rutledge reversed. Back on the High Street again,

he saw Hickam weaving an uncertain path along the pavement. His head down, he was muttering to himself, once or twice flinging out an arm in a gesture of disgust. He looked half drunk now, a man without pride or grace or spirit. Neither Rutledge nor Davies made any comment, but both could see that there was no need to stop.

Still driving in the direction he had taken to Mallows earlier, Rutledge saw Smithy Lane some thirty feet ahead, just as Davies pointed it out to him. An unpaved street, it ran between the busy blacksmith's shop and a livery stable on the right and the ironmonger's on the left. Beyond these businesses were six or seven run-down houses straggling up the slope of the hill toward the fields beyond. Where the last house stood, the lane became a cart track and soon the cart track narrowed into a country path of ruts and mud puddles. Rutledge drove gingerly, his attention on tires and axles.

But then the cart track eventually lost its way in a tangle of hawthorns and wild cherry, and here they left the car. As Davies got out, he said, "It's here I found Hickam—he'd fallen asleep in the leaves yonder. And there," he said, pointing to the last open ground before the track faded into the path, "is where he claims he saw the Colonel talking to Captain Wilton."

"Did you look for signs of a horseman here? Or the prints of Wilton's boots in the dust?"

"Inspector Forrest came to look the next morning, and then said we'd best leave this business to Scotland Yard."

"But were there signs of the two men?"

"Not that he could see."

Which probably meant that he hadn't wanted to

find anything. Rutledge nodded and they moved on, soon afterward passing the point where the rather overgrown track from the east met this one.

"And that's the bar of the H, sir, like I said."

Skirting a field of marrows, they came at length to the hedgerows. Sergeant Davies quickly found his way through them, into the fields of young wheat beyond.

"We're on Mallows land now," he said. The edges of the fields where they walked were still heavy with wet earth, clinging to their boots in great clots. The hayfield higher up was a wall of tall wet stalks rimmed with weeds. Burrs stuck to their trousers and wild roses caught at their coats. Davies swore once with fervent imagination as he was stung by nettles, and then they were in the copse, where walking was easier, almost silent on a cushion of damp leaves. They came out of the stand of trees into a small, sunny meadow, where the sound of bees filled the air.

The rain had washed away any signs of blood, but the grass was still bruised and trampled from the many feet that had milled around the body.

"He lay just about there, chest down, toward the wood, one arm under him and the other outflung. His legs were straight, slightly bent at the knees but that's all. I'd say he fell from the horse and never moved, not even a twitch. So his attacker must have come out of the trees, just as we did. Say, just *here*," Davies explained, moving a few feet away from where the body had been found. "Not more than ten feet, anyway, from where the body fell, depending on whether the shot knocked him out of the saddle or he fell out of it."

"If he was knocked out of it, why was he on his face—chest? If he was shot from the front, the force of the blast would have driven him out of the saddle backward. Even if the horse had bolted in terror, his feet would slip out of the stirrups and he'd have come off backward. On his *back*, Sergeant! Or his side. But not facedown."

Davies chewed his lip. "I thought about that myself. That Harris must have been shot from the back, to fall forward on his chest. But that doesn't fit with the horse—I saw it, there was blood all over the saddle and its haunches, but not on its ears or mane. You'd have thought, if Harris's head had exploded from behind, not the front, that the horse's mane would have been matted with blood and brains."

"Then someone turned him over. The search party?"

"They swear they never touched the corpse. And there was no question but that he was dead—they didn't need to move him."

"The killer, then?"

Davies shook his head. "Why would he do that? He'd be wanting to get as far away as he could, in case someone heard the shot and came to see what it was."

Rutledge looked around. "We've come two miles, or thereabouts. How far is the other track from this wood?"

"Two miles, a little more than that. Shorter if you don't mind rougher going than we just had."

"So Wilton could have reached the meadow either way—from the lane where we came up, if Hickam is right, or from the churchyard path, if Wilton walked that way, as *he* claims he did."

"Aye, but it isn't likely, is it? Somehow I just don't see the Captain waiting in the trees to shoot the Colonel from ambush! Besides, when Hickam saw him, he wasn't carrying a shotgun, was he? So where did he get the gun, and where is it now?"

"A good question, that. You've scoured the area looking for it?"

"Aye, as soon as possible we had men in the trees there and in the tall grass. But by that time, who knows what might have become of the weapon. The killer's hidden it somewhere, most likely."

Looking about him, Rutledge thought, It isn't where he's hidden it that's half as important as where he got it.

Davies pointed and said, "Look, if you go down *this* hill, over the fields yonder, and across the stile when you come to another line of hedgerows, you soon find yourself in the orchard behind Mallows, and that takes you to the gardens and the house itself. Of course, you can't see it from here, but the going's fairly straight if you know your way. The land's a pie wedge, like. Mallows is out on the Warwick road, and we've come up from the High Street. The crust, so to speak, runs from Upper Streetham to Warwick. Up here now, we're at the point of the wedge, having come up one side. If we followed the other side, that would be the Haldane property over there."

He turned to point generally in that direction, then faced the way they had just come. "Behind the church are the smallholdings you saw from the churchyard. Beyond them is Crichton land. This meadow then is farther from Mallows—the house, I mean—and the village, than any other part of the Harris property."

"Which means the killer chose this place because he felt sure the shot might not be heard. There aren't any other houses in this area?"

"No."

Rutledge walked around the meadow for a while

longer, not knowing what he expected to find and finding nothing. Finally, satisfied, he called to Davies and they started back toward the car.

But he changed his mind when he reached the field of marrows and said, "We'll walk along the track—the crossbar of the H—as far as that other path coming up from the churchyard. I want to see for myself how these two connect."

The track meandered, but bore mainly eastward through plowed fields, crops already standing greenly after the rain. It joined the churchyard path in the middle of a stretch of fallow land, more or less out in the open. They were standing there while Davies described how they could continue over the ridge to the mill ruins when they saw a woman in the distance, her skirts blowing in the wind as she crested the ridge, her stride long and competent and graceful.

Sergeant Davies shaded his eyes. "That's Miss Sommers—Miss Helena Sommers. She and her cousin live in a little cottage that belongs to the Haldanes. They let it for the summer, now and again, when there's no other tenant."

"She's the woman who encountered Wilton on his walk?"

"Aye, she's the one."

Rutledge moved in her direction. "Then we'll see if we can talk to her now."

Davies hailed her in a baritone that carried clearly, and she turned, acknowledging the shout with a wave.

Miss Sommers was in her late twenties or early thirties, her face strong and her eyes a clear and untroubled gray. She stood waiting for them, calling, "Good morning!"

"This is Inspector Rutledge from London,"

Davies said, more than a little short-winded after the fast pace Rutledge had set. "He's wanting to ask you some questions if you don't mind."

"Of course. How can I help you?" She turned toward Rutledge, shielding her eyes from the sun as she looked up at him.

"Did you see or hear anything unusual on Monday morning when Colonel Harris was shot? I understand you were out walking."

"Yes, I was. But this part of the country is rather hilly, and the echoes do funny things with sound. I didn't hear a gunshot, but once over the crest of the hill there, I wouldn't be likely to if it came from this side." She smiled, indicating the fine pair of field glasses around her neck. "I enjoy watching birds, and when I first came here, I was forever getting confused. I'd hear a song and swear my quarry was in *that* tree, only to discover he was nothing of the sort, he was in a bush over *there*. And the next time it would be just the opposite." The smile faded. "They say Colonel Harris was shot in a meadow—the small one beyond a copse of trees. Is that true?"

"Yes."

She nodded. "I know where it is then. I followed a pair of nesting robins there one afternoon. I wouldn't have been very likely to hear any sounds from there, I'm afraid."

"Did you see anyone?"

"Captain Wilton," she answered with some reluctance. "I didn't speak to him, but I did see him, and he waved."

"At what time was this?"

She shrugged. "I don't know. Early, I think. Around eight, I imagine, or a little after. I was engrossed in tracking a cuckoo and was mainly glad that Wilton wasn't the sort who'd want to stop and chatter."

"Which way was he going?"

"The same way you are."

"Toward the old mill, then."

"Yes, I suppose so. I wasn't really paying much attention, he was just walking along here. I saw him, realized who it was, waved, and then went on my way."

"Did you know the Colonel well?"

"Hardly at all. We've been here since April, and he very kindly asked us to dinner one evening. But my cousin is shy, almost a recluse, and she didn't want to go. I did, enjoyed the evening, and that was that. We spoke to each other on the High Street, and I waved if I saw him out riding, but that's about all I can tell you."

"And you know the Captain well enough to be certain you did see him and not someone else?"

She smiled, the gray eyes lighting within. "A woman doesn't forget Mark Wilton, once she's seen him. He's very handsome."

"How would you describe the Colonel?"

She considered his question, as if she hadn't given much thought to the Colonel before now. "He was younger than I expected. And rather attractive in a quiet way. Widely read for a military man—we had a very interesting discussion over dinner about American poets, and he seemed to know Whitman quite well." She brushed a strand of windblown hair out of her face. "He seemed a likable man, on short acquaintance. A very gracious host. I can't tell you much more, because I talked mostly to Lettice Wood after dinner and then to Mrs. Davenant, and shortly after that, the party broke up."

"How would you describe relations between Wilton and Colonel Harris?"

"Relations? I hardly know." She thought back to that evening for a moment, then said, "They seemed comfortable with each other, like men who have known each other over a long period of time. That's all I can remember."

"Thank you, Miss Sommers. If you should think of anything else that might help us, please get in touch with Sergeant Davies or me."

"Yes, of course." She hesitated, then asked, "I've gone on with my walks. I suppose that's all right? My cousin frets and begs me to stay home, but I hate being cooped up. There's no—well, danger—is there?"

"From the Colonel's killer?"

She nodded.

"I doubt that you have anything to fear, Miss Sommers. All the same, you might exercise reasonable caution. We still don't know why the Colonel was killed, or by whom."

"Well, I wish you luck in finding him," she said, and went striding off.

"A pleasant lady," Davies said, watching her go. "Her cousin, now, she's as timid as a mouse. Never shows her face in the village, but keeps the cottage as clean as a pin. Mrs. Haldane was saying that she thought the poor girl was a half-wit at first, but went over to the cottage one day to ask how they were settling in, and saw that she's just shy, as Miss Sommers said, and on the plain side."

Rutledge was not interested in the shy Miss Sommers. He was tired and hungry, and Hamish had been mumbling under his breath for the last half hour, a certain sign of tumult in his own mind. It was time to turn back.

What bothered him most, he thought, striding

along in silence, was the Colonel himself. He'd actually seen the man, heard him inspire troops who had no spirit and no strength left to fight. A tall persuasive figure in an officer's greatcoat, his voice pitched to carry in the darkness before dawn, his own physical force somehow filling the cold, frightened emptiness in the faces before him. Convincing them that they had one more charge left in them, that together they could carry the assault and take the gun emplacement and save a thousand lives the next morning—two thousand—when the main thrust came. And the remnants of a battered force did as he had asked, only to see the main attack fail, and the hill abandoned to the Hun again within twenty-four hours.

Yet here in Upper Streetham Charles Harris seemed to be no more than a faint shadow of that officer, a quiet and "thoroughly nice" man, as Mrs. Davenant had put it. Surely not a man who was likely to be murdered.

How do you put your fingers on the pulse of a dead man and bring him to life? Rutledge had been able to do that at one time, had in the first several cases of his career shown an uncanny knack for seeing the victim from the viewpoint of the murderer and understanding why he or she had had to die. Because the solution to a murder was sometimes just that—finding out why the victim had to die. But here in Warwickshire the Colonel seemed to elude him. . . .

Except to acknowledge the fact that once more he would be dealing with death, he, Rutledge, had never really thought through the problems of resuming his career at the Yard. At least not while he was still at the clinic, locked in despair and his own fears. To be honest about it, he'd seen his return mainly as the answer to his desperate need to stay busy, to shut out Hamish, to shut out Jean, to shut out, indeed, the shambles of his life.

Even back in London, he had never really considered whether or not he was good enough still at his work to return to it. He hadn't considered whether the skills and the intuitive grasp of often frail threads of information, which had been his greatest asset, had been damaged along with the balance of his mind by the horrors of the war. Whether he *could* be a good policeman again. He'd simply expected his ability to come back without effort, like remembering how to ride or how to swim, rusty skills that needed only a new honing. . . .

Now, suddenly, he was worried about that. One more worry, one more point of stress, and it was stress that gave Hamish access to his conscious mind. The doctors had told him that.

He sighed, and Sergeant Davies, clumping along through the grass beside him, said, "Aye, it's been a long morning, and we've gotten nowhere."

"Haven't we?" Rutledge asked, forcing his attention back to the business in hand. "Miss Sommers said she did see Wilton walking this track. But where was he coming from? The churchyard, as he claims? Or had he walked by way of the lane, as Hickam claims, met the Colonel, and then crossed over this way? Or—did he go after Harris, follow him to the meadow, with murder on his mind?"

"But this way leads to the ruins by the old bridge, just as he told us, and Miss Sommers saw him here around eight, she thought. So we're no nearer to the truth than we were before."

"Yes, all right, but since Miss Sommers saw him here, he'd be bound to tell us that he was heading for the *mill*, wouldn't he? No matter where he'd actually been—or was actually going."

"Do you think he's guilty, then?" Sergeant Davies couldn't keep the disappointment out of his voice.

"There isn't enough information at this point to make any decision at all. But it's possible, yes." They had reached the car again, and Rutledge opened his door, then stopped to pick the worst of the burrs from his trousers. Davies was standing by the bonnet, fanning himself with his hat, his face red from the exertion.

Still following a train of thought, Rutledge said, "If Miss Sommers is right and Wilton was up there in the high grass early on, say eight o'clock, he might well have been a good distance from the meadow by the time the Colonel was shot. Assuming, as we must, that the horse came straight home and the Colonel died somewhere between nine-thirty and ten o'clock, when Royston went down to the stables looking for him."

"Aye, he would have reached the ruins and the bridge in that time, it's true. So you're saying then that it still hangs on Hickam's word that Captain Wilton was in the lane, and when that was."

"It appears that way. Without Hickam, there's no evidence where the Captain had come from before he ran into Miss Sommers. No evidence of a further quarrel. And no real reason except for what Johnston and Mary overheard in the hall at Mallows for us to believe that the Captain had any cause to shoot Harris."

Sergeant Davies brightened. "And no jury in this county is going to take a Daniel Hickam's word over that of a man holding the Victoria Cross."

"You're forgetting something, Sergeant," Rutledge said, climbing into the car.

"What's that, sir?" Davies asked anxiously, coming around and peering into the car from the passenger side so that he could see Rutledge's face.

"If Wilton didn't shoot Harris, then who did? And who turned the corpse over?"

After lunch at the Shepherd's Crook, Rutledge took out the small leather notebook, made a number of entries, and then considered what he should do next. He had sent Davies home to his wife for lunch, while he lingered over his own coffee in the dining room, enjoying the brief solitude.

What was Harris like? That seemed to be the key. What lay buried somewhere in the man's life that was to bring him to a bloody death in a sunlit meadow?

Or to turn it another way, why did he have to die that morning? Why not last week—last year—ten years from now?

Something had triggered the chain of events that ended in that meadow. Something said—or left unsaid. Something done—or left undone. Something felt, something glimpsed, something misunderstood, something that had festered into an angry explosion of gunpowder and shot.

Royston, Wilton, Mrs. Davenant, Lettice Wood. Four different people with four vastly different relationships to the dead man. Royston an employee, Wilton a friend, Mrs. Davenant a neighbor, and Lettice Wood his ward. Surely he must have shown a different personality to each of them. It was human nature to color your moods and your conversations and your temperament to suit your company. Surely one of the four must have seen a side to his character that would lead the police to an answer.

It was hard to believe that Charles Harris had no sins heavy on his conscience, no faces haunting his dreams, no shadows on his soul. There was no such thing as a perfect English gentleman—

Hamish had started humming a tune, and Rutledge tried to ignore it, but it was familiar, and in the way of songs that run unbidden through the mind, it dragged his attention away from his own speculations. And then suddenly he realized what it was—a half-forgotten Victorian ballad called "The Proper English Gentleman" written by a less well known contemporary of Kipling's—less popular perhaps because his sentiments were bitter and lacked Kipling's fine sense of what the reading public would put up with, and what it would turn from. But the ballad had been popular enough in the trenches during the war:

> *He's a proper English gentleman who never*
> *   spills his beer.*
> *He dines with all the ladies and never shows*
> *   his fear*
> *Of picking up the wrong fork or swearing at*
> *   the soup*
> *When it's hot enough to burn him, or jump-*
> *   ing through the hoop*
> *Of English society, and all it represents.*
>
> *But he's a damned good soldier in front of all*
> *   the troops*
> *And marches like a gentleman in his fine*
> *   leather boots*
> *And eats in the reg'lar mess and calls the*
> *   men by name*
> *And shares the dirty work with 'em, what's*
> *   called the killing game*
> *Of English Imperialism and all it represents.*

But by his own hearthside he's a very
    different sort
And he beats his tenants quarterly and no
    one dares retort,
He takes their wives and daughters, and
    never stops to think
That a man might someday shoot him when
    he's had enough to drink!
Of English duplicity, and all it represents,

He's the finest of examples, and there's others
    of his kind
Who keep their secrets closely and never
    seem to mind
That the man who sits at table and has their
    deepest trust
Might carry in his bosom the foulest kind
    of lust,
Not English respectability, and all it represents.

So watch your step, my laddies, keep your
    distance, ladies dear,
Watch out for English gentlemen and don't
    ever let them near.
Their faces won't betray them, their deeds
    are fine and true,
But put them near temptation and it really
    will not do—
For certain English gentlemen and all they
    represent.

What was the secret behind Charles Harris's very proper face? What had he done, this apparently "thoroughly nice" man, that had made someone want to obliterate him, and to choose a shotgun at point-blank range to do it?

·   ·   ·

Barton Redfern was just removing the coffee things and turning to limp back to the kitchen when Dr. Warren came through the dining-room door and, seeing Rutledge at the table by the window, crossed hurriedly to him.

"You'd better come," he said. "They're about to lynch that stupid devil Mavers!"

5

Mavers, sprawled in the dust by the worn shaft of the village's market cross, was bloody and defiant, spitting curses as a dozen men tried to kick and drag him toward the broad oak tree that stood outside a row of shops. There was murder in the angry faces encircling him, and someone had found a length of rope, although Rutledge wasn't sure whether the initial intent was to hang Mavers or tie him to the tree for a sound thrashing. One man was carrying a horsewhip, and when in the confusion a heavy blow intended for Mavers caught him on the shin instead, he wheeled and lashed out in retaliation. The whip flicked across several heads, and for an instant it looked as if a general battle might ensue, while Mavers called them all every unprintable name he could think of. It was noisy, dangerous chaos on the verge of turning even nastier as other men came running toward the scene, shouting encouragement.

Women had hurried into the safety of the nearest shops, their pale faces peering out of windows in horror, while the shopkeepers stood in their doorways, demanding that this nonsense stop. Children clinging to their mothers' skirts were crying, and four or five dogs attracted by the din had begun to bark excitedly.

As Hamish growled over the odds in some far corner of his mind, Rutledge reached the melee and began forcing his way through with rough disregard for victim or victimizer. He used his voice with coldly calculated effect, the officer commanding discipline, Authority in the flesh, a man to be reckoned with. "That's enough! Let him go, or I'll have the lot of you up before the magistrate for assault! Touch me with that whip, you fool, and you'll be flat on your back with your arm broken. . . ."

His unexpected onslaught scattered the attackers for an instant, and Rutledge quickly had Mavers by his collar, yanking him to his feet with blistering impatience. "Now what's this all about?"

Dr. Warren had followed Rutledge as fast as he could, and reaching the market cross, began catching men by the arm and calling them by name. "Matt, don't be stupid, put that whip down. Tom, George, look at the lot of you! Your wife will take a flatiron to you for ripping that coat, Will, wait and see if she doesn't!"

Mavers, wiping his bloody nose on the sleeve of his shirt, said to Rutledge, "I don't need the likes of you to fight my battles for me! A policeman stinks of his masters, and I can smell oppression, London's bourgeois fist in the backs of the people—"

Rutledge gave a jerk of his collar that silenced Mavers with a choking grunt. Warren had stopped tongue-lashing the disgruntled villagers still milling around the market cross and was already casting a professional eye over cuts and bruises and one swelling lip.

Then the affair was over as quickly as it had

begun, and Warren said, "Take Mavers to my surgery. I'll be there in five minutes."

Rutledge's eyes swept the circle of faces, grimness changing slowly to sullen mortification on most of them, and decided that there would be no more trouble here. With one hand still gripping the rumpled collar, he marched Mavers down the street and across to the doctor's surgery, ignoring the man's protests and the stares of latecomers. Warren's housekeeper, prim and neat in starched black, was waiting in the doorway. She looked at Mavers's condition with disgust and said, "Don't you dare drip blood on my clean floor!" before going off to fetch cold water and a handful of cloths.

"What the hell were you trying to do out there, take on half the village?" Rutledge asked, standing in the entrance hall waiting for the housekeeper to come back, one eye on the street.

"I told the fools what they didn't want to hear. I told them the truth." His voice was thick and muffled from the swelling nose, like a man with a head cold.

"Which was?"

"That they were too blind to see their chance and take it. That their precious war hero had feet of clay. That the Colonel was nothing but an oppressor of the workingman and deserved what he got." Warming to his theme, he went on, "It's the fate of all landlords, to be taken out and shot and their lands given to the peasants. And here somebody has already gone and done the peasants' bloody work for them."

"I'm sure Matt Wilmore liked being called a peasant," Dr. Warren said, coming through the door behind Rutledge, "just when he's bought his own farm and is proud as punch of it." His housekeeper arrived with a basin of water and wads of lint to use packing Mavers's nose, but it wasn't broken, only thoroughly bloodied. "That was Tom Dillingham's fist, I'll wager," Warren said with some satisfaction as he cleaned up Mavers's truculent face. "He's something of a legend around here," he added to Rutledge, "made enough money as a pugilist to buy a bit of land down by the Ware. *He's* not likely to take to being called a peasant either. Even those who are tenants—Haldane's or Mrs. Crichton's—aren't going to swallow it. Peasants went out with Wat Tyler in 1340 or whenever the hell it was."

Rutledge smiled. Mavers said, "Can I go now?"

Warren washed his hands. "Yes, be off with you, I've got more important things to do. Ungrateful fool!"

Rutledge led him outside and said, "Don't be in any hurry, Mavers, I want to talk to you."

"About the Colonel's death?" He grinned, the bloodshot eyes as yellow as a goat's. Mavers was not a big man, and had the wizened look of poor food and bad health in early childhood, his face pointed and sallow, his hair thin and a dusty brown. But his eyes were vivid, their color giving his face its only character. "You can't accuse me of touching him. I was here in Upper Streetham that morning, lecturing all those busy market goers on the evils of capitalism. Ask anybody, they'll tell you as much."

But there was a gloating in the way he said it that made Rutledge wonder what he was hiding. Mavers was very pleased with himself, and not above taunting the police.

A born troublemaker, just as everyone had said. Still, such a man could put that sort of reputation to good use, hiding behind it quite easily. People might shake their heads in disgust, but their perception of Mavers gave him the freedom to make a nuisance of himself without fear of retribution. *"What do you expect? That's Mavers for you!"* or *"What's the damned fool going to get up to next?"* People ignored him, expecting the worst and getting it. Half the time not seeing *him*, seeing only their own image of him . . .

"What do you do for a living?"

Caught off guard, Mavers shot Rutledge a glance out of the corner of those goat's eyes. "What do you mean?"

"How do you find the money to live?"

Mavers grinned again. "Oh, I manage well enough on my pension."

"Pension?"

Sergeant Davies came running toward them, a smear of mustard like a yellow mustache across his upper lip. "I've taken care of that lot," he said. "Damned fools! What have you been about this time, Mavers? The Inspector yonder should have let them hang you and be done with it!"

Mavers's grin broadened. "And you'd get fat, wouldn't you, without me to keep you from your dinner?"

"The trouble is," Davies went on, paying no heed to Mavers, "they've all been in the war, or had family that was, and the Colonel was looked up to. *He* tried to tell them the Colonel had squandered the poor sod in the trenches while keeping his own hide safe, but *they* know better. The Colonel kept up with every man from the village, and visited them in hospital and saw to the families of the ones that didn't come back, and found work for the cripples. People remember that."

"Money's cheap," Hamish put in suddenly. "Or

was he thinking of standing for Parliament? Our fine Colonel?"

But no one heard him except Rutledge.

It was decided to take Mavers home, to give the villagers time to cool off without further provocation, and Rutledge went back to the Shepherd's Crook for his car. He had just reached the walk in front of the door when someone called, "Inspector?"

He turned to see a young woman astride a bicycle, her cheeks flushed from riding and her dark hair pinned up inside a very becoming gray hat with curling pheasant's feathers that swept down to touch her cheek.

"I'm Rutledge, yes."

She dismounted from the bicycle and propped it up against the railing by the horse trough. "I'm Catherine Tarrant, and I'd like to talk to you, if you have the time."

The name meant nothing to him at first, and then he remembered—she was the woman Captain Wilton had courted before the war. He led her inside the Inn and found a quiet corner of the old-fashioned parlor where they wouldn't be interrupted. Waiting until she seated herself in one of the faded, chintz-covered chairs, he took the other across from her and then said, "What can I do for you, Miss Tarrant?" Behind him a tall clock ticked loudly, the pendulum catching sunlight from the windows at each end of its swing.

She had had the kind of face that men often fall in love with in their youth, fresh and sweet and softly feminine. Rutledge was suddenly reminded of girls in white gowns with blue sashes around trim waists, broad-brimmed hats pinned to high-piled curls, who had played tennis and strolled on cropped green lawns and laughed lightheartedly in the summer of 1914, then disappeared forever. Catherine Tarrant had changed with them. There was a firmness to her jaw and her mouth now, signs of suffering and emerging character that in the end would make her more attractive if less pretty. Her dark eyes were level, with intelligence clearly visible in their swift appraisal of him.

"I have nothing to tell you that will help your enquiries," she said at once. "I don't know anything about Colonel Harris's death except what I've heard. But my housekeeper is Mary Satterthwaite's sister, and Mary has told her about the quarrel between the Colonel and Captain Wilton. I know," she added quickly, "Mary shouldn't have. But she did, and Vivian told me. I just want to say to you that I've known Mark—Captain Wilton—for some years, and I can't imagine him killing anyone, least of all Lettice Wood's guardian! Lettice adored Charles, he was her knight in shining armor, a father and brother all in one. And Mark adores Lettice. He'd never let himself be provoked into doing anything so foolish!"

"You think, then, that the quarrel was serious enough to make us believe that the Captain is under suspicion?"

That shook her quiet intensity. She had come in defense of Wilton and found herself apparently on the brink of damning him. Then she collected her wits and with a lift of her chin, she said, "I'm not a policeman, Inspector. I don't know what is important in a murder enquiry and what isn't. But I should think that a quarrel between two men the night before one of them is killed will be given your thorough consideration. And you don't know those two as well as I do—did."

"Then perhaps you should tell me about them."

"Tell you what? That neither of them had a vile temper, that neither of them would hurt Lettice, that neither of them was the sort of man to resort to murder?"

"Yet they quarreled. And one of them is dead."

"Then we've come full circle again, haven't we? And I'm trying to make you understand that however angry Charles might have made him at the moment, Mark wouldn't have harmed him—least of all, killed him so savagely!"

"How do you know what might drive a man to murder?" he asked.

She studied him for a moment with those dark, clear eyes, and said, "How do you? Have you ever killed a man? Deliberately and intentionally? Not counting the war, I mean."

Rutledge smiled grimly. "Point taken." After a moment he added, "If we scratch Wilton from our list of suspects, have you got a name to put in his place?"

"Mavers," she said instantly. "I wouldn't trust him as far as I could see him!"

"But he was in the village on Monday morning. In plain view of half a hundred people."

She shrugged. "That's your problem, not mine. You asked me who might have shot Charles, not how he did it."

"It appears that Wilton was seen by several witnesses in the vicinity of the meadow where Harris died."

"I don't care where he was seen. I tell you he wouldn't have touched Charles Harris. He's madly in love with Lettice. Can't I make you understand that? Why would he risk losing her?"

"Are you still in love with him?"

Color rose in her face, a mottled red under the soft, fair skin. The earnestness changed to a clipped tension. "I was infatuated with Mark Wilton five years ago. He came to Upper Streetham one summer, and I fell in love with him the first time I saw him—any girl with eyes in her head must have done the same! Mrs. Davenant's husband had just died, and Mark stayed with her for a while, until the estate was settled and so on. I envied her, you know, having Mark's company every day, from breakfast to dinner. She's only a few years older than he is, and I was sure he'd fall in love with her, and never notice *me*. Then we met one Sunday after the morning service, he called on me later, and for a time, I thought he was as in love with me as I was with him."

She stopped suddenly, as if afraid she'd said too much, then went on in spite of herself. "We made quite a handsome pair, everyone said so. He's so fair, and I'm so dark. And I think that was part of my infatuation too. The trouble was, Mark wanted to fly, not to find himself tied down with a wife and family, and at that point in my life I wanted a rose-covered cottage, a fairy-tale ending."

For a moment there was a flare of pain in her dark eyes, a passing thought that seemed to have no connection with Wilton but was directed at herself—or at her dreams. "At any rate, I had several letters from Mark after he went away, and I answered a few of them, and then we simply didn't have anything more to say to each other. It was over. And it wouldn't have done. For either of us. Does that answer your question?"

"Not altogether." Her color was still high, but he thought that it was from anger as much as anything else. And that intrigued him. He found himself wondering if Mark Wilton had been having an affair with his widowed cousin—and using Catherine Tarrant as a blind to mislead a village full of gossips. If she'd guessed that, her pride might have suffered more than her heart. And she might defend him now to protect herself, not him. "Are you still in love with him?" he asked again.

"No," she said after a moment. "But I'm still fond enough of him to care what happens to him. I've got my painting, I've made quite a success of that, and any man in my life now would take second place." He could hear a bleak undercurrent of bitterness behind the proud declaration.

"Even the fairy-tale prince?"

She managed a smile. "Even a prince." She had stripped off her soft leather gloves when she came into the Inn, and now she began to draw them on again. "I have the feeling I've only made matters worse. Have I?"

"For Captain Wilton? Not really. So far you haven't told me anything that would point in his direction—or away from it. Nothing has changed, as far as I can see."

Frowning, she said, "You must believe this, if nothing else. Mark wouldn't have harmed Charles Harris. Of all people."

"Not even if Lettice now inherits Mallows?"

Startled, she laughed. "Mark inherited his own money years ago, quite a lot of it. That's what made it possible for him to learn to fly, to buy his own aeroplane. He doesn't need hers!"

As she rose and said good-bye, he considered for a moment whether she had come for Captain Wilton's sake—or for some private motive. And what that motive might be. Not her own guilt, as far as he could see. If she still loved Wilton, killing Charles Harris was not the way to bring the Captain back to her. And jealousy would have been better served by shooting Wilton himself. Or Lettice.

Then why was it that the bitterness and pain

he'd read in Catherine Tarrant's voice seemed far more personal than the altruistic act of coming to a friend's defense?

"Women," Hamish said unexpectedly. "They always ken the cruelest way to torment a man for what's he's done, witting or no'."

Rutledge thought of Jean and that day in the hospital when she had abandoned him to his nightmares. She'd intended to be kind—that's what had hurt him most.

Outside, picking up her bicycle and leading it away from the railing, Catherine Tarrant paused, biting her lower lip, busy with her own thoughts. Mrs. Crichton's estate agent came out of the Inn and spoke to her as he passed, but she didn't hear him.

"Oh, damn," she accused herself silently, "you've muddled everything. You should have had the sense to leave well enough alone, to stay out of it. Now he'll start to pry and probe—" If Inspector Forrest had been handling the enquiry, *he* would have listened to her. He'd known her family for ages, he would have believed her without bringing up what happened in the war. Why on earth had they sent for someone from London instead of leaving this business to the local people!

But she knew the reason. The finger of suspicion must be strongly pointing toward Mark already, and everyone in Warwickshire was running for cover. There had been a dozen photographs of the King and Mark together, he'd dined with the Prince of Wales, was invited to Scotland to shoot, had even accompanied the Queen to a home for soldiers disabled by mustard gas—and questions were going to be asked when he was arrested for a bloody murder involving another war hero. Buckingham Palace would be icily furious.

Then where was their case? Not just that stupid quarrel. Surely you wouldn't arrest a man simply because he had a roaring argument with the victim the night before. There had to be more damning evidence against him than that. And who were these people who claimed to have seen Mark near the place where Charles Harris had died? What else had they seen, if someone had the wit to ask them the right questions? . . .

For a moment she debated going straight to the Davenant house and asking Mark himself who the witnesses were. But Sally Davenant would be there, smiling and pretending not to notice how badly Catherine wanted to speak to Mark alone. Making the unexpected visit seem more like a ploy, an emotional excuse to come back into his life. And that would be hard to explain away.

She hadn't told Rutledge the whole truth about Mrs. Davenant either. But she didn't care about anyone else if Mark could be protected. She still wasn't certain why she was so determined to help him. In the wild tangle of her emotions, he was the man who had opened her eyes to passion and prepared her for what had come later. And for that alone perhaps she owed him something.

There must be a better way of getting to the bottom of this. She'd find Inspector Forrest and make him tell her everything she wanted to know. He wouldn't be like the Londoner, stark and unfeeling. A man to watch, that one!

Steadying the bicycle, she began to pedal, absorbed in the question of how best to handle Forrest.

·   ·   ·

Catherine met him just coming home from Lower Streetham and looking tired. He was middle-aged, thin and stooped, more the university don than a village policeman. He smiled when she hailed him, and waited by the steps of his house.

"Miss Tarrant. That's a fetching hat you've got on, my dear. Don't let my wife catch a glimpse of it or she'll be pestering me for one just like it."

Which was kind of him, because his wife, like many of the women in Upper Streetham, cared nothing for Catherine Tarrant, with or without a fetching hat on her head. And it gave her the excuse she needed to say, "Then will you walk along with me a little way? I'd like to speak to you."

"I've missed my lunch and I've got a headache you could toss the churchyard through. Will it take long, this talking?"

"No, not really." She gave him her most winning smile, and he said, "All right, then. Ten minutes!"

She had dismounted and he took the bicycle from her, leading it himself as she strode down the quiet street beside him. "What's this all about then?"

And Catherine Tarrant began to work her wiles.

Mavers and Sergeant Davies were glaring at each other by the time that Rutledge finally drove up in front of the doctor's surgery. They climbed into the car in silence, and Rutledge said, "How do I find your house, Mavers?"

"Like the birds in the air, you'll have to fly to it. Or walk. I live up behind the churchyard. There's a path to the house that way. Did you buy this car from the wages of wringing the necks of felons, or have you got private means?"

"Does it matter either way? I'm still an oppressor of the poor."

Mavers grinned nastily, his goat's eyes alight with the zeal of his favorite subject. "Horses earn their keep. What does this bleeding motorcar do for mankind?"

"It keeps workmen employed putting it together, and others earn their livings in the factories that supply the materials to those workmen. Have you considered that? Every person driving a motorcar is a benefactor." He turned into the short street leading to the church.

"And those workmen could be better employed building homes for the poor and growing food for the hungry and making clothes for the naked."

"Which of course you spend every free moment of *your* time doing, a shining example to us all?"

Mavers growled, "You'll have to leave the motor here, by the lych-gate, and get your boots dirty on the path like the rest of us poor devils."

Which they did, marching behind Mavers up the bare track that Rutledge had seen just that morning. It had begun to dry out in the sun, although a thin coating of mud clung halfheartedly to their shoes. But soon they turned off on a small, rutted path that went over another rise and across an unplowed field to a shabby cottage standing in a clump of straggling beech trees. The yard before it was bare of grass and a dozen equally shabby chickens scratched absently there, paying no heed to their owner or his visitors when the three men arrived at the cottage door.

From somewhere around back a pig grunted, and Mavers said, "He's not mine, he belongs to one of the farmers over on the Crichton estate. Too ill-tempered an old boar to keep within sight of a sow, but he still breeds fine. And I'm not home long enough to notice the smell." Which was a good thing, all in all. As the breeze shifted, the essence of pig was nearly breathtaking.

He went inside, and Rutledge followed. The cottage—surprisingly—was not dirty, though it was as shabby inside as the exterior and the chickens. There were four rooms opening off a short central hall, the doors to each standing open. In the first of them on the left side the only windows were over-hung by beech boughs, cutting off the sunlight, and Rutledge blinked in the sudden dimness as he crossed the threshold. Papers were scattered every-where, most of them poorly printed political tracts and handwritten tirades, covering floor and furnish-ings impartially like grimy snow. Mavers walked through and over them, regardless, and flung him-self down in a chair by a small mahogany table at the corner of the hearth. There was a lamp on it, its smoke-blackened chimney surrounded by stacks of books, an inkstand of brass, and a much-used blotter.

"Welcome to Mavers Manor," he said, adding with heavy sarcasm, "Are you planning to stay to dinner? We don't dress here, you'll do as you are." He didn't ask them to sit.

"Who killed Colonel Harris?" Rutledge asked. "Do you know?"

"Why should I? Know, I mean?"

"Somebody knows something. It might be you."

"If I knew anything I'd more likely shake the fool's hand than turn him in to you."

Which Rutledge believed. "Why did you feud with the Colonel? All those years?"

Suddenly Mavers's face turned a mottled red,

which gave the darkening bruises a garish air, and he snarled, "Because he was an arrogant bastard who thought he was God, and never cared what he did to other people. Send that great lump, Davies, out into the yard with the rest of the dumb animals and I'll tell you all about your fine Colonel Harris!"

Rutledge glanced over his shoulder and nodded at Davies, who clumped out and slammed the door behind him, as near as he could ever come to insubordination.

Mavers waited until he could see Davies fuming in the yard, well out of hearing, and then said, "He thought he was lord and master around here, Harris did. Mrs. Crichton never comes to Upper Streetham, she's so old she hardly knows her arse from her elbow, and the Haldanes—well, the Haldanes were so well bred they've nearly vanished, a bloodless lot you can't even be bothered to hate. But the Colonel, now he was something else."

There was pent-up venom in the thick voice, and Mavers was having trouble breathing through his nose as his anger mounted, almost panting between words. "He came into his own early, after his father had a stroke and wound up being confined to a chair for the rest of his life—which wasn't all that long—and in *his* eyes his precious son could do no wrong. Harris had the first motorcar in this part of Warwickshire, did you know that? Drove like a madman, terrified old ladies and horses and half the children. Then he got his commission in the family's Regiment, and he came home swaggering in his fine uniform, telling every man he met that the army life was for them. Had any girl he wanted, paid his way out of trouble, and raised hell whenever he felt like it. My older brother joined the Army to please him, and he died in South Africa with a Boer musket ball in his brain."

He stopped, but Rutledge said nothing, and after a time, Mavers went on more quietly. "My mother never got over that—he was her favorite. A big strapping lad like her own father. And my sister drowned herself in the pond one day because Harris stopped fancying her. I went to Mallows to horsewhip him and got thrashed by the grooms instead. Ma called me a worthless whelp for daring to blame Harris for Annie's weakness. So I ran off to join the Army myself, and somehow he found out about it, and he had me sent home for lying about my age. But he wouldn't give me my job back in the stables at Mallows—he told that bootlicking fool Royston that they didn't want me there anymore because I was a troublemaker. So that's just what I became, trouble. A thorn in his flesh! And if you believe that one fine morning I'd shoot him down, depriving myself of that lifelong pleasure, you're a greater fool than you look!"

Rutledge heard two things in Mavers's diatribe—the ring of truth, and the echo of envy. "You're talking about a boy. Twenty, perhaps? Not much older than that. And you were what? Fourteen? Fifteen?" he said carefully.

The red flush returned to Mavers's face. "What does age have to do with it? Is there some special dispensation for cruelty if you're rich and under twenty?"

"You know there isn't. But a man generally isn't judged by what he did as a boy, he's judged by what he did as a man."

Mavers shrugged. "Boy or man, he's the same. Besides, the damage is done, isn't it? And the man at forty may be a saint, but the rest of us are still bleeding from what he did when he was twenty. Who's to put that right? Who's to bring Annie back, or Jeff? Or Ma. Tell me!"

Rutledge looked around the room, at the worn, plain furniture and the threadbare carpet on the floor, half hidden by the papers, at the damp-stained walls and the windows streaked with dust, all of it dappled by the tree leaves outside as a passing wind stirred them and let in a little light. He'd met men like Mavers before. Hungry for something they didn't have, and ignorant of how to go about getting it, hating those who had had life given to them easily. Lost men, angry men, dangerous men . . . because they had no pride of their own to bolster their self-esteem.

"Hating doesn't put it right either, does it?"

The goat's eyes were hard. "It does give life a purpose, all the same."

Preparing to go, Rutledge said, "As long as it doesn't lead to murder. There's never an excuse for murder."

He was nearly out the door into the hall when Hamish said under his breath, "But who's a murderer, then? The man who carried that shotgun yonder, or the officer who shoots his own men?"

Startled, Rutledge half turned as if Mavers had spoken, not the voice in his own head. And as he looked back, he saw what had been concealed behind Mavers's chair and by Mavers's body and by the books piled on the table—a shotgun, leaning against the wall where it met the jutting corner of the hearth, almost lost in the deep shadow there.

6

Satisfied after her conversation with Inspector Forrest, Catherine Tarrant rode slowly back down the High Street, threading her way through the late-afternoon shoppers and the workmen going about their business. Her eyes quickly scanned their faces, but no one spoke to her and she didn't stop to ask the whereabouts of the one person she sought. Turning her head to glance down Smithy Lane, she almost ran down a small boy dragging his dog behind him on a rope. The dog was too interested in the smells along their route to pay much heed to its master, and looked up with a wide, sloppy grin when she braked hastily to avoid them.

"George Miller, you've got that rope too tight," she said, but the boy gave her a frightened glance and tugged all the harder. The dog followed him good-naturedly, and she sighed in exasperation. Then she saw Daniel Hickam come out of one of the run-down houses beyond the smithy.

Upper Streetham turned a blind eye to the profession of the two women who occupied this particular house as long as they comported themselves with reasonable dignity elsewhere. It was whispered that they made a very good living at their trade because they could be depended on to pass their best customers on the High Street the next day without a flicker of recognition. Catherine had once tried to hire the older of the two, who had hair black as coal and eyes the color of the sea, to pose for a portrait she was painting of an aging courtesan, but the woman had turned her away in a fury.

"I don't care what you're painting, I have my pride, Miss Tarrant, and I'd rather starve than take money from the likes of *you*."

The words had hurt. Catherine had gone to London for her model, but within three weeks had abandoned the portrait because her vision of it had somehow gone astray. The face on the canvas had become a mockery, color and lines without a soul, technical skill without depth of expression.

Pretending to inspect her tire to give Hickam a head start, Catherine waited until he was beyond the last house, finally disappearing among the shadows cast by the first of the hawthorns, at the end of the stand of long grass. Then she began to pedal slowly after him, taking her time so that no one would suspect what she was about to do.

"Whose weapon is that?" Rutledge asked, his eyes on Mavers's face now. "Yours?"

"What weapon?"

"The one just behind you," Rutledge snapped, in no mood for the man's agile tongue. Why the hell hadn't Forrest found this shotgun? If Mavers was a suspect, then he could have obtained a warrant, if necessary.

"What if it is?" Mavers asked belligerently. "I've a right to it, if it was left in a Will!"

"In whose Will?"

"Mr. Davenant's Will, that's whose."

Rutledge walked across the room and carefully broke open the gun. It had been fired recently, but when? Three days ago? A week? Like the rest of the cottage, it was worn, neglected, the stock scratched and the barrel showing the first signs of rust, but the breech had been kept well oiled, as if Mavers was not above a bit of quiet poaching.

"Why did he leave the gun to you?"

There was a brief silence; then Mavers said with less than his usual abrasiveness, "I expect it was my father he meant. My father was once his game-keeper, and Mr. Davenant's Will said, 'I leave the old shotgun to Bert Mavers, who is a better bird-man than any of us.' My father was dead by then, but the Will hadn't been changed, and Mrs. Davenant gave the gun to me, because she said it was what her husband wanted. The lawyer from London wasn't half pleased, I can tell you, but the Will didn't say *which* Bert Mavers, did it? Alive or dead?"

"When was the last time it was fired?"

"How should I know? Or care? The door's always open, anybody can walk in here. There's naught to steal, is there, unless you're after my chickens. Or need a shotgun in a bit of a hurry." His normal nastiness resurfaced. "You can't claim I used it, can you? I've got witnesses!"

"So everyone keeps telling me. But I'll take the gun for now, if you don't mind."

"First I'll have a piece of paper saying you'll bring it back!"

Rutledge took a sheet from his notebook and scribbled a sentence on it, then signed it under the man's baleful eye. Mavers watched him leave, and then folded the single sheet carefully and put it in a small metal box on the mantel.

Inspector Forrest was waiting for them in the magpie cottage beyond the greengrocer's shop that served as the Upper Streetham police station. There was a small anteroom, a pair of offices, and another room at the back used as a holding cell. Seldom occupied by more serious felons than drunks and disturbers of the peace, an occasional wife beater or petty thief, this cell still had a heavy, almost medieval lock on its door, with the big iron key hanging nearby on a nail. The furnishings were old, the paint showing wear, the color of the carpet on the floors almost nondescript now, but the rooms were spotless.

Leaning across a battered desk to shake hands, Forrest introduced himself to Rutledge and said, "I'm sorry about this morning. Three dead in Lower Streetham, another in critical condition, two more seriously injured, and half the village in an uproar. I didn't like to leave until things had settled a bit. I hope Sergeant Davies has told you everything you wanted to know." He saw the shotgun in Rutledge's left hand and said, "Hello, what have we here?"

"Bert Mavers says this was left to him in a Will—or rather, left to his father."

"Good Lord! So it was! I'd forgotten about that. And Mrs. Davenant didn't mention it either, when I went to see her about her husband's Italian guns. It's been *years*—" His face was a picture of shock and chagrin.

"We probably can't prove it's the murder weapon, but I'm ready to wager it was."

Reaching for the shotgun, Forrest said with

sudden enthusiasm, "Used by Mavers, do you think?"

"If so, why didn't he have the wit to put it out of sight afterward?"

"You never know with Mavers. Nothing he does makes much sense." Forrest examined it carefully, as if half expecting it to confess. "Yes, it's been fired, you can see that, but there's no saying when, is there? Still—"

"Everyone claims he was in the village all morning. Is that true?"

"Unfortunately, it appears to be." Forrest fished in the center drawer of his desk and said, "Here's a list of people I've talked to. You can see for yourself."

Rutledge took the neatly written sheet and glanced at the names, nearly two dozen of them. Most were unfamiliar to him, but Mrs. Davenant's was among them, and Royston's. And Catherine Tarrant's.

"Each of these people heard him ranting. That's clear enough," Forrest went on. "He was plaguing everyone who came within earshot, and each one will swear to that. Although the shopkeepers were too busy to pay much heed to him, they remember that he was making the usual nuisance of himself, and their customers were commenting on it. Putting it all together, you can see that he arrived in the market square early on and was still there at midmorning." He rubbed his pounding temples and gestured to the two barrel-backed oak chairs across from the desk. "Sit down, sit down."

Rutledge shook his head. "I must find Daniel Hickam."

Inspector Forrest said, "Surely you don't intend to take his statement seriously? There's bound to be other evidence more worthy of your time than anything Hickam can say! If we keep looking hard enough?" He could see that the man from London was far from well, and suddenly found himself worrying about that. You don't have the patience and the energy to give to a thorough investigation, is that it? he thought to himself. You want an easy answer, then back to the comforts of London. That's why the Yard sent you, then, to sweep it all under the rug for them. And it's my fault. . . .

"I won't know that until I've spoken to him, will I?"

"He can't tell you what day of the week it is half the time, much less where he came from before you ran into him or where he might be going next. Mind's a wasteland. Pity he didn't die when that shell exploded—no good to himself or anyone else in his condition!"

"You took down his statement," Rutledge pointed out. Hamish, relishing Forrest's remark, was repeating it softly, an echo whispering across a void of fear. ". . . *no good to himself or anyone else in his condition. . . .*" He turned away abruptly to shield his face from Forrest's sharp gaze, and unintentionally left the impression that he was putting the blame squarely where it belonged.

"I don't see what else I could have done. Sergeant Davies reported the conversation, and after that I *had* to pursue the matter," Forrest answered defensively, "whether Hickam is mad or not. But that doesn't mean we have to believe him. I can't see how Wilton could be guilty of this murder. You've met him. It's just not like the man, is it?"

"From what I can see, it wasn't like the Colonel to find himself the victim of a murder either."

"Well, no, not when you get right down to it. But he *is* dead, isn't he? Either his death was accidental or it was intentional, and we have to start with murder because no one has come forward to tell us any differently. No one has said, 'I was standing there talking to him and the horse jostled my arm, and the gun went off, and the next thing I knew the poor devil was dead.'"

"Would you believe them if they did?"

Forrest sighed. "No. Only an idiot carries an unbroken shotgun."

"Which brings us back to Mavers and his weapon. If Wilton was on either of those tracks on the morning of the murder, he could have taken the gun from Mavers's house, fired it, then put it back before Mavers came home from the village. Hickam's evidence is still important."

"And if Captain Wilton could do that, so could anyone else in Upper Streetham for all we know," Forrest retorted doggedly. "There's still no *proof*."

"There may be," Rutledge said thoughtfully. "Captain Wilton came to stay with his cousin when her husband died. He undoubtedly knew about the Will, and the provision regarding the old shotgun. It caused some problems at the time, I understand."

"*I* knew about it as well, and had forgotten it—so might he have. It's all circumstantial! Guessing—"

"What if the Colonel was the wrong victim?"

That sent Forrest's eyebrows up in patent disbelief. "What do you mean, 'wrong victim'? You don't shoot a man at point-blank range and get the wrong one! That's foolery!"

"Yes, so it is," Rutledge answered. "It's also foolery that the Colonel was flawless, a man with no sins on his conscience. When people begin to tell me the truth, Captain Wilton will be far safer.

Assuming, of course, that you're right and he's innocent."

Leaving Sergeant Davies to check on Royston's dental appointment in Warwick, Rutledge went searching for Hickam on his own, but the man seemed to have disappeared.

"Drunk somewhere, like enough," Hamish said. "Yours is a dry business, man. I'd as soon have a bottle myself."

Which was the only time Rutledge had found himself in agreement with the voice in his mind.

He turned the car toward the Inn and his thoughts toward dinner.

Which turned out to be interesting in its own way. He had hardly cut into his roast mutton when the dining room's glass doors opened and a man with a clerical collar came in, stood for a moment surveying the room, then made his way across to where Rutledge sat.

He was nearing thirty, of medium height, with fair hair, a polished manner, and a strong sense of his own worth. Stopping by the table, he said in a rich baritone, "Inspector Rutledge? I'm Carfield. The vicar. I've just called again at Mallows, and Miss Wood is still unwell. Then I thought perhaps it might be wiser to ask you anyway. Can you tell me when the Colonel's body will be released for burial?"

"We haven't held an Inquest yet, Mr. Carfield. Sit down, won't you? I'd like to talk to you, now that you're here."

Carfield accepted the offer of coffee and said, "Such a tragic business, the Colonel's death."

"So everyone says. Who might want to kill him?"

"Why, no one that I can think of!"

"Yet someone did."

Studying Carfield as the man stirred cream but no sugar into his cup, Rutledge could see that he had the kind of face that would show up well on the stage, handsome and very masculine beyond the twentieth row, but too heavily boned to be called more than "strong" at close quarters. The voice too was made to carry, and grated a little in ordinary conversation. The actor was lurking there, behind the clerical collar, Sergeant Davies had been right about that.

"Tell me about Miss Wood."

"Lettice? Very bright, with a mind of her own. She came to Mallows several years back—1917, after she'd finished school. And she's been an ornament to the community ever since. We're all very fond of her."

Over the rim of his cup, Carfield was quickly assessing the Inspector, noting his thinness, the lines of tiredness about the mouth, the tense muscles around the eyes that betrayed the strain behind his mask of polite interest. But Carfield misunderstood these signs, putting them down to a man out of his depth, one who might prove useful.

"She's taken her guardian's death very hard."

"After all, he was her only family. Girls are often very attached to their fathers, you know."

"Harris could hardly be termed that," Rutledge commented dryly.

With a graceful wave of his hand, Carfield dismissed the quibble over ages. "In loco parentis, of course."

"From all I hear, he may well have walked on water."

Carfield laughed, but it had an edge to it. "Harris? No, if anyone fits that description it's Simon Haldane, not the Colonel. *He* was too good at killing, you know. Some men become soldiers because they've no imagination, they don't know how to be afraid. But Charles Harris had an uncanny aptitude for war. I asked him about that once, and he said that his skills, such as they were, came from reading history and learning its lessons, but I found that hard to believe."

"Why?"

"The Colonel was the finest chess player I've ever met, and I have no mean skills at the game myself. He was born with a talent for strategy that few of us are given, and *he* made the choice about how to use it. He fully understood that choice, that war meant playing with men's lives, not with prettily carved pieces on a game board, but battle was an addiction he couldn't rid himself of."

Rutledge said nothing. Carfield sipped his coffee, then added as if he couldn't stop himself, "Men from Warwickshire who served under him worshiped him; they tell me that on the battlefield he was charismatic, but I call it more a gift for manipulation. I don't suppose you were in the war, Inspector, but I can tell you that sending other men into battle must rest heavily on one's soul in the end."

Hamish stirred but made no remark. He had no need to. Rutledge found himself saying, "Then the Kings of Israel must not be sleeping peacefully in Abraham's bosom. As I remember, they were at war most of the time."

Carfield nodded graciously to parishioners who had just come in, a man and his wife, then turned back to Rutledge. "Make light of it if you wish. But something deep down in Charles Harris was frightened by the man he was. He was a Gemini, you see, two forces in one body. In my opinion he needed to come home to Mallows from time to time because it brought him peace, a sense of balance, proof that he wasn't a man who actually *enjoyed* killing, however good he might be at it. His much-vaunted devotion to the land was perhaps merely a charade for his troubled conscience."

"And Captain Wilton? What do you think of him?"

"An intelligent man. And a brave one—one would have to be to fly, don't you think? When Ezekiel saw the wheel, high in the middle of the air, he claimed it was God at work. We've come a long way since then, haven't we? Man has finally set himself on a par with the archangels. The question is, are we morally ready for such heights?"

Hamish made a derisive snort and Rutledge busied himself with the caramel flan. When he had choked down his amusement, Rutledge asked, "But would he kill a friend?"

"Wilton? None of us can see into the souls of others, Inspector, least of all me. I've always tried to understand my parishioners, but they still have the power to surprise me. Just the other day—"

"Is that a yes or a no?" Rutledge asked, looking up and catching an expression in Carfield's eyes that interested him. The man was ably playing the role of wise village priest, enamored by the part, but his eyes were cold and hard as he answered Rutledge's question.

"I would be lying if I said I liked the man. I don't. He's a private person, keeps himself to himself. I think that may be why he enjoys flying—he's there alone in his aeroplane, out of reach and accountable to no one. And a man who likes his own company more than he ought is sometimes dangerous. Hermits have been known to come out of

their isolated cells and lead crusades, haven't they?
But murder?" He shook his head. "I don't know.
Possibly. If he were angry enough and determined
enough, or if it was the only possible way to get exactly what he wanted. I think he's been used to
that, getting his own way. People tend to idolize
handsome daredevils."

For "people," substitute Lettice Wood, Rutledge thought to himself. But discounting the jealousy, Carfield had offered a better evaluation of
Harris and Wilton than anyone else.

Sometimes hatred saw more clearly than love.

And it might be a very good idea to add
Carfield's name to the very short list of possible
suspects, though what purpose Harris's death
might have served in the Vicar's eyes was yet to be
seen.

He went over his notes after dinner, sitting in his
room until the walls seemed to close in on him. No
illumination came, no connections. Faces. Voices.
Yes. But so far leading nowhere. Except, possibly, to
Wilton? He remembered his father saying once, after a tiring day in court, "It isn't actually a question
of guilt or innocence, is it? It's a matter of what the
jury *believes*, once we've told them what evidence
there is on either side. Given the proper evidence,
we could probably convict God. Without it, Lucifer
himself would walk free!"

It was late when he got up to walk off a restless-
ness that prodded him into activity, useful or not.

Before the war it had been the case that drove
him night and day—partly from a gritty determi-
nation that murderers must be found and punished.
He had believed deeply in that, with the single-
minded idealism of youth and a strong sense of

moral duty toward the victims, who could no longer speak for themselves. But the war had altered his viewpoint, had shown him that the best of men could kill, given the right circumstances, as he himself had done over and over again. Not only the enemy, but his own men, sending them out to be slaughtered even when he had known beyond any doubt that they would die and that the order to advance was madness.

And partly from his fascination with a bizarre game of wits. Like the Colonel, who was far too good at strategy, he'd had a knack for understanding the minds of some of the killers he had hunted, and he had found the excitement of the hunt itself addictive. Man, he'd read somewhere, was the ultimate prey. And the police officer had the reinforcement of Society to indulge in that chase.

Rutledge had tried to explain his reasons to Jean once, when she had begged him to leave the Yard and take up law instead, like his father before him. But she'd stared at him as if he had spoken to her in Russian or Chinese, then laughed and said, "Oh, Ian, do stop teasing me and be serious!"

Now it was his own uncertainties that left him with no peace, his illusions as shattered as his mind. Why could he feel *nothing* about this murderer? *Why?*

He heard something in the shadowy alley to his left, between the baker's shop and a small bootery, a muffled cough. And then Hickam stumbled out, singing to himself. Drunk again. If anything, worse than before, Rutledge thought with exasperation. But at least he wasn't back in an imaginary France, and there might still be a chance of getting a little sense out of him.

Overtaking him in five strides, Rutledge put a hand on the man's shoulder to stop him, speaking his name. Hickam shrugged it off irritably. "I want to talk to you. About Colonel Harris," Rutledge said firmly, prepared to block his retreat down the alley or a dash across the street. "I've come from London—"

"London, is it?" Hickam asked, slurring the words, but Rutledge suddenly had the feeling that he wasn't as drunk—yet—as he wished he was. "And what does London want now? A pox on sodding London! A pox on sodding everybody!"

"The morning that the Colonel died, you were in the lane, drunk. That's where Sergeant Davies found you. Do you remember?" He forced the man to face him, could smell the alcohol on his breath, the unwashed body. The fear.

Hickam nodded. His face was ghastly in the moonlight, tired and strained and hopeless. Rutledge looked into eyes like black plums in a pudding, and flinched at what he read there, a torment much like his own. "Did you see the Colonel? Charles Harris. Or anyone else?"

"I didn't shoot him. I had nothing to do with it!"

"No one claims you did. I'm asking if you saw him. Or saw anyone else that Monday morning."

"I saw them—the two of them." He frowned. "I saw them," he added, with less certainty. "I told Forrest—"

"I know what you told Forrest. Now tell me."

"He was angry. The Captain. Pleading. They were sending us across to take the guns, and he didn't like it. You could hear the shells—the bombardment had started." He was beginning to shake. " 'I won't give up that easily,' he said. 'I'll fight. Whatever you've done, I'll fight you every step of the way!' The guns were ours at first, but then the Hun answered, and they were close, I could hear the screaming and I couldn't find my helmet. And the Colonel said, 'Don't be a fool. Whether you like it or not, you'll have to learn to live with it.' And I saw the Captain's face, and knew we were going to die—"

He was crying, tears running down his face like the shiny trails left by garden slugs, his mouth turned down in an agony of terror. "They sent me down the sunken road, to see that the flankers found their way, and the Colonel rode off, leaving the Captain behind, and I knew he'd kill me if he caught me hiding there from the guns—I didn't want to die—God help me—"

Arms wrapped protectively around his body, he bowed his head and wept with a bottomless grief that silently racked him, his shoulders shaking, all dignity and identity gone.

Rutledge couldn't take any more. He fished in his pocket for coins and gave them to the man, forcing them into the hand nearest him. Hickam lifted his head, staring at him, bewildered by this interjection of reality into his desolation, feeling the coins with his fingers like a blind man. "Here. Buy yourself something else to drink, and go home. Do you hear me? *Go home!*"

Hickam continued to stare at him, at a loss. "They're moving up, I can't leave—"

"You're out of it," Rutledge said. "Go find the aid station and tell them you need something to drink. Tell them I said you could have it. Tell them—for God's sake, *tell them to send you home!*"

And without a backward glance, Rutledge wheeled and strode angrily down the walk to the Inn, Hamish hammering at his senses like all the Furies.

• • •

Rutledge lay awake for hours, listening to the murmurs of a pair of doves nesting under the eaves. They were restless, as if a prowling cat or an owl worried them. The village was quiet, the public bar had closed, and only the big church clock, striking the quarters, disturbed the stillness of the night. He had himself under control again, and only Redfern had seen him return, taking the stairs three at a time. He'd nearly stopped to tell the man to bring him a bottle of whiskey, but had enough sense left to remember where—and who—he was.

Staring at the ceiling, he decided he would call for an immediate Inquest and have it adjourned.

Hickam had been too befuddled to know what he was saying, and God alone could imagine what sort of witness he would make in court. Yet Rutledge was sure now that there was *something* locked in his mind, tangled with the war, tangled with his confusion and the fumes of alcohol, and if Dr. Warren could get the man sober—and sane— long enough to question, they might get to the bottom of this business.

For all they knew, it might clear Wilton as easily as it might damn him, in spite of Forrest's dithering.

The trouble was, there was too much circumstantial evidence and not enough hard fact. The quarrel with Harris at Mallows, the possible— probable—encounter with Harris again in the lane the next morning, the shotgun sitting in Mavers's unlocked house, the direction Wilton had chosen for his walk, all appeared to point to the Captain. And the *time* sequence itself fit, all quite neatly.

But this hadn't been a neat killing. It had been angry, vengeful, passionate, bloody.

Where, except for Mavers's tired rhetoric, had there been such passion on a quiet June morning?

And where had it disappeared, once Charles Harris had been cut down with such savage fury? That was the mystery he was going to have to solve before he could find the killer. So much passion . . . it had to be there still, banked like a fire . . . and aroused, it might kill again. . . .

He fell asleep on that thought, and didn't hear the bustle in the street at two o'clock in the morning.

7

Although Rutledge went out directly after breakfast in search of him, Hickam was nowhere to be found.

After a fruitless waste of time, Rutledge decided that the man probably didn't want to be found, and gave up, cursing his own maudlin stupidity for not hauling him directly to the doctor's surgery last night while he had the chance, and forcibly sobering up the poor devil.

Picking up Sergeant Davies at the station after giving Forrest instructions for the Inquest, Rutledge said as they got into the motorcar, "I've been to the cottage, checked every street in town, and the outlying lanes as well, not to mention the churchyard and the livery stables. Is there any place I haven't thought of?"

Davies scratched his chin. "That about covers it, I'd guess. But there's high grass, hedgerows, and any number of sheds about, and we could send half the army out looking and still not find him. Drunks have a way of vanishing, but when he's slept this one off and needs more gin, he'll surface soon enough."

He glanced at the Inspector, and decided that he hadn't slept well. Changing the subject, he said, "I checked with the dentist in Warwick. It's true, Royston had an appointment on the morning of the murder, but he never came in. Of course that's not surprising."

"No. I think I should speak to Helena Sommers again, before she hears about Mavers's shotgun coming to light. How do we get there?"

Davies had just had a very unpleasant discussion with Inspector Forrest about duty. It was his *duty* to assist London, and equally his duty to stay out of Scotland Yard's way as much as possible, which seemed to his mind a simple contradiction of terms. Forrest hadn't been pleased either that Rutledge failed to bring his own sergeant along, and before the interview had ended, a chastened Davies was beginning to feel that that was his fault as well. But there was no escape. Constable Reardon in Lower Streetham couldn't be spared, and Warwick wasn't about to send over one of their men, and Constable Miliken from Upper Streetham was still at home with a leg broken in two places from the kick of a half-wit horse that had accidentally poked its nose into a hornet's nest and run amok afterward.

Trying to make the best of a bad situation and feeling uncomfortable in the lengthening silence that was beginning to sound very loud in the car, Davies cleared his throat and offered a suggestion that he had been mulling over while shaving that morning.

"I was thinking, sir, about who might have shot Colonel Harris, and it seems to me we've overlooked one thing. What if the killer hadn't come from Upper Streetham at all? I mean, someone from Warwick, or London, or as far as we might know, from Canterbury or Liverpool?"

"It's possible, of course," Rutledge answered. "For that reason I don't rule it out. But we're short on motives, aren't we?"

"Well, sir, it seems to me we're short on motives for everyone else. I mean, the Colonel might have done something in the war, someone might hold him responsible for the loss of a leg or a son's death or a wrecked career. Somebody we'd never heard of in Upper Streetham. And would have no way of knowing existed."

"Before we could leave the case as 'person or persons unknown,' we'd still have to clear every suspect in Upper Streetham. Including the Captain."

Davies sighed. "Aye, that's true."

Rutledge glanced across at him. "Tell me something. Why is everyone so determined to believe Wilton is innocent?"

Surprised, Davies said, "He's a war hero, isn't he? Admired by the King and a friend of the Prince of Wales. He's visited Sandringham, been received by Queen Mary herself! A man like that doesn't go around killing people!"

With a wry downturn of his lips, Rutledge silently asked, How did he win his medals, you fool, if not by being so very damned good at killing?

With Davies to guide him, Rutledge found the narrow road cutting into the Haldane property that led to a small, picturesque cottage standing isolated on a hillside, surrounded by fields and trees. Wild roses climbing over low stone walls set off the grounds, their scent filling the air with sweetness. On the north side, the wall was a good two feet higher, a windbreak for the gardens that lay at its foot. Someone had made a valiant effort to rescue them from weeds, and lupines stood like sentinels behind the sweet williams and the irises.

Drawing up in front of the cottage, Rutledge got out and was immediately attacked by an irate gray goose that took instant exception to invasion by unexpected strangers in motorcars.

Fending off the goose, he called, "Miss Sommers?"

No one answered, and after a moment, neatly outdistancing the irate fowl by doubling back the other way around the car, he made it to the steps and knocked on the cottage door.

No one came, and he was on the point of leaving when a sixth sense, that intuitive feeling that someone is there in the stillness on the other side of a door, made him knock again, louder this time. The sound attracted the goose, and she ceased her attack on her reflection in the car's wing, bearing down on Rutledge with neck arched. But Davies had the presence of mind to blow the car's horn, and she wheeled in midrun to hurry back to her first victim.

Finally the door was opened a narrow crack and a soft voice said, "Yes?"

"Miss Sommers? Inspector Rutledge. I'm looking for your cousin. Is she in?"

Reluctantly the door opened wider, and a pale face stared out. "She's not here just now. There was a bird's nest she wanted to check this morning."

He noted the strong family resemblance in features, but this cousin was quieter, dowdier, younger. Her hair was a mousy brown, her eyes wide and fearful, her dress a muted gray-green that did nothing for her complexion or her coloring. "Do you know when she'll be back?" he asked.

Maggie Sommers shook her head quickly, not wanting to encourage him to wait. She peered over his shoulder, saw the goose attacking the front tires of the Inspector's car, saw Sergeant Davies laughing out of the passenger's side, and then ducked back almost as if recoiling from any responsibility for what was happening on her lawn.

"She's Helena's pet," she said defensively. "I don't like her, she terrifies me."

"Shall I put her in a pen or somewhere?" Rutledge asked, wondering how he was going to manage that feat, but Miss Sommers shook her head again.

"No, she'll leave me alone if I'm not hanging out the wash. She hates that. Why do you wish to see Helena?"

"I wanted to talk with her about Captain Wilton. She saw him the morning that Colonel Harris was shot."

Tears filled her eyes, and he thought for a moment she was going to start crying. "That was awful—I was never so terrified in my life as when I heard about it. He seemed like such a nice man."

"You knew the Colonel?" Rutledge asked in surprise.

"Oh, no. No. But sometimes he rode this way—through the fields there," Maggie Sommers said, pointing. "That's his land, just beyond the high wall. The two estates meet there. If I was out in the gardens or something, he'd wave. At first I was afraid he'd want to stop and chat, but he never did, and Helena said I ought to wave back. It was—neighborly. She said he probably thought it was she anyway. She'd met him—at a dinner party." She smiled timidly, giving her face a little more life and color, the tears forgotten. "I was invited too."

He could see why she had been called a recluse, why there had even been the suspicion that she was simple. But she was only unimaginably shy, almost childlike. He thought that all he would have to do was shout at her in a harsh voice, and she'd scurry back inside and shut the door and hide under the bed. Torn between sympathy and irritation, he wondered where someone as brisk and active as Helena found the patience to cope with Maggie for an entire summer. Or perhaps she wasn't quite so timorous when left alone.

She was saying anxiously, "Should I offer you tea or—or coffee? I don't know when Helena's coming back, truly I don't, it would be useless to wait, and there's the cleaning still to be done. . . ."

Taking pity on her, he left, dodging the goose again, but he was sorely tempted to sideswipe it after one last onslaught as he cranked the car. The heavy wings had caught the side of his head a nasty clip as he bent over.

"At least it wasn't a goat," Davies said, enjoying himself. "You'd have sailed over yon wall like one of the Captain's aeroplanes."

When they reached Upper Streetham again, they found a message from Dr. Warren saying that he must see them urgently.

He was in his surgery when they arrived and he took them upstairs to a small room with an iron bedstead, a table, a single chair, and a very still form under starched sheets.

"Hickam," Warren said shortly.

"What the devil's happened to him?" Rutledge demanded, drawing up the only chair and sitting down to stare at the closed, gray face. "He looks half dead!"

"He is. Alcoholic poisoning—he drank enough to kill himself. A miracle he didn't. I've never seen a man so full of gin in all my years of practice. Hickam must have the constitution of an ox."

Rutledge felt a surge of guilt. "Where did you find him? How?"

"I was coming home last night from the Pinters' farm—just over the ridge, one of Haldane's tenants, little girl's in rough shape, and I'd stayed until the sedative finally started to work. This was about two in the morning. Hickam was lying in the middle of the road. He'd crawled that far, though God knows from where, and then passed out. I damned near ran over him, to tell you the truth of it, didn't see him until the last minute because he was in the darker shadows cast by the trees along the High Street there, and I didn't have my headlamps on—there's something wrong with the fool things. I was so tired that I thought it was a sleeping dog and swerved to miss it, and damned near rammed the horse trough outside Miss Millard's dress shop. Then I realized it was Hickam, and for a brass farthing would have just left him there in the road to sleep it off. But I got the car started again, managed to haul him into it, and brought him here. And a good thing too, or we'd have lost him for a fact."

Rutledge could see the man's unsteady breathing, the sheet over his chest rising and falling with soft but ragged irregularity, and said, "Are you sure he'll live?" He found himself torn between wishing Hickam dead and keeping him alive. But if he died, and it was Rutledge's doing—he cursed himself savagely.

Warren shrugged. "Nothing is sure in medicine. But at least the odds are on his side now. God knows, there must have been a pint of gin still in his belly when I pumped him out. And that would have killed him for certain before morning."

"Where did he find enough money to drink that much?" Davies demanded, leaning over Rutledge's shoulder for a closer examination of the sunken eyes, the scraggle of beard, the slack mouth.

Without answering him, Rutledge glanced up at Warren. "Did you know I've been looking for him? Most of this morning?"

"Forrest said something about it when I spoke to him about Hickam. That's when I left the message for you. But if you're thinking of questioning him now, you're mad. He's too weak to know what he's saying—even if he could manage to speak."

Rutledge nodded. He could see that much for himself. But he said, "Then I want you to keep him here until I can question him. Use any pretext you can think of, tie him to the bed if you have to, but keep him here, out of harm's way. And no visitors, absolutely none."

"You don't seriously believe he can tell you anything useful!" Warren scoffed. "A man like Hickam? Nonsense!"

Rutledge's eyes were dark with anger as he said, "Why? Because he's a drunk? A coward? Out of his head? You might be the same in his shoes. I've seen more shell shock cases than you'll ever attend, Doctor, and they're tormented people with no way out of the prisons of their minds. You weren't in France or Gallipoli or Palestine, and there's nothing in your medical practice to tell you what it was like."

"And I suppose you know?" Warren snapped.

Rutledge caught himself on the brink, realized in time where his outburst was carrying him, and said only, "*I was there.*"

Still angry when he reached the car, Rutledge said to Davies, "Tell Forrest I'm holding Dr. Warren responsible for Hickam, and if for any reason whatsoever he leaves the doctor's care, he's to be arrested on sight. Is that clear?"

"Where'll you be, then?" Davies asked warily.

"I'm going back to Mallows." To see what Lettice Wood might tell him, alone and with no notes being taken.

Glad not to be included in that visit, Davies hurried off to find Forrest. And Rutledge was left with Hamish's company on the drive out to the Colonel's home.

This time he was shown directly to Miss Wood's sitting room, and Rutledge found it empty. She came in through a connecting door after a few minutes, still wearing black, but with her face no longer invisible to him. The drapes were drawn back, and the sun's warm reflection filled the room with a softness that was kind to her grief-shadowed eyes.

And this time she offered him a chair facing the couch where she chose to sit, in the opposite corner, with her back to the light from the windows. More, he thought, for her own comfort than from any desire to make the interview difficult for him. But she was braced for something—he could see the tenseness in her body, the clenched line of her jaw.

"Have you brought me any news?" she asked, her voice still husky. As she looked directly at him he noticed that her eyes were not the same color. One was a smoky hazel, a green flecked with brown and gray, the other a warm green touched with gold. Startlingly odd, yet very beautiful.

"Not yet. We're still exploring several avenues. I'm trying to build a picture in my mind of Colonel Harris. The sort of man he was, the sort of life he led."

She brushed that aside with angry impatience. "I've told you. He had no enemies."

"Someone killed him," he reminded her. "*Someone* wanted him dead. He must have done something, if only that one single act, to rouse such terrible hate."

She flinched as if he'd struck her. "But surely you've made progress?" she asked again after a moment. "You must have talked to other people. Laurence Royston? Mark? Inspector Forrest?"

Lettice Wood was fishing, he realized suddenly. She wanted to know what had been happening, what had been said. . . .

"They've told me very little, actually. Everyone says that your guardian was a very fine man. Everyone, that is, except Mavers." He said nothing about Carfield.

She smiled a little, more in irony than amusement. "I'd have been more surprised if he hadn't. But Charles *was* a very nice man. He needn't have been my guardian, you know. He was barely grown himself at the time, and it must have seemed a dreary job, taking on the responsibility of a parentless child—a little girl at that!—just when there was a war to go to. To me he seemed as old as my father. I was even a little frightened of him, clinging to my nanny's skirts and wishing he'd go away. Then he dropped to one knee and held out his arms to me, and the next thing I knew I'd cried myself dry and he was ordering a tea with all my favorite things and afterward we went riding. Which scandalized the household, I can tell you, because I was supposed to be in deepest mourning, shut away in darkness and in silence. Instead I was out in the fields laughing and racing him on my pony and—" Her voice cracked, and she looked away hastily.

He gave her time to regain her composure, then asked, "What sort of mood had the Colonel been in, the last few days before his death?"

"Mood?" she repeated quickly. "What do you mean?"

"Was he happy? Tired? Worried? Irritable? Distracted?"

"He was happy," she said, her thoughts fading where he couldn't follow her. "Very, very happy . . ."

"Why?"

Disconcerted, she said, "What do you mean, why?"

"Just that. What had made him so happy?"

Lettice shook her head. "He just was."

"Then why did he quarrel with Mark Wilton?"

She got to her feet and walked across the room. For a moment he thought she was leaving, that she would disappear into her bedroom and shut the door on him. But she went to the windows instead, looking out at the drive and seeing, he thought, very little. "How could I know the answer to that?" she countered. "You harp on it as if it was important."

"It might be. It might decide whether we must arrest Captain Wilton or not."

Turning back to him, a dark silhouette against the light, she said after a moment, "Because of *one* quarrel? When you claim you don't even know what it was about?" Was it a statement? Or a question? He couldn't be sure.

"We have a witness who says they quarreled again. The next morning. Not far from where your guardian was killed."

Even with her back to the window he could see how shaken she was, her shoulders hunched suddenly, her body tense. Her hands were still. He waited, but she said nothing, as if she'd run out of words.

And still no defense offered on behalf of the man she loved.

"If Captain Wilton is guilty, you'd wish to see

him hang for it, wouldn't you?" Rutledge asked harshly. "You told me before that you wanted to see the killer hanged."

"Then why haven't you arrested him?" she demanded huskily. "Why have you come here instead, and told me these things, why are you adding to my grief—" She stopped, somewhere finding the will to go on, to make her voice obey her brain. "What is it you want of me, Inspector? Why are you here? Surely not to ask my opinion of quarrels I didn't witness, or to speculate on Mark's hanging as if he were someone I'd never met. There has to be more reason than that!" She was insistent, almost compellingly so.

"Then tell me what it is." He was angry with her, and wasn't sure why.

"Because," Hamish whispered, "she's got courage, hasn't she? And your Jean never did. . . ."

She crossed to the hearth, restless with pent-up emotions, fingers mechanically rearranging the flowers there as if their relative positions mattered, but he knew that she wasn't aware of what she was doing. "You're the man from London, the one they sent to find my guardian's murderer. What have you been doing since you got to Upper Streetham? Searching for scapegoats?"

"That's odd," he said quietly. "Catherine Tarrant said nearly the same thing. About making the Captain a scapegoat for someone else's crime."

In the mirror above the hearth he saw her face flame, the warm blood flooding under the pale skin until she seemed to be flushed with a fever, and her eyes sparkled as they met his in the glass. "Catherine? What has she to do with this?"

"She came to me to tell me straightaway that she was certain Captain Wilton was innocent." He was intrigued with the way her eyes darkened with emotion, until you couldn't see the difference in them. "Though why she might have done that, before anyone had actually accused him of murder, is still something of a mystery."

Lettice Wood bit her lip. "It was to spite me," she said, looking away from him. "I'm sorry."

"Why should Catherine Tarrant wish to spite you? At Wilton's expense?"

"Because she thinks I let the man she loved die. Or at least was in a sense responsible for his death. And I suppose this is her way of striking back at me. Through Mark." She shook her head, unable to speak. Then she managed to say, "It's rather appalling, isn't it, considering—" She stopped again.

"Tell me about it." When she hesitated, he said, "I've only to ask someone else. Miss Tarrant herself, Captain Wilton—"

"I doubt if Mark even knows the story."

"Then tell me about her relationship with Wilton."

"She met him before the war—when he came to Upper Streetham after Hugh Davenant's death. And I suppose there was a mutual attraction. But nothing came of it, neither of them was ready for marriage. He could think of nothing but flying and she's quite a fine artist, did you know? She hadn't sold anything at that point, I don't think she'd even tried, but soon afterward one of her paintings received a great deal of attention in a London show, and she moved up to Town."

The name suddenly clicked. He'd seen C. Tarrant's work, powerful, memorable studies of light and shadow, of faces with strength and suffering written in each line, or scenes where color richly defined the landscape with a boldness that brought Turner to mind. His sister Frances admired her enormously, but somehow he'd thought of the artist as older, a woman of experience and style, not the earnest girl he'd talked to in the Inn parlor.

Lettice Wood was saying, "When her father died early in 1915, she came back to run their estate on her own."

"That must have been a heavy responsibility."

"It was. But there was no one else to take over. And the only men left to work the land were either very old or very young. Or like Laurence Royston, were trying to keep the large estates afloat, food and meat quotas filled." She looked down at her hands, slim and white in her lap. "I admired her—I was only a schoolgirl, and I thought she was something of a heroine. A part of the war effort, doing a man's work when she'd rather be in London, painting, going to parties and exhibitions."

"Was her lover someone she'd left behind in London?"

She shook her head. "You must ask Catherine, I tell you."

He was watching her closely. She had stopped taking the sedatives, he was sure of it now. But she was still dazed, a little unsteady, as if the first shock of her guardian's death hadn't really worn off. Or as if something was tearing her apart inside, crowding out all other emotions except grief, and she was struggling to find a way to cope. "You brought up the subject in the first place. Why, if you won't tell me the rest of it?"

"I was trying to explain, that's all—that she was turning the other cheek, if you like, showing magnanimity. She was doing for me what I failed to do for her." Lettice swallowed hard. "Or rubbing salt into the wound, for all I know."

He continued to look at her, his face cold with speculation. Lettice lifted her chin, her eyes changing again as she refused to be intimidated. "It has nothing to do with Charles. And certainly not with Captain Wilton," she said firmly. "It's between Catherine and me. A debt . . . of a sort."

"Nothing seems to have anything to do with Charles Harris, does it?" Rutledge stood up. "Why didn't you go riding with your guardian that last morning?"

Her mouth opened and she gulped air, as if he had struck her in the stomach with his fist. But no words came. And then with a courage he could see, she got herself in hand and answered him. "Are you telling me that he might still be alive if I had? That's very *cruel*, Inspector, even for a policeman from London!"

"There was no thought of cruelty, Miss Wood," he said gently. "In our first interview you yourself seemed to emphasize the fact that you hadn't gone riding that morning. I wondered why, that's all."

"Had I?" Her dark brows drew together and she shook her head. "I don't remember—I don't know in what context I might have left that impression. . . ."

"When I asked you if you'd seen the Colonel since his quarrel with the Captain. You answered, 'I didn't go riding that morning.' As if that was somehow important."

"Important! If he had asked me, I would have gone! But I know—knew—how much his early rides meant to him, and I thought there was all the time in the world—" She checked, shook her head wordlessly, and then after a moment said in exasperation, "Oh, do sit down! We can't both prowl this room like tigers in a small cage!"

"I'd like to speak to Mary Satterthwaite before I go, if I may."

She said, "Of course," as if it was a matter of indifference to her, and rang the bell, then watched him silently as they waited. Hamish, grumbling deep inside Rutledge's mind, was uneasy with Lettice Wood, his Scottish soul disturbed by those strange eyes and the intensity that churned behind them. But Rutledge found himself drawn to her against his will, to the emotions that seethed just beneath the surface and somehow seemed to reflect his own. A woman of passion . . .

When Johnston answered her summons, she said, "The Inspector wishes to speak to Mary. Could you take him to the small parlor, please?"

Five minutes later, Rutledge found himself in a pleasant room overlooking the gardens and face to face with a woman of thirty, neatly dressed and primly correct. She had fair hair and pale blue eyes, and her cheeks were pink from nervousness.

Rutledge asked her to describe what she had seen and heard coming down the stairs the night of the quarrel, and she answered readily, giving him almost verbatim the same words he'd heard from Johnston. But he wanted more.

"You have no idea what the two men were quarreling about?"

"No, sir. None."

"Was it the sort of quarrel that might have led to blows? Or to hard feelings?"

Mary frowned, trying to bring back the scene as she remembered it. "They were very angry, sir. Their voices were deeper, rougher, if you know what I mean? I wouldn't have recognized it for the Captain's, not if I hadn't seen him with my own eyes. It wasn't a small matter they'd quarreled over—I've never seen either of them that upset. But they're gentlemen, both of them, it would never have come to blows, however bad it was!" There was a naive certainty in her words, and Rutledge found himself suppressing a smile.

"What reason did Miss Wood give you for coming upstairs early?"

"She didn't give any, sir, but as I was brushing her hair she said she'd left the gentlemen to discuss the marriage, and I asked if she'd be going up to London soon. She said she didn't feel like thinking about what all had to be done in London, not tonight. So I thought she must have a headache starting, especially when she asked for a cloth to cool her face. She was that tense, the way she always is when something's troubling her, so I helped her get ready for bed, and left her to sleep."

"Strange, isn't it, that she wouldn't have wished to be present if it was an important discussion? Headache or not."

"You must ask Miss Wood that, sir. But if they was to talk about business matters, now, the settlement or such, it wouldn't have been proper, would it? And she'd seemed a little restive all evening, to tell the truth of it, as if there were things on her mind or the headache was coming on. The first fitting for the gown was next week, and they say brides often get edgy over that."

"Miss Wood herself never mentioned a headache? Or that she was feeling unwell?"

"No, sir. But I can always tell when there's something bothering her. She doesn't need to say anything."

"How long have you worked at Mallows?" he asked, as if that was more important to him than the evidence she had given. Her eyes flickered in surprise, but she answered readily. "Since I was twelve, sir."

"Was the Colonel a good master?"

"The best, he was. Always considerate, always polite, saying please when he had no need to." She bit her lip. "We're all that upset. . . ."

"Yes, I understand. I hear that you have a relative who is housekeeper to Miss Tarrant?"

"That's right, yes, sir. My sister."

"How long has she been in Miss Tarrant's employ?"

The pale eyes narrowed warily. "Since 1910, sir, if you please. Or I should say, she was Mr. Tarrant's housekeeper then."

"Is she happy enough there?"

"It would seem so, sir."

"And she met Captain Wilton when he was here in Upper Streetham before the war?"

The wariness vanished. "Oh, yes, sir. Vivian thought very highly of him."

"He was very much interested in flying even then, I understand."

"Indeed, sir. Mad for it, she said. And teasing Miss Catherine about taking her up, making her laugh and plead with him not to dream of it."

"A pleasant man, was he? Good-natured, well-mannered?"

"Yes, sir. A gentleman. Not like—" She stopped short.

"Yes? Not like Charles Harris?"

She turned a deep red, and he realized that it was with anger, not embarrassment. "Oh, no, sir! The *German*, not the Colonel!" And then, with grave dignity, she added, "I'll say no more, sir, if you please."

And although he persisted for a time, she was true to her word.

8

So he went to see Catherine Tarrant, and found her in her studio. It was a tiled, high-ceilinged room that had been converted from an Edwardian conservatory, with light that illuminated without blinding. And there was an earthy smell about it, mixed with the odors of paint and of turpentine— and oddly enough, the ghostly scent of roses.

She was stretching a canvas when Vivian, who bore a faint resemblance to her sister Mary, led Rutledge there and then left, shutting the door quietly.

"I didn't know, at the Inn," he said, "that you were C. Tarrant. My sister is a great admirer of your work." He looked around at the paintings drying against the wall, their colors gleaming like jewels in various corners of the room.

"That's always nice to hear. You never tire of praise. The critics are generous enough with condemnation." She glanced up and said, "But that isn't what brought you here, is it? What's happened?" Her face was tense, prepared.

"Nothing has happened, that I'm aware of. I've

come to ask you about something that has been puzzling me, that's all. The German."

The slender stretcher in her hands snapped, and she stared at him with a mixture of anger and exasperation. "I might have known! As a general rule I find that men who were at the Front are the least prejudiced, in spite of what they've suffered. Or saw their friends suffer. I'm sorry you aren't one of them."

He found a smile for her, although she had made him angry in turn. "How do you know? To tell you the truth, I don't have any idea what I'm supposed to be prejudiced about. Why don't you tell me, and then we'll see where I stand."

Putting down the canvas, she walked over to one of the open windows, her back to him. "As a matter of curiosity, who told you? About the German?"

"Several people have alluded to him," he said carefully.

"Yes, I expect they have," she answered, weary patience in her voice. "But I really don't see what it has to do with this enquiry." She turned around, lifted one of the paintings stacked against the wall beside her, and began to study it as if she saw something she didn't like about it.

"How can I be sure, until I hear your side of the story?"

She glanced up wryly. "You've been talking to Lettice, I think. Well, everyone else has pawed over what happened with salacious enthusiasm, why not Scotland Yard? At least you'll hear the truth from me, not wild conjectures and the embroideries of gossip." She put that painting down and picked up another, keeping her voice coolly detached, but he could see the way her hands gripped the canvas as she held it at arm's length.

"It's very simple, really. During the war, when there weren't enough men to do the heavy work on the farms, the government allowed people to take on German prisoners of war to help on the land. Most of them were glad to do it, it was better than being cooped up in camp all day with nothing to occupy them. Mallows was allowed three Germans to bring in the harvest one year."

"And you?"

She turned the painting a little, as if to see it better. "Yes, I applied for one, but he didn't work out—I don't think he'd ever seen a cow before, much less a plow! He'd been a clerk in a milliner's shop, and although he was willing, I spent most of my time trying to show him what *he* was supposed to be doing."

Rutledge said nothing, and after a moment she went on reluctantly. "So they sent me a new man, and then someone to help him. *He* was marvelous. He could do anything—make repairs, plow, birth a foal, milk, whatever was needed—and he seemed to take pleasure in it. He had grown up on the land, but he hadn't actually worked it, someone else did that for him. He was a lawyer in Bremen. Rolf was his name—Rolf Linden. And—I fell in love with him. It wasn't an infatuation this time. It wasn't at all like my feelings for Mark. But Rolf was a German—and as far as everyone in Upper Streetham was concerned, the only good German was a dead one. And he was a prisoner, he went back to the camp every night. Hardly the stuff of high romance, is it?"

"Nothing came of it, then?" he prompted after a time. She seemed to have forgotten the painting in her hands, and after a moment absently put it back in its place.

"Not at first. Then I realized that *he* loved me."

"Did he tell you that?" If so, Rutledge thought to himself, the man was an opportunist, whatever she had been led to believe.

"No, it happened rather prosaically. He was gored by the bull we'd brought in for the dairy herd, and he couldn't be moved. So I nursed him, and when he was too ill to know what he was saying, he said too much. After that, well, somehow we managed to keep it a secret from everyone else. But he was terrified that I'd find myself pregnant, and late in 1917 I wrote to Lettice to ask her to contact Charles for me—I thought he might use his influence to let us be married."

She walked aimlessly across the studio, straightening the canvas on her easel, picking up a dry brush and running the tip through her fingers, frowning at a palette as if the colors on it were entirely wrong. And all the while her eyes were hidden from him. "In all fairness," she said, as if to the palette, "I do believe Lettice when she says she wrote to him. I think she kept her promise."

Behind the unemotional voice was a well of anguish, and Rutledge found himself thinking again of Jean. He knew what loss was, how the mind refuses to believe, the way the body aches with a need that can't be satisfied, and the awful, endless desolation of the spirit. And as always when he was under stress, Hamish stirred into life.

"You rant about your Jean," he said, his voice seeming to echo in the high ceiling of the studio. "What about my Fiona? She promised to wait. But I didna' come back, did I? Not even in a box. There's nae grave in the kirkyard to bring flowers to, so she'll sit in her wee room and cry, with no comfort to ease her grief. Not even a kiss did we have in that room, though I saw it once. . . ."

Desperate to silence him, Rutledge said aloud,

and more brusquely than he'd intended, "Go on. What happened?"

"It all went wrong. He was taken away, sent elsewhere, they wouldn't tell me where he had gone. And then, around Boxing Day—no one was quite certain of the date because so many people were ill and the records were all botched—he came down with influenza. No one told me that either."

She looked up suddenly, her eyes hot with unshed tears. "It wasn't until the war ended and I had searched half of England for him that I finally discovered he'd been dead for over a year—a *year*! I went a little mad, I blamed Lettice and Charles— for Rolf being taken away, for his death, for no word being sent to me—for all of it. I told myself she hadn't *tried* to make Charles understand how much Rolf and I loved each other. I was certain that Charles never did anything more than glance at her letter and then send it straight to the War Office. It was the only way they could have learned the truth about Rolf and me, the only reason they would have punished us by taking him away. Charles had done *nothing*—except betray us."

In the brightness of the skylight over her head, he could see that her breathing was ragged, her face settling into taut lines as she fought for control. And she won. No tears fell, because the remembrance of anger had burned them out instead.

"Did you ever ask Harris what he'd done—or not done?"

"No." It was uncompromising. "Rolf was dead. Nothing would bring him back. I had to learn to forget, or I knew I'd be dead as well. Emotionally, I mean."

Which gave her a powerful motive for murder. And could explain why she'd defended Wilton at the Inn.

He looked around him at Catherine Tarrant's work, at the strength of her lights and darks, the daring use of spaces, the power of her colors. At the emotions her subjects evoked. Even the bold black of her sketches set the imagination ablaze.

A mother and child locked in each other's arms, fierce protectiveness in the mother's face, terror in the child's. He had seen refugees on the roads of France who might have posed for that. An old man, clutching a folded British flag in his arms and fighting back tears as he stood in a small, overgrown country churchyard staring down at the raw earth of a new grave. If you wanted to capture the waste of war, Rutledge thought, what better expression was there than this, the very antithesis of the dashing recruitment posters? A girl in a rose-splashed gown whirling in ecstasy under the spreading limbs of an aged oak. The lost world of 1914, the innocence and brightness and abandonment to joy that was gone forever.

There were landscapes heavy with paint, storm clouds thrusting upward, wind racing wildly through a high meadow, waves lashing a rocky coast where watchers waited for stormbound ships, to lure them inland.

He saw enormous control in each work, the sure knowledge of exactly how much and how little made enough. A natural gift of talent honed to a cutting edge by long experience. The same control she had exerted just now.

But there was not a single still life among them. . . .

As if the whirlwind in the painter's mind couldn't be leashed that far?

He was finding it hard to relate the woman before him and the art he could see with his own eyes.

"It's unwomanly," Hamish said uneasily. "I'd not take my ease with one of those hanging above my hearth!"

As if she'd heard him, Catherine seemed to collect herself with an effort. She saw Rutledge examining her work. Brushing the dark hair aside, she said with a sigh, "Yes, I know, no one expects *me* when the artist is introduced. Everyone thinks C. Tarrant must be a man. Or one of those masculine women who wear trousers everywhere and smoke strong Russian cigarettes. I've considered wearing a patch over one eye and walking about with a trained ocelot on a leash. Were you listening at all?"

"I was listening. And you're wrong, I would have had no objection to your marriage. Not, at least, on the basis of Linden's nationality. I didn't know the man himself."

"But I did. And if you believe I might have shot Charles out of some twisted need to revenge Rolf, I suppose I could have. But what good would it have done, I ask you?"

"A life for a life?"

Her mouth twisted in a sardonic smile. "Charles Harris for Rolf Linden. Do you think that's why I came to see you about Mark? To make certain that he didn't hang for my crime?" She laughed, but there was no amusement in it. "It would be a terrible irony, wouldn't it, if Mark was punished for what I'd done? The two men I've cared for dead because of me."

"Who were the women in Charles Harris's life?"

The change of direction sobered her. "How should I know? He spent so little time here, and when he was at home, Mallows absorbed him completely."

"Was he ever in love with anyone in Upper Streetham? Mrs. Davenant, for instance?"

"Why on earth do you ask that?"

"Most soldiers carry a woman's image in their minds."

"Like the photos of Gladys Cooper each man wore next to his heart, in the trenches?" She considered that, head on one side. "I've never really understood why Sally married Hugh—yes, he was attractive, if you liked the ne'er-do-well dashing romantic. Enormous fun, always exciting, and he could make your heart absolutely flutter when he wanted to be charming. But as a husband, he was hopeless. For a time Laurence Royston was in love with her, I'm sure of it. I couldn't believe at first that Mark wasn't! But Charles?" She shook her head slowly. "I'll have to think about that. . . ."

With a smile to take the sting from his words, he asked, "And you? Were you ever in love with Charles Harris?"

She laughed, this time a contralto laugh that rippled with humor. "Of course. When I was sixteen and went to my first ball. It was at the Haldanes'. And Charles rescued me from the possessive clutches of my father, who thought every man in the room must have designs on my virtue. It would have been far more exciting if they had, but Charles was there, splendid in his dress uniform, and took pity on me. So I promptly fell in love with him and slept with my dance card under my pillow for at least a month afterward. He was a terribly attractive man, not strikingly handsome like Mark, of course, but with something about the eyes, and the mouth, that you remembered."

"How much would you say your art was influenced by your relationship with Linden. Before—and after?"

"Now there's an interesting question!" she said, biting her lip as she gave it her attention. "I'd say he softened it, if anything. Love teaches you humility—patience—understanding. And acceptance. Charles told me once that I'd have made a good soldier on the battlefield because I didn't know the meaning of fear. You aren't afraid until you've got something to lose. But when you love someone or something, you're terrified—there's so much at stake, then, so much at risk, you see. . . ."

Driving back toward Upper Streetham, Rutledge saw Laurence Royston coming toward him on a magnificent bay hunter. Royston waved, then drew rein, indicating that he wanted Rutledge to stop as well. Leaning down to speak to him, Royston said, "While you're out in this direction, come to Mallows with me and I'll give you that Will."

So Rutledge followed him back to Mallows. This time he was taken to a small doorway on the western side of the house nearly hidden by a giant wisteria whose faded blossoms still bore a whisper of lingering scent. Royston unlocked it and then down a short, stone-flagged passage unlocked another heavy door.

They entered a large room, dark with paneling and bookshelves and tall cabinets, but with a pair of windows behind the desk looking out on a pleasant shrubbery. Royston went to one of the cabinets beside the desk, unlocked that with another key, and brought out several bundles of papers. Sorting them with the swiftness of familiarity, he quickly found what he was looking for and handed over a bundle tied in dark ribbon.

"Sit down, man. That's the more comfortable chair over there. I use this one when I've got to read the riot act. It's hard enough to numb the bones! You'll notice the seal of this document hasn't been broken. The Will is just as it was when Charles brought it up from London to put in the cabinet."

Rutledge examined the seal carefully, and agreed. "No, it hasn't been touched as far as I can see." He opened it and began to read. Ten minutes later, he looked across at Royston and said, "It seems rather straightforward. The estate is left as you would expect, and there are the usual bequests in addition to that."

Royston smiled wryly. "I hope they include a sum for the church. We'll have Carfield ranting on the doorstep if there isn't. He's very determined to have a new organ, and something has to be done about the roof as well. The old parsonage could come down around his ears for all he cares, but the church is a different matter."

A proper setting for a proper man of God.

"Why isn't he interested in the parsonage? He lives there, doesn't he?"

"To tell you the truth, I always believed that he had his eye on Mallows. By way of Lettice, of course. Charles said he would as soon see her married to a giant slug."

Rutledge laughed. It was cruel but apt.

He retied the ribbons and said, "I'll keep this if I may. When are the solicitors coming down from London?"

"Not until after the funeral. I've spoken with them, and there are contingency measures to see to the running of the estate, that's no problem. Frankly, I don't think Lettice is up to hearing the Will read, and I told them as much."

"I expect to have the Inquest tomorrow."

"Adjourned, of course?" he asked, one eyebrow raised.

"For the time being. Yes." Rutledge considered him. "Did you ever have a falling-out with Harris?"

Royston shrugged. "We didn't always see eye to eye on management of the estate. But you don't kill a man over marrows and hay. Or a new barn."

"Did you envy him? After twenty years, Mallows must carry your imprint more than his. But Harris survived his wars. He came home, eager to take charge. If Miss Wood inherited, you'd be master here again. In all but name."

"No," he said tightly. "That's ridiculous." But then he glanced away.

"Are you in financial trouble of any sort?" There was a sizable bequest to Royston in the Will, following the recommendation that he be kept on as agent.

Royston flushed but said, "No. I don't gamble, I haven't time for wasting my money in other pursuits, and I'm well paid."

"Have you ever borrowed money from Harris?"

Unprepared for that, Royston's eyes flickered. "Once," he said tightly, "Many years ago, when I got into the devil of a scrape and couldn't get out of it on my own. I was twenty-one."

"What did you do?"

Royston hesitated. "I borrowed his car without his knowledge. There was a girl I desperately wanted to see down in Dorset because I thought I was madly in love with her. Colonel Harris—Captain, he was then—was in Palestine, and at the time it didn't seem like such a crazy thing to do, taking the car." He stopped, and then added quickly, "There was an accident. I wasn't a very experienced driver, and so it was my fault, whatever the law said. I paid for what I'd done—in more ways than one. And there were hospital bills. Among other things I'd badly damaged a kidney. That's what kept me out of the war, later. Charles lent me the money to settle it all. Within five years I'd paid him back every penny."

"It must have been a large sum."

"Any sum is large when you're twenty-one and frightened out of your wits. But yes—it was large. The car wasn't mine, remember. And—someone was hurt. It took every ounce of courage I had to confess to Charles. All he said was, 'You've had a bad experience. But there's no going back to change it. So try to learn from it. That's the only restitution you can offer.' "

"And did you?"

The eyes meeting his were level and sober. "For eight years or more I had nightmares about it. The accident, I mean. Reliving it. I don't hold with Freud's nonsense about dreams, but I can tell you that nightmares strip the soul."

Rutledge found no answer for that.

Sally Davenant watched her cousin for a while, then said, "Mark, that's the fifth time you've read that page. Put the book down, for God's sake, and tell me what's wrong."

"Nothing," he said, smiling up at her. "I was thinking, that's all."

"Don't tell me 'nothing' when I know there *is* something. You've walked around like a man in torment for days now. And why aren't you at Mallows? Lettice must be frantic with grief, and surely there's something you can do for her, if only to hold her. You did that for me after Hugh died, and it was all that got me through those first ghastly days. And there are practical considerations—who's arranging the funeral? You can't leave it to that dreadful man Carfield, he'll give us a sickeningly long eulogy comparing poor Charles to Pericles or Alexander. And the solicitors in London could do worse, with something coldly formal and military. Lettice will know best what Charles would have wanted—the right scripture, hymns, and so on."

"She's still under Dr. Warren's care—"

"Do you think being drugged into helplessness is going to solve anything for her? What's wrong, I ask you again. Something is! You spent every free moment at Mallows until the day Charles died, and it's going to look decidedly *odd* if you aren't there now!"

He took a deep breath, then said, "If I'm suspected of the murder—and they wouldn't have brought in Scotland Yard, would they, if they'd believed it was Mavers, they'd have hauled him to jail and been done with it!—I can hardly go to Lettice with that sort of thing being whispered all through the county."

She regarded him thoughtfully, half in amusement and half in exasperation. "Mark, my dear, that's carrying good manners to absurd extremes! Do you think Lettice will care what the county believes? She'll want you beside her, and that in itself will silence most of the gossips!"

There was such desperate grief in his eyes now that she was suddenly appalled. "Mark—," she began, anxiety changing her voice, making it strained and wary.

"The first time I went, I was turned away—if I go again, and it happens a second time, what do you think will be made of that?"

Almost weak with relief, she said, "She'd been given a sedative! Did you expect Dr. Warren to invite you to her bedroom, with no chaperone in the house? Betrothed or not, he wouldn't have countenanced that!" Rising from her chair, she came to kneel beside his, taking his hands in hers. "My dear. Lettice probably has no idea what's been said. Who's going to tell her?"

"Rutledge for one."

She bit her lip. "Yes. Rutledge. The man's a menace, probing and digging."

"He's no fool, Sally. And he won't leave until he's got what he wanted."

"If only you and Charles hadn't quarreled so publicly that last night—"

"How were we to know that the servants were still about? Besides—" He stopped, then lifted her fingers, kissed the tips, and let them go. She didn't rise, but stayed there beside him, her hands dropping to her lap.

"I wish you would tell me what that was all about. How can I help you if I don't *know*?"

He rubbed his eyes, and they burned as if he hadn't slept for a week. They had felt that way in France, he remembered, when there was a push on, and the planes went up as long as the pilots could stay awake to man them. Until blind exhaustion sent you stumbling back to quarters and the nearest bed. "It wasn't even a quarrel, come to that. We never got to the point of quarreling. He said something that took me completely off guard, and the next thing we knew, we were both murderously angry."

Mark looked at her, his eyes bloodshot from the rubbing, his tiredness there for her to see. "It died with Charles. At least pray God it did," he added vehemently.

"But the timing—"

"Yes, I know, there's no getting around that, is

there, Sally? And Rutledge will have me exactly where he wants me if he ever finds out the whole of it. Hickam was a bloody nuisance, but I could have dealt with him. As it is, Charles might still reach out from the grave and take me with him."

She got to her feet and said with conviction, "Then you *must* go to Lettice! Now, before everyone in Upper Streetham notices that you *aren't* there! Mark, don't you see? You're being very foolish!"

Rutledge went to find Johnston before he left Mallows, but instead came face-to-face with Lettice as she slowly descended the main staircase. It was, he thought, the first time she'd left her room since Dr. Warren had taken her there, and she seemed abstracted, her body moving without the volition of her mind, which was turned inward toward private visions no one else could share. Whatever they were, she drew no comfort from them, for she looked tired, empty.

"I thought you had gone away," she said, frowning as she saw him and recognized him. "Well? Did you want something—or someone?"

"I've just spoken to Royston. I wanted to let you know that the Inquest will be tomorrow—"

"I won't be there," she said quickly, with an edge of panic. "I won't attend!"

"I shan't expect you to attend. There will be— we must address certain formalities, and then I intend to ask for an adjournment," he amended, to spare her. There was no need to go into more detail than that, since Royston had identified the body, not Lettice.

She turned to go back the way she'd come, and he stopped her. "I went to see Catherine Tarrant."

With her hand on the banister as if she gained strength from its support, she came down the rest of the stairs. "And?" she asked when she was on eye level with him. It was almost as if she thought he might be tricking her.

"She told me about Linden."

"And?" she repeated.

"And I understand the debt you referred to this morning—your fiancé's life for her lover's. But there's another aspect of the situation, one less pleasant. Could Miss Tarrant have shot Colonel Harris in revenge for Linden's death? Brooding over what happened and convincing herself that he *might* have saved the German if he'd tried? Punishing him—and indirectly, you?"

Lettice Wood began to laugh, bitterly at first, and then in wild denial. "Oh, God," she said, "that's too diabolical to contemplate!" The laughter turned to tremors that racked her body. *"No, I won't think about it!* Go away, I don't want to talk to you anymore!"

Rutledge had seen soldiers close to the breaking point begin to shake after a battle, and he moved quickly to lead her to one of the ornate chairs standing against the wall. Once he got her seated, he gripped Lettice's shoulders firmly and said, "Stop it! That's enough." His voice was quiet, but pitched to reach her through the emotional frenzy.

She fought him, then collapsed in tears, and for a moment he knelt by her chair and simply held her, offering what comfort he could. She smelled of lilies of the valley, and her hair was soft against his face.

It was not professional, and Hamish was clamoring in the back of his head about the seduction of witches, but there was nothing else he could do.

When the worst was over, he went into the drawing room to ring for Mary Satterthwaite.

Waiting for his summons to be answered, he stood by the high back of the chair with one hand on Lettice's shoulder, knowing from experience that the warmth of human contact was often more important than words.

And thinking to himself that this rather blew to the four winds his earlier impression that Lettice Wood knew who had killed her guardian. . . .

9

Dr. Warren had spent a harried morning in his surgery, and added to that had been a sleepless night attending to Hickam. He was tired, irritable, and behind in his schedule. As he started out on his rounds, he was grumbling about a retirement long overdue and the ingratitude of villagers who seemed to think he was on call twenty-four hours of the day.

He looked in on the new baby he had delivered and found it flourishing, but tongue-lashed the father when he discovered that the mother had spent her morning bent over a full tub of washing.

"I've told you Mercy had a hard birth," Warren finished, "and you'd have seen it for yourself if you hadn't been ten parts drunk that whole day. Now either you find someone from the village to lend a hand in the house or I'll find a good woman and bill you for her. If Mercy hemorrhages, she's as good as dead. And then where will you and that child be?"

He stumped back to his car and swore as he barked his knuckles trying to start it.

The next stop was briefer, to call on an elderly widow ill with shingles, and this time he left her a stronger powder to help with the pain from the long ropes of fluid-filled blisters that looped down her arm. It was all he could do, but the old, cataract-clouded eyes smiled up at him with a pathetic gratitude.

Finally he reached the cottage on the Haldane property where Agnes Farrell's daughter Meg lived. Agnes was tall, spare, and capable, the most level-headed woman he'd ever met and—in his opinion—wasted as a housemaid when she'd have made such an excellent nurse. Meg had married well; her husband, Ted Pinter, would be head groom on the estate when his father retired, and the cottage was as pretty as she could make it. Warren had always looked forward to his visits here because Meg was as healthy as her mother and had gone through two pregnancies with no trouble at all, the last one four years ago. She was also a very respectable cook and never failed to send him away with a slice of cake or scones for his tea.

But the kitchen no longer smelled of baking, and the woman who met him at the door had lost the bloom of youth and health. Meg looked forty, and her mother twice that.

Lizzie was a pretty little thing, he thought, bending over the narrow crib to peer down at the pale little face staring blankly at the wall. But she wouldn't be for long if something didn't work soon. She was, as far as he could tell, exactly as he'd left her the day before, and the day before that as well—he'd lost count of the string of days he had come here, and yes, nights too, trying to break through that blank stare. Lizzie reminded him even more strongly now of those round-cheeked marble cherubs that the Haldanes seemed to want carved on all their family tombs—and nearly as white and cold where once her skin had had the soft warmth of ripe peaches.

Lizzie didn't move, she didn't speak, she never seemed to sleep, and food pressed into her mouth dribbled out it as if she'd somehow forgotten how to swallow.

Except for an array of bruises that were already fading, there was not a mark on her. Warren had looked with great care. No sign of a head injury, spinal injury, bee sting, spider's bite. No rash, no fever, no swellings. Just this deathly stillness that was broken by fits of wild thrashing and screaming that went on and on until Lizzie was exhausted and dropped suddenly back into stillness again.

Agnes watched him watching the child, and said, "There's no change. Not that we can see. I got some milk into her again, and a little weak tea. Most of the broth ended up on her gown."

Meg, her hands twisted tightly together, added, "We thought, Ma and I, that it was darkness she was afeared of, but the screaming only happens when Ted is near her. He's got so he won't come into the room." After a moment she added anxiously, "Why should she be afeared of her own father?"

"She probably isn't," Warren said shortly. "Where's the boy?"

"I sent him over to my sister Polly. The screaming was bothering him, he wasn't getting any rest at all." Teddy, six, was the image of his father and seemed to be made entirely of springs, like a jack-in-the-box.

"It doesn't seem to disturb her when I come near her," Warren went on thoughtfully. "Who else has been in the house? Men, I mean?"

"No one," Agnes said. "Well, Polly's husband,

come to get Teddy. He stopped on his way home
from the mill, and was too dusty to set foot in
the door. But Lizzie must have heard him." She
grinned tiredly. Saul Quarles was the bass in the
church choir, with a chest to match. Local wits
claimed that his voice carried farther than the
church's bell. "She couldn't miss him, could she?"

"But she didn't cry? Scream?"

"Not a peep. Is she going to die?" Meg asked,
striving for calmness and failing wretchedly. "What's
wrong with her?"

Warren shook his head. "She needs a specialist. I
saw a woman like this once, early in my practice.
She'd lost her baby, and couldn't face it. The spell
passed in a week, a little longer perhaps. Grief,
fright, sudden changes—they can do things to the
brain."

Meg began to cry softly, and Agnes put her arm
around the girl's shaking shoulders. "There, there,"
she whispered, but the words carried no comfort.

Mary Satterthwaite, answering the summons of the
drawing room bell, was startled to find Rutledge
back at Mallows when she'd seen him out the door
two hours earlier. He was standing by one of the
hall chairs, a hand on Lettice Wood's shoulder as if
holding her there, and the girl was shaking like a
tree in the wind.

Bristling at the sight of her mistress in such dis-
tress, she rounded on the Inspector from Scotland
Yard and said, "What's happened, then?"

Rutledge replied quietly, "I think you should
ask Miss Wood."

Lettice had stopped crying before Mary came
through the servants' door, but she accepted the
fresh handkerchief the maid thrust into her hand

and pressed it to her eyes almost as if to form a barrier between herself and the two people standing over her—a shield. When she lowered it, Rutledge could see that she was thinking again, that she'd used that brief instant of withdrawal to take a firmer grip on self-control. The trembling had stopped, but shock still showed in the pinched whiteness of her face, and in the effort she was making to overcome it. She said huskily, "I'm all right, Mary. Truly I am! It's just—"

Lettice glanced up quickly at Rutledge's unreadable face. Mary's sister was Catherine Tarrant's housekeeper. Did *he* know that? She wasn't sure how he might respond to the lie she was about to tell. If he would understand *why*. But she had to keep Catherine Tarrant out of this investigation, if she could, and the first step was preventing Mary from gossiping. "There's to be an Inquest. And I expect—something must be done about the services—"

Mary eyed Rutledge accusingly. "Mr. Royston will see to all that for you, Miss, *and* the Captain! Don't worry your head about it. The Inspector shouldn't ought to have sprung that on you. It was ill done, sir, if you ask me!"

To Lettice's relief, Rutledge said nothing.

"Shall I get one of Dr. Warren's powders for you, Miss? It'll help, I'm sure it will!"

Lettice shook her head vehemently. "No, no more of those! I can't abide them. The Inspector is leaving, Mary. Will you see him to the door?"

She stood up in dismissal, then faltered, catching her breath, her face even whiter if that was possible, her eyes wide with alarm. Rutledge, still carefully watching her, reached out to steady her. But Mary was there before him, quickly taking

Lettice's arm and chiding, "You *must* eat something, Miss, to keep up your strength. I keep telling you, it won't do, sending your tray back untouched. Sit yourself down in the small drawing room and let me talk to Cook, she'll find something you can fancy, see if she doesn't!"

Lettice said, "Yes, all at once I feel as if I'm floating, I hadn't realized—" She made an effort to smile. "Anything will do, it doesn't matter. Goodbye, Inspector." She was gradually overcoming the shock, her training and her own fierce will coming to her aid, and as she turned to Rutledge, her chin lifted a little. Pride, he realized. "About that other matter, I'm sure you're wrong. You took me by surprise, but it's a horridly convoluted theory, isn't it, and not very realistic if you actually think about it—"

The bell at the front door sounded. Rutledge could hear it pealing distantly in the servants' hall downstairs. Lettice closed her eyes, as if shutting out the sound. "I don't want to see anyone!" she said quickly.

Distracted, Mary turned to the policeman. "It's my duty to answer that, sir, Mr. Johnston isn't here just now, he's gone into Upper Streetham—"

"Take care of your mistress, I'll see to it," Rutledge said curtly, and moved to the door before she could stop him. Lettice stepped just across the threshold into the drawing room, a sanctuary of sorts.

He opened the heavy door only far enough to see who was on the step, prepared to be equally curt with the caller.

It was Mark Wilton, and the man's face mirrored his own surprise.

"Where's Johnston? What's happened?" the

Captain said sharply, and shoved the door wide with a suddenness that caught Rutledge off guard. "Is Lettice—?"

Lettice stood in the drawing-room doorway, her pale, troubled face turned in alarm toward the sound of the Captain's voice. Her emotions were still raw, and Rutledge had seen her reaction, swiftly covered though it was. More to the point, so had Wilton.

Stepping into the hall, he seemed suddenly at a loss for words, his eyes sweeping her with a mixture of love and something else. Concern? Or fear?

Rutledge, intensely interested, watched the pair of them. For an instant neither of them moved, neither spoke. But a question was asked, an answer given, in a wordless exchange that lasted for no more than a matter of seconds.

He would have sworn, before God and in a crowded courtroom, that it was the look of silent conspirators that he saw pass between them.

And then Mark was striding across the marble floor toward her, while Lettice came forward to meet him under the glorious painted Venus overhead.

She moved with exquisite grace, a tall, slim woman in rustling black, her hands held out before her, palms down, a blind look in her eyes, a mixture of emotions in her face.

Mark grasped her hands in his as if they were lifelines, before leaning forward to kiss her gently on her left cheek. "This is the last thing that should have happened," he said quietly, to her alone. "You know I mean that."

Yet Rutledge could sense the suppressed feeling

in the man, an intensity that was both physical and emotional. And was confused by his own reaction to it. As if his hackles rose . . . Then he remembered, with a jolt, the way he'd felt the last few times he'd seen Jean—wanting to hold her, desperately in need of her warmth to keep the darkness away, and yet afraid to touch her. Afraid of her rejection.

Hamish, deep in his mind, said ominously, "She's a witch, man, this one'll have your soul if you let her! *Are ye no' listening!*"

Mary hesitated, then quickly made herself scarce, disappearing down the passage toward the servants' door. Rutledge, drawn into the scene before him, held his ground.

Lettice gave a quick little shake of her head, as if she couldn't think of anything to say in response to Wilton's words. Or in denial?

Still holding Lettice's hands, Wilton turned to Rutledge and asked, "When will you—er—permit us to make arrangements for the funeral?" Rutledge saw Lettice flinch, in spite of Wilton's careful words.

"Tomorrow," he replied briefly, "after the Inquest."

Wilton stared at him, wariness behind his eyes. But he said only, "Then I'll speak to you later. At the Inn?"

Rutledge nodded. Wilton was right; this was neither the time nor the place to discuss what form the Inquest was going to take.

There was an awkward silence, as if no one quite knew what to say next. Then Wilton went on, speaking to Lettice now, the words stilted, meaningless, even to his own ears. "Sally sends her dearest love. She wanted to come before this, but Dr. Warren insisted you were to have quiet and rest. If there's anything she can do, please tell me. You know how fond she was of Charles."

Lettice said huskily, "Thank her for me, will you? I don't know what's to be done next—the service, for one thing. I don't think I can face the Vicar." She made a wry face. "Not just now! Or the lawyers. But I ought to send word to someone in the Regiment—"

"Leave Carfield to me. You needn't see him or anyone else, if you'd rather not. And I'll deal with the Army, if you like. They'll want a memorial service, of course, when you're up to it. But that can wait."

Rutledge walked away from them, to the still-open door.

And Lettice said unexpectedly, raising her voice a little as if suddenly afraid he was leaving, "I expect you and I must also give some thought to the wedding, Mark. I can't—the white gown—I'm in mourning. All the arrangements must be canceled, the guests notified."

Rutledge missed the look on Wilton's face, but the Captain said only, "My love, I'll see to it as well, you needn't worry about any of that now."

But her eyes were on Rutledge, and as he stopped by the door, he could see that they were nearly the same color.

"Something must be done," she said insistently. "I can't go through with it. So many people—the formality—"

"No, of course not! I understand, I promise you," Wilton said quietly. "You can trust me to take care of it." Taking her elbow, he tried to lead her down the passage by the stairs, toward the room where Rutledge had spoken with Mary earlier that morning.

There was a frown between Lettice's eyes now, as if they weren't focusing properly. "Mary was going to bring me something—some soup. I haven't eaten—I feel *wretchedly* lightheaded, Mark. . . ."

"Yes, I'm not surprised. Come and sit down, then I'll see what's keeping her."

Rutledge quietly let himself out, finally satisfied.

But Hamish wasn't.

"She's up to something!" he said uneasily. "Yon Captain, now, he's nobody's fool, is he? But that one will lead him a merry dance before he's finished, wait and see. Aye, you'll find a woman at the bottom of this business, and a terrible hate."

"Which woman?" Rutledge asked, getting into the car. "Or haven't you made up your mind? The witch? The painter? Or the widow?"

Hamish growled softly. "Oh, aye, I've made up *my* mind. It's you that won't see where the wind's blowing. You're the wrong man for this murder, and if you had any wit left, you'd drive straight to London and ask to be relieved!"

"I can't—if I quit now, you'll have won. I've got to see it through or put a pistol to my head."

"But you know what will happen if you drag that poor sod, Hickam, into court. They'll crucify him, and you along with him. Because the women will protect yon fine Captain, mark my words! And there's no one left to protect you."

Turning out of the gates, Rutledge said between his teeth, "When I've finished, there won't be any need to drag Hickam anywhere. I'll have other proof."

Hamish's derisive laughter followed him the rest of the way back to Upper Streetham.

•   •   •

Bowles had called from Scotland Yard.

When Rutledge rang him back, Bowles said, "You've had two days, what's happened?"

"We're holding the Inquest tomorrow. And it will be adjourned. I need more time," he answered, trying to keep the tenseness, the uncertainty out of his voice.

There was an appreciative silence at the other end of the line, and then Bowles asked, "I'm being pushed for results myself, you know; I can't put them off with 'Rutledge needs more time.' What kind of progress *have* you made?"

"We've found the shotgun. At least, I think we have. The owner has witnesses that place him elsewhere at the time of the murder, but the general consensus is, he's got the best motive for killing the Colonel. The problem is, I don't see what it achieved—why *now*? This feud between them is of long standing. Why not twenty years ago, when it all started? But the man's house is unlocked, it's isolated, and anyone who knew about the shotgun could have walked in and taken it. And several people did know. It would have been a simple matter to put it back afterward. I'm presently exploring who had the best opportunity."

"Not Captain Wilton, I do hope?"

Rutledge answered reluctantly. "Among others, yes."

"The Palace will have a collective *stroke* if word of that leaks out. For God's sake, say nothing until you're absolutely sure!"

"Which is why I need more time," Rutledge pointed out reasonably. "Can we afford to make a mistake? Either way?"

"Very well. But keep me informed, will you? I've got people breathing down *my* neck. I can go out on a limb for you at the moment, but we'll need something soon or heads may start to roll. Mine among them!"

"Yes, I understand. I'll call you on Monday morning. At the latest."

He waited, let the silence drag on, but Bowles had finished and cut the connection.

Rutledge hung up, unable to see the pleased smile at the other end of the line as Bowles replaced the receiver. The situation in Warwickshire, in Bowles's opinion, was progressing exactly as he had planned.

Still turning their conversation over in his mind, Rutledge told himself that the exchange had gone well enough. The Yard wanted answers, yes, but it was also prepared to accept his judgment in the field rather than forcing him into hasty decisions. A sign that nothing had been held back intentionally?

Badly needed encouragement, then, whether the Yard realized it or not—he should feel only a sense of relief.

But Hamish, who had a knack for cutting to the heart of Rutledge's moods, asked softly, "Why hasn't he asked about Hickam, then?"

Stopping by Warren's surgery as he walked toward the Inn, Rutledge asked the housekeeper for a report on Hickam.

"He's still alive, if that's any help. But he just lays there, for all the world a dead man. Do you want to know what I think?" She gave him a penetrating look. "He's gone away, so far back into that mad war he came from that he can't find his way home again. While he's there on the bed, not moving, not seeing, not hearing, I keep wondering what's happening inside his head. Where we can't follow him."

"God only knows," Rutledge answered her, not wanting to think about it.

She frowned. "Do you suppose he's afraid? I watched him on the street sometimes, and saw the anger in him, and the strangeness that unsettled everybody—well, of course it was unsettling, we didn't know what to do about it, whether to ignore him or shout at him or lock him up! But when he was sober I saw the fear too, and that worried me. I'd not like to think that wherever he's gone, he's taken the fear with him, as well as the horrors of the war. When he can't *move*, he can't run from it."

Rutledge considered her. "I don't know," he told her honestly. "You're probably the only person in the town who cares."

"I've seen too much suffering in my life not to recognize it, even in a drunkard," she said. "And that man suffered. Whatever he did in the war, good or evil, he's paid for it every hour since. You'll remember that, won't you, when and if you can talk to him? I don't suppose you were in the war, but pity is something even a policeman ought to understand. And like him or not, that man deserves pity."

She grasped the door firmly, ready to shut it, her face suddenly still as if she regretted offering opinions to a stranger. "Call again after dinner, if you want. I don't expect he'll come around before then, if he comes around at all." Her voice was crisp again, businesslike. "It won't do any good to try before that, mind!" She closed the door, leaving him standing there on the pavement.

Hamish, stirring again, said, "If he dies, and it's proved you gave him the money that brought him to his grave, a man with your past, what do you suppose they'll do to you?"

"It will be the end of my career. If not worse."

Hamish chuckled, a cold, bitter sound. "But no firing squad. You remember those, now, don't you? The Army's way of doing things. A cold gray dawn before the sun rises, because no man wants to see a shameful death. That bleak hour of morning when the soul shrivels inside you and the heart has no courage and the body shrinks with terror. You remember those, don't you! A pity. I'd thought to remind you. . . ."

But Rutledge was striding toward the Inn, head down, nearly blundering into a bicycle, ignoring the women who hastily moved out of his path and the voice of someone saying his name. The world had narrowed down to the agony that drove him and the memories that devoured him. Back in France, back to the final horror, the disintegration of all he had been and might be, in the face of blazing guns.

The machine gunner was still there, and the main assault was set for dawn. He had to be stopped before then. Rutledge sent his men across again, calling to them as he ran, and watched them fall, his sergeant the first to go down, watched the remnants turn and stagger back to their lines through the darkness, cursing savagely, eyes wild with pain and fury.

"It's no' the dying, it's the *waste*!" Corporal MacLeod screamed at him, leaping back into the trench, faces turning his way. "If they want it taken out so badly, *let them shell it*!"

Rutledge, pistol in hand, shouted, "If we don't silence it, hundreds of men will die—it's *our* lot coming, we can't let them walk into that!"

"I won't go back—you can shoot me here, I won't go back! I won't take another man across that line, never again, as God's my witness!"

"I tell you, there's no choice!" He looked at the mutiny in the wild eyes surrounding him, looked at the desolation of spirit in weary, stooped shoulders, and forced himself to ruthless anger: "There's never a choice!"

"Aye, man, there's a choice." The Corporal turned and pointed to the dead and dying, caught in a no-man's-land between the gunner and the lines. "But that's cold-blooded murder, and I'll no' be a part of it again. Never again!"

He was tall and thin and very young, burned out by the fighting, battered and torn by too many offenses and too many retreats, by blood and terror and fear, tormented by a strong Calvinistic sense of right and wrong that somehow survived through it all. It wasn't courage he lacked; Rutledge knew him too well to think him a coward. He had quite simply broken—but others had seen it. There was nothing Rutledge could do for him now, too many lives were at stake to let one more stand in the way. Grief vied with anger, and neither won.

He'd had Hamish MacLeod arrested on the spot, and then he'd led the last charge out into the icy, slippery mud, challenging them to let him do it alone, and they'd followed in a straggle, and somehow the gun had been silenced, and there was nothing left afterward but to see to the firing party. Then he'd sat with Hamish throughout what was left of that long night, listening to the wind blowing snow against the huts they'd somehow rigged in the trenches. Listening to Hamish talk.

A hideously long night. It had left him drained beyond exhaustion, and at the end of it he'd said,

"I'll give you a second chance—go out there and tell them you were wrong!"

And Hamish had shaken his head, eyes dark with fear but steadfast. "No. I haven't got any strength left. End it while I'm still a man. For God's sake, *end it now*!"

The shelling had started down the line when Rutledge summoned six men to form the firing party. It rocked the earth, shook men to their souls, pounding through the brain with a storm of sound until there was no thought left. He'd had to shout, had to drag them, reluctant, unwilling, through the falling snow, had to position them, and will them to do his bidding. And then he'd gone to fetch Hamish.

One last time, he'd said, "It isn't too late, man!"

And Hamish had smiled. "Is it my death you're fearing, then? I don't see why; they'll all die before this day's out! What's one more bloody corpse on your soul? Or do you worry I'll haunt you? Is it that?"

"Damn you! Do your duty—rejoin your men. The Sergeant's dead, they'll need you, the push will come in less than an hour!"

"But without me. I'd rather die now than go out there ever again!" He shivered, shrugging deeper into his greatcoat.

It was the darkness that blinded them, and the snow. But dawn would come soon enough, and Rutledge had no choice, the example had to be made. One way or another. He took Hamish's arm and led him up the slick, creaking steps and to the narrow, level place where men gathered before an assault.

"Do you want a blindfold?" He had had to bring his mouth to Hamish's ear to be heard. He was shaking with cold, they both were.

"No. And for the love of God, untie me!"

Rutledge hesitated, then did as he asked.

There was a rumble of voices, strangely audible below the deafness of the shelling. Watchers he couldn't see, somewhere behind the firing party. The six men didn't look around, standing close together for comfort. Rutledge fumbled in his pocket and found an envelope to mark the center of Hamish's breast, moving by rote, not thinking at all. He pinned it to the man's coat, looked into those steady eyes a last time, then stepped away.

He could hear Hamish praying, breathless words, and then a girl's name. Rutledge raised his hand, dropped it sharply. There was an instant in which he thought the men wouldn't obey him, relief leaping fiercely through him, and then the guns blazed, too bright in the darkness and the snow. He turned, looked for Hamish. For a moment he could see nothing. And then he found the dark, huddled body. He was on the ground.

Rutledge reached him in two swift strides, barely aware of the shifting of the noises around him. The firing party had melted away quickly, awkward and ashamed. Kneeling, he could see that in spite of the white square on the man's breast, the shots had not entirely found their mark. Hamish was bleeding heavily, and still alive. Blood leaked from his mouth as he tried to speak, eyes dark pools in his white, strained face, agony written in the depths, begging.

The shelling was coming closer—no, the Germans were responding, rapidly shifting their range, some falling short. But Rutledge knelt there in the dirty snow, trying to find the words to ask forgiveness. Hamish's hand clutched at his arm, a death grip, and the eyes begged, without mercy for either of them.

Rutledge drew his pistol, placed it at Hamish's temple, and he could have sworn that the grimacing lips tried to smile. The fallen man never spoke, and yet inside Rutledge's skull Hamish was screaming, *"End it! For pity's sake!"*

The pistol roared, the smell of the powder and blood enveloping Rutledge. The pleading eyes widened and then went dark, still, empty. Accusing.

And the next German shell exploded in a torrent of heat and light, searing his sight before the thick, viscous, unspeakable mud rose up like a tidal wave to engulf him.

Rutledge's last coherent thought as he was swallowed into black, smothering eternity was, "Direct hit—Oh, God, if only—a little sooner—*it would have been over for both of us—*"

And afterward—afterward, London had given him a bloody *medal*—

10

$\mathscr{I}$t was an hour or more later that Rutledge walked down the stairs to the dining room for his lunch. He wasn't sure how he had reached the Inn, how he'd made it to his room, whom he might have encountered on the way. It had been the worst flash of memory he'd suffered since he left the hospital, and it had unnerved him, shaken his fragile grip on stability. But as the doctor had promised him, in the end it had passed, leaving him very tired, very empty.

Bracing himself as he opened the French doors, he was prepared for Redfern to comment, or worse still, for the other diners to stare at him in speculation and disgust. But the room was nearly empty, and Redfern had a tight, inward look about his eyes. The limp was more pronounced as he came to take Rutledge's order, and he leaned against the table.

"Been on it too much," he said, aware of Rutledge's perception. Then he shrugged. "It's the stairs that are the worst. The doctors say it will pass in time."

But he sounded dejected, as if he had stopped believing in them.

Rutledge spent what was left of the afternoon talking to Inspector Forrest in his office about the names in his notebook. It was better than being alone, better than letting Hamish reach him again too soon, and it was a way of thinking aloud that might lead to something that the local man knew and he didn't. An idle hope, he realized, when he'd finished and Forrest sat there in silence, reflectively scratching his chin and staring at the ceiling as if half expecting to find an answer written there.

"What do you think?" Rutledge repeated, trying to keep his impatience out of his voice.

"None of them is likely to be your murderer," Forrest said, unwittingly emphasizing *your* as if setting himself apart from the whole business. "Take Miss Wood, for a start. I've never seen a cross word pass between her and the Colonel, no, nor ever heard of one. And he'd have given her whatever she wanted; there'd be no need for trouble over it."

"What if she wanted what he couldn't give her?"

Forrest laughed. "And what would that be? I can't think of a thing she didn't already have! She's a lovely girl, nothing mean or selfish or strong-headed about her."

"Well, then, Wilton?"

"He was marrying the girl. The surest way to lose her would be doing a harm to the Colonel, much less killing him. Here, just before the wedding? It would be insanity! And what if they did argue the night before the murder? What if it *is* true? You can't make much out of that—not enough for murder, if you ask me! Not without more evidence than we've got."

"Then why won't Wilton come straight out with the truth and tell me what caused the quarrel?"

Forrest shrugged. "It could be something that happened in France, something only the two of them know about. Maybe something that Captain Wilton thinks the Colonel wouldn't want known, even after his death. A personal matter."

"Yes, that's what he said," Rutledge replied, and got up to pace, unable to sit still while he talked. "But we don't *know*, do we, and as long as we don't, I intend to keep the quarrel in mind. Mrs. Davenant?"

"A very well respected lady. *She* wouldn't be very likely to have a hand in murder. And what reason could she have for it anyway?"

"I don't know. Was she ever in love with the Colonel? Or with Wilton?"

"There's never been a hint of gossip. If she was in love with anyone but her husband, she kept it to herself. And somehow I can't picture her stalking the Colonel with a loaded shotgun in her hand. If she was jealous of Lettice Wood, killing the Colonel wouldn't help her any."

"Unless the Captain—or Lettice Wood—was blamed for it."

"If the Captain's blamed for it, she's going to lose him to the hangman, isn't she? And I can't see *how* she'd put the blame onto Miss Wood. Besides, if there was any real threat to Miss Wood, I can see Wilton stepping in and saying it was *his* doing, the Colonel's death—to protect the girl. And Mrs. Davenant ought to know that as well as I do. It would be a *risk*, wouldn't it? One she'd have to consider."

"And Catherine Tarrant?"

Forrest was suddenly wary. "What's she got to do with this, then?"

"I know about the German. Linden. She wanted to marry him, and she wanted Harris to clear the way for them. Instead, Linden was taken away and he died. Women have killed for less, and what she felt for Linden wasn't a girl's infatuation, it was passionate and real."

"You're on the wrong track! Miss Tarrant might have wanted somebody else to suffer too, once she found out what had happened to the German—she was that upset. Yes, I'll grant you that much. But you don't bide your time, you don't wait for a year or two, not when you feel the way she did then! You come in a rage for revenge, hot and furious."

"Then you think she's capable of seeking revenge?"

Forrest flushed. "Don't put words into my mouth where Catherine Tarrant is concerned! I said she was that hurt, she might have done something foolish straightaway, out of sheer mad grief and shock. But not murder."

Rutledge studied him. "You like her, don't you? You don't want to think of her as a killer."

Forrest answered stiffly, "I've always been fond of the girl, there's nothing wrong in that. And you don't know how people in Upper Streetham shunned her when they found out about her and the German. Treated her like dirt, the lot of them. My wife among them. As if she'd done something unforgivable."

"How did they find out? About Linden?"

"I never did learn how. But I had my suspicions. She tried to move heaven and earth to find out where they'd sent the German, and people started to talk. Gossip, speculation, but nothing anybody could pin the truth on. So I think Carfield was to blame—he was in Warwick when she came back from London on the train, and he offered to drive her home. She was half sick with grief—she may have blurted out the whole story without thinking. And he's one to pry, he could have gotten around her. At any rate he made some pious remarks on the next Sunday about loving our enemies and healing the wounds of war, just when the reality of the war was coming home to all of us, the cripples and the wounded—and the dead. And the next thing I knew, the story was racing all over Upper Streetham that Catherine had been expecting to marry the prisoner, only he'd died. That there had been something between them. That she'd even slept with him. And the damage was done."

"I've heard Carfield was courting Lettice Wood."

"Oh, yes, indeed. He'd have *liked* to marry the Colonel's ward—but how much he cared for Miss Wood is anybody's guess. There are those would say it was little enough, that he isn't capable of loving anybody but himself. And it's true, I've never seen a man so set on his own comfort." His mouth turned down in distaste. "All right, he's a man of God, but I don't like him, I never have."

"Royston? What do you know about him?"

"A good man. Hardworking, reliable. There was a time when he sowed his share of wild oats, his place at Mallows going to his head a bit, and he was one for the girls too. But he settled down and got on with his life soon enough." Forrest smiled. "Well, we're none of us free of that charge."

"Nothing between him and the Colonel that you know about, which might have led to murder?"

"I can't think of any reason for Mr. Royston to shoot anybody."

"He hasn't married?"

"He's married to Mallows, you might say. There was a girl years back. When he was about twenty-six or -seven. Alice Netherby, a Lower Streetham lass, pretty as they come and sweet with it, but frail. She died of consumption and that was that. He's always gotten on very well with Catherine Tarrant, but he's not her sort, if you know what I mean. A countryman. And she's a lady. A famous artist. I've a cousin, living in London. He says her work's all the rage."

"Which brings us back to Mavers, doesn't it?"

"Aye," Forrest answered with regret. "And it doesn't seem very likely that we'll prove anything against *him*, worst luck!"

The interview with Forrest left Rutledge feeling dissatisfied, a mood reinforced by an encounter with Mavers on his way back to the Inn.

"You don't look like a successful man," Mavers said, his goat's eyes gleaming with maliciousness. "You've got my shotgun, but you haven't got me. And you won't, mark my words. I've got witnesses, as many as you like."

"So you keep reminding me," Rutledge said, taking his own malicious pleasure in the sight of Mavers's swollen nose. "I wonder why?"

"Because I enjoy seeing the oppressors of the masses oppressed in their turn. And you might say that I have an interest in this business—a *professional* interest, you could even call it."

Rutledge studied him. "You enjoy trouble, that's all."

"The fact is, I like to think I can take some of the credit for the Colonel's death. That all those hours of standing in the market square speaking out against the landlords and capitalists—while those village fools reviled me—weren't wasted. Who knows, I might have put the idea into some mind, the first glimmer of the Rising to come, and the salvation of the masses from the tyranny of the few." He cocked his head, considering the possibility. "Aye, who knows? It might just have its roots in my words, the Colonel's killing!"

"Which makes you an accessory, I think?"

"But it won't stand up in a court of law, will it? I bid you a good day—but I hope you won't be having one!" He started to walk off, pleased with himself.

Rutledge stopped him. "Mavers. You said something the other day. About your pension. Is that how you live? A pension?"

Mavers turned around. "Aye. The wages of guilt, that's all it is."

"And who pays you?"

The grin widened. "That's for me to know and you to discover. If you can. You're the man from London, sent here to set us all straight."

There was a little dogcart standing in the road outside the Inn when Rutledge strode up the steps, and Redfern came to meet him in the hall, hastily wiping his hands on a towel. "Miss Sommers, sir. I've put her in the back parlor. Second door beyond the stairs."

"Has she been here long?"

"Not above half an hour, sir. I brought her tea when she said she'd wait awhile."

Rutledge went down the passage to the small back parlor and opened the door.

It was a pleasant room, paneled walls and drapes faded to mellow rose at the long windows. There was a writing desk in one corner, several chairs covered in shades of rose and green, and a small tea cart on wheels.

Helena Sommers stood, back straight, at one of the windows, which overlooked a tiny herb garden busy with bees. She turned at the sound of someone at the door and said, "Hallo. Maggie told me you wanted to see me. Strangers at the house make her uncomfortable, so I thought it best to come into town."

Rutledge waited until she sat down in one of the chairs and then took another across from her.

"It's about Captain Wilton. The morning you saw him from the ridge. The morning of the murder."

"Yes, of course."

"What was he carrying?"

"Carrying?" She seemed perplexed.

"A rucksack. A stick. Anything."

Helena frowned, thinking back. "He had his walking stick. Well, he always does, and that morning was no different from the other times I've glimpsed him."

"Nothing else. You're quite sure?"

"Should he have had something else?"

"We're trying to be thorough, that's all."

She studied him. "You're asking me, aren't you, if the Captain carried a shotgun. Has your investigation narrowed down to him? Why on earth would *he* kill Colonel Harris? The Captain was marrying the Colonel's ward!"

"Wilton was there, not a mile from the meadow, shortly before the murder. We have reason to think he wasn't on the best of terms with Colonel Harris that morning."

"And so the Captain marched up the hill hoping to run into Charles Harris, carrying a shotgun through the town with him, in the unlikely event he'd have an opportunity to use it? That's absurd!"

Rutledge was very tired. Hamish was growling restlessly at the back of his mind again.

"Why is it absurd?" he snapped. "Someone killed the Colonel, I assure you; we've got a body that's quite dead and quite clearly murdered."

"Yes, I understand that," she said gently, seeming to understand too his frustration. "But why—necessarily—is the murderer someone in Upper Streetham? Colonel Harris served in a regiment on active duty. He was in France for five years, and we've no idea what went on in his life during the war—the people he met, the things that might have happened, the soldiers who died or were crippled because of his orders. If *I* wanted revenge—and expected to get away with it, of course!—I'd shoot the man on his home ground but not on mine. You can take a train to Warwick from anywhere in Britain, then walk to Upper Streetham."

"Carrying a shotgun?"

She was momentarily at a loss, then rallied. "No, certainly not. Not out in the open. But people do have things they carry without arousing suspicion. A workman with his kit of tools. Salesmen with sample cases. Whatever. And you don't wonder what's inside, do you, when you see someone carrying something that belongs with him. You assume, don't you, that it's all aboveboard?"

Rutledge nodded grudgingly. She was right.

"I'm not suggesting that it happened this way. I'm merely pointing out that Mark Wilton needed a very powerful reason to kill his fiancée's guardian, practically on the eve of their wedding.

And he had heard Lettice, only hours ago, putting off the marriage. Because she was in mourning.

It made sense, what Helena Sommers had said. And it gave him a very sound excuse for ignoring Hickam's statement. But her argument also left him with the whole of England to choose from, and nothing to go on in the way of motive or evidence. Bowles would not be happy over that!

Helena seemed to appreciate his dilemma. She said ruefully, "I'm sorry. I have no business interjecting my views. I'm an outsider here, I don't know any of these people very well. But I *have* met them, and I'd hate to think one of them is a murderer. 'Not someone *I* know, surely!' You must have heard that often enough!"

He had. But he answered, "I suppose it's human nature."

As the clock in the other parlor began to chime the hour, she got up quickly. "I've been away longer than I intended. Maggie will be wondering what's become of me. I must go." Hesitating she added, "I've never been to war, of course, and I know nothing about it except what one reads in the news accounts. But Colonel Harris must have had to do many things as an officer that he as a man wouldn't care to talk about—was ashamed of, even. When you find his murderer, you may discover that his death has its roots in the war. Not in the affairs of anyone we know."

The war.

But if she was right, the war also brought him full circle to Mark Wilton, who had known Harris in France.

Or to Catherine Tarrant . . .

When he'd seen Helena to the dogcart and watched the Haldane pony trot off down the main street, Rutledge went back to the station to rout out Sergeant Davies. He sent him off to Warwick to find out, if he could, about anyone who had arrived there by train shortly before the murder and come on to Upper Streetham.

A wild-goose chase, Sergeant Davies thought sourly as he set out. He knew his own ground, and there hadn't been any unexplained strangers in Upper Streetham or even in Lower Streetham for that matter—before, during, or after the killing. Except for that dead lorry driver who'd been accounted for. There were always eyes to see, ears to hear, if anyone passed through. And news of it reached him, directly or indirectly, within a matter of hours. Strangers stood out, nobody liked them, and word was passed on. But going to Warwick, waste of time though it was, kept him out of the Inspector's clutches, and that counted for something.

As he was finishing his dinner, Rutledge looked up to see Mark Wilton standing out in the hall of the Inn. The Captain saw him at the same time and crossed the dining room to Rutledge's table.

"I've come to speak to you about the Inquest. And the release of the body."

"I was just on my way out to see Dr. Warren. But that can wait. Can I offer you a drink in the bar?"

"Thanks."

They went through to the public bar, which was half empty, and found a table in one corner.

Rutledge ordered two whiskeys and sat down. "The Inquest will be at ten o'clock. I don't expect it will last more than half an hour. After that, you can speak to the undertakers."

"Have you seen the body?" Wilton asked curiously.

"Three days after death, I didn't expect it to tell

me very much. I wasn't there to see it in place, which is what counts."

"I was there. Before they moved it. Half the town came to look. I couldn't believe he was dead. Not after going through the war unscathed."

"Oddly enough, that's what Royston said."

Wilton nodded. "You sometimes meet people who appear to have charmed lives. There was a pilot in my outfit who was at best a mediocre flier, shouldn't have lasted a month, but he was the damnedest, luckiest devil I've ever known. Invisible in the air, the Germans never could see him for some reason, and he'd find the field in any weather, instinct almost. Crashed five times, and walked away with no more than a few bruises. I'd thought of Charles as having a charmed life too. I knew my own chances for surviving were slim, but we'd plan to meet, Charles and I, in Paris on our next leave, and I always knew he'd be there, waiting. Whatever happened to me." Wilton shrugged. "That was comforting, in a strange way—certainty in the midst of chaos, I suppose."

Rutledge knew what he meant. There had been a Sergeant in one company who always came back, and brought his men back with him, and men wanted to serve with him because of that. The Sergeant's reputation spread across the Front, and someone would say, "It was a bad night. But Morgan made it. Pass the word along." A talisman— bad as the assault was, it hadn't been bad enough to stop Morgan.

He'd asked the sergeant once how he'd managed it, when he ran into him on a mud-swallowed road out in the middle of nowhere, moving up for the next offensive. And Morgan had smiled. "Now, then, sir, if you believe anything hard enough," he said, "you can make it happen."

But by that time, Rutledge had lost his own will to believe in anything, and Morgan's secret wasn't any help to him. He often wondered what had become of the man after the war. . . .

Wilton looked at the light through his glass, almost as if it held answers as well as liquid amber, then said quietly, "I was as surprised as anybody when I made it through to the end of the war."

Rutledge nodded in understanding. He himself had gone from being terrified he'd die to not caring either way, and then to the final stage, *wishing* it would happen, bringing him to a peace that was more desirable than life itself.

Returning to Charles Harris, as if he found murder an easier subject than war memories, Wilton cleared his throat and went on. "As I said, I had to see for myself. My first thought was, My God, Lettice, and my second was, I still don't believe it's true—"

He stopped. "Sorry, you can ignore that," he went on, when Rutledge made no comment. "I wasn't trying to sway your judgment."

"No."

Wilton took a deep breath. "I hear that Hickam is dead drunk at Dr. Warren's. Or ill. The story varies, depending on which gossip you listen to."

"What else does gossip say?"

"That you haven't found much to go on. That you're floundering in the dark. But that's not true. I know what's in the back of your mind." He smiled wryly.

"If you didn't kill Harris, who did?"

"The comfortable answer would be, 'Mavers,' wouldn't it?"

"Why not Hickam, who claims he saw you speaking to Harris—arguing heatedly with him, in his words—in the lane? Why isn't it possible that he knew where to find a shotgun, and decided, in that confused mind of his, that he was off to shoot the Boche? Or to kill an officer he hated? He wouldn't be the first enlisted man to do that. In fact, he might just as easily have chosen you as his target as Charles Harris. A toss-up, given his drunken state."

The look of stark surprise on Wilton's face was quickly covered, but it told Rutledge one thing—that Hickam's story might very well be true, that he'd seen the Captain and the Colonel quarreling. For Wilton had taken the bait without even questioning it. He'd immediately recognized the twist that could be put on Hickam's evidence, and his mind had been busily considering that possibility just as alarm bells had gone off reminding him that—in his own statement—Hickam hadn't witnessed any meeting at all, angry or not.

"I suppose I'd never thought he was capable of such a thing," Mark answered lamely. "Shell-shocked—mad, perhaps—but not particularly dangerous." Feeling his way carefully, he added, "And it probably wouldn't matter whether he actually saw Charles that morning or just thought he did. Well, it does make a certain sense out of this business. I can't imagine anyone in his *right* mind shooting Charles. It would have to be a Mavers. Or a Hickam."

Which was all very interesting. Taking another shot in the dark, Rutledge said, "Tell me about Catherine Tarrant."

Wilton shook his head. "No." It was quiet, firm, irreversible. He emptied his glass and set it down.

"You knew her well when you were in Upper Streetham before the war. You were, in fact, in love with her."

"No, I thought I was in love with her. But her father was wise enough to see that it wouldn't do, and he asked us to wait a year or two before we came to any formal understanding." He turned in his chair, easing his stiff knee. "And he was right; a few months apart, a dozen letters on each side, and we soon discovered that they were getting harder and harder to write. I think we both realized what was happening, but there was never any formal ending. The letters got shorter, then further apart. I'm still quite fond of Catherine Tarrant, I admire her, and I like her work."

"Was she painting then?" There was a clatter in the kitchens, someone dropping a tray, and then Redfern's voice, sharply taking whoever it was to task.

"Oddly enough, nobody seemed to recognize how talented she was. Yes, she'd mention something about a painting. But you know how it was before the war, most well-bred girls tried their hand at watercolors or music—it was rather expected of them."

Rutledge recalled his sister's lessons, and smiled. Frances could sing beautifully, but her watercolors had generally been a welter of slapdash color sent running over the paper with an enthusiastic and generous hand. Not one, to his certain knowledge, had ever seen a frame. She had studied assiduously, searching for subjects and giving grandiose names to her work, but her teacher had finally written, "Miss Rutledge makes up in spirit what she lacks in talent," and to everyone's relief, the lessons had ended there.

Wilton was saying, "And no one thought anything about it when Catherine said, 'I'm doing a portrait of that old woman who used to milk cows for us, remember her? She's got a wonderful face.' " He glanced wryly at Rutledge. "Least of all me! I wasn't interested in anything that didn't have wings to it! But that one later won a prize in London. When I went to her first exhibit, I was stunned. I wondered where in God's name Catherine had found such power of expression, such depth of feeling. How she'd come to change so much in such a short time. But she hadn't changed— it was there all along, and apparently I'd been blind to it. I suppose that's the difference between infatuation and love, if you come down to it."

"And Linden? Had he brought any of these changes about? Found the woman somewhere inside the sweet, untouched girl you'd met before the war?"

Wilton's mouth was grim. "I've told you. Ask Miss Tarrant about her personal life."

"Then you disapproved of the affair?"

"I was in France, trying to stay alive. I couldn't have approved or disapproved, I didn't know. Until much later. In fact, it was Charles who told me, the first time he brought me down to Mallows. He thought I should be aware of it, before I ran into her. But Catherine has never spoken of Linden to me."

"Did she blame Colonel Harris for not handling their case properly with the Army? Or blame Lettice for not making it clear to her guardian that Catherine was serious about this man?"

"I don't know, I tell you. Except that Charles would have done what he could. If he'd *known*. For Catherine's sake if nothing else. He'd been fond of her."

"But he didn't know?"

"I can't answer that. I can tell you his headquarters was swamped with people's letters, wanting news about their sons, their husbands, their lovers. He said once it was the hardest part of his job, reading such letters. Sometimes they were sent to the wrong place, or lost."

"Surely not a letter from his ward? That wouldn't have been shoved in a sack with dozens of others and forgotten?"

This time Wilton stood up. "You're putting words into my mouth, Rutledge. I don't know what went wrong over Linden. I don't suppose anyone does. I'm sure that Charles would have done his best for the pair of them, he would try to help Catherine. My God, he did what he could for anyone in Upper Streetham in one way or another, so why not *her*? What the War Office did is anybody's guess. Some ignorant fool sitting at a cluttered desk in Whitehall might have felt it his personal duty to prevent any relationship between prisoners and the home population, whatever the Colonel said about it. Bad for morale and all that. And come to that, it wouldn't have mattered; the war was nearly over, and if he'd lived, Linden could have spoken for himself. Who could have guessed that Linden would die of *influenza*. Still, it decimated the country, for God's sake, no one was immune."

"But because he was sent from here, he died alone, and no one told Catherine. Not until long afterward."

Wilton laughed harshly. "In war you can't keep up with every poor sod you send out to die. I was a squadron leader, I knew the hell of that. A man's blown to bits in a trench, shot down in flames, chokes on gas and lies rotting in the mud. You do your best, you write letters about his bravery, how much he'd done for his country, how much his comrades looked to him for an example—and you don't even recall his name, much less his face! Linden took his chances, like any soldier. At least she *knows* what became of him, where he's buried!"

Rutledge watched his face, remembering how Catherine Tarrant had looked when she spoke of searching for Linden. And remembering what Sally Davenant had said about Wilton's love of flying changing to agony in the heat of battle and death and fear.

"That's cold comfort to a grieving, passionate woman."

"Is it? After all the killing, I came home to a hero's welcome. Safe and whole. Invited to the Palace and to Sandringham. Treated like royalty, myself. But I was there in a hospital in Dorset when they brought in a man they'd found wandering in France. Didn't even know who he was, whether he was British or German—a shell of a man, starving and begging on the roadside for a year or more, more animal than human, worse than Hickam, and I looked at him, and thought, I used to have nightmares about burning to death in a crash, but *there are worse things than that*! Worse than being blind or without a limb, lungs seared with gas, face shot away, guts rotted. Coming home safe—*and not knowing it's over*—that's the bleakest hell I'm capable of picturing!"

Rutledge felt the blood run cold in his body. Wilton nodded and walked away, unaware of what he'd done.

In the dark recesses of his mind he heard Hamish laughing, and finished his whiskey at a gulp. It burned going down, almost bringing tears to his eyes as he fought to keep from choking. Or were the tears for himself?

Think of anything, he commanded himself

roughly. *Anything but that!* His mind roiled with emotion, then settled into the dull pain of grief and despair. *Think, man, for God's sake!*

What was it they'd been talking about? No, who? Catherine Tarrant.

What to do about Catherine Tarrant, then, how to find a key to her? Waving Redfern away and getting to his feet, the whiskey still searing his throat, he walked out of the bar.

The person to answer that question was another woman. Sally Davenant.

11

The next morning just before the Inquest Rutledge had an opportunity to ask Inspector Forrest if he knew the source of Mavers's pension. But Forrest shook his head.

"I didn't know he had one. But that explains why he's never had to lift his hand to a stroke of work if he didn't feel like it. His father served the Davenants. Ask Mrs. Davenant if she knows anything about it."

The Inquest, held in one of the Inn's parlors, was crowded with a cross-section of spectators who settled in early for the best seats and waited with patient expectation for something interesting to happen. They quietly took note of who was—and was not—present, and wondered aloud how the man from London would present his findings, and more importantly, what they would be. No one knew anything about an arrest—never a good sign—but rumor claimed that Sergeant Davies had spent most of the night in Warwick, and this could mean that the killer hadn't been an Upper Streetham man after all. More than a few had pinned their hopes on Bert Mavers. Such expectations were destined for disappointment.

The Coroner's Court progressed with smooth timeliness, from the finding of the body to the request for an adjournment while the police pursued their inquiries. Half an hour, and it was finished. The coroner, an elderly man from Warwick, agreed to the police request, stood up with decision, and said, "That's it, then," before nodding to Forrest and walking out to find his carriage. A murmur of dissatisfaction trailed him like ghostly robes as he went.

Sergeant Davies had returned from Warwick around six o'clock that morning, since he had to give evidence about finding the Colonel's body. It had been a long night, he was tired and irritable, and his trip had been for nothing.

"There's no reason to believe the killer came on the trains," he said. "All strangers are accounted for, and there aren't any reports of stragglers along the road from Warwick. That's not to say someone couldn't have come from another direction, but I'd give you any odds you like that he didn't arrive from Warwick."

Which was more or less what Rutledge had expected. He thanked the Sergeant and then hurried to catch up with Sally Davenant, who was walking along with another woman, dark haired and neatly dressed in gray. They parted just as Rutledge reached them, and Sally turned to him, smiling politely.

"Good morning, Inspector."

It *was* a beautiful morning, the sky that particular shade of blue that comes only in June. The air was scented with roses, wild in the hedgerows and blooming in gardens, birds everywhere, children laughing. Not a day to consider the ramifications of a man's death.

"I'd like to speak with you," he said. "May I offer you a cup of tea?"

"Yes, I'd like one, after that ordeal." She turned to walk with him back toward the Shepherd's Crook. "I only came for Mark's sake. I'm glad you didn't require Lettice's presence. Mark says she's had a very rough time."

Refusing to be drawn, Rutledge said, "I wanted to ask you about Mavers. About a pension he may have received from your husband. Or rather, a pension that might have been left to his father, as the shotgun was."

Sally frowned. "I don't know anything about a pension, Inspector. Hugh had a very high regard for the man's father—he was dependable, honest, and knew his job. Quite different from his son. In every respect. I can tell you, Hugh had no such regard for the Mavers you've met."

"Yet he left him a shotgun."

"He left it to the *father*, and no one ever thought to change that article in the Will. When the Will was read, I made no objection to letting the shotgun go to the son because it was easier at the time than trying to fight over it. I had many problems with my husband, Inspector. He was a man who could charm anyone, but he wasn't easy to live with. That doesn't mean I didn't love him—I did. But his death was a difficult time for me. Emotionally, I was torn between grief and relief, to be honest. And the problem of dealing with someone like Mavers was beyond me. I'd never have heard the end of it anyway, whatever the lawyers promised, and I wasn't going to put up with a lifelong vendetta, as Charles did. How that man endured the endless bickering and trouble I'll never know! Probably because he was never here long enough to be driven crazy. But I was, you see."

When they were seated in the dining room, where Redfern was trying to keep up with the demand for refreshment, Rutledge ordered tea, then said to Mrs. Davenant, "What can you tell me about Catherine Tarrant?"

Her surprise showed in her face. "Catherine? Whatever does she have to do with Charles's death?"

"I don't know. I'd like a woman's opinion of her."

Sally Davenant laughed wryly. "Ah yes, the men flock to her defense, don't they? I don't know why. Not that they shouldn't, you understand!" she added quickly. "It's just that men and women see things quite differently."

Which still told him very little about Catherine.

When the tea things had been set before them, and Sally had poured, Rutledge tried again. "Did you know the German? Linden?"

"As a matter of fact, I did. He worked on her land, and several times when I went to call he came around to take my horse. Tall, fair, quite strong." She hesitated, then added, "He was a little like Mark, you know. I don't know quite how to put my finger on the likeness. I'd never have mistaken one for the other. But a *fleeting* resemblance— something you felt rather than saw?"

Rutledge said nothing, reaching for one of the little cakes on a gold-rimmed china plate. They were amazingly good, he discovered.

After a moment, she went on, "He was an educated man—a solicitor, I was told later—and in the ordinary way, an acceptable suitor. If he'd been one of the refugees, Belgian or French, there wouldn't have been any comment at all. Well, very little! But he was German, you see, those horrible monsters who shot Edith Cavell, spitted babies on their bayonets, killed and maimed British soldiers—the casualty lists were awful, and when they came out, you sighed with relief because someone you loved or knew wasn't on it this time—then felt guilty for feeling relieved! We hated the Germans, and to think of *loving* one—of marrying one—seemed—unnatural." A woman coming through the dining room spoke to Sally and walked on.

Rutledge waited until she was out of hearing. "I understood that no one knew of their relationship at the time Linden was taken away."

"That's true. But there was no doubt how Catherine felt, after the war. She went a little mad, trying to find him, and then when she learned he was dead, she was hardly herself for months. Carfield made matters worse by trying to make them better, and the town has shunned her ever since. Most of the women, and more than a few of the men, won't even speak her name."

"You said that Linden reminded you of Mark. Did he remind Catherine too? Was she, do you think, still in love with Mark?"

Sally Davenant shook her head. "No, that was over long ago. I could have told you at the time that it wouldn't last. Mark *always* falls in love with the wrong women—" She stopped, her mouth closing firmly, her eyes defying him.

Rutledge waited. She shrugged after a moment and went on. "I didn't mean that the way it sounds, of course."

But he thought she had. "What did you mean?"

"Catherine hadn't discovered her talent when she met Mark. She painted, yes, but it wasn't the focus of her life, if you see what I mean. I think it would have come between them, when she did. And she hated his flying. Even if the war hadn't come along to separate them, what chance would such a marriage have?" Carfield came in, smiled warmly at Mrs. Davenant, then nodded briskly to Rutledge.

"And Lettice?"

She hesitated, then answered carefully. "I don't think it would have worked. Not in the end. There was Charles, you see, and Lettice was devoted to him. No man enjoys living in the shadow of such a devotion. If he'd been older, yes, Mark could have relegated him to the father's role. Mark could never bear to be second best. It would have been 'Charles this' and 'Charles that' every time he turned around."

"Did Lettice fall in love with Wilton because he was the handsome hero her guardian had brought home for her? An infatuation, like Catherine's, years ago?"

"No, of course not. She's rather mature for her years, have you noticed? Probably it has to do with being orphaned so young, she had to learn to be independent early on. Charles more or less cultivated that too. Well, he could have been killed at any time, and he wanted her to be capable of carrying on alone! She wasn't a dewy-eyed girl, and I think that's what attracted Mark to her. He's been through too much to fall in love with a silly twit who thought he was dashing and exciting. And Mark is a very private man, he would have to be, to spend so much time alone in the air. Charles seemed so—open. Where Hugh had devastating charm, shallow though it was, Charles was the most—I don't know, the most physically compelling man. He could walk into a room and somehow dominate it just by being there. Men deferred to him, women found him sympathetic. That combination of strength and tenderness that's quite rare."

"But of the three, Mark Wilton was surely the most attractive?"

She laughed as she poured herself another cup of tea, then refilled his cup. "Oh, by far. If he came in here right now, every woman in the room would be aware of it! *And* preen. I've seen it happen too many times! Hugh had charm, Mark has looks, Charles had charisma. The difference is that Hugh and Charles knew how to wield what they'd been given. Mark isn't a peacock, and never has been. It's his greatest failing. People expect too much from beauty."

"Which is why you feel he couldn't have lived in Charles Harris's shadow."

"Of course. I think that's why he never fell in love with me—Hugh was one of those men who dominated with charm. To tell you the truth, Hugh used it as a weapon to have his own way, Sending you to the skies one minute, tearing your heart out the next. And although I was close to hating him at the end, it was too late, I'd lost the ability to trust. I'd have made a shrew of a wife for Mark Wilton! And he knew it."

The words were said lightly, with a smile, but there was pain behind them, in her eyes and in her voice. Rutledge heard it, but his mind was occupied by what she'd told him the first day he'd spoken to her—that Mark Wilton would have been a fool to harm Lettice's guardian, it was the surest way to lose her.

And yet just now she'd contradicted that.

Whether she had realized it or not, she'd given him a motive for murder—not her own motive, but Mark Wilton's.

Unless you turned it the other way about—and asked yourself if the most complete revenge was to destroy all three of them, Lettice, Charles, and the Captain, in one single bloody act whose repercussions would leave Lettice as alone and empty as Sally Davenant herself. Could she also have betrayed Catherine and her German lover? Women often sensed such things—his sister Frances always knew before the gossips what the latest scandal was.

Almost as if she heard his thoughts, Sally said quietly, "But you wanted to hear about Catherine, not me. Her father taught her to shoot, you know. If she'd wanted to shoot Charles, she'd have known how to go about it. But why now? Why after all this time? I'd always thought of her as hot-blooded, to paint like that. Not cold-blooded . . ." She let the thought trail off.

It was a wearing day. Hickam was still too ill to question, and Dr. Warren was testy from lack of sleep. A child he was tending was dying, and he didn't know why. When Rutledge tried to prod him over Hickam, he said, "Come with me and see this child, and then tell me, damn you, that Hickam's life is worth hers!"

So Rutledge went back to the meadow, walking up and down it, trying to see the murder, the frightened horse, the falling man. He tried to feel the hatred that had led to murder, worked out angles to see how the horseman and the killer had come together here in this one spot. How long had the killer waited? How sure had he been that Charles Harris would come this way? Had he known, somehow, where the Colonel was riding that morning? Which would bring suspicion back to Royston, surely. Or Lettice. Unless, before the quarrel, something had been said over dinner about his plans, and Wilton had remembered. Or perhaps the killer had simply followed Harris from the lane. Wilton again. Or Hickam? What would bring Catherine Tarrant out so early on that particular June morning, shotgun in hand, murder on her mind? Or Mrs. Davenant?

The damnable thing was, except for Catherine Tarrant's dead lover and Mark Wilton's quarrel, and possibly Mrs. Davenant's jealousy, there was nothing to make Colonel Harris a target. Not if Mavers was out of the running, and Rutledge had to admit there was too little chance there of proving opportunity.

Why couldn't he get a grip on the emotions of this case?

Because there was something he hadn't learned? Questions he should have asked and hadn't? Relationships he hadn't found?

Or because his own ragged emotions kept getting in his way?

Why had he lost that strong vein of intuition that once had made him particularly good at understanding why the victim had to die? At understanding why one human being had been driven to kill another. Was it lost innocence, the knowledge that he himself was now no better than the killers he hunted? No longer siding with the angels, cut off from what he once had been?

He laughed sourly. Maybe it had only been a trick, a game he was good at when he could stand back dispassionately from the searing flame of emotions. A trick he'd used so often he'd come to believe in it himself. He could hardly bring back an image of the man he'd been in 1914. A realist, he'd told himself then, accustomed to the darkest corners of human experience. Well, he'd discovered in the trenches of France that hell itself was not half so frightening as the darkest corners of the human mind.

Not that it mattered. All they expected of him now was that he do his job. No frills, no flamboyance, no magician's artifice, just answers.

If he couldn't do his job, what would he do with his life?

He began to walk, making his way from the meadow down to Mallows, trying to think which way the horse might have come, what path had led Harris here.

But that didn't work, did it? If Harris had been in the lane speaking to Wilton, he must have been *returning* to Mallows, not starting out on his ride! And why hadn't Lettice chosen to go riding with her guardian that morning? Why had she said, with such pain, "I didn't go riding with him," as if in her mind this time had been somehow different?

He walked on, following the contour of the land, using his sense of direction to lead him toward the house. In the distance he could see the chimneys of the cottage the two Sommers women had rented for the summer, and from one particular spot, the church steeple rising among the treetops, marking the village. Could you also see this part of Mallows' land from the church tower? It was an interesting thought. . . .

And farther along, the distant rooftops of Mallows itself, and the stables. What could be seen of the hillside from that vantage point?

Could you follow Colonel Harris's progress and be certain of meeting him at one particular place? Or had the encounter been happenstance?

No, because the killer had come armed, *ready to kill.* . . .

Skirting the plowed fields where new growth was dark green and strong, he found the orchards, and the stile, and a shrub-bordered path. At a fork that divided into one path of hard-packed earth pointing in the direction of the stables and sheds, the other paved now and passing through a hedge to the landscaped grounds, he came first to the kitchen gardens, the herbs, the flowers for cutting, and then the formal beds that marked the lawns.

Sure of his way now, Rutledge strode around a hedge, badly startling a gardener on his knees in a patch of vegetables. The man scrambled to his feet, pulled off his cap, and stared. Rutledge smiled. "I've come to see Mr. Royston."

"I—he's not at home, sir, Mr. Royston isn't, he hasn't come back from the Inquest that I know."

"Then I'll go along to the house and wait. Thank you." He nodded, and the gardener stood staring after him, perspiration unheeded running into the frown lines on his sun-red forehead.

Rutledge crossed the lawns to the drive and rang the bell, finding himself asking to see Lettice, not Laurence Royston.

12

To Rutledge's surprise, Lettice Wood asked him to come up to the small sitting room and was waiting for him there in the sunlight from the windows.

"The Inquest is over, Miss Wood," he said formally. "I haven't any information to give you."

"No, I can see that," she told him quietly, gesturing for him to be seated. There was a large crystal bowl of flowers on the table. From Sally Davenant's gardens? Or from Mallows'? Next to the severe black of her mourning the colors were richly bright, making her face all the paler. "Is it so hard a thing, to find a murderer?"

"Sometimes. When he—or she—doesn't want to be found, and the trail is cold, as it were." He sat down in the chair facing her, back to the window.

Her eyes were dark with pain. "Have you seen my—the Colonel's body?"

Caught off guard, he said, "No. I haven't."

"Neither have I." She stopped. "I read a story once, when I was a child. It was about medieval Norway or perhaps Scotland—an outlandish place, it sounded to me, where people didn't behave as *Englishmen* did. There was a death in the village, and the chief couldn't discover who'd killed the person. And so he ordered everyone who came to the funeral to walk past the bier where the body lay, and put their hand on the wound. Everyone did, and nothing happened. But the chief wasn't satisfied, and then he found a man hiding under an overturned boat. *He* didn't want to see or touch the dead, he was afraid of what might happen if he did. Afraid the wound would cry out and accuse him of a sin that had nothing to do with murder. And so he'd run away. I was too young to understand when I read the story. I thought the frightened man was wiser than the rest—not to want to touch the dead." She had been toying with a small silver box she had taken up from the table beside her. Now she looked up at him. "But I wanted to go to Charles. Hold him—tell him again that I loved him—tell him good-bye. That's when the doctor explained what had been done to him. And now I can't bear the thought of it—I can't bear to think of Charles at all, because when I do, I see a— a *monster.* You can't imagine how guilty it makes me feel—how bereft of comfort of any kind."

Rutledge remembered the first corpses he'd seen in France, obscene, smelling things, inhuman grotesques that haunted his dreams. Stiff, awkward, ugly—you couldn't feel compassion for them, only disgust, and the dreadful fear that you'd turn out like them, carted off in the back of a truck, like boards.

"Death is seldom tidy," he said after a moment. "Sometimes for the very old, perhaps. Nothing is finished by a murder, whatever the killer may expect."

She shook her head. "Laurence Royston told me that he had killed a child once. Quite accidentally. She'd run in front of his motorcar, there was nothing he could do, it was over in an instant. But he still remembers it quite vividly, the faces of the parents, the grief, the small crumpled body. Two children, playing a game, and suddenly, death." She smiled wryly at Rutledge. "It was meant to help me see that none of us is spared pain. Meant *kindly*. He's a very kind man. But it was small comfort." A bird began to sing in the trees beyond an open window. The sound was sweet, liquid, but oddly out of place as a background to a quiet discussion of death.

"Do you still wish to see Charles's murderer hang?" He watched her face.

Lettice sighed and asked instead, "Do you truly believe Catherine Tarrant could have killed him?"

"I don't know. The field is still wide. Catherine Tarrant? Mark Wilton? Or Mrs. Davenant. Royston. Hickam. Mavers."

She made a dismissive gesture. "Then you've made no progress at all. You're whistling in the dark."

"You, then." He couldn't decide if the scent that wafted to him on the slight breeze coming in the window was her perfume or from the flowers.

"*Me?*"

Rutledge said only, "I must keep an open mind, Miss Wood."

"If I were planning to kill anyone—*for any reason*—I would not have used a shotgun! *Not in the face!*"

"There are many ways to kill," he said, thinking suddenly of Jean. "Cruelty will do very well."

Her face flamed, as if he'd struck her. On her feet in an instant, she stood there poised to leave.

"What are you talking about? No, I don't want to hear it! Please—just leave, I've nothing more to say to you." Her odd eyes were alight with defensive anger, giving her face a wild and passionate force. "Do what you came to do, and go back to London!"

"I'm sorry—that wasn't what I intended to—" He found himself apologizing quickly, a hand out as if to stop her from ringing the bell for Johnston.

Hamish stirred. "She'll enchant ye, wait and see! Go while you can!"

But Rutledge paid him no heed. "Look at this from my point of view," he went on. "So far, the best evidence I can find leads me to Mark Wilton. I don't want to make a mistake, I don't want to arrest him now and then have to let him go for lack of proof. Can you see what that could do to his life? Or yours, if you marry him, now or later. Chances are, you knew Charles Harris as well if not better than anyone. The man, not the soldier, not the landowner, not the employer. Help me find the Colonel's killer! If you loved him at all."

She stared at him, still very angry. But she hadn't rung the bell. Instead, she walked with that long graceful stride toward the window, swinging around, making him turn as well to see her. "What is it you want, then? For me to damn someone else?"

"No. Just to help me see that last evening as clearly as I can."

"I wasn't there when the quarrel began!"

"But you can judge what might have happened. If I ask the right questions."

She didn't answer him, and he made himself think clearly, made himself consider what might have happened.

Three women. Three men. Catherine Tarrant,

Lettice Wood, Sally Davenant. Charles Harris, Mark Wilton, and a German called Linden. He hadn't found a link that satisfied him. And yet there *were* ties between them, of love and hate. Linden was dead. Harris was dead. And if Hickam's testimony in court was damning enough, Wilton would be hanged. The men gone. All three of them.

Which in a way brought him back again to Catherine Tarrant. . . .

"Is it possible," he began slowly, "that, whatever they may have discussed just after you went up to your room, your guardian and Captain Wilton argued that night over Miss Tarrant? That somehow the subject of Miss Tarrant—or Linden, for that matter—came up after they'd finished the discussion of the wedding?"

The defensive barrier was there again. She answered curtly, "I can't imagine what you're talking about! Why should they've argued about Catherine?"

"Could the Colonel have warned the Captain that Catherine Tarrant still felt strongly about Linden's death and was likely to do something rash? To harm one of them? To spoil the wedding, perhaps? Could the Captain have refused to hear anything said against her? Defended her, and made Harris very angry with him?"

"If Charles had been worried, he would have said something to *me*. But he didn't—"

"But you didn't go riding with him that morning. There was no opportunity to tell you what was on his mind."

She opened her mouth to say something, and decided against it. Instead, she replied, "You're chasing straws!"

"A witness saw them together, still arguing, that morning shortly before the Colonel died. If they weren't arguing over the wedding, then over what? Or over whom?"

With her back to the windows, her eyes shadowed by the halo of her dark hair, she said, "You're the policeman, aren't you?"

"Then what about Mrs. Davenant?"

"Sally? What on earth does she have to do with anything?"

"She's very fond of her cousin. Your guardian might have worried about that. Or conversely, Mark Wilton might have been jealous of the place Harris held in *your* life—"

Lettice turned to the flowers in the vase, her fingers moving over them as if she were blind and depended on touch to know what varieties were there. "If Mark had wanted to marry Sally, he could have done it any time these last eight years. When he had leave during the war, she went to London to meet him. He's fond of her, of course he is. He's fond of Catherine Tarrant, as well. As for Charles, Mark knows how I feel—felt—about him." She bit her lip. "No, *feel*. I won't put it in the past tense, as if everything stopped with his death! As if you stop caring, stop giving someone a place in your life. I want him back again, so desperately I ache with it. And yet I'm afraid to *think* about him—I can only see that awful, terrible *thing*—"

She lifted her head, forced back the tears. "Do you dream of the corpses you've seen?"

Taken aback, he said before he thought, "Sometimes."

"I dreamed about my parents after they died. But I was too young to know what death was. I saw them as shining angels floating about heaven and watching me to see if I was good. In fact, the first time I saw the Venus above the hall here at Mallows, I thought it was my mother. It was a great comfort, oddly enough." After a moment she said in a different voice, "You'll have to chase your straws without me. I'm sorry. There's nothing else I can do."

This time he knew he had to go. He stood up. "I'd like to question your staff again before I leave. Will you tell Johnston that I have your permission?"

"Question them, then. *Just put an end to this.*" It was a plea; her anger had drained away into pain and something else that he couldn't quite identify.

And so he spent the next hour talking to the servants, but his mind was on the lonely woman shut up in grief a few walls, a few doors from wherever he went in that house.

Mary Satterthwaite nervously told him she wasn't sure what the master and the Captain were arguing about, but Miss Wood had said they were discussing the wedding, and it appeared to have given her the headache; she wanted only to go to bed and be left alone.

"Was it common for the Colonel and the Captain to argue?"

"Oh, no sir! They never did, except over a horse race or how a battle was fought, or the like. Men often quarrel rather than admit they're wrong, you know."

He smiled. "And who was wrong in this instance? The Colonel? The Captain?"

Mary frowned, taking him seriously. "I don't know, sir." She added reluctantly, "I'd guess, sir, it was the Colonel."

"Why?"

"He threw his glass at the door. I mean, he couldn't throw it at the Captain, being as *he* was already gone. But he didn't like it that the Captain had had the last word, so to speak. So he threw his glass. As if there was still anger in him, or guilt, or frustration. Men don't *like* to be wrong, sir. And I doubt if the Colonel was, very often."

Which was a very perceptive observation. He asked about relations between the Captain and the Colonel. Cordial, he was told. Two quite different men, but they respected each other.

In the end, he asked to be taken upstairs to any rooms overlooking the hillside where the Colonel had been riding.

In theory, the hill was in view from a number of windows, both in the family quarters and on the servants' floor. At this time of year, with the trees fully leafed out, it was different. You'd have to be lucky, Rutledge thought, peering out from one of the maids' windows—the best of the lot—to catch a glimpse from here. You'd have to know where the Colonel was riding, and be watching for the faintest flicker of movement, and then not be certain what you'd seen was a horse and man. Possible, then. But not likely.

Tired, with Hamish grumbling in the back of his mind, Rutledge left the house and began the walk back to the meadow, the far hedge, and the lane where he'd left his car two hours or more before.

He glimpsed Maggie, the quiet Sommers cousin, hanging out a tablecloth on the line. He waved to her, but she didn't see him, the breast-high wall and the climbing roses blocking her view. He walked on. Somewhere behind her he could hear the goose honking irritably, as if it had been shut away for the morning and was not happy about it. Rutledge smiled. Served the damned bird right!

Back in the meadow where Charles Harris had been found, Rutledge ignored Hamish and began to quarter the land carefully. But there was nothing to be learned. Nothing that was out of the ordinary. Nothing of interest. He went back over the land again, moving patiently, his eyes on the ground, his mind concentrating on every blade of grass, every inch of soil. Then he moved into the copse where the killer might have stood waiting.

Still nothing. Frustrated, he stood there, looking back the way he'd come, looking at the lie of the land, the distant church steeple. Hamish was loud in his mind, demanding his attention, but he refused to heed the voice.

Nothing. *Nothing*—

Except—

In the lee of the hedge, near where he and the Sergeant had cut through on their first visit. Something dull and gray and unidentifiable. Something he hadn't been able to see from any other part of the meadow. What was it?

He walked down to the hedge, keeping his bearings with care, and found the place, the thing he'd seen. He squatted on his heels and looked at it, thinking it was a scrap of rotting cloth. Nothing . . . Ignoring the brambles, he pushed his way nearer to it. Closer to, it had shape, and staring eyes.

Reaching into the brambles, he touched it, then pulled it forward.

A doll. A small wooden doll, in a muddy, faded gown of pale blue flowered print, the kind of cloth that could be bought in any shop, cheap, cotton, and favored by mothers for children's clothes. A girl's dress, with the leftover cloth sewn into a gown for her favorite doll.

Hadn't Wilton said something about seeing a child who had lost her doll?

Rutledge picked up the little bundle of cloth and stared down at it.

Hickam might not be fit to testify against the Captain. Would a child be any more reliable as a witness? He swore. Not bloody likely!

Making his way through the hedge, Rutledge went striding down to the lane, ignoring the high grass and brambles, his mind working on how to deal with the child, and with Wilton. Hamish was silent now, but somewhere he still moved about restlessly, waiting.

When he got to his car, left in the brushy, overgrown lane, Rutledge swore again. With infinite feeling.

One of his tires was torn. As if viciously slashed with a knife or a sharp stick. Deliberately and maliciously damaged.

Rutledge didn't need a policeman to tell him who had done this.

Mavers.

13

$\mathcal{R}$utledge sent the blacksmith to bring his car back to the village and then went to find Inspector Forrest. But he wasn't in—he'd been called back to Lower Streetham on the matter of the lorry accident. Fortuitously, Rutledge told himself irritably.

It was long past time for luncheon, and Rutledge turned back toward the Inn. After a hasty meal, he crossed to Dr. Warren's surgery to look in on Hickam. He was no better—awake, but without any awareness in his eyes. A dead man's stare was focused on the ceiling of the tiny room, blank and without knowledge or pain or grief.

Dr. Warren came in as Rutledge was leaving. "You've seen him? Well, it's something that he's still alive, I suppose. I've got enough on my hands—I can't stand over him. You might see if the Vicar will pray for him"—he snorted—"it's about all *he's* good for!"

"Can you tell me if any young children live near the meadow where Harris was found?"

"Children?" Dr. Warren stared at him.

"Girls, then. Young enough to play with something like this." He held out the muddy wooden doll.

Dr. Warren transferred his gaze to the object in Rutledge's hand. "There must be seven or eight on the estate itself, servants' and tenants' children. More, scattered on the farms thereabouts. The gentry have china dolls, not wooden ones. As a rule. Why?"

"I found this under a hedge. Captain Wilton says he saw a child that morning, that she'd lost her doll."

"Then ask the Captain to find her for you! I've got a breech birth to see to, and after that, a farmer whose ax slipped and damned near took off his foot. If I save the limb, it'll be a miracle. And he won't have the Army to provide him with a false one if I don't."

Rutledge stood aside and let him walk into the small surgery, where Warren restocked his bag and then set it on the scrubbed table. "You understand, don't you, that if Hickam lives, he may not have enough of a mind left to testify at all? Everything that's happened could be wiped out?"

Rutledge replied, "Yes. I know. You've served the people of this town for most of your life. Who do you believe might have killed Charles Harris?"

Warren shrugged. "Mavers, of course. That would be my first thought. I don't know your Captain well enough to judge *him*. Still, Lettice was going to marry him, and Charles was damned careful where she was concerned; he wouldn't have stood by and let a fool sweep her off her feet."

"Catherine Tarrant?"

Warren shook his head. "Because of the German? Don't be an idiot, man. I can't see her lurking behind a tree with a shotgun, can you? If she had

wanted Harris dead, she'd have come for him at
Mallows, the first day he was back from the war.
Why wait until *now*? But I'm not paid to find murderers. That's your job. And if you ask me, you're
damned slow going about it!"

Hamish, chuckling deep in his mind, said deri-
sively, "You're half the man you were, that's what
it is. Ye left the better half in the mud and terror,
and brought back only the broken bits. *And London knows it!*"

Rutledge turned on his heel and strode out, the
doll still in his hand.

He tracked down Wilton having a whiskey in the
Inn's bar, morosely staring at the glass in his hand.
Rutledge sat down at the small corner table and
said, "Early in the day for that?"

"Not when you've come from the under-
taker's," Wilton said, turning his glass around and
around in his fingers. "The fool had never dealt
with a headless man before. He was half titillated,
half revolted. Would we be wanting the Colonel in
his dress uniform? And how was that cut, sir, with
a high collar or low? Would we wish a silk scarf to
cover what was—er—the remains? Would we wish
for a *pillow* in the coffin? To rest the shoulders
upon, of course, sir. And will you be wanting to inspect the—er—deceased, before the services?" The
Captain shuddered. "My good God!" He looked at
Rutledge. "When Davenant died, the old vicar was
still alive, and he went with me to attend to matters. Before we left, Davenant's valet handed us a
box with suitable clothing in it, and that was that.
It was civilized, simple."

"An ordinary death." Rutledge shook his head
as Redfern started toward them, to indicate that he

didn't wish to be disturbed. Then he put the doll on the table.

Mark Wilton stared at it, frowning. "What the hell is that?"

"A child's doll."

"A doll?"

"You told me that on the morning Harris was killed, you ran into a child who'd lost her doll. On the path near the meadow."

"Oh, yes. I remember her. She'd been picking flowers or some such thing, and then couldn't find the doll—she'd put it down somewhere or other. I see she found it."

"I found it. Now I want to find her."

Wilton smiled tiredly. "To ask her if I was carrying a shotgun when she and I crossed paths? First a drunken madman, then a child. Good God!"

"Nevertheless."

"I have no idea who she was, or what her name was. Small, fair, cheerful—a *child*. I've had very little experience with them. I'm not even certain I'd know her again if I saw her."

"But you won't mind accompanying the Sergeant to visit the tenants on Mallows' land and in the farms above the church." It was not a question.

Wilton regarded him for a time. "You're quite serious about this?"

"Entirely."

Mark Wilton sighed. "Very well."

"That night, when Lettice Wood left you and Harris together in the drawing room, she said you were discussing the wedding. Where did the conversation turn after that? To Catherine Tarrant?"

Wilton was surprised. "*Catherine?* Why on earth should we have discussed *her*—much less quarreled over her? Charles and I admired her."

"If not Catherine Tarrant, what about Mrs. Davenant?"

Wilton laughed. "You are in desperate straits, aren't you? Did you think I'd shoot Harris over the good name of my cousin? What has *she* done to merit your attention?"

Rutledge shrugged. "Why shouldn't I grasp at straws?" He realized that he was quoting Lettice Wood. Had her words rankled that much? "There hasn't been a rush of people breaking down the police-station door to volunteer information about Harris's killer, has there? I've decided there's a conspiracy to keep me from finding out what's best hidden."

Wilton stared at him, eyes sharp and searching. The thin, weary face before him was closed and unreadable. What had made this man so ill, consumption? War wounds? The sickly often had a way of piercing to the heart of a matter, as if their close brush with death made them more sensitive to the very air around them.

Rutledge had spoken out of irritation, exasperated with Wilton and himself. But the reaction had been completely unexpected.

"Yon pretty hero isn't what he seems," Hamish growled. "Unlucky in love and good for nothing but killing. But *very* good at that. . . ."

Finally Wilton said carefully, "A conspiracy to murder Harris?"

"A conspiracy to hide the truth. Whatever it may be," Rutledge amended.

Wilton finished his whiskey. "I thought you were an experienced man, one of the best London had. That's what Forrest told us. If you can find one person in Warwickshire—other than that fool Mavers—who wanted Harris dead, I'll willingly be damned to the far reaches of hell! Meanwhile, I'll find the Sergeant and we'll tour the nurseries of Upper Streetham for this child who lost a doll. Little good may it do you!"

He left, lifting a hand to summon Redfern. Rutledge sat where he was, watching the stiff, angry set of his shoulders as the Captain stalked off. "Unlucky in love," Hamish had said.

He considered that again. Catherine Tarrant's German. Lettice Wood's guardian. And Sally Davenant, who might not have forgotten what had become of her husband's old shotgun.

If Charles Harris had died of poison, Rutledge might believe in simple jealousy more easily. But a shotgun? That took rage, hatred, a need to obliterate, as Lettice had put it.

He could feel the fatigue dragging at him, the stress and the loneliness. The fear. Looking around for Redfern, Rutledge saw that he was alone in the bar. And then Carfield was coming through the doorway, glancing his way.

"Inspector. I've spoken with Mark Wilton," he said, crossing over to Rutledge's table. "We've settled on Tuesday for the services. I understand that Dr. Warren hasn't lifted his embargo on visits to Lettice. I really feel, as her spiritual adviser, I should go to her, offer her comfort, prepare her for the very difficult task of attending the funeral. Could you use your good offices to persuade him that seclusion is the worst possible thing for a young woman with no family to support her?"

Rutledge smiled. *Pompous ass* didn't begin to describe the Vicar. "I have no right to overturn a medical decision unless it has a bearing on my duties," he said, remembering Lettice's dread of having to cope with Carfield.

"And there's the matter of the reception after the service. It should be held at Mallows. I sincerely believe Charles would have wished that. Naturally I shall take charge; I know the staff well enough, they'll do my bidding."

"Why not at the Vicarage?" Rutledge asked. "After Miss Wood has greeted the guests, she can go quietly home. Wilton will see to that, or Royston."

Carfield sat down uninvited. "My dear man, one doesn't serve the funeral's cold baked meats at the *Vicarage* for a man like Charles Harris, who has his own quite fine residence! That's what staff is *for*, you know, to do the labor. One doesn't expect dear Lettice to shoulder such a burden."

"Have you suggested to Wilton that you wish to arrange the reception at Mallows?"

Carfield's eyebrows rose. "It isn't his home, is it? The decision is for others to make, not for Captain Wilton."

"I see." He considered the Vicar for a moment. "Who told Upper Streetham that Miss Tarrant was in love with a German prisoner of war and wished to marry him?"

The heavily handsome face was closed. "I have no idea. I tried to make the village see that she had done nothing wrong, that loving our enemies is part of God's plan. But people are sometimes narrow-minded about such matters. Why do you ask?"

"Could she have killed Charles Harris?"

Carfield smiled. "Why not ask me if Mrs. Davenant did it?"

"All right. Did she?"

The smile disappeared. "You're quite serious?"

"Murder is a serious business. I want to solve this one."

"Ah, yes, I can understand your dilemma, with Wilton so closely connected to the Royal Family,"

Carfield answered with a shrewdness that narrowly escaped shrewishness as well. "I shouldn't have thought that a shotgun was a woman's weapon."

"Nor should I. But that doesn't mean it wasn't a woman. Behind it at the very least, even if she never touched the trigger."

With a shake of his head, Carfield replied, "Women are many things, but obliterating a man's face in that fashion is a *bloody*, horrible business even for a man. Catherine, Mrs. Davenant, Lettice—they are none of them farmwives who can take an ax to a chicken without blinking."

"Catherine Tarrant ran her father's estate throughout the war."

"Ran it, yes, but do you suppose she butchered cattle or dressed a hen?"

"Perhaps she didn't know how bloody the results would be. Perhaps she intended to aim lower, but the kick of the weapon lifted the barrel."

Carfield shrugged. "Then you must take into account the fact that during the last three years of the war, Sally Davenant volunteered to nurse the wounded at a friend's house in Gloucestershire, which had been turned into a hospital. She has no formal training, you understand, but Mrs. Davenant did tend her husband through his last illness, and the—er—intimacies of the sickbed were familiar to her. Dressing wounds, taking off bloody bedclothes, watching doctors remove stitches or clean septic flesh—I'm sure you learn to face many things when you have to."

No one, least of all Sally Davenant, had seen fit to mention that. Rutledge swore under his breath.

"But I can't think that it would lead her to commit a murder!" Carfield was saying. "And why should she wish to kill the Colonel, I ask you!"

"Why did anyone want to kill him?" Rutledge countered.

"Ah, now we're back to why. Whatever the reason, I'm willing to wager that it was deeply personal. Deeply. Can you plumb that far into the soul to find it?"

"Are you telling me that as a priest you've heard confessions that give you the answer to this murder?"

"No, people seldom confess their blackest depths to anyone, least of all to a priest. Oh, the small sins, the silly sins, even the guilty sins, where a clean conscience relieves the weight of guilt. Adultery. Envy. Anger. Covetousness. Hate. Jealousy."

He smiled, a rueful smile that belittled himself in a way. "But there's fury, you know. Where someone acts in a blind rage, and only then stops to think and feel. Or fright, where there's no time for second thoughts. Or self-defense, where you must act or be hurt. I hear of those afterward. From the man who hits a neighbor in a rage over a broken cart wheel. From the woman who takes a flatiron to her drunken husband before he beats her senseless. From the child who lashes out, bloodying a bully's nose. And sometimes these things can also lead to murder. Well, you've seen it happen, I needn't tell you about that! But what's deeply burned into the soul, what's buried beneath the civilized layers of the skin, is the more deadly because often there's no warning it even exists. No warning, even to a priest."

Which was more truth than Rutledge had expected to hear from the Vicar.

"However," Carfield went on before Rutledge could answer him, "I'm not here to solve your problems but to attend to my own. Which brings me back again to Mallows."

"I'd speak to Royston or to Wilton, if I were you. I'd leave Miss Wood out of it. If they agree, they can break the news to her."

"I'm her spiritual adviser!"

"And Dr. Warren is her physician. It's his decision, not yours."

Carfield rose, eyes studying Rutledge, the tired face, the lines. "You carry your own heavy burdens, don't you?" he said quietly. "I don't envy you them. My God, I don't! But let me tell you this much, Inspector Rutledge. When you return to London, this will still be my parish, and I must still face its people. The reception *will* be at Mallows. I promise you that."

He turned and strode through the bar, ignoring Redfern. The younger man came limping across to Rutledge's table. "Now there's a man I'd not want to cross," he said, glancing over his shoulder at the sound of the outer door slamming. "I'd turn Chapel before I'd tell him what was going on in my head!"

Rutledge laughed wryly. He wondered if Redfern had overheard part of the conversation or was simply, unwittingly, confirming the Vicar's words.

Redfern picked up the empty glasses and wiped the table with his cloth. "It isn't easy, is it? Being from London and not knowing what's happening here. But I'll tell you, there's no reason I can think of for any of us to shoot Colonel Harris. Save Mavers, of course. Born troublemaker! There was a private in my company, a sour-faced devil from the stews of Glasgow, who was bloody-minded as they come! Never gave us any peace, until the day the Germans got him. I heard later that the ambulance carrying him to hospital was strafed. Everybody killed. I was sorry about that, but I was relieved that Sammy wasn't coming back. Ever. Tongue as rough as the shelling, by God!"

"I understand that Mrs. Davenant was a nurse during the war. Is that true?"

It was Redfern's turn to laugh, embarrassed. "You could have knocked me over with a feather when she walked into the ward the day I was brought in, still too groggy from what they'd been doing to my foot to know where I was. God, I thought somehow I'd landed back home! The next day she was there again, changing dressings. I told the sister on duty I'd not hear of her touching *me*! Sister said that was enough nonsense out of me. Still, they must have spoken of it, because she left me alone."

"You recognized her?"

"Oh, aye, I did. Well, why not? I grew up in Upper Streetham!"

"And she never said anything? Then or later, when you'd both come back here, to the village?"

"No, and I can tell you it was a relief the first time she passed me on the High Street without so much as a blink! We've spoken since, of course, when she's been here to dine, just good evening, and what will you have, and thank you—no more nor less than is needed."

"Did she work primarily with the surgical patients, or only wherever she was most useful?"

"I asked one of the younger sisters about her. She said that Mrs. Davenant had shown a skill with handling the worst cases, and the doctors often asked for her. No nonsense, and no fainting, Tilly said. She was best with fliers, she knew how to talk to them. And we got any number of those. Of course, with her own cousin one of them, I expect it was natural for her to find it easy to talk to them."

"Amputations, cleaning septic wounds, burns— she didn't shirk them?"

"No, not that I ever saw. But she's not one the lads would feel free to chat up and laugh with, not the way you did with Tilly. Good-natured nonsense, that's all it was, but not with the likes of Mrs. Davenant!"

"Yet the fliers were comfortable with her?"

"Yes. She'd ask news of the Captain, and then they'd soon be easy around her."

She'd ask news of the Captain. . . .

It always came back to the Captain. But he was beginning to think that whatever her feelings about Mark Wilton, it would take more skill than he possessed to bring them to the surface.

Rutledge went upstairs and along the passage to his room. The sun was bright, showing the worn carpet to worst advantage, dust motes dancing in the light as he passed the windows. The vegetable garden looked like a vegetable garden again, not a sea of temples. He thought the onions had grown inches since his arrival. Even the flowers in the small private garden between the Inn and the drive, surrounded by shrubbery, were no longer flat and drooping from the rain, but stood tall and full of blossom heads. The lupines were particularly glorious. His mother had liked them and filled the house with them as soon as they began to bloom. She'd had a way with flowers, a natural instinct for what made them thrive. His sister Frances, on the other hand, couldn't have grown weeds in a basket. But she was known throughout London for her exquisite flower arrangements, and was begged to lend her eye for color and form to friends for parties and weddings and balls.

His door was ajar, the maid finishing making his bed. She apologized shyly when he stepped in, saying that luncheon had been such a busy time they'd needed her in the kitchens.

"No matter," he said, but she hastily finished her task, picked up her broom and the pile of dirty linens, and bobbed a curtsy of sorts as she left. Rutledge sat down by the windows, wondering what he would say to Bowles on Monday.

Possibilities weren't evidence. Possibilities weren't guilt. Bowles would have a fit if he knew how few facts Rutledge possessed.

He wondered what luck Wilton would have tracking down the child who'd lost the doll. He set it on the windowsill and looked at it. Too bad you couldn't bring a doll into the courtroom. What could it tell? What had it seen, lying there in the hedgerow? Or heard? Rutledge grimaced. A drunken, shell-shocked man, a small child, and a doll, versus a war hero wearing the ribbon of the Victoria Cross. Every newspaper in the country would have a field day!

He needed a motive . . . a reason for murder. A reason why the Colonel, riding out that sunny morning, had to die. What had brought about his death? Something now, something in the war, something in a life spent largely out of England? So far such questions had gotten him nowhere.

Rutledge leaned his head against the back of the chair, then closed his eyes. He needed to find a young sergeant at the Yard and train him. Someone he could trust. He'd ask Bowles for names of likely men. Someone who could work with him. Davies was too busy trying to stay out of sight. Davies had his own commitments to Upper Streetham, and like the Vicar, he had to live here long after Rutledge was gone. It was understandable. But he needed someone to talk to about this case. Someone who was impartial, whose only interest was finding the killer and getting on with it. Someone to share the loneliness—

"And what would you tell yon bonny Sergeant about me? Would you be honest with him? I'll not go away, you can't shut me out, I'm not your un-happy Jean, who wants to be shut out. I'm your conscience, man, and it wouldn't be long before yon bonny young Sergeant knows you for what you are!"

Getting quickly to his feet, Rutledge swore. All right, then, he'd do it alone. But do it he would!

Outside the Inn, he met Laurence Royston. Roys-ton nodded, and was about to walk on, when Rut-ledge said, "Have you spoken with the Vicar?"

Royston turned. "Damned fool! But yes, I have, and yes, he's right. Charles would have expected to have the reception at Mallows. I've told him I'll take the responsibility, and I'll see to the arrange-ments. He needn't disturb Lettice. Miss Wood."

"Can you tell me if Sally Davenant worked as a nurse during the war? At a convalescent hospital?"

"Yes, she did. In a friend's home in Gloucester-shire. Charles ran into her there once or twice, vis-iting one of his wounded staff officers. He felt she was very capable, very good at what she did."

"Why do you think she volunteered?"

"Actually, she spoke to me about it before she wrote to Mrs. Carlyle." He grinned. "I told her she'd hate it. Well, I thought she might, you see, and if she expected to hate it, it wouldn't be quite such a letdown. She said then that she wasn't cut out to run a farm the way Catherine Tarrant was doing, and she was damned if she'd roll bandages or serve tea to the troop trains leaving London—ladies' make-work, she called it. But she thought she might be useful with the wounded. And she was worried about her cousin. Pilots didn't have a long life expectancy; by rights Wilton should have been killed in the first year—eighteen months. She felt that staying busy would make the news easier to bear. When it came."

There was a commotion in the street as two boys came swooping past, chasing a dog with a bone nearly as large as its head in its mouth. A woman on the other side of the street called, "Jimmy! If you've let that animal into the house—"

Royston watched the boys. "Father died on the Somme. They're growing up wild as hellions. What was I saying? Oh, about Mrs. Davenant. I couldn't serve," he went on quietly. "I have only the one kidney, as I told you. The army wouldn't have any part of me, and I suppose it was for the best. Hard on a man, when everyone else is serving, even the women. Charles told me I was doing my bit keeping Mallows and the Davenant lands productive."

"You worked Mrs. Davenant's land?"

"Yes, her steward left before Christmas in 1914. Mad to fight, mad to be there before it was all over. He never came back. And the old steward wasn't up to the work. I did it, and he kept an eye on things when I couldn't be there."

"Did you know Hugh Davenant well?"

Royston shrugged. "Well enough. Hugh Davenant made a wreck of his marriage. One of those selfish, careless bastards who go through life leaving grief in their wake, never taking notice."

"Was she ever in love with her cousin?"

He frowned. "I've wondered. Well, it was natural, I suppose, to wonder. But there was never anything to support speculation. She's fond of him."

"What was Wilton planning to do after he married Lettice? Live here at Mallows?"

"No, he has a home of his own in Somerset— I've seen it, a handsome house, good rich land."

"I can't picture the Captain quietly growing lettuces and wheat."

With a laugh Royston said, "His father was an architect, his mother's family's in banking in the City. Even if he never flies again, he'll hardly be reduced to growing lettuces."

But when he came back to Warwickshire, he'd stay at Mallows, not with his cousin. . . .

"Right, thank you, Royston." Rutledge stepped out of the way of a woman pushing a pram. She acknowledged Royston with a pleasant smile and walked on, glancing at Rutledge out of the corner of her eyes at the last minute.

Royston waited until she was out of hearing. "You've made no progress, then?" He shook his head. "I keep thinking about it—how someone could shoot the Colonel down and then disappear so completely. Unless he's left the County. But if he's still here, there's been no change in his manner, nothing to point to him. It was a bloody, vindictive sort of crime, Inspector. And yet it doesn't seem to have changed the killer at all. Either to make him happier or make him angrier. Somehow I find that particularly horrifying. Don't you? That someone could kill and not be marked by it?"

14

$\mathcal{R}$utledge watched Laurence Royston walk away down the busy street, then brought his mind back to the task he'd set himself. He stepped out into the afternoon traffic, following a woman with a pram. Standing by the market cross, he looked up and down the main street. Two boys on bicycles passed him, grinning, trying to attract his attention, but he ignored them.

Mavers, that Monday morning when Harris was shot, had been busily haranguing the market goers. Both Mavers and any number of witnesses had sworn to it.

But Sally Davenant, for one, had suggested that it was possible for him to disappear for a short time without anyone noticing his absence.

Rutledge considered first of all Mavers's cunning, and the distance from here to the meadow where Harris died.

The gun was a problem. If Mavers went to his house first, retrieved the shotgun, then went to the meadow, waited for Harris, shot him, put the gun back, and returned to Upper Streetham, he would need at the very least some ninety minutes, possibly even two hours.

Too long. He'd have been missed.

All right then, what if he'd taken the shotgun and left it somewhere along the hedge before coming down to the village? Harangued the crowds, disappeared, and after the killing, concealed the shotgun again in the high grass before returning to his post? A long hour? Could he have done it that quickly? It was a risk, a calculated risk, and Rutledge wasn't sure that Mavers was willing to run it. On the other hand, Mavers liked nothing better than thumbing his nose at his betters. . . .

Rutledge nodded to the woman he'd seen earlier with Sally Davenant, his attention on Mavers's movements. And then he brought himself up sharply and caught up with her as she crossed the street in the direction of the greengrocer's. Touching her arm to attract her attention, he introduced himself and said, "Were you in Upper Streetham last Monday morning? Did you by any chance hear the man Mavers speaking out here in the street?"

She was a pleasant-faced woman, dressed well and carrying a small basket nearly full of parcels. But she grimaced as Rutledge asked his question. "You can't miss him during one of his tirades," she said. "More's the pity!"

"Could you tell me if he was there, by the market cross?"

"Yes, he was, as a matter of fact."

"All the time? Part of the time?"

She frowned, considering, and then called to another woman just coming out of the ironmonger's shop. "Eleanor, dear—"

Eleanor was in her fifties, with short iron gray

hair and a look of competence about her. She came across to them, head to one side, her stride as brisk as her manner.

"Inspector Rutledge from London, Eleanor," the first woman said. "This is Eleanor Mobley, Inspector. She might be able to help you more than I can—I was here only very early that morning."

Rutledge remembered the name Mobley from Forrest's list of witnesses. He repeated his questions, and Mrs. Mobley watched his face as she listened. "Oh, yes, he was here by the market cross very early on. At least part of the time. He went down along the street there, closer to the shops and the Inn, for a while. Later I saw him near the turning to the church. But he came back to the cross, he usually does." She gave him a wry smile. "I was trying to line up tables for the Vicar's summer fete. A fund-raiser for the church. You know how it is, everyone *promises* to contribute something for the sale. All the same, you can't let it go at that, can you—you have to pin them down. Not my favorite task, but this year I'm on the committee, and market day brings most everyone into town, I just catch them as I can. I must have been up and down this street a dozen times or more."

"He moved from place to place, but as far as you know, he didn't leave? To go to the pub, for instance, or step into the Inn?"

"Not as far as I know. But since I wasn't paying him much heed, I can't be certain that I'm right about that. He just seemed to be underfoot wherever I turned, putting people's backs up, spoiling a perfectly lovely morning."

Someone passing by spoke to the other woman, calling her Mrs. Thornton. She acknowledged his greeting, adding, "I'll be along directly, tell Judith for me, will you, Tom?"

Mrs. Mobley was saying to Rutledge, "Is that any help at all?"

"Yes, very much so. What was on his mind that morning? Do you recall anything he might have been saying?"

Mrs. Mobley shook her head. "He was running on about the Russians, you can usually depend on that. Something about the Czar and his family. I remember something about unemployment too, because I was thinking to myself that he was a lovely one to talk! The strikes in London."

"You don't really listen, do you? He's not a very pleasant man at the best of times!" Mrs. Thornton put in. "And riding his hobbyhorse, he's—repellent. As Helena Sommers put it, any good he might do is lost with every word that comes out of his mouth!"

"Was Miss Sommers here on Monday?"

"Yes, just around noon, I think it was, buying some lace for her cousin," Mrs. Mobley said. "I put her down for two cakes; I was glad to have them."

Mrs. Thornton bit her lip, then said, "You'll think it silly of me, but I don't feel it's safe for two women in a cottage in the middle of nowhere. Since the Colonel's death, I mean. Since we don't *know*— And Helena might as well be alone, her cousin is such a ninny! I went out there to call one afternoon, and Margaret was working in the garden. Well, that goose gave my horse such a fright, and she was absolutely too terrified even to drive the silly thing away with a broom!"

"I think they're probably safe enough," Rutledge said, refusing to be drawn.

"If you say so." Mrs. Thornton seemed unconvinced. "Now, if there's nothing else, Inspector?"

He thanked them both and went back to the

market cross, threading his way between a buggy and a wagon piled with lumber.

If Mavers had moved from place to place that Monday morning, and given some forethought to the shotgun, he might—just might—have killed Harris and gotten away with it. . . .

From the market cross, Rutledge made his way to the lane where Hickam had seen the Captain and the Colonel together. Where Sergeant Davies had found Hickam drunk and rambling about the two men.

He looked about the lane for several minutes, then walked to the first house and knocked on the door, asking questions.

Did you see Daniel Hickam in this lane on the Monday morning that Colonel Harris was shot? Did you see Captain Wilton in this lane, walking? Did you see the Colonel, on his horse, riding through here, stopping to talk to anyone? Did you see Bert Mavers anywhere in the lane, coming or going toward the main street?

The answer was the same at every house. No. No. No. And no.

But at one of the doors, the woman who answered raised her eyebrows at finding him on her doorstep. "You're the man from London, then. What can I do for you?" She looked him up and down with cool eyes.

He didn't need to be told what she was, although she was respectably dressed in a dark blue gown that was very becoming to her dark hair and her sea-colored eyes. A tall woman of middle age and wide experience, who saw the world as it was, but more important, seemed to take it as it was.

Rutledge asked his questions, and she listened

carefully to each before shaking her head. No, she hadn't seen Hickam. No, she'd not seen the Captain that morning, nor Mavers. But the Colonel had been here.

"Colonel Harris?" Rutledge asked, keeping his voice level as Hamish clamored excitedly. "What brought him this way, do you know?"

"He came to leave a message by the door, knowing it was an early hour for Betsy and me, but he wanted to put our minds at rest about the quarrel we'd had with the Vicar." Her mouth twisted, half in exasperation, half in humor. "Mr. Carfield is often of a mind to meddle; he likes to be seen as a thunderbolt, you might say, flinging the moneylenders out of the temple, the whores out of the camp. Not that there's that much to go on *about* in Upper Streetham. It's not what you'd call a regular Sodom and Gomorrah."

She caught the responsive gleam in Rutledge's eyes. "The Colonel, now, he was a very decent man. We pay our rent, regular as the day, but Vicar had been onto that Mr. Jameson about us, and *he* called around, talking eviction. I could have told him who put him up to it! But there was no changing his mind. So the next time I saw the Colonel on the street, I stopped him and asked him please to have a word with Mr. Jameson about it."

"Jameson?"

"Aye, he's the agent for old Mrs. Crichton, who lives in London, and he manages her holdings in Upper Streetham. Well, the short of it was, Mr. Jameson agreed he'd been a little hasty over the evicting."

"Do you still have the message?"

She turned and called over her shoulder to someone else in the house. "Betsy? Could you find that letter of the Colonel's for me, love?"

In a moment a thinner, smaller woman came to the door, apprehension in her eyes and a cream-colored envelope in her hand. She handed it silently to the older woman. "Is everything all right, Georgie?"

"Yes, yes, the Inspector is asking about the Colonel, that's all." She gave the envelope to Rutledge, adding, "He never came here—as a caller. He was a proper gentleman, the Colonel, but *fair*. Always fair. If you'd asked me, I'd have said I knew most of the men in Upper Streetham better than their own wives, and I can't think of one who'd want to shoot Colonel Harris!"

There were two words on the front: Mrs. Grayson.

"That's me, Georgina Grayson."

Rutledge took the letter out of its envelope, saw the Colonel's name engraved at the top, and the date, written in a bold black hand. Monday. He scanned it. It said, simply, "I've spoken to Jameson. You needn't worry, he's agreed to take care of the matter with Carfield. If there should be any other trouble, let me know of it." It was signed "Harris."

"Could I keep this?" he asked, speaking to Mrs. Grayson.

"I'd like it back," she said. "But yes, if it'll help."

Turning to Betsy, Rutledge went over the same questions he'd asked earlier, but she'd seen no one, not Mavers—"He knows better than to show his face around here!"—not Hickam, not Harris, not Wilton—"More's the pity!" with a saucy grin. "But," she added, a sudden touch of venom in her voice, "I did see Miss Hoity-toity just the other day, Thursday it was, following after that poor sot, Daniel Hickam. He'd spent the night on the floor here, too drunk to find his way home, and we got a little food into him, then let him go. She was onto him like a bee onto the honey, slinking after him into the high grass toward the trees." She pointed, as if they had only just disappeared from sight, down toward the track that eventually led up the hill to Mallows.

The one called Georgie smiled wryly at Rutledge. "Catherine Tarrant."

"What did she want with Hickam?" Rutledge asked. Thursday was the day she'd come into town to speak to him about Captain Wilton.

Betsy shrugged. "How should I know? Maybe to pose for her—she asked Georgie to do it once, and Georgie told her sharpish what she thought about that! But it was him she did want! She caught up with him where she didn't think I could see, and stopped him, talking to him, and him shaking his head, over and over. Then she took something from her pocket and held it out to him—money enough to get drunk again, I'll wager! He turned away from her, but after only a few steps turned back and began speaking to her. She interrupted him a time or two, and then she gave him whatever it was she was holding, and he shambled off into the trees. She walked back down to where she'd left her bicycle, head high as you please, like the cat that got the cream, and then she was gone. She's a German lover, that one. Maybe she's got a taste for drunks as well!"

The eyes of hate and jealousy . . .

Mrs. Grayson said, "Now, then, Betsy, it won't help the Inspector to do his job if you run on like that. Miss Tarrant's business is none of ours!"

He left them, the letter in his pocket, his mind on what it represented—the fact that the Colonel had been in the lane on Monday morning, just when Hickam had said he was. And Catherine Tarrant had given Hickam money. . . .

When Rutledge arrived at the Inn, Wilton and Sergeant Davies were waiting. There was a distinctly sulfurous air about them, as if it hadn't been a pleasant afternoon for either of them. But Sergeant Davies got to his feet as soon as he saw Rutledge, and said, "We *think* we've found the child, sir."

Turning to Wilton, Rutledge said, "What does he mean? Aren't you sure?"

Wilton's temper flashed. "As far as I can be! She's—different. But yes, I feel she must be the one. None of the others matched as well. The problem is—"

Rutledge cut him short. "I'll only be a minute, then." He went up to his room, got the doll, and came down again, saying, "Let's be on our way!"

"Back there?" Wilton asked, and the Sergeant looked mutinous.

"Back there," Rutledge said, walking down the rear hallway toward his car. He gave them no choice but to follow. "I want to see this child for myself."

He said nothing about Georgina Grayson as he drove to the cottage. While it was, as the crow flies, only a little farther from Upper Streetham than the meadow where the Colonel's body had been found, it was necessary to go out the main road by Mallows, through the Haldanes' estate, and up the hill, the last hundred yards on rutted road that nearly scraped the underpinnings of the car.

On the way, he asked instead for information about the child's family.

"She's Agnes Farrell's granddaughter," Davies answered. "Mrs. Davenant's maid."

"The one we met at her house on Thursday morning?"

"No sir, that was Grace. Agnes was home with the child. Lizzie's mother is Agnes's daughter, and the father is Ted Pinter, one of the grooms at the Haldanes'. They live in a cottage just over the crest of the hill from where the Captain says he was walking when he saw Lizzie and Miss Sommers that Monday morning. When Meg Pinter is busy, the little girl sometimes wanders about on her own, picking wildflowers. But she's quite ill, now, sir. Like to die, Agnes says."

Rutledge swore under his breath. When one door opened, another seemed to close. "What's the matter with her?"

"That's just it, sir, Dr. Warren doesn't know. Her mind's gone, like. And she screams if Ted comes near her. Screams in the night too. Won't eat, won't sleep. It's a sad case."

The car bumped to a stop in front of the cottage, a neatly kept house with a vegetable garden in the back, flowers in narrow beds, and a pen with chickens. A large white cat sat washing herself on the flagstone steps leading to the door, ignoring them as they walked by.

Agnes Farrell opened the door to them. He could see the lines of fatigue in her face, the worry in her eyes, the premature aging of fear. But she said briskly, "Sergeant, I told you once and I'll tell you again, I'll not have that child worried!"

"This is Inspector Rutledge, from London, Agnes. He needs to have a look at Lizzie. It won't be above a minute, I promise it won't," he cajoled. "And then we'll be on our way."

Agnes looked Rutledge over, her eyes weighing

him as carefully—but in a different manner—as Georgina Grayson's had done. "What's a policeman from London want with the likes of Lizzie?" she demanded.

"I don't know," Rutledge said. "But I believe I've found the child's doll. It was in the hedge near the meadow where Colonel Harris was killed. Captain Wilton here says he met her on his walk that morning, and she was crying for the doll. I'd like to return it, if I could." He held out the doll, and Agnes nodded in surprise. "Aye, that's the one, all right! Whatever was she doing in the meadow?"

"Looking for Ted, no doubt." Meg Pinter came forward and touched the doll. Her face was drawn with lack of sleep and a very deep fear for her child. "She goes out to pick flowers, and that's all right, she comes to no harm. But once or twice she's gone looking for her father because he lets her sit on one of the horses in the stables, if the Haldanes aren't about."

Rutledge said, "Do you think she was in the meadow that morning? When the Colonel was killed?"

"Oh *God*!" Meg exclaimed, turning to stare at her mother. "I'd never even thought—" Agnes's face twisted in pain, and she shook her head.

"She might have seen something," he added, as gently as he could. "But I'd like to have a look at her, give her the doll."

"No, I'll take it!" Meg said quickly, tears in her eyes, but he refused to part with it.

"I found it. I'll return it."

The two women, uncertain what to do, turned to the Sergeant, but he shook his head, denying any responsibility. In the end, they led Rutledge through the neat house to the small room with its silent crib.

Lizzie lay as quietly as a carved child, covers tidily drawn over her body, her face turned toward the wall. It was a bright room, very pleasant with a lamp and a stool and a small doll's bed in one corner, handmade and rather nicely carved with flowers in the headboard. It was very much like the crib, and empty. Even from the door he could see how the little girl's face had lost flesh, the body bony under the pink coverlet. There had been so many refugee children in France with bones showing and dark, haunted eyes, frightened and cold and hungry. They had haunted him too.

Rutledge walked slowly toward the child. Wilton stayed outside the door, but the Sergeant and the two women followed him inside.

"Lizzie?" he said softly. But she made no response, as if she hadn't heard him. As if she heard nothing. A thin thread of milk drained out of her mouth on the sheet under her head, and her eyes stared at the wall with no recognition of what she was seeing.

"Speak to her," he said over his shoulder to Meg. She came to the bed, calling her daughter's name, half cajoling, half commanding, but Lizzie never stirred. Rutledge reached out and touched Lizzie on the arm, without any reaction at all.

Meg's voice dwindled, and she bit her lip against the tears. "I'd never thought," she said softly, as if Lizzie could hear her, "that she might have been *there*. Poor little mite—poor thing!" She turned away, and Agnes took her in her arms.

Rutledge went around to the other side of the crib, between the child and the wall. He stooped to bring his face more in line with her eyes, and said, with a firmness that he'd learned in dealing with children, "Lizzie! Look at me."

He thought there was a flicker of life in the staring eyes, and he said it again, louder and more peremptorily. Agnes cried out, telling him to mind what he was doing, but Rutledge ignored her. "Lizzie! I've found your doll. The doll you lost in the meadow. See?"

He held it out, close enough for her to see it. For an instant he thought that she wasn't going to respond. Then her face began to work, her mouth gulping at air. She screamed, turning quickly toward the door, her eyes on the Sergeant, then on Wilton beyond. It was a wild scream, terrified and wordless, rising and falling in pitch like a banshee's wail. Deafening in its power from such a small pair of lungs. Curdling the blood, numbing the mind. Agnes and Meg ran toward her, but with a gesture Rutledge held them back. But the screaming stopped as quickly as it had started. Lizzie reached out and Rutledge put the doll in her open arms. She clasped it to her with a force that surprised him, her eyes closing as she rocked gently from side to side. After a time one hand let go of the doll and a thumb found its way to her mouth. Sucking noisily, she clutched the doll and began a singsong moan under her breath.

Agnes, watching her, said, "She does that when she's falling to sleep—"

There was the sound of a voice, then the front door slamming. A man's voice called, "Meg, honey— I saw the car. Who's come? Is it that doctor Warren was going on about?"

Lizzie opened her eyes, wide and staring, and began to scream again, turning her back to the doorway. The sound ripped through the silence in the small room, ripped at the nerves of the people standing there. Meg ran out of the room, and Rutledge could hear her speaking to her husband, leading him away from Lizzie, then the slamming of the front door.

After a time, Lizzie stopped screaming and began to suck her thumb again, the doll held like a lifeline in her other hand. After a minute or so the singsong moaning began as well. The child's eyes began to drift shut. A deep breath lifted her small chest, and then she seemed to settle into sleep. Or was it unconsciousness?

"That's the first time she's rested." Agnes stood watching for a time, then shook her head slowly, grieving. "She adored her father—it's cut him to the heart to have her like this, carrying on so when he comes into the house, not wanting him near her."

Rutledge studied the child. "Yes, I think she really is asleep," he said, gesturing to the Sergeant and Agnes to leave. "Let her keep the doll. But I'll need it. Later."

He followed them out of the room, and saw Wilton's white face beyond the Sergeant's stolid red one. The screams had unnerved Davies, but Rutledge thought that it was the doll, and the child's reaction, that had worried Wilton more.

Agnes said, her voice shaking, "What's to be done, then? If she saw the man, what's to be done?"

"I don't know," Rutledge told her honestly. "I don't know."

Out by the car, a horse was standing, reins down. In the middle of the yard, Meg was holding her husband in her arms. As they came out of his house, he stared over her head at them, raw pain in his eyes.

"I want to know what's going on," he said, "what's happening to Lizzie."

"She—your daughter was possibly a witness to Colonel Harris's murder," Rutledge said. There was no easy way to break the news. "She may have seen him shot. I found her doll in the meadow there. Captain Wilton"—he gestured toward Mark—"saw Lizzie that morning as well. Crying for the doll. I'm not sure yet how all of this fits together, but that child is frightened to death of you. Can you think of any reason why?"

Ted shook his head vehemently. "I've nothing to do with it. She was like that when I came home Monday from the stables for lunch. Meg found her wandering lost like, and brought her home. She didn't speak, she wasn't herself. Meggie put her to bed, and she's—it's been like that ever since." His voice was husky with feeling. "Are you sure about this? I'd not like to think of her there in that meadow with a murderer. Or a man killed. She's never had a harsh word spoken to her in her life, she's been a quiet, cheerful, good little thing—" He stopped, turned away.

The horse he'd been riding ambled over and nudged his shoulder. Ted reached up to its muzzle without thinking, stroking the soft nose. Rutledge watched him.

"Does your daughter like horses?"

"Horses? Aye, she's been around them most of her life. Not to ride, but I've let her sit on their backs, held her in front of me. Let her touch them. She likes to touch their coats, smooth it, like. Always has."

Rutledge gestured to Davies and Wilton to get into the car. "If you want my advice, send for Dr. Warren and let him take another look at her. And stay away from her for a few days, Pinter, if you can. There's a chance that she can sleep now. It ought to help. When she wakes up, if she's at all capable of talking, send for me. Do you understand? It could be very important! For your sake and for hers."

Ted nodded, his wife and mother-in-law watchful, wary. But Rutledge, looking at them, thought they'd do it. "Stay away from her, mind!" he added. "Let her heal, if she can."

Agnes said, "I'll see to it. For now."

"I've seen men suffer like that. In the war," he added. "Shock can do that. If that's what's wrong with her. But don't let her be frightened, don't let her scream. That means she's remembering. Keep her warm and quiet and at peace. Let her sleep. That's the main thing now."

He turned toward the car. Hamish, silent throughout the half hour in the house, said, "You ought to know about sleep. It's the only time *you're* safe. . . ."

The drive back to Upper Streetham was quiet, only the sound of the tires along the road, and once a dog barking furiously as they passed. When they reached the Inn, Wilton said only, "God, I'm tired! It's been a damned long day."

Sergeant Davies got out stiffly and said, "I'd best say something to Inspector Forrest about this. Unless you'd rather speak to him yourself, sir?"

It was the last thing Rutledge wanted to do. He said, "No, that's all right, I'll see him tomorrow. There's not much more we can do tonight anyway."

Davies nodded to Wilton and said, "Until tomorrow, then, sir," to Rutledge, before marching off down the street toward his own house.

Wilton waited, making no move to get out of the car, but Rutledge said nothing, leaving him to break the silence. In the end he did.

"Does the child damn me? Or clear me?"

Aware of the envelope in his pocket, Rutledge said only, "I don't know. Do you?"

"I didn't kill him, Inspector," Wilton said quietly. "And I don't know who did." He got out, closed the car door behind him, and walked away, his limp more pronounced than usual, a measure of the tension in him.

Rutledge sighed. A child, a doll, a drunkard. The evidence was still slim. But the letter from Harris to Mrs. Grayson was something else.

It could very well send the handsome Captain to the gallows.

15

That night Rutledge lay in his bed, listening to the street noises dwindle into silence, then the sound of the church bell marking the passage of time.

He couldn't get Lizzie out of his mind. She was terrified. But of what? The roar of a shotgun? The bloody death of a man? Of a killer she'd seen—and somehow recognized?

Then why hadn't she screamed in terror at sight of Mark Wilton?

Her father, not the Captain, frightened her most. Why?

He wrestled with the puzzle for an hour or more and came no closer to an answer.

Bowles. He was supposed to call London on Monday and speak to Bowles. A drunk, a child, a whore. Witnesses against the Royal Family's favorite war hero. He, Rutledge, was going to look a right fool at the Yard!

"Aye, and is it why they've sent you to Warwickshire, then?" Hamish asked. "A sick man who's not up to the business in hand? Who'll be blamed for muddling the evidence and give them a reason to let the Captain off the hook? Is that what London wanted when it let you take on this bluidy murder?"

Rutledge felt cold. *Was* that the reason he'd been given this case? As the scapegoat for failure? Was that why they hadn't mentioned Hickam? Hoping that the shock of discovering the truth might be too much for the balance of Rutledge's mind as well? Or, alternatively, if he was successful . . . he was also expendable? When he brought the wrath of Buckingham Palace down on the Yard's head, he could be quietly returned to the clinic, with regret that the experiment hadn't worked out. For the Yard. For Rutledge. For the doctors who'd had faith in him.

It was a frightening prospect. While Hamish rattled gleefully around in the silence, Rutledge fought his anger. And his fear. And the dreadful loss of hope, a hope that'd buoyed him through the worst days at the clinic as he fought for survival and the harsh reality of returning to London. . . .

He promised himself that he wouldn't return to the clinic. He wouldn't go back to failure. There were other choices. There always were. To a man who feared living more than he feared death.

Sunday morning was overcast, a misting rain fading into low, heavy clouds that hung about Upper Streetham like ghosts. The heat was oppressive, wrapping the damp around people making their way to the church and wreathing the air inside with a breathlessness that even the open doors couldn't drain away.

Rutledge went to see Hickam before walking down to the church. The man was sleeping when he arrived, but the housekeeper was a little more optimistic about his condition. Still, she wouldn't let Rutledge come in.

"Stronger. That's all I can tell you. But the doctor, now, he was dragged out to the Pinter farm last night, tired as he was, and he said it was all your doing!" Her voice was sharp with condemnation. "He's not going to church this morning either, I can tell you that! Not if you haven't roused him up with your banging on the door."

"But the child's all right? She seems better?" he asked. "Did she sleep?"

"No thanks to you! Get on with your own business, and leave doctoring to those who know what's best!"

Rutledge thanked her and went on to the church. The last of the parishioners were hurrying through the lych-gate and he could hear the sound of the organ as he walked quickly down the Court. He'd found before the war that going to the church the victim had attended sometimes gave him a better feeling for the atmosphere of the town or the part of London in question. Anything that brought the victim into better perspective was useful.

The oppressiveness of the morning hung around the church door, and a flush of claustrophobia left him suddenly breathless. He shook his head at the usher ready to lead him down the aisle to a seat and stepped instead into the last one on the back row, where he could escape the heat and the crush of bodies.

Before the first prayer, someone slipped in beside him. Looking up, he met Catherine Tarrant's equally surprised eyes. Then she sat down and ignored him as she fumbled for her prayer book. It was an old one, he saw, and she found her place without trouble.

The service was High Church, which befitted the image of a man like Carfield. He brought to everyone's attention the fact that the funeral for Charles Harris would be held on Tuesday morning at ten, then spent several minutes lauding the dead man in a sonorous voice that echoed around the stone arches and through the nave. You'd have thought, Rutledge told himself, that they were burying a saint, not a soldier.

He let his eyes wander, taking in the high-vaulted ceiling, the slender pillars, and a small but very fine reredos behind the altar. Above that was a rather plain east window. The reredos was of stone, a representation of the Last Supper, and the figures had a grace about them that was pleasing.

The Haldane family tombs were just visible from where he sat; they were ornate marble, with clusters of cherubs as mourners around the bases. Several of the figures were medieval, a handful were Elizabethan, while the Victorian representations were almost lavishly ugly.

The Vicar's sermon was on making the best of one's life, using each idle minute with care, recognizing that death might sweep in at any moment to wipe out the hopes and dreams of the future. He never mentioned Charles Harris's name, but Rutledge was sure that every parishioner present knew exactly what his reference was. Rutledge spent most of the long exhortation studying the townspeople in the body of the church. He could see Catherine Tarrant only out of the corner of his eye, but several rows away was Helena Sommers, with Laurence Royston just ahead of her; Captain Wilton and Sally Davenant were down near the front; and to their left were the two women Rutledge had met near the market cross the day before,

Mrs. Thornton and Mrs. Mobley, with their husbands. To his surprise, he caught sight of Georgina Grayson as well, sitting alone in one corner, a very fine hat on her head and wearing a dress of the most conservative cut in a most becoming but decorous summery green.

When the last prayer was said, Rutledge was on his feet and out of the church door, away from the rising tide of people coming toward him. He found a vantage point under a tree in the churchyard and watched for a time.

Catherine Tarrant had also come out almost as quickly as he had, making her way toward a car with a driver waiting by the lych-gate. But the others were taking their time. Laurence Royston came out, strode down the walk, and called to Catherine as she was getting into the car. She waited for him, and he went to speak to her. She shook her head, smiling but firm.

Mavers was lingering behind the lych-gate, watching. Rutledge saw him and wondered what had brought him there. Sergeant Davies came out of the church and stopped to speak to Carfield, effectively damming the flow of people for the moment. Royston said good-bye to Catherine Tarrant, and her driver went to the end of the Court to turn the car. Mavers came quickly to Royston and began to speak very earnestly.

Royston listened, head to one side, watching Catherine's departure. Then his attention came back to Mavers, and after a time he began to shake his head.

Mavers's reaction was interesting. A flush of anger spread over his face, and he began to bob almost frantically, demanding something.

But Royston seemed to take pleasure in telling

him that it was no use. Rutledge was not close enough to hear, but the movements of both men told enough of the tale.

Mavers was furious. For an instant, Rutledge thought he was going to lash out with his clenched fists, and Royston must have thought so too because he stepped back, wary.

Suddenly Mavers turned toward the church and raised his voice, making himself heard by the fresh flood of people moving out into the mist.

"Has God refreshed your spirits?" he demanded, the fury mounting in him almost slurring his words. "Do you feel sanctified? Or have you seen yon fat toad for what he is, a *mountebank*, a fool leading other fools down the path of lies and high-flown words covering the emptiness of every soul here?"

With their attention riveted on him, he swung around to where a stunned Royston was standing, watching him, and included him in the fierce denunciation.

"There's not a *Christian* in the lot of you. Not one soul not already damned, and no one safe from the fires of hell! Here's a murderer of children, hiding behind the coattails of a man who went to wars to do *his* killing. Aye, you think you see the Colonel's fine agent, but I know him for what he is, a man who paid his way out of the law's clutches, a rich man's *money* for the bloody deed, and the Colonel, like a pied piper, leading your sons off to war and maiming the lot of them in soul or body! His funeral ought to be a time of rejoicing that he's dead before his time! And yonder's a whore, wearing the dress of a proper lady while you—and you—and you"—he was pointing to a handful of appalled men—"make your way to her bed any chance you've got! Aye, I know who you are, *I've seen you there!*"

He whirled to face another group of emerging worshipers. "And you, lusting after your cousin, while he's busy with moneyed ladies, sucking up to wealth, and you watching him like a starved woman!"

Sally Davenant's face flushed with a mixture of anger and speechless embarrassment. Wilton started toward Mavers, but the man said, "And the Sergeant, there, the Inspector over yonder, quaking in their boots to arrest the King's *friend*, who shot down the Colonel in cold blood *with a stolen shotgun*! And the man from London who lurks in shadows and tackles the pathetic likes of Daniel Hickam instead of doing his duty!"

Almost foaming at the mouth in his terrible need to hurt, Mavers paid no heed to the effect his words were having on the targets of his wrath; he poured them out in torrents, spilling over one another in a tangle. Rutledge began to move toward him, cutting across the churchyard, one eye on Mavers, the other on his feet among the damp, tilted tombstones.

"You, with the feebleminded cousin, who ought to be shut away for her own good! And that artist, the one who took a German to her bed and reveled in it—that other one with the witch's eyes, hiding in her bedchamber, with her lascivious desires, and the Inspector yonder with his cold, sexless wife, and Tom Malone, the butcher, who keeps his thumb on his scales. The bloodless Haldanes dead and not even *knowing* it. Ben Sanders, whose wife killed herself rather than go on living with him, the Sergeant who—"

But Wilton and Rutledge had reached him by

that time, dragging him away from the lych-gate, bending his arms behind him until he choked from pain and stopped lacerating the townspeople with a tongue as sharp as a lash. They hauled him with them down the length of the Court, his aggrieved cries echoing off the facades of the almshouses, raising the rooks in the fields beyond the trees.

The look on Wilton's face was murderous. Behind them, Rutledge could hear Forrest running to catch up and the Sergeant's bull roar, telling everyone at the church to pay no heed, that the fool had run mad, like a rabid dog.

But Rutledge thought he had done no such thing. Stopping at the corner to hand Mavers over to Forrest, Rutledge turned on his heel and went back to the lych-gate, searching for Royston in the crowd gathered there, silent and avoiding one another's eyes, their faces stiff with shocked dismay, unable to think of any way out of the churchyard that wouldn't take them past the rest of the parishioners equally paralyzed with indecision.

As Rutledge scanned their faces, he saw tears in Sally Davenant's eyes, though her chin was high and her cheeks still flushed. Helena Sommers seemed to be trying to find something in her handbag, her expression hidden by the wide-brimmed hat she wore, her hands shaking. Georgina Grayson had moved away from the crowd to the tree where Rutledge had been standing earlier, her back to the churchyard, her head tilted to watch the rooks soaring around the church tower.

Royston was gripping a post on the lych-gate, staring at the worshipers on the other side of the wall, a defensive look in his eyes, his mouth turned down in shame.

As Rutledge reached him, he said, "It's my fault. I shouldn't have told him. I should have thought about what he'd do. And now look what's happened—I'll never be able to face any of them again!"

"What did he want?"

Royston turned to Rutledge as if surprised to find him there. "He wanted to know if we'd read the Will. Charles's Will. He wanted to know if his pension was going to continue."

"Pension?"

"Yes. Charles gave him a pension years ago."

"Why?"

Royston shrugged expressively. "It was his sense of responsibility. The other son—there were two boys and a girl in the family, the mother had worked at Mallows as a maid before she married Hugh Davenant's gamekeeper—the other son died in South Africa. The daughter drowned herself. When Mavers ran off to join the army, Charles had him sent home. He was told that as long as he stayed there and looked after his mother, he'd be paid a pension. After the mother died, Charles didn't stop it, he let it go on. Against my better judgment. He felt he could stop Mavers from getting into worse trouble than he had already. It was threatening to cut off the pension as much as the threat of sending him to an institution that stopped the poisoning of the cattle and Charles's dogs. A lever. But Charles planned to let it end with his death."

It wasn't quite the same version of the story Mavers had told, but Rutledge thought that it was very likely that Royston's was closer to the truth.

Some of the color was coming back to Royston's face, and with it, the shuddering acceptance of the immensity of Mavers's revenge. "I've never felt quite so deliberately spiteful as I did when I told him that. I was thinking that it was one of the few times in my life when I actually *relished* causing pain. What I didn't realize was that I would cause so much! God, I feel—*filthy*!"

Rutledge answered harshly, "Don't be a fool! They're all so horrified they don't know how it began or why. Leave it at that. Let them blame Mavers. Don't give them a scapegoat! It will ruin you, and only a bloody idiot is that self-destructive."

After a moment, Royston nodded. He turned and walked away, joining the others who were now coming, by ones and twos and threes through the lych-gate, heads down, hurrying toward the safety of home. On the church steps, Carfield was alone, staring after his flock with an empty face.

He hadn't come forward in a heaven-sent rage to defy Mavers and protect his parishioners. He'd stood there, missing the opportunity of a lifetime to play the grand role of savior and hero, waiting in the shadows of the church door geared for flight and not for fight. Planning to make a hasty and unseen departure if need be, unwilling to do battle with the powers of darkness in the form of one wiry little loudmouth with amber goat's eyes.

A mountebank, Mavers had called him.

He looked across the churchyard and saw Rutledge watching him. With a swirl of his robes he vanished inside the church, shutting the door firmly but quietly behind him.

Rutledge walked slowly behind the last of the parishioners hurrying down the lane. By the time he reached the High Street, he was alone.

That afternoon Dr. Warren allowed him to visit Daniel Hickam. Rutledge stood in the doorway, looking down at the man in the bed, thin, unshaven, but clean and as still as one of the carved Haldanes on the church tombs.

Then as Rutledge stepped into the room, the heavy eyelids opened, and Hickam frowned, knowing someone was there. He moved his head slightly, saw Rutledge, and the frown deepened, with incipient alarm behind it.

Dr. Warren moved out from behind Rutledge's shoulder and said briskly, "Well, then, Daniel, how are you feeling, man?"

Hickam's eyes moved slowly to Warren and then back again to Rutledge. After a moment he said in a croak that would have made a frog shudder, "Who are you?"

"I'm Rutledge. Inspector Rutledge, Scotland Yard. Do you remember why I'm here?"

Alarm widened his eyes. Warren said testily, "Oh, for God's sake, tell the man he's done nothing wrong, that it's information you want!"

"Where am I?" Hickam asked. "Is this France? Hampshire—the hospital?" His glance swept the room, puzzled, afraid.

Rutledge's hopes plummeted. "You're in Upper Streetham. Dr. Warren's surgery. You've been ill. But someone has shot Colonel Harris, he's dead, and we need to ask people who might have seen him on Monday morning where he was riding and who he was with."

Dr. Warren started to interrupt again, and this time Rutledge silenced him with a gesture.

"Dead?" Hickam shut his eyes. After a time he opened them again and repeated, "Monday morning?"

"Yes, that's right. Monday morning. You'd been drunk. Do you remember? And you were still hungover when Sergeant Davies found you. You told him what you'd seen. But then you were ill, and we haven't been able to ask you to repeat your statement. We need it badly." Rutledge kept his voice level and firm, as if questioning wounded soldiers about what they'd seen, crossing the line.

Hickam shut his eyes again. "Was the Colonel on a horse?"

Rutledge's spirits began to rise again. "Yes, he was out riding that morning." He heard the echo of Lettice Wood's words in his own, then told himself to keep his mind on Hickam.

"On a horse." Hickam shook his head. "I don't remember Monday morning."

"That's it, then," Warren said quietly, still standing at Rutledge's shoulder. "I warned you."

"But I remember the Colonel. On a horse. In the—in the lane above Georgie's house. I—was that Monday?" The creaking voice steadied a little.

"Go on, tell me what you remember. I'll decide for myself what's important and what isn't."

The eyelids closed once more, as if too heavy. "The Colonel. He'd been to Georgie's—"

"He's lost it," Warren said at that. "Let him be now."

"No, he's right, the Colonel had been to the Grayson house!" Rutledge told him under his breath. "Now keep out of it!"

Hickam was still speaking. "And someone called to him. Another officer." He shook his head. "I don't know his name. He—he wasn't one of our men. A—a captain, that's what he was. The Captain called to Colonel Harris, and Harris stopped. They stood there, Harris on the horse, the Captain by his stirrup."

And then there was silence, heavy and filled only with the sound of Hickam's breathing. "There was a push on, wasn't there? I could hear the guns, they were in my head—but it was quiet in the lane," he began again. "I tried, but I couldn't hear what they were saying. I could see their faces—angry faces, low, angry voices. Clenched fists, the Colonel leaning down, the Captain staring up at him. I—I was frightened they'd find me, send me back." He stirred under the sheet, face agitated. "So angry. I couldn't hear what they were saying."

He started to repeat over and over, "The guns—I couldn't hear—I couldn't hear—I couldn't *hear*—"

Warren clucked his tongue. "Lie still, man, it's done with, there's nothing to be afraid of now!"

The unsteady voice faded. Then Hickam said, so softly that Rutledge had to lean toward the bed to hear him while Warren cupped his left hand around his ear: "*I'll fight you every step of the way. . . .*"

Rutledge recognized the words. Hickam had repeated them to him in the dark on the High Street the night he'd given him enough money to kill himself.

"*Don't be—fool—like it or not—learn to live with it.*"

"Live with what?" Rutledge asked.

Hickam didn't answer. Rutledge waited. Nothing. The minutes ticked past.

Finally Dr. Warren jerked his head toward the door and took Rutledge's arm.

Rutledge nodded, turned to go.

They were already in the hall, Rutledge's hand on the door, preparing to close it. He stopped in the act, realizing that Hickam's lips were moving.

The thready voice was saying something. Rutledge crossed the room in two swift strides, put his ear almost to the man's mouth.

"Not the war . . . *it wasn't the war.*" A sense of amazement crept into the words.

"Then what? What was it?"

Hickam was silent again. Then he opened his eyes and stared directly into Rutledge's face. "You'll think I'm mad. In the middle of all that fighting—"

"No. I'll believe you. I swear it. Tell me."

"It wasn't the war. The Colonel—he was going to call off the *wedding*."

Dr. Warren said something from the doorway, harsh and disbelieving.

But Rutledge believed.

It was, finally, the reason behind the quarrel. It was, as well, the Captain's motive for murder.

16

$\mathcal{T}$he Inn was remarkably quiet, but Rutledge stopped Redfern in the hall and asked to have sandwiches and coffee brought to his room. He wanted to think, without distraction or interruption, and Redfern must have sensed this, because he nodded and hurried off toward the kitchens without a word.

Rutledge took the stairs two at a time. In the passage near his room, he paused as the first rays of a sultry, overly bright sun broke through the heavy clouds. Storm signs, he thought, watching the light play across the gardens and then flicker out again. They'd had a remarkable run of good weather as it was.

His eyes caught a splash of color in the small private garden, and he looked down. A woman in a broad-brimmed hat was standing there, her back to the Inn, hands on her arms, head bowed. He tried to see who it was, but in the gray light he wasn't sure he recognized her. Searching his mind for someone at the morning church service wearing a hat like that, he drew a blank. He'd been more interested in faces than apparel. And in reactions to Mavers's vicious denunciations. Leaning his palms on the windowsill, he cocked his head to one side for a better line of sight.

Behind him he heard limping footsteps—Redfern bringing up his lunch. He straightened and turned to meet him.

Redfern carried a tray covered with a starched white napkin, a pot of coffee steaming to one side, cream and sugar beside it, the sandwiches a large and uneven mound.

Rutledge gestured to the woman in the garden. "Do you know who that is, down in the private garden? The woman with her back to us."

Redfern handed the tray to Rutledge and looked out. "That's—aye, that must be Miss Sommers. The Netherbys brought her into town for the morning services. But she's worried about her sister with a storm coming, doesn't want to stay for lunch after all. Jim—that's the stable boy—went to see if Mr. Royston or the Hendersons or even the Thorntons might take her home."

He reached for the tray again, going on into Rutledge's room to set up the table. Rutledge stayed where he was for a moment longer.

He'd have sworn it was Catherine Tarrant.

The small table by the window overlooking the street was ready for him when he followed Redfern to his room. "If you don't mind, sir, you can just leave the tray in the hall when you go. I'll be back to pick it up when the dining room is closed. We're not all that busy today, but you never know; if it starts to rain, we could be full."

He was already out the door when Rutledge stopped him. "Redfern. Did the Colonel come here often to dine? Or did Captain Wilton bring Miss Wood?"

Redfern nodded. "Sometimes. But I think they went into Warwick as often as not, if they wanted a dinner. Lunch, now, that was different. If the Colonel had business in the town, he'd often stop in. Always left a generous tip. Never fussy. Mrs. Haldane, Simon's mother, was the fussiest woman alive! There was no *pleasing* her! The Captain's not one to demand service, but he expects you to do a proper job, and he knows when you don't. Miss Wood"—he smiled wryly—"Miss Wood is a lady, and you don't forget that, but she's a pleasure to serve, never makes you feel like a wooden post, with no feelings. Nicest smile I've ever seen. I enjoy having her come in."

"How did she and Wilton get on?"

He thought about it for a moment. "Comfortably. You could see that they were happy. Never holding hands or anything like that, not in public, but the way he held her coat or took her arm, the way she'd tease him—the closeness was there. I was sometimes—envious, I suppose. My own girl married another chap while I was in hospital and they thought I'd soon be having my foot taken off. When you're lonely, it can hurt, watching others in love." There was a wistfulness in his voice as he finished.

Hamish, in the back of Rutledge's mind, growled. "You'd know about that, then, wouldn't you? How it hurts? And all you've got to ease your loneliness is *me*. . . . If there's a more dismal hell, I haven't found it."

Rutledge almost missed Redfern's next words.

"The last time I ever saw the Colonel, he'd come here for lunch."

"What? When was that?"

"The Tuesday before he died. It was another day like this one. Overcast, you could *feel* the storm coming. Everyone was jittery, even the Colonel. Didn't say two words to me all through his meal! Frowned something ferocious when Miss Wood came in looking for him. He left his pudding and took her into that garden where you saw Miss Sommers just now. I came up here to fetch some fresh linens for the maids, and they were still there. He had his hands on her shoulders, saying something to her, and she was shaking her head as if she didn't want to hear. Then she broke away and ran off. As I came back down the stairs, the Colonel was just walking in from the garden, looking exasperated, and he said, 'Women!' But I had the feeling there was—I don't know, an exhilaration there too, as if in the end he expected to have his way. I brought him another cup of coffee, but he was restless, and after drinking half of it, he was gone."

"You don't know what had upset Lettice Wood? Or the Colonel?"

"It mustn't have been too important," Redfern answered. "I saw her the next day, looking radiant. Walking down to the churchyard with Mr. Royston. I ought to be back in the dining room—"

Rutledge let him go with a nod of thanks.

He sat there, biting into the thick beef sandwiches, not even aware of the taste or the texture, absently drinking his coffee. There was a slice of sponge cake for dessert.

Wilton had motive, he had opportunity, and he had access to a weapon. All that was left was to clear up loose ends and then make the arrest. And to explain to Bowles on Monday morning the reasons behind the decision.

Was Tuesday the day that the Colonel had told

his ward what he was planning to do? To call off the wedding?

But why? It was an excellent marriage from any point of view, as far as an outsider could tell. Wilton and Lettice were well matched in every way—socially, financially, of an age. Unless there were things about Wilton that Charles Harris knew and didn't like. Then why allow the engagement to take place seven months ago? Because he hadn't known at the time?

What could he have learned in the last week that would have made him change his mind? Something from Wilton's past—or present?

The only other person who could answer that question was Lettice herself.

Rutledge drove out to Mallows in sunlight that poured through large cracks in the heavy black clouds, bringing heat in waves with it.

Lettice agreed to see him, and he was taken up to the sitting room by Johnston.

There was a little more color in her face this afternoon, and she seemed stronger. As he came into the room, she turned to him as she'd done before and said at once, "Something's happened. I can tell."

"It's been a rather busy morning. Mavers was on the loose as services ended at the church. He raked most everyone there over the coals, as vicious a display of hate as I've ever seen. Royston, the Captain, Mrs. Davenant, Miss Sommers, the Inspector—even people I don't know."

Lettice frowned. "Why?"

"Because he'd just discovered that his pension from Charles Harris ended with the Colonel's death. And he was furious."

She was genuinely surprised. "Charles paid him a *pension*?"

"Apparently."

Lettice gestured to one of the chairs and sat down herself. "It's the sort of thing Charles might do. Still—*Mavers*!"

"And a very good reason for Mavers *not* to kill him."

"But you said Mavers didn't know the pension would end."

"That's right. He stopped Royston as he came out of the church and asked if the Will had made any provision for the pension to continue. All those months when he agitated for Harris's death, Mavers doesn't seem to have considered the fact that he might lose his own golden goose."

She sighed. "Well. You said there were witnesses who claimed Mavers was haranguing everyone on Monday morning. He wasn't in the running anyway, was he?"

"I've discovered that he could have been. With a little planning. But he isn't high on my list. Tell me, what did you and Charles Harris argue about on Tuesday at the Inn? Or rather, in the garden there?"

The swift change in subject caught her unprepared, and her eyes widened and darkened as she stared at him.

"You might as well tell me about it," he said gently. "I already know what Harris and Mark Wilton quarreled about on Sunday evening after dinner. And again on Monday morning in the lane. Harris was planning to call off the wedding. I have a witness."

Her color went from flushed to pale and back again. "How could you have a witness," she demanded huskily. "Who is this *witness*?"

"It doesn't matter. I know. That's what's important. Why didn't you tell me before? Why did you
pretend, when Mark Wilton came to the house, and
I was there to overhear, that you were calling the
wedding off because you were in mourning? If
Charles had already ended your engagement?"

She met his eyes, hers defiant, challenging.
"You're fishing, Inspector. Let me meet this witness face-to-face! Let me hear it from him—or
her!"

"You will. In the courtroom. I believe Mark
Wilton shot Charles Harris after he was told on
Sunday night that the wedding was off and the
Colonel refused again on Monday morning to listen to reason. All I need to know now is *why*. Why
your guardian changed his mind. What Wilton had
done that made it necessary."

Lettice shook her head. "You don't go out and
shoot someone because a wedding has been called
off! In another year, I'd have been my own mistress. It wasn't necessary to murder *Charles*—" She
stopped, her voice thick with pain.

"It might have been. If the reason was such that
Wilton could never have you. Mrs. Davenant has
said she'd never seen him so in love—that you'd
given him a measure of peace, something to live for,
when he'd lost his earlier love of flying. That he'd
have done anything you asked, willingly and without hesitation. A man who loves like that might
well believe that in a year's time, your guardian
would have convinced you that he'd made the right
decision, breaking it off. Even turned you against
Wilton while he wasn't there to defend himself.
When he thought he was in love with Catherine
Tarrant, Wilton waited for her because her father
felt she wasn't ready for marriage—and in the end
she changed her mind. It came to nothing."

"That was different!"

"In what way?" When she didn't answer, he asked instead, "Is that why you didn't go riding with your guardian Monday morning? Because you were as angry as Wilton over what was happening?"

She winced, closing her eyes against his words. But he inexorably went on. "Is that why you had a headache, and left the two men alone to discuss the wedding? Because you'd already lost the battle?"

Tears rolled silently down her cheeks, silvery in the light from the windows, and she made no attempt to wipe them away.

"I will have to arrest Wilton. You know that. I have enough evidence to do it now. But I'd prefer to spare you as much grief as I can. Tell me the truth, and I'll try to keep you out of the courtroom." His voice was gentle again. Behind it, Hamish was restlessly stirring.

After a moment, he took the handkerchief from his pocket and, going to her, pressed it into her hand. She buried her face in it, but didn't sob. Outside he heard the first roll of thunder, distant and ominous. Rutledge stood by the sofa where she sat, looking down at the top of her dark head. Wondering whether she grieved for Mark Wilton. Her guardian. Herself. Or all three.

"That first day I was here, you thought, didn't you, that Mark had shot him. I remember your words. You didn't ask *who* had done the shooting—instead you were angry about *how* it was done. I should have guessed then that you were a part of it. That you already knew who it was."

She looked up at him, such anguish in her face that he stepped back. "I am as guilty as Mark is," she told him, holding her voice steady by an effort of will. "Charles—I can't tell you why it was stopped.

The wedding. But I can tell you what he said to me on that Tuesday at the Inn. He said I was too young to know my own heart. That he must be the one to decide what was best for me. All that week I begged and pleaded—and cajoled—to have my way. Saturday evening, when Mark had gone home, Charles and I sat up well into the night, thrashing it out."

Thunder rolled again, much nearer this time, and she flinched, startled. The sunlight was fading, an early darkness creeping in. Outside the windows the birds were silent, and somewhere Rutledge could hear a rustle of leaves as if the wind had stirred, but the heat was oppressive now.

Taking a deep, shaking breath, Lettice went on. "Charles was a very strong man, Inspector. He had a fiercely defined sense of duty. What he did on Sunday evening wasn't easy for him. He liked Mark—he respected him. It was for my sake—not because of any weakness in Mark!—that he changed his mind about the wedding."

"Charles doted on you—he'd have given you anything you wanted. Then why not this one thing—the man you planned to marry?"

"Because," she said softly. "Because he *did* put my happiness above everything else. And he finally came to believe that Mark Wilton wasn't the right man."

"And Wilton, who believed as strongly that he *was* the right man, turned on his friend, shot him out there in the meadow, and with that one act, lost *any* hope he might have had of marrying you! I don't see how he gained anything by killing Charles that he couldn't have gained by waiting. Unless there was something else—some reason powerful enough that silencing Charles Harris was worth the risk of losing you forever. Something that might have destroyed Captain Wilton personally or professionally."

She looked up at him, eyes defensive but resolute. It was a strange test of wills, and he wasn't sure exactly where it was leading. Or even if she knew the answer he wanted to hear.

"All right, I did think it was Mark at first—not because I saw him as a murderer, but because of my own sense of responsibility over what had happened, the feeling that he'd done it to obliterate Charles, to get even. I was half drugged, ill with grief, not knowing where to turn or what to do. Charles was dead, they'd quarreled over the marriage—one thing on the heels of the other—what else *could* I think? But I'm not as sure now. When Mark finally came here, I couldn't sense *guilt*, I couldn't find any response in him—or in me—that ought to have been there if he'd killed. Only—a terrible emptiness."

"What did you expect? Shivers of premonition?"

"No, don't offer me sarcasm! Give me credit for a little sense, a little knowledge of the man I was planning to marry!" A flush of anger in her cheeks made her eyes glitter, the unshed tears brightening them.

"But still you called off the wedding! In my presence."

"You don't marry while you're in mourning!"

"Then you'll go ahead and marry him after you've mourned a decent length of time? If he isn't hanged for murder?"

Shocked, she stared at him. "I—I don't—"

"Lettice. You aren't telling me all of the truth." He gave her time to answer him, but she said nothing, her eyes holding his, unreadable, once more defiant. "Who are you protecting? Mark? Your-self? Or Charles?"

The wind had picked up, lashing at the house, sending a skirl of leaves rattling across the windows. She got up quickly and went to close them. From there, she turned to face him again. "If you want to hang Mark Wilton, you'll have to *prove* he's a murderer. In a court of law. With evidence and witnesses. If you can do that, if you can show that he was the one who shot Charles Harris, I will come to the hanging. I've lost Charles, and if I truly thought Mark had killed him, and no one could actually prove it, even though that was the way it *had* happened, I'd go through with the wedding and spend the rest of our lives making him pay for it! I care that much! But I won't betray him. If he's innocent, I'll fight for him. Not because I love him—or don't love him—but because Charles would have expected me to fight."

"If Mark didn't shoot Harris—who did?"

"Ah!" she said, smiling sadly. "We're back to where we were, aren't we? Well, I suppose it comes down to one thing, Inspector. What mattered most to Mark? Keeping me? Or killing Charles? Because he knew—*he knew!*—he couldn't do both. So what did he have to gain?"

The storm broke then, rain coming down with the force of wind behind it, rattling shutters and windows and roaring down the chimney, almost shutting out the flash of the lightning and a clap of thunder that for an instant sounded as if it had broken just overhead.

17

The rain was so intense that he stopped at the end of the drive, in the shelter of overhanging trees. Rutledge's face was wet, his hair was matted to his head, and the shoulders of his coat were dark with water. But he felt better out of that house, away from the strange eyes that told him the truth—but only part of the truth. He didn't need Hamish whispering "She's lying!" to tell him that whatever Lettice Wood was holding back, he'd find no way of forcing it out of her.

As the storm passed, the rain dwindled to a light drizzle, the ground steaming, the air still humid and unbreathable. He got out and started the car again, then turned away from Upper Streetham toward the Warwick road. He drove aimlessly, no goal in mind except to put as much distance between himself and the problems of Charles Harris's murder as he could for the moment.

"You're drawn to her, the witch," Hamish said. "And what will Jean have to say about that?"

"No, not drawn," Rutledge answered aloud. "It's something else. I don't know what it is."

"Do you suppose, then, that she bewitched the Captain and the Colonel as well? That somewhere she had a hand in this murder?"

"I can't see her as a murderess—"

Hamish laughed. "You ought to know, better than anyone, that people kill for the best of reasons as well as the worst."

Rutledge shivered. What was it about Lettice Wood that reached out to him in spite of his better judgment?

Reluctantly, bit by bit, she had confirmed Hickam's rambling words. And Wilton's own behavior, his unwillingness to come to Mallows after the quarrel or explain what it had been about, reinforced the picture all too clearly. And it was slowly, inevitably developing. The child's part in it still—

Rounding the bend, he saw the bicycle almost too late, coming up on it with a suddenness that left decision to reflexes rather than conscious action. He got the brake in time to skid to a stop in the mud, wheels squealing as they locked, sending him almost sideways.

Hamish swore feelingly, as if he'd been thrown across the rear seat.

Standing on the road was Catherine Tarrant, bending over her bicycle. She looked up in startled horror as he came roaring down on her, driving far faster than he'd realized, faster than the conditions of the road dictated. His bumper was not five feet from where she stood as the car came to a jarring halt, killing the engine.

Recovering from her shock, she demanded angrily, "What do you think you're doing, you damned fool! Driving like that? You could have killed me!"

But he was getting out of the car, and she recognized him then. "Oh—Inspector Rutledge."

"What the hell are you doing in the middle of the road? You deserve to be run down!" he responded with a matching anger, marching toward her, fists clenched against his rising temper. The unpleasant drizzle wasn't helping.

"The chain's broken—I don't know if something came loose or if I jammed it when I skidded. Oh, for pity's sake, don't just stand there, put my bicycle in the back of your car before we're both wet to the skin, and take me home!" She was in a foul temper as well, but dry, he noticed, as if she'd found shelter somewhere from the worst of the rain.

They stared at each other, faces tight with self-absorbed emotions; then she managed a wry smile. "Look, we'd better both get out of the way, or someone else will fly around that bend and finish us off! Take me home and I'll offer you some tea. You look as if you could use it. I know I could."

He walked past her, lifted the bicycle, and carried it to his car. She helped him put it in the back—he had an instant's sharp sense of the ridiculous, thinking that it would crowd Hamish out—and then came around to the passenger side, not waiting for him to open her door.

He cranked the car, got in, and said, "Did you miss the rain?"

"I was at the Haldanes' house. They're away, I just went by to pick up a book Simon promised to lend me." She lifted a large, heavily wrapped parcel out of the basket behind her and set it in her lap. "He brought it back from Paris and thought I might want to see it. Something on the Impressionists. Do you know them?"

They talked about art as he backed the car and drove to her house, and she left a servant to deal with the bicycle, striding past the handsome staircase and down the hallway toward her studio without looking over her shoulder to see if he followed. Setting the borrowed book on a stool, she took off her hat and coat, then said, "Get out of that coat, it will dry faster if you aren't in it."

Rutledge did as he was told, looking about for a chair back to drape it on.

Catherine sighed. "Well, Mavers most certainly put the wind up everyone in Upper Streetham this morning! What did you think of his little show?"

"Was it a show? Or was he upset?"

She shrugged. "Who knows? Who cares? The damage is done. I think he rather enjoyed it too. Lashing out. It's the only way he can hurt back, with words. Nobody pays any attention to his ideas."

"Which is one of the reasons he might have shot Charles Harris."

"Yes, I suppose it is—to make us sit up and take notice. Well, I wouldn't mind seeing him arrested for murder and taken off to London or wherever! *I* didn't enjoy having my own life stripped for the delectation of half of Upper Streetham—the whole of it, come to that! Everyone will talk. Not about what he said of them, but about everyone else. Those who weren't there will soon be of the opinion that they were." Catherine moved about her paintings, touching them, not seeing them, needing only the comfort of knowing they were there.

"That's a very bitter view of human nature."

"Oh, yes. I've learned that life is *never* what you expect it will be. Just as you come to the fringes of happiness, touching it, feeling it, tasting it—and desperately hoping for the rest of it—it's jerked away."

"You have your art."

"Yes, but that's a compulsion, not happiness. I

paint because I must. I love because I want to be loved in return. Wanted to be."

"Did you ever paint Rolf Linden?"

Startled, she stopped in midstride. "Once. Only—once."

"Could I see what you did?"

Hesitating, she finally moved across to a cabinet in one wall, unlocking it with a key she took from her pocket. She reached inside and drew out a large canvas wrapped in cloth. He moved forward to help her with it, but she gestured to him to stay where he was. There was a little light coming in through the glass panes overhead, and she kicked an easel to face it, then set the painting on it. After a moment, she reached up and undid the wrappings.

Rutledge came around to see it better, and felt his breath stop in his throat as his eyes took it in.

There was a scene of storm and light, heavy, dark clouds nearer the viewer, a delicate light fading into the distance. A man stood halfway between, looking over his shoulder, a smile on his face. It was somehow the most desolate painting that Rutledge had ever seen. He'd expected turbulence, a denial, a fierce struggle between love and loss, something dramatic with grief. But instead she'd captured annihilation, an emptiness so complete that it echoed with anguish.

He knew that anguish. And suddenly he was convinced that Lettice Wood knew it also. That that was what he'd responded to in her.

Catherine was watching his face, unable to hear Hamish but seeing the flicker of fear and recognition and a deep stirring of response, while Hamish— Hamish wept.

"It's never been shown—" It was all he could manage to say into the silence.

"No," she answered with certainty. "And never will be."

A maid brought in the tea, and Catherine quickly covered the painting, putting it carefully back into its vault, like a mausoleum for her love. Turning back to pour a cup for Rutledge and then for herself, she said unsteadily, "You've been there, haven't you?"

He nodded.

"The war?"

"Yes. But she's still alive. Sometimes that's worse."

She put sugar into her tea and handed him the bowl. He helped himself, finding relief in the ordinary movements of his hands, then accepted the cream.

"Where were you going when you nearly ran me down?" she asked, finally sitting down, allowing him to do the same. It was an overt change of subject. She had closed the door between them again.

"Anywhere. Out of Upper Streetham."

"Why?"

He reached for one of the small, iced tea cakes as an excuse not to meet her eyes. "To think."

"What about?"

"Whether or not I have enough evidence to arrest Mark Wilton tomorrow morning. For Harris's murder."

He could hear her suck in her breath, but she didn't say anything.

Looking up, he asked, "Why did you track down Daniel Hickam? On the Thursday you spoke to me? No, don't bother to deny it! I have witnesses. You stopped him, talked to him, and then gave him money."

"I felt sorry for him. . . . Most people have forgotten that before the war he was a very good cabinetmaker. Better than his father ever was. He made the frames for my first paintings. And that easel. Now—he probably shakes too much to drive a nail straight, much less do finer work. I try to keep an eye on him."

"No. You wanted to know what he'd said about Wilton. I don't know yet how you found out about Hickam. Possibly from Forrest." He watched that guess go home. She wasn't as good at hiding her thoughts as Lettice Wood.

"Yes, all right. I was afraid for Mark. I still am. He wouldn't have killed Charles! You come in here from London, asking questions, making assumptions. You *judge* people even though you know very well they're under a great deal of stress. But it isn't the same as getting under the skin, is it? You can't do that, you can't *know* them. Not in a few days' time. You haven't got that skill!"

He'd had it. Once. Refusing to be sidetracked, Rutledge said only, "He had means. Opportunity. Motive. It's all there now. Out into the open."

"Then why are you telling me this? If you know so much!" She cocked her head to one side, considering him. "Why were you driving out on the Warwick road when you had all the evidence you need? Why are you involving me?"

"Because I wanted to know what you would say when you heard."

She set down her teacup. "And are you satisfied?" He didn't answer. After a moment she asked, "Have you told London yet?"

"No. Not yet. I'll call Superintendent Bowles early tomorrow morning. I'd prefer to have everything finished before the funeral services on Tuesday. Upper Streetham will be full of people then. Harris's friends, fellow officers, dignitaries. They shouldn't be distracted from their mourning by police business."

"There'll be a great hue and cry when you do it. It will upset the King, and everyone else, including the Prime Minister. He's got enough on his plate right now, with the peace talks. It will bring the wrath of Scotland Yard down on your head. It will ruin Mark. It could very well ruin you! I'd be very careful before I did something I couldn't undo."

She was a very perceptive woman. And she knew London.

"That doesn't matter. If he shot Charles Harris, why should Mark Wilton go scot-free?"

"He couldn't have shot Charles! He's marrying the man's *ward*! You don't seem to understand the importance of that!"

"The wedding has been called off."

"Of course it has, Lettice is in mourning. But by next spring—or in a quiet ceremony at Christmas, since she's got no family and needs Mark's support—"

"No. Charles himself stopped the wedding. And that's why he was killed."

Catherine shook her head. "Called off the wedding? Before he died? You can't be serious!"

"Why would he joke about that? Why should I?"

"No, Mark was going to marry her! And he will, once this nonsense is finished. I'll help him find someone in London to take his case if you go through with this. I refuse to believe that Mark could have done anything of the sort! Or Charles, for that matter! Whoever told you such a thing is either crazy or vindictive. Or both. I absolutely refuse to believe it!"

• • • •

He left soon afterward, stiffly thanking her for the tea and then finding his own way out. Catherine said good-bye with equal reserve, and added as he reached the solarium doorway, his coat over his arm, "Don't be hasty, Inspector. You owe that to Mark. You owe it to Charles. Be very sure before you act!"

Rutledge drove back to Upper Streetham and left the car at the rear of the Inn, going in by the door he'd used on the night of his arrival. The back stairs were empty, the Inn silent.

He felt bone weary. Emotion was drained out of him, and his body ached with tension.

I need to find Forrest, he told himself. I need to attend to that warrant, bring Wilton in. The sooner the better.

"And where's he going?" Hamish demanded. "He's no' the kind of man who'll run, or he wouldn't have been so good at killing Germans."

"Shut up and keep out of it! I thought you wanted to see the dashing Captain hanged!"

"Aye," Hamish said, "I do. But I'm not ready to see you crawl back to yon clinic, and doctors that will stuff your mind full of drugs. Easing you into oblivion where there's no pain and no memory and no guilt to savage you. I've not finished with you yet, Ian Rutledge, and until I have, I won't let you crawl away and hide!"

An hour later, Rutledge found himself at Sally Davenant's door. The maid Grace opened it to his knock and said, "Yes, sir?"

"I've come to see Captain Wilton. Will you tell him Inspector Rutledge is here. On official business."

She caught the nuances in his voice and her face lost its trained mask of politeness. Concern filled her eyes, and she said, "Is there anything wrong, sir?"

"Just tell the Captain I'm here, if you please."

"But he's in Warwick, sir. He and Mrs. Davenant have gone to dine there. She wasn't herself all afternoon, and the Captain suggested an outing to take her mind off the unpleasantness at the church this morning. I doubt they'll be back much before eleven o'clock, sir."

He swore under his breath. "Very well. Tell him I'll expect to see him here at eight o'clock tomorrow morning." He nodded and walked off down the scented path, among the peonies and the roses.

There was, actually, a certain irony about that appointment, he thought, driving back to the Inn. It was exactly one week from the time Charles Harris died.

The rain came back in the night, and Rutledge lay there listening to it, unable to sleep, his mind turning over everything he'd learned in the past four days. Thinking about the people, the evidence, the way it was coming out now. One or two loose ends to finish tomorrow, and then he'd be on his way back to London.

But the funeral was on Tuesday, and he found himself wanting to be there, to watch Lettice walk down the aisle of the church on—on whose arm? To see her one more time, and in the light. To exorcise the witchery Hamish had been so worried about? He could contrive it; there was enough to do, he needn't hurry back to that tiny cubicle in London, where his mind was dulled by routine and Hamish had freer rein.

It wasn't a night for sleeping, in spite of the rain drumming lightly on house roofs and muffling the normal sounds of the village. Rutledge could hear the gutters running, a soft, ominous rush that echoed in his head, and once, a carriage rattling down the High Street. The church clock tolled the quarter hours, and still his mind moved restlessly in a kaleidoscope of images.

Of Catherine Tarrant's paintings, vivid reflections of her inner force. Of Lettice Wood's unusual eyes, darkening with emotion. Of Royston's shame as he watched the faces of parishioners outside the church. Of Carfield's swift retreat from confrontation. Of Wilton's lonely grief, and a child's terror. Of a woman hanging out clothes in the sunlight, a goose penned in the yard behind her. Of Sally Davenant's cool shell, hiding emotions she couldn't afford to feel. Of Charles Harris, man and monster, alive and bloodily dead . . . Of Mavers with his amber goat's eyes . . .

At Mallows, Lettice Wood lay on her bed and wished with the fervor of despair that she could turn back the slowly moving hands of the ornate porcelain clock on the table by her pillow. Turn them back to that moment when she had said, with the blitheness of loving, "I've never *known* such happiness—I want it to go on and on forever—I want to feel it in old age, and look back on *years* full of it, and you, in the center of it."

And his warm indulgent voice, laughing at her,

promising. "My dear girl, when have I ever been able to deny you anything you wanted? We'll be together always, as long as the seas run and the stars shine and the earth lasts. Is that pledge enough for you?"

The seas still ran, the stars still shone, and the earth was there still. But her happiness had poured out with a man's blood in a field of wildflowers, and there was no way she could put it back again. And there was nothing—*nothing*—that would turn back time to that single, glorious gift of love.

Catherine Tarrant sat in her studio, in a darkness lit by heat lightning, the patter of rain on the surrounding glass a counterpoint to her tears. On the easel in front of her was the wrapped portrait of Rolf Linden. She didn't need to take the cloth off, she knew it by heart. But it was Mark Wilton she was thinking about, and Charles Harris—and how the body ached with longing for a man who would never come back to her. She could forget, sometimes, when she was painting, or in London. Somehow Charles's death and Mark's dilemma had stirred her feelings into life again, and left her vulnerable. While memories, like long-buried ghosts, crept around her in the silence, she made herself remember too what she owed Mark.

He was awake as well, metaphorically setting his house in order, arranging his affairs and steeling himself to meet what was coming. There was no way out for him, he had to accept that. Still, he'd found the courage he needed in France, and it hadn't deserted him yet. It would be there when he needed it now. From hero to gallows' bait, a great comedown for a proud man, he thought with heavy irony. If only he could guess what Lettice would do— But there was one final duty to perform, and after a while, he decided that the best way to achieve it was with honesty rather than guile. . . .

But in a cottage on a hillside above Upper Streetham, a small child slept with the deepness of death, without dreams for the first time in days.

18

The rain had drifted away by morning, and a watery sun soon broke through the clouds, strengthening rapidly until there was a misty, apricot light that warmed the church tower and touched the trees with gold.

Rutledge walked out of the Inn door and stood for a moment watching the early market goers hurrying to set up booths or find a bargain. A low murmur of voices and laughter, the noises of traffic, people coming and going—he'd seen markets like this in a hundred English towns, peaceful and bustling. A week ago a man had died on market day, Mavers had made his way through the crowds shouting, agitating, locked in hatred, and a child had been frightened nearly to death. But a traveler, strolling through Upper Streetham this pleasant summer morning, wouldn't hear about it, wouldn't be touched by it. None of the drama, none of the misery, none of the lasting pain showed.

He turned and moved briskly down the sidewalk, stopping at Dr. Warren's for a report on Hickam. The man had had rather a restless night,

Warren's housekeeper reported, but he'd eaten a decent enough breakfast and seemed a little stronger.

"That's when the craving for gin will return, as he improves," she added. "The poor soul isn't out of the woods yet, I can tell you! And what he'll do with himself when he's well enough to go home is another worry."

"I'm told he was a cabinetmaker before the war," Rutledge said.

Surprise spread across her face. "Aye, that's true. I'd forgotten. And very good he was! But not anymore, not with hands that shake like leaves." She picked up the broom she'd leaned against the wall while talking to him. "They've already started. The tremors. But he's stronger than he looks, which is a good thing!"

Rutledge thanked her and turned back to the Inn, walking around past the small gardens to the car. Ten minutes later he was pulling up in front of the Davenant house.

Grace let him in, and Sally Davenant came to meet him as soon as she heard his voice. She quickly glanced behind him to see if Rutledge had brought Sergeant Davies with him, looking decidedly relieved to discover that he was alone. "Good morning, Inspector! We've been sitting on the terrace, having a last cup of coffee. Won't you join us?"

He let her lead him to the French doors that opened onto a slate-floored stone terrace overlooking the gardens. There was a wide sweep of lawn, edged by trees and set with beautifully manicured borders, a graceful and pleasing design that someone—he wondered if it had been Mrs. Davenant herself—had chosen to match the architectural grace of the house. An air of peace pervaded it, with birds singing in the trees and a low hum of bees working their way through the blossoms.

Beyond the balustrade, the flower beds looked rather bedraggled from the storm, but the scent of stock and peonies and lavender drifted softly on the morning air. Someone had swept the rain from the terrace and a set of white chairs cushioned in a pattern of gray, rose, and white encircled a wrought-iron table. The breakfast things had already been taken away, but a coffee tray gleamed brightly in the center.

Wilton got to his feet as they came out into the sunlight and stood by the table, not speaking, his eyes on Rutledge.

"Another cup for the Inspector, please, Grace," Sally was saying over her shoulder. Then, "Do sit down, Inspector. Mark." They sat, and when the cup came, Sally poured Rutledge's coffee, passing it to him with a practiced smile.

"Well, I don't suppose that half of Upper Streetham will dare to show their faces at market this morning!" she began, hiding her own feelings quite well under a pose of wry humor. "I told you before, that man Bert Mavers is a danger to himself and everyone else! How Charles—" She stopped, then said, "How anyone put up with him for this many years is a mystery to me!"

"I don't think the Inspector came to discuss Mavers," Wilton said. "You wanted to see me last night, Rutledge?"

He tasted his coffee and then answered, "Yes, as a matter of fact. But it will keep. For the moment. Have you and Royston and Carfield completed the arrangements for tomorrow's services?"

Wilton stared out over the lawns. "Yes, everything's in hand. I—was planning to see Lettice this morning, to show her what we'd done, what was expected of her, who would be here. There has been a great deal of mail, telephone calls, wires. Royston and Johnston have kept up with it between them, but I know most of these people personally. Who they are, what they represent. Sally can help Lettice with the proper acknowledgments afterward. As for the reception, we've kept Carfield out of it as much as possible." Disgust tightened his mouth as he turned to Rutledge. "The man's a threat to sanity! He told Johnston he'd be there most of today to oversee the preparations, the flowers, and so on. Royston had to tell him to his face that he wasn't needed, that the church was his responsibility and nothing else. And he'll do that well enough! Writing the funeral oration probably kept him awake most of the night."

Sally said generously, "He means well, Mark. He's been a great comfort to Agnes, worried about poor little Lizzie. And when Mary Thornton's mother died he took care of everything. But I understand how you feel; he's had his eye on Lettice since she came here in 1917."

Wilton glanced at Rutledge but said nothing. Rutledge finished his coffee and pushed back his chair. "I'd like to speak to you, privately, Wilton. If you don't mind."

Sally rose. "No, no, stay here, I've things to see to."

But there were too many windows overlooking the gardens and the terrace, voices carried. Wilton put his hand on her arm. "Enjoy the sun, my dear; I won't be long."

He couldn't see the look she gave him as he got to his feet and courteously waited for Rutledge to follow. It was a mixture of emotions. Dread. Love. And indecision.

Wilton took Rutledge to the small parlor where

they'd talked on his first visit and closed the door, standing there, his back to it, as he said, "I expected you to come with the Sergeant. And a warrant for my arrest."

"I had planned to. But it occurred to me that marching you to jail in front of all those people coming in to market would cause Miss Wood and your cousin unnecessary embarrassment. If you go with me now, of your own accord, we'll see to this business as quietly as possible."

"So it's finished, is it?" He moved away from the door and crossed to a chair, gesturing impatiently for Rutledge to be seated.

"I know what you and Harris quarreled about. After dinner Sunday evening. In the lane Monday morning. He was calling off the marriage, and you were furious with him."

There was no reaction in his face. "Who told you this?"

"I have two witnesses. I think they're reliable enough. A third can prove that Harris was there, in the lane. Another saw him speaking to you."

"And Lettice? Have you talked to her?"

"Yes. At first she denied it. Then she admitted that Charles had, for reasons of his own, changed his mind about the marriage."

"I see." He faced Rutledge quietly enough, but a nerve at the corner of his mouth twitched. After a time, he said, "Yes, all right, Charles changed his mind. I thought he was wrong, and I told him so. We argued. I didn't think this was information that the world needed to know, that's why I wouldn't explain it to you. I felt that—given time—Lettice and I could work out the problem of what to do. Charles Harris was a very strong influence in her life. I had to keep that in mind."

"Then she went along with his decision?"

Wilton shook his head. "I never had the chance to ask her how she felt. Charles was shot—she was given sedatives by Warren—and the wedding had to be called off anyway. My God, she was grieving, I couldn't very well barge in there and say, 'I love you, I still want to marry you, will you go through with it and be damned to Society!' And then there was the funeral to discuss—hardly the proper ambience for a declaration of love, is it? Now—I haven't much to offer her now, have I?"

Listening, Rutledge could hear the ring of truth—and the suspicion of a lie. He had to remind himself that Mark Wilton had spent four years in the air over France, surviving on his wits, surviving *because* he was intelligent, kept his nerve, never let himself be outwitted or outmaneuvered.

"Did she ask you if you'd shot her guardian?"

"No." It was curt, haughty. Pride speaking.

"What will you tell her when she does? When you've been arrested?"

"That you've decided I did shoot Harris. That I'll fight you in court, and with any luck make you look like a fool." He frowned. "I'm not a barrister, but I've got a chance, I think. The evidence against me is circumstantial, no one saw me with a gun, no one saw me actually shoot the Colonel. Calling off the wedding might damn me, but we'll see about that." He caught the fleeting expression in Rutledge's eyes and said, "Oh, yes, I've thought it all through! Most of the night. I've also considered something else. You'll probably win in the long run; the trial will end with 'not proved' rather than an acquittal. And that doubt, that shadow will hang over me for the rest of my life. *Did I or didn't I kill Harris?* In some respects that's worse than the gallows. I can't possibly expect Lettice to marry me, knowing she might wonder in the middle of the night if I had done it."

"Then you won't come with me now, and give yourself up."

"If I do, it's an admission of guilt. In the view of most people." He rubbed his eyes tiredly. "I can't afford to damn myself. You'll have to arrest me. Without fanfare, I can promise you there will be no trouble over it. But it will have to be a warrant."

"Why did Charles Harris change his mind about you? About the wedding? What had you done to turn him against the marriage?"

To Rutledge's surprise, a smile flickered deep in Wilton's eyes. "Ah. I expect *that* information did die with Charles Harris!"

Then the smile faded, and he said quite soberly, "I need a favor from you, Rutledge. I don't know if you can grant it, but I'm asking you at least to consider it. I want to go to the funeral with Lettice. She needs someone besides that idiot Carfield. Or Simon Haldane, who's kind enough but damned ineffectual. The Regiment is sending a representative, but Lettice doesn't know him, he's a stranger. It won't be easy for her, with her guardian dead and her fiancé in jail. You can lock me in a room in the Inn tonight, if that's any use. I'll agree to any terms you like. Just let me do this one thing, and I'll be very grateful."

"I can't postpone an arrest."

"Why? Do you think I'll shoot myself when you aren't looking? Or run to France? The only hope I have of a normal life is proving I *didn't* shoot Charles! A trial is as important to me as it is to you. Give me twenty-four hours!"

Rutledge looked at him, trying to read the man. Behind the handsome face was an extraordinary strength. And a gambler's instincts? High in the clouds, pitting his wits against another man, with death as the price of losing, he had come through duel after duel almost unscathed. It was a remarkable record, and his nerve had never broken—

Hamish, who'd been silent most of the morning, stirred to life. "But yours did! That's why you've lost your skills, man, you've broken. Nerve, mind, spirit. You aren't the hunter anymore, you're the prey!"

He forced himself to think, ignoring the voice in the back of his mind. Wilton was waiting, patient, watchful. He wanted this very badly. And he didn't like begging.

Dredging up his own instincts, Rutledge sorted them out. And made his decision.

"All right, then. Twenty-four hours. But if you trick me, by God I'll crucify you!"

Wilton shook his head. "It isn't for me. It's for Lettice."

And driving back to the Inn, Hamish was raging. "The witch again! She's cast a spell on you with those strange eyes, and you've lost your soul—"

"No," Rutledge said, concentrating on the road. "I'm beginning to think"—he dodged a big yellow dog ambling peacefully across his path—"I'm beginning to think I might have found it."

"You've got the man—witnesses—the shotgun— the reason why yon fine Colonel needed to die that morning. You've done your work, man, don't throw it away!"

"On the contrary. I've stumbled around in the dark, letting other people tell me what was happening. I've been terrified that someone might see my own terrors and turn them against me. I've dreaded failure and done very little to prevent it. I was lost—*lost!*—and couldn't find my way back to 1914. If I can't do any better than this, I deserve to be locked away in that damned clinic with the other wretched dregs of humanity. If I want to survive, I've got to fight for it...."

He spent the day organizing his evidence, finishing his report. Before he began he put in a call to Bowles in London and said, "I've got enough proof to ask for a warrant. Tomorrow at noon. The case is as strong as I can make it, but not without some problems. I think a good KC can fill them in, and we'll have our conviction."

Bowles, listening, finally interrupted. "I hope to God you aren't telling me we're going to arrest Wilton! The Palace called this morning; they want to know whether to send a representative to the funeral. Wilton's marrying Harris's ward—"

"Tell them to send someone who knew Harris. He was a good soldier, he served the King well. It doesn't matter about Wilton."

"Rutledge, if you've got this wrong, the Yard will have your head. Do you hear me? Leave the man alone unless you've got such proof that Christ Himself couldn't find a way out of it! I won't be responsible if you humiliate the Palace and disgrace the Yard!"

"I won't," Rutledge said, with more firmness than he felt. "If I do, you'll have my resignation on your desk by Wednesday morning."

"A hell of a lot of good that will be, man! After the damage is done!"

"I know. That's why I'm taking my time."

Rutledge hung up. So much for the confidence and support of his superiors. He felt suddenly isolated, alone.

But loneliness was also a strength. When you trusted, you were more vulnerable. You gave yourself away. He would have told someone about Hamish long ago, if he'd trusted. As long as it was his own private hell, he was, in a sense, far safer. No one could reach him. No one could destroy him. Except he himself, in the muddle that was now his life.

By late afternoon he'd covered sheet after sheet with notes and a framework for his evidence. Satisfied that he'd been thorough, he reread the pages. It wasn't a clever work of detection, nor was it complete, since there were no eyewitnesses to the death itself.

Except for the child, and the doll. She had been in the meadow. Not surprisingly, the shock of what she'd seen had frightened her into the blankness of withdrawal, the secure world of no feeling, no thought, no memory.

And yet she hadn't responded to Wilton at all when he came to her room. It was her father who terrified her, her father who couldn't come near her without provoking wild and mindless screams.

He got up from the table he'd been using as a desk and moved restlessly around the room. He'd never been a man to enjoy being shut up indoors all day long; he thought that that had, unconsciously, been one of several reasons why he'd failed to follow in his father's footsteps at the bar. But the war, the aftermath of being buried alive in a trench, had turned an ordinary dislike into an almost rabid claustrophobia, and police work at least took him outside much of the time, before the walls began to close in upon him. As they were now.

Picking up his coat, he went out and down the stairs, planning to walk no farther than the lane in front of the church.

Outside the Inn the market was drawing to a close, stalls shut up and ready to load on wagons, the last of the market goers straggling from shop to shop. In front of the milliner's he saw Helena Sommers in earnest conversation with Laurence Royston. She was standing on the sidewalk and he was in one of Charles Harris's cars. And she was wearing the same hat Rutledge had glimpsed in the Inn garden on Sunday after Mavers's malicious attack on everyone in the churchyard.

Then she smiled at Royston, stood back, and he drove on. Noticing Rutledge on the sidewalk, he waved.

Charles Harris had been fortunate in his steward, Rutledge thought. Few men worked so devotedly on another man's property without a stake in it for themselves. He'd probably spent more time and love on Mallows than Harris had ever been able to give. Was that because he'd never had a wife to lavish time and love on? It was an interesting possibility.

Helena crossed the street, saw Rutledge, and paused. "Good afternoon, Inspector." She indicated a large box in her left hand. "I didn't bring a black hat with me. And I felt I ought to attend the funeral tomorrow. I didn't know the Colonel well, but I was a guest in his home. It seems—courteous—to attend. Mr. Royston has been kind enough to promise to send a car for me."

She looked tired. As if aware of it, she added, "The storm yesterday left us mired in mud. I had to walk into town today, there was no way to take out my bicycle. Maggie is always terrified of thunder, so she didn't sleep much, and neither did I. But it seems to have cleared the air, in more ways than one."

"A beautiful day," he agreed.

"And I've spent enough of it indulging myself. I'll be on my way."

"Before you go, I wonder—did you notice a child out in the fields, a little girl picking wildflowers, on the morning of Harris's death? Either before or after you saw Captain Wilton on the path?"

She frowned thoughtfully. "No. But that doesn't mean she wasn't there. I was using my field glasses. I could well have missed her. There are often children about, and I try to avoid them—well, they frighten off the birds I'm watching! The Pinter children are usually wandering here and there. The little girl is a charmer, but with any encouragement at all, the boy talks your ear off." She smiled wryly to take the sting out of her words. "He'll make his mark as a politician, I've no doubt at all about that! Maggie will be looking for me, I must go."

She walked away with a countrywoman's clean, swift stride. He watched her, wondering again how much of her interest in birds was real and how much was an excuse to be out of the cottage as often as she could. Or perhaps her cousin preferred to have the house to herself. Safe, familiar ground in a rather frightening world. Make-believe in the place of reality. He felt a sense of pity, knowing how harsh life could be for the Maggies, ill-equipped to cope with anything more demanding than domestic chores and small comforts.

Glancing at his watch, he saw that he'd have

time for a drink before dinner. He'd earned it. Time enough afterward for the last task on his list.

Rutledge was greeted at the door of the Pinter house by a wary Agnes Farrell. Long rays of the sun, still warm at nine-thirty, gave her face a glow that faded as soon as she stepped back to allow him to enter. The thinness of long nights of no sleep, the sallowness of stress were marked in the dimness of the narrow passage between the door and the parlor.

"How is the child?" he asked, smiling down at her, trying to be reassuring.

"Well enough," she answered doubtfully. "Eating. Sleeping. But grieving somehow, clutching that doll as if it was a lifeline."

Meg appeared behind her mother, wiping her hands on a dishcloth. "Inspector?" she asked anxiously. The child's illness had worn her too, the confidence of youth lost, the dread of death haunting her, buoyed only by a blind hope that soon it would all be back as it had been, normal and comforting.

"Good evening, Mrs. Pinter. I've come to have a look at Lizzie," he said, as if it was an ordinary thing to do on a Monday evening. "If I may?"

She glanced at her mother and then said, uncertainly, "Yes, sir?" Both women stepped back, allowing him to enter, and from their attitude he gathered that they were alone in the house, that Ted Pinter hadn't returned from the Haldane stables. He had chosen his time well, he thought with relief.

He began to move toward Lizzie's small room, saying something about the lovely day that had followed the rain, in an attempt to set them at ease.

They followed, close together for comfort. A lamp was burning on the low table, and the child stared up at him as he came in with large, sober dark blue eyes. He wasn't really sure she saw *him*, in the sense of comprehending that he was a stranger, someone she didn't know and wasn't used to, because there was no spark of curiosity, no quick look at her mother to see if all was well. Instead there was an apathy about her still. But she wasn't screaming, and he took that as a good sign.

"What did Dr. Warren have to say?" he asked over his shoulder.

Agnes answered, "He said it was what he'd *hoped* might happen, but didn't expect. And we'd have to see if this new quietness lasted. In truth, sir, I think he was more than worried she might die, she was wasting so fast."

Meg added, "She's not in the clear yet—" as if hoping Rutledge might take the hint and go, now that he'd done what he came to do.

Instead he walked over to the bed. "Lizzie? I'm—er—a friend of Dr. Warren's. He asked me to come and see you tonight. In his place."

Her eyes had followed him, watched him, but she said nothing.

He went on, talking to her for several minutes, telling her he'd seen a woman with a basket of strawberries at market, and a man with a dog that did tricks. But nothing touched the blankness on her face.

Rutledge wasn't accustomed to children. But he'd seen enough of the sad refugees on the roads of France—hungry, frightened, tired—to know that it wasn't very likely that he'd be able to break through the barrier of her silence on his own. Not without days of careful groundwork to gain her confidence.

He thought about it for a time, watching those

blue eyes, wondering what the best way of reaching her might be. He didn't have days to give.

Hamish said softly, "Your Jean has such eyes; your children might have been fair and very like Lizzie. . . ."

Turning to Agnes, Rutledge said, "Do you have a rocking chair?"

Surprised, she answered, "Aye, sir, a nursing rocker. In the kitchen."

"Show me." She did, and he saw that he had come just at the end of their meal; there was a chicken partly carved on the counter, a bowl of potatoes sat on the table next to a half loaf of bread and a plate of pickles, and dishes were stacked in a wash pan in the sink, while a big kettle whistled softly on the stove. The nursing rocker—small and without arms to allow a woman to breast-feed comfortably—stood by the hearth, worn but serviceable.

He carried it back to the bedroom, turned it with its back to the doorway, and said to Meg, "You'll want to finish in the kitchen. Then I'll have a cup of tea, if I may. And a few questions for you."

She didn't want to leave, but Agnes said, "Go on, Meg. I'll call you if I need you." But Meg still went out reluctantly, looking back over her shoulder at Rutledge with worried eyes.

Rutledge waited until he could hear the familiar clatter of dishes and then said to Agnes, "I don't want to frighten the child. Or make her uncomfortable. But if you'll sit here and hold her, rock her as you must do, sometimes?" She nodded. "Good! I'll be here by the door. And when she's settled, at ease, I'll tell you what to say to her."

"I don't know, sir!"

"It won't harm her. It might help. And—I need to know what she saw! There in the meadow where Colonel Harris was shot!"

"I can't take the chance! What if she saw the *murder*? What if that's the thing that sent her into this decline? We don't want to lose her! Not now!" She was an intelligent woman; she knew the risk he was going to run.

"Trust me," he told her gently. "Let me at least try."

And so she went to the bed, lifted the child in her arms, talking in that soft singsong mothers the world over know by heart. Lizzie whimpered, but seemed content enough when Agnes went no farther than the chair, sat down, and began slowly to rock, humming under her breath.

Afraid she'd soon put the child to sleep—in fact, he thought that might be her intention—Rutledge said quietly, "Ask her if she saw a man with a shotgun."

"Did you see a man carrying a gun, love? A big long gun that made a big noise? Did you see that, love?"

Lizzie didn't stir.

"Did the noise scare you? Loud and nasty, was it?"

Nothing.

Agnes repeated her questions, varying the words, probing over and over again, but Lizzie was silent. And still awake.

"Ask her if she remembers losing her doll."

That elicited no response, although Agnes tried several variations on that theme too. But Lizzie began to pluck restlessly at the front of Agnes's apron.

"It's no good, sir!"

"We'll try a different tack, then. Ask her—ask her if she saw the big horse."

Agnes crooned to the child to soothe her, and

then said softly in the same tones, "Was there a big horse, my lamb? A big shining horse in the meadow? Was he standing still or riding along? Did you see the big horse?"

Lizzie stopped sucking her thumb, eyes wide, tense. *Listening.*

Rutledge could hear Meg in the kitchen, speaking to someone in a low voice or singing to herself. He couldn't tell which it was. He swore silently, irritated by the distraction. "And a man on its back?"

"Did the big horse carry a man on its back? High in the saddle the way you ride with your pa? Did you see the man, love? Just like Papa on the horse? Did you see his face—"

The words were hardly out of her mouth before Lizzie went rigid and began to scream. The sudden change was alarming in the quiet room, and Agnes cried out, "Now, now, lovey—don't fret! *Sir!*"

"Papa! Papa! Papa! Papa! No—no—don't!" Lizzie screamed, the words tumbling over one another, the doll clutched tight as she struggled in her grandmother's arms.

Meg came running, and behind her were other footsteps.

Rutledge had gone to Agnes, his back to the door and was bending over the child, speaking to her, when he was caught from behind and thrown hard against the wall, scraping his cheek and all but knocking the breath out of him. A man's voice was roaring, "Don't touch her—let her be! Damn you, *let her be*!" Rutledge wheeled, and Ted Pinter, face distorted with rage, charged at him again. Lizzie was standing rigidly in her grandmother's lap, eyes squeezed shut, shrieking, "No—no! No!" over and over again.

Rutledge was grappling with Pinter, Meg was shouting, "Ted! Don't!", and her husband was yelling, "She's suffered enough, God blast you, I won't have her hurt anymore!"

And then the little girl stopped screaming so suddenly that the silence shocked them all, halting Pinter in his tracks. Over his shoulder, Rutledge could see the child's face, startled, mouth wide in a forgotten scream. Her eyes were half scrunched closed, half opened. But the lids were lifting, until they were wide, unbelieving. And then she was holding her arms out, straining against her grandmother's shoulder, a huge and shining smile on her tear-streaked face. Ted had turned toward her, and as she said in wonder, "Papa?" he made a wordless sound in his throat and went to her, pulling her into his arms against his chest. His features were crumpled with tears, his head bent over his daughter. Meg was hanging on his arm, half cradling both of them, weeping too.

Agnes, both hands over her heart as if to keep it from leaping out of her chest, was on her feet also, staring at Rutledge with consternation in her eyes.

Rutledge, as stunned as they were, stared back, uncertain what he'd done.

Behind his eyes, Hamish was saying over and over again, "She's naught but a child—a *child*!"

19

The sunset was a thin red line on the western horizon as Rutledge drove back into Upper Streetham. His body was tired, his mind a tumult of images and probabilities. He made his way though the quiet Inn and upstairs to his room, shutting the door behind him and standing there, lost in thought.

If the child's evidence was right—and he would have wagered his life that it was—Mavers couldn't have shot Harris. Well, he'd been almost sure of that from the perspective of timing! An outside possibility, a dark horse, attractive as Mavers was as a suspect, but a close-run thing if he'd actually done the killing.

But what else had Lizzie changed?

The doll had been beside the hedge at the edge of the meadow, half hidden under the spill of branches and leaves. From that vantage point, then, Lizzie had seen a horse and rider.

The man she was most accustomed to seeing on a horse was her own father. Living in the little cottage over on the other side of the hill, at the end of a long and rutted road, the Pinter family was more or less out of the mainstream of village life. Yes, Lizzie had seen any number of horses, Lizzie had seen any number of men—and women—riding. But the man she was *most accustomed* to seeing . . .

And when she heard the horse coming toward her out there in the fields where she'd been searching for wildflowers, she had run toward the sound, expecting to find her father.

But it wasn't Tom Pinter on that horse, it was Charles Harris thundering toward her, his horse already frightened and bolting.

Only she hadn't known that, for she hadn't been able to see the rider's face.

Instead she'd seen only a bloody stump on a man's body. And if her sudden screams had startled the horse, making it shy away from her, the gruesome burden on its back might finally have fallen out of the saddle.

Face—or rather chest—down on the grass?

But Lizzie, in terror, believing that the awful thing covered in blood was her own father, had fled, dropping the doll. . . .

Or had she been in the meadow earlier, dropped the doll, remembered where she'd left it, and on her way to fetch it, encountered the specter of death?

He wasn't sure it mattered. What did matter was that Lizzie had been in the meadow, had seen Charles Harris on horseback, already dead. But she hadn't seen the gun, she hadn't seen Wilton, she hadn't been frightened by a loud noise at close range.

And the killer hadn't see her. . . .

Which meant that Charles Harris might not have been killed in that meadow.

Sergeant Davies had said from the beginning

that he wasn't sure exactly where Harris had been shot, but assuming that the pellets driving into his head and body had thrown him violently out of the saddle, he would have dropped no more than a few feet either way from the scene of the killing.

I should have looked at the body—

And something else—the fact that Harris had been found on his chest, not his back. If he'd been shot out of the saddle, he'd have gone down on his back. If he fell out of the saddle after his horse had bolted, the dead man's knees spasmodically gripping the animal's sides in the muscle contractions of death . . . if he fell out, he might well have gone down on his face.

Hamish, whispering in the darkness that filled the room, said, "You remember Stevens, don't you? He was hit and ran on for a yard or more, without a head to lead him, and you had to pry the rifle out of his hands, they were gripping it so tight. As if he were still killing Germans, even though he didn't know it. And MacTavish, who was heart shot, and Taylor, who got it in the throat. Death seized them in an instant, *but they held on!*"

It was true, he'd seen it happen.

Moving toward the bed, he turned up the lamp and then walked across to the windows, rested his hands on the low sill, and looked out into the silent street. A cool breeze touched the trees, then brushed his face in the open window, but he didn't notice.

Where had Harris been killed?

Not that it mattered—if the Colonel hadn't been shot in the meadow, it simply gave Wilton more time to reach Mavers's cottage, pick up the gun, and track him down.

But closer to the house, someone might have

seen him pull the trigger or heard the shot. Yet no one had come forward.

Mark Wilton had the best possible motive. Still, Rutledge had been involved with other cases where the best motive wasn't necessarily the one that counted. Mark Wilton was, by his own admission, near the scene. He'd quarreled with the Colonel because the wedding was going to be called off . . . which made the timing of the death *right*: to kill Harris before he'd made public what he'd decided to do.

All the same, Rutledge knew he'd feel better when he'd answered the final two questions: One, why had Harris called off the wedding? And two, where precisely had Harris been shot?

Rutledge straightened, pulled off his tie, and took off his coat. There wasn't very much he could do tonight. In the dark. When everyone else was sound asleep . . .

But he found himself retying his tie, picking up the coat again. Almost driven to action, when it wasn't possible to take any action at all. Buffeted by the strongest feeling that time was running out.

Wilton had said he wouldn't shoot himself, he wouldn't take the gentleman's way out before he was arrested, convicted, and hanged. But that was assuming he was innocent, and could see that there was truly a chance for a very bright barrister to prove that there wasn't enough evidence to bring in a conviction. If he was guilty, however—

Rutledge was almost sure that Wilton wouldn't do anything rash before the funeral. For Lettice's sake, rather than his own. But afterward . . .

Bowles and the Yard—and the King—would probably rejoice if Wilton never came to trial. But Rutledge, far from wanting his pound of flesh, was determined to have that trial. To prove or disprove his evidence, to finish what he'd begun. With a carefully constructed suicide note left behind, Wilton could appear to be the victim, not the villain. He could leave behind enough doubt to overshadow anything Hickam and that child and Mrs. Grayson might say. The case couldn't be closed in such uncertain circumstances.

Without turning down the lamp, Rutledge walked out of the room, down the stairs, and out the garden door to his car. It made a racket starting up in the stillness, but there was nothing he could do about it. The first of the funeral guests to arrive were probably sleeping and wouldn't hear it anyway.

He turned toward Mallows, driving fast, his headlamps scouring the road with brightness. But at the estate gates, he changed his mind and stopped just inside them, turning off his headlamps and pulling off into the rhododendrons that grew high and thick under the trees. Getting out of the car, he stood still for a time, listening.

A dog barking off in the far distance. A lonely bark, not an alarm. An owl calling from the trees behind the house. The light breeze sighing overhead. He started to walk then, giving the house as wide a berth as he could, and soon found himself in the fields above it, lying between Mallows proper and the Haldane lands.

Moving through the darkness, minding where he put his feet, he kept the house to his right. It was dark, and the windows of Lettice's rooms shone like black silver in the night. In the back there was a single light in one of the upper rooms, where he'd seen the servants' quarters. He could hear horses moving quietly in the stables, stamping a foot, rustling about in the straw, and somewhere a groom coughed. He'd done enough reconnaissance missions during the war to move as silently as the night around him, his dark clothes blending with the trees and the shrubs and the hedges, and he was careful never to cast long shadows or hurry.

For an hour or more he roamed the fields above Mallows, looking for a likely place where a killer was safe, out of sight of the house, out of hearing, where none of the tenants might stumble over him accidentally and see that shotgun. But there was nothing that spoke to him, no vantage point that caught his fancy.

Look at it again, Rutledge told himself. You were a ground soldier. You'd see it differently. Wilton flew. His eye for terrain might not be as sharp as yours.

All right, then. A clump of saplings here. A high hedge full of summer-nesting birds there. A dip in the land, like a bowl or dell, where someone might quietly loiter. A section of the rose-clotted wall that separated the Haldane land from Mallows. They were all possibilities. The saplings in particular offered a shield from the house and thick brambles in which to conceal a shotgun. And the hedgerow in one or two spots was almost as good. For the most part the wall was too open, especially on this side, and the dell had no cover at all.

Another thought struck him. Betrothed to Lettice or not, Wilton would attract more notice on Mallows land than would, say, Royston, who had every reason to move about in his daily tasks. Or Lettice, who lived there and had had the run of the place since she was a child. In the spring with the fields plowed and the crops growing, you left tracks—

But Davies and Forrest had assumed that Charles

was killed in the meadow, and hadn't looked for tracks. Or blood. Or bits of flesh and bone . . .

Finally he turned back, still uneasy, still driven by something he couldn't define. Not so much knowledge as a sense of alarm, a distinct frisson that rippled along his nerves like the breeze rippling softly through his hair.

In front of Mallows, in the open where there was just enough ambient light, he looked at his watch. It was after two.

"Decent Christian folk are all in their beds," Hamish began.

Rutledge ignored him. Mallows was a house of mourning, and Charles had no close relatives. Most of the funeral's guests would be staying the night in Warwick, or at the Shepherd's Crook in Upper Streetham. Lettice would be alone, as she had been for the past week since her guardian's death.

There wouldn't be an opportunity to see her in the morning before the services began—and it would be callous to try. Afterward there was the reception that the Vicar had his heart set upon. No opportunity to speak to her then . . . and after the reception, time might have run out. . . .

He turned and walked across the gravel of the drive to the front door with its black wreath darker than the night on the wooden panels. After a moment, he rang the bell, and in the stillness, fancied he heard it echo through the house like some gothic tale of late-night callers bringing bad tidings. His sister had gone through a stage of reading them just before bedtime, shivering under the covers with a mixture of horror and delight, or scratching at his door for comfort when she'd succeeded in terrifying herself too much to sleep.

Rutledge was still smiling when Johnston opened

the door, eyes heavy with sleep, clothes stuffed on haphazardly.

He stared at Rutledge, recognizing him after a moment, then said, "What's happened?"

"I have to speak to Miss Wood, it's urgent. But don't frighten her, there's nothing wrong."

"Inspector! Do you know what time it is, man! I can't wake Miss Wood at this hour—there's the funeral tomorrow, she'll need her sleep!"

"Yes, I know, and I'm sorry. But I think she'd rather see me now than just as she's leaving for the church."

It took persuasion, and a pulling of rank, but in the end Johnston went up the stairs into the darkness, leaving Rutledge in the half-lit hall.

After a time he could hear someone coming, heels tapping on the floor. It was Lettice, face still flushed with sleep, hair falling in dark waves down her back, a dark green dressing gown on over her night wear. She came slowly down the stairs with her eyes on him, and he said, "I'm sorry. I wouldn't have come if it hadn't been so important. It won't take long, I promise you."

"What's wrong, is something wrong?" she asked.

"No. Yes. I'm in a quandary of sorts. I need to talk to you."

She hesitated at the foot of the stairs, looked toward the door of the drawing room, then made up her mind. "Come this way. To the small parlor."

He followed her there, and she found the lights, bringing an almost blinding brightness into the room. Turning in the middle of the floor, she gestured to a chair for him and then curled up on the sofa, drawing her legs under her as if for warmth. Without the sun the room did seem chill, comfortable to him after his long walk in the fields, but cold to her after the warmth of bed. As he sat down he saw that the soles of his shoes and one trouser leg had mud on them. She saw it too, and asked, "Where have you been?"

"Walking. Thinking. Look, I'll tell you what's bothering me. I went to arrest Captain Wilton this—yesterday—morning, and he asked me to wait until after the funeral tomorrow—this—morning. It made sense. I could see no reason to cause any more grief or embarrassment for you."

Frowning, she said, "Yes, that's true, I'd rather not face it alone. But you're telling me that the man who's accompanying me to the services is Charles's murderer. The man who'll be sitting beside me while I grieve—I don't see how that will make it any easier for me. Or for Mark! Do you think I only care about *appearances*? I survived last Monday morning alone. I can survive this."

"I hadn't expected to be telling you any of this. Not until afterward. But you know where my suspicions—and the evidence—have been pointing."

She brushed a heavy fall of hair out of her face and said quietly, "Yes."

"You know I've learned about the source of the quarrel. That the marriage was being called off. You told me yourself that Charles had decided to do it."

"Yes."

"It's motive, Miss Wood. It explains why Charles had to die that particular morning—*that* Monday, not seventeen years ago or six months from now or next Friday."

"All right. I can see that. I—I'd considered it myself."

Which brought him back to his first impression of her—that she'd known who the killer was.

"But I need to know *why* your guardian called off the marriage."

"What does Mark say?" she countered.

Rutledge leaned forward in his chair, trying to reach her with his words, with the sense of haste driving him. "He says the reason isn't important. That it died with Charles. But I think it may be very important. In fact, it's crucial. I'm concerned, you see, that if the cause was serious enough, Wilton might prefer not to stand trial and have it brought out into the open, afraid that in the end we'd discover what it was and use it in court, and the whole world would hear what it was. I'm afraid that he might—choose the gentleman's solution instead."

"Shoot himself?" Tears came to her eyes, darkening them, but hovered behind the lids, not spilling over. "Are you quite sure, Inspector?"

"I wouldn't have come tonight if I hadn't been sure it could happen. Not that it would—but that it could," he said, forcing himself to honesty.

"But if I tell you—*you're* the police, you'll know what it is, and then it'll happen just as he's afraid it might. And I'll be the cause of it!" Before he could deny it, she said, "No, I can't tell you something, and then afterward say that I didn't mean it, that you must forget I'd said it. You *can't* forget it. It's your job, you see—there's no separating the man from the *job*!"

"Lettice—" He wasn't even aware that he'd used her name.

"No! I've lost Charles, nothing will ever bring him back. I'm going to lose Mark, one way or another. I feel enough guilt already, I won't add to it, I tell you I *won't*!" The tears spilled over, and she ignored them, her eyes on his face. "Have you ever been in love, Inspector, so in love that your very life's blood belonged to someone else, and then just when it seemed that everything was wrapped in joy, and you were the luckiest, most fortunate, most *cherished* person in the world, had it snatched away without warning, stripped from you without hope or sense or explanation, just *taken*?"

"Yes," he said, getting to his feet and walking to the window where she couldn't see his face. "It would be easy to say that the war came between us, Jean and me. All those years of separation. But I know it's something deeper than that. She's frightened by the—the man who came back. The Ian Rutledge she wanted to marry went away in 1914, and the Army sent a stranger home in his place five years later. She doesn't even recognize him anymore. As far as that goes, I'm not sure that she's the girl *I* remember. Somehow she's grown into a woman who lives in a world I've lost touch with. And I can't find my way back to it. I came home expecting to turn back the clock. You can't. It doesn't work that way." He stopped, realizing that he'd never even told Frances that much.

"No," she said simply, watching him, seeing—although he wasn't aware of it—his reflection in the dark glass. "You can't turn back the clock. To where it's safe and comfortable again."

His back was still toward her, his thoughts far away. She said, "Don't put this burden on me, Inspector Rutledge. Don't ask me to make a decision for Mark Wilton."

"I already have. Just by coming here."

"*Damn you!*"

He turned, saw the flush of anger and hurt on her face.

And then, out of nowhere he had his answer, as if it had come through the night to touch him, but he knew how it had come—from his own recognition of the pain and the loss he'd sensed from the start in her.

Lettice Wood wasn't grieving for Mark Wilton. She was grieving for Charles Harris. And it was Charles Harris that she loved, who had come between her and the wedding in September, who had called off the wedding because he wanted his ward and—she wanted him.

She saw something in his expression that warned her just in the last split second. She was off the sofa in a flash, on her way out of the room, running away from him to the safety and comfort of her own apartments.

Rutledge caught her arm, swung her around, held her with a grip that was bruising, but she didn't notice, she was struggling to free herself, her dark hair flying in swirls around his face and hands.

"It's true, isn't it? *Tell me!*"

"No—no, let me go. I won't be a part of this. I've killed Charles, I've got his blood on my soul, and I won't kill Mark as well! *Let me go!*"

"You loved him—didn't you!" he demanded, shaking her.

"God help me—oh, yes, I loved him!"

"Were you ever in love with Mark?"

She stopped struggling, standing almost frozen in his hands. Then she began speaking, wearily, disjointedly, as if it took more strength than she could muster. And yet she didn't try to hide her face or those strange, remarkable eyes.

"Did I ever love him? Oh, yes—I thought I did. Charles brought him home, he believed I'd like him, love him. And I did. I told myself that what I'd felt for Charles was only a girl's crush, a silly thing you grow out of, and I'd better hurry before I'd harmed what we'd had between us since the beginning, when I was a small, frightened child—an affection that was deep and caring and wonderfully comforting."

She took a deep breath as if steadying herself. "But Tuesday—two weeks ago now—I was in the drawing room, just finishing with flowers for the vases there, and Charles came in, and I—I don't know, one of the bowls slipped somehow as I was lifting it back onto the bookshelf, and he reached for me before it could fall on me and hurt me, and the next thing I knew—I was in his arms, I was being held against his heart and I could hear it beating as wildly as mine, and he kissed me."

Her eyes closed for a moment, reliving that kiss; then they opened, and he saw emptiness in them, pain. "He stopped, swearing at himself, telling me it was nothing—*nothing*! And he was gone, just like that. I searched everywhere. I finally found him, he was having lunch at the Inn, and he took me outside into the garden where no one could overhear and he said it wasn't love. It was just that he'd been away from London too long, he'd needed a woman too long, and touching me had made him forget who I was, it was only his need speaking. But it wasn't true, it wasn't *Charles*, it was what we both felt, and I was sure of it. He wouldn't speak to me about it for days, wouldn't listen to me, stayed away from me as if I had the plague or something, and then on Saturday—I waited until he'd gone up to his room, and I came to the door and said I wasn't marrying Mark, that it wasn't fair to Mark, and that the wedding would have to be called off anyway. And he just said, 'All right,' as if I'd told him the cat had just had kittens or the rain had brought grasshoppers with it— something that didn't matter. . . . But on Sunday— on Sunday I went to his room again when he was

dressing for dinner, and he didn't hear me come in,
I caught him by surprise, standing there buttoning
his cuff links, and when he looked up—and I saw
his face—I ran. There was such—such depth of
love in his eyes as he looked up at me, I couldn't
bear it. He came after me, told me he was sorry
he'd frightened me, and then he was kissing me
again, and the room was whirling about, and I
couldn't breathe, I couldn't think—Mark had
never, ever made me feel like that, he—he was
aloof, somehow, as if his head was still in the
clouds, with his planes. As if his heart was shut off
somewhere and I couldn't touch it. But Charles
wasn't that way, and I didn't care then whether
Charles married me or not, there wouldn't be anyone else in my life. He let me go, he told me to
think clearly and carefully, not to make a quick
judgment, that there was such a difference in our
ages that I couldn't be sure, and neither could he,
what we were feeling. He talked about honor and
duty—about going away for a while—and I smiled
and said I'd not be hasty. But I knew I didn't need
to consider, and I was the happiest—the happiest
woman on earth at that moment. I didn't even
think about Mark! And I paid for it the next morning, because we had one night together, Charles
and I, and that was all. All that I'll have to take
with me as far as my grave, because it was beyond
anything I've ever known and could ever hope to
feel, whatever happens to me. . . ."

   "*I didn't go riding that morning. . . .*" Rutledge
heard those words again in the far corners of his
mind, Lettice answering his question about how
Charles had behaved on the morning after the
quarrel. She hadn't lied, she'd told him the truth,
only in a fashion that she alone knew was an eva-
sion. For she *had* seen him that morning.

"I didn't want pity. I didn't want people point-ing at me, saying I'd had a love affair with Charles and was the cause of his death. I thought there would be enough evidence—something—witnesses—that would lead you to his killer without me. When you came that first time, I thought the only happiness I'd ever have again was seeing Mark hang. And then I realized, with Sergeant Davies standing there by the door, that anything I said would be common knowledge in the village before dinner."

"And now? How do you feel about Wilton now?" Rutledge asked, breaking the silence.

Lettice shook her head. "I know he must have killed Charles. It makes sense, the way it happened. But—I still can't see Mark shooting him down in hot blood, obliterating him, wreaking such a *ter-rible* vengeance. He's not—devious by nature, not passionate or impulsive. There's an uprightness in him, a strength."

"He wouldn't have fought to keep you?"

"He'd have fought," she said quietly. "But in his own way."

20

It was after eight when Rutledge woke up the next morning, head heavy with sleeplessness that had pursued him most of the night. He'd heard the church clock chime the hours until it was six o'clock and light enough to see the birds in the trees outside his window before he'd drifted into a drowsing sleep that left him as tired as he'd been when he went to bed.

He'd stayed with Lettice an hour or more, sitting with her until she felt able to sleep. He thought it had been a relief to talk, that she'd feel better afterward. But her last words to him, as he began to close the heavy front door behind him, were, "If I had it to do over, I'd have loved him just the same. I only wish I hadn't lost my courage now, and said more than I meant to say."

"I know."

She'd cocked her head to one side, looking at him, her eyes sad. "Yes. I think you do. Don't humiliate Mark. If he's guilty, hang him if you must, but don't break him."

"I give you my word," he'd said, and Hamish

had quarreled with him all the way back to Upper
Streetham.

Rutledge had a hasty breakfast and went directly to
the Davenant house. But Grace, the maid, informed him that the Captain had already left for
Mallows, and Mrs. Davenant had gone with him as
far as the church, to see to the flowers. He came
back to town and found that there was already a
gathering of people in the lane near the church,
though it was only a little after nine. Cars and carriages were lined up, having brought guests from
Warwick and elsewhere, and small groups were
standing about talking quietly.

The church bell began to toll soon after nine-
thirty, deep, sonorous, welling out over the countryside. The hearse had already drawn up, and the
casket, oak and bronze, had been carried inside by
men from Charles's Regiment acting as pallbearers,
their uniforms red as blood in the sunlight.

Rutledge walked about, looking to see if Sally
was indeed in the church, and found her giving
instructions about the placement of wreaths in
front of the coffin. Carfield, magnificent in flowing
robes, was already greeting the mourners, moving
among them like a white dove in flocks of crows.
He went back outside.

Catherine Tarrant arrived, saw him, nodded,
and walked quickly to the church, not looking
to the right or left. The women from Upper
Streetham made a point of cutting her dead as she
passed, but several people from London spoke to
her as if they knew her.

Rutledge stopped Sergeant Davies when he
arrived and asked, "Have you seen Royston? I
need to speak to him." He wanted an invitation to

the reception, to keep an eye on Wilton. And he wanted to ask Royston about the place where Charles might have been killed.

Davies shook his head. "He was supposed to be here and greet these people. Mr. Haldane is over there, speaking to some of them. Beyond Carfield. The one with the fair hair."

Rutledge could see the tall, slim figure moving quietly from group to group. Sally Davenant came out to join Haldane just as the car arrived with Lettice Wood and Mark Wilton. She got out, swathed in veils of black silk, moving gracefully toward a half dozen officers who had turned to meet her. She spoke to them, nodding, her head high, back straight, Wilton just behind her with a quiet, thoughtful expression. Someone from the War Department came over—Rutledge recognized him from London—and then she moved on, impressively calm and leaving behind her looks of admiration and warmth.

"It's a bloody show," Hamish was saying. "We stacked our dead like lumber, or buried them to keep them from smelling. And here's a right *spectacle* that'd shame an honest soldier."

Rutledge ignored him, scanning the gathering crowd as they moved through the lych-gate and up the walk toward the open doors of the church. Overhead the bell began to count the years of the dead man's life, and he saw Lettice stumble. Wilton took her arm to steady her, and then she was herself again.

He let them go inside and walked down to where the Mallows car had been parked near the lych-gate, ready to take Lettice back in time for the reception.

"Where's Royston?" Rutledge asked the neatly

uniformed groom sitting in the driver's seat. "Has he already arrived?"

"I don't know, sir. I haven't seen him at all," the man said, touching his cap. "Mr. Johnston was looking for him just before we left."

Inspector Forrest came hurrying by on his way to the service. The tolling had stopped, and from inside the church the organ rose in solemn majesty, the lower notes carrying the sense of loss and sorrow that marked the beginning of a funeral's salute to the dead.

Rutledge called to him, "Keep an eye on Wilton. Don't let him out of your sight. It's important."

"I'll do that, sir," he promised over his shoulder, not stopping.

Uncertainty, that same sense of time passing, of tension and of waiting, swept him. He wasn't sure why. Looking up, he saw Mavers hurrying past the end of the Court, head down and shoulders humped.

Dr. Warren's car, turning in to the Court, moved quickly to a space in front of one of the houses across from the lych-gate. Warren got out, saying to Rutledge as he passed, "Hickam's the same— neither better nor worse, but holding on and eating a little. Why aren't you in the church?"

"I don't know," Rutledge answered, but Warren had gone on, not hearing.

On impulse, Rutledge walked around the church, trying to see if Mavers had taken the path up to his house in the fields. But the man had vanished. He kept on walking, climbed over the churchyard wall, and struck out into the fields. But by the time he'd reached the crossbar of the H that led to the other path—the one that skirted Charles Harris's fields and Mallows land—he turned that way instead, his

back to Mavers's house. Soon he came to the hedge,
and the meadow and the copse of trees where the
body had been found. It had seemed very different
last night in the dark. Somehow thicker, more sinis-
ter, full of ominous shadows. Now—it was a copse,
open and sunlit, shafts of light like spears lancing
down through the trees. Butterflies danced in the
meadow.

Rutledge moved on. Dozens of feet and two
rainstorms had swept the land clean of any signs
that might have led him to the answer he needed.
Where had Charles Harris died? Where was the
blood, the small fragments of bone?

The sun was warm, the air quiet and still. Some
quirk of the land brought the sound of singing to
him from the church, a hymn he remembered from
childhood. "A Mighty Fortress." Appropriate to a
soldier's death.

Hamish, who had been quiet, tense, and watchful in his mind, like something waiting to pounce
in the vast, secretive recesses of emotion, said suddenly, "I don't like it. I've been on patrol on nights
when the Huns were filtering like smoke out of the
trenches, and my skin crawled with fear."

"It isn't night," Rutledge said aloud. The sound
of his voice was no comfort, only intensifying his
sense of something wrong.

He moved from field to field. It hadn't taken
long, not more than twenty minutes since he'd left
the churchyard. Unconsciously he'd lengthened his
stride early on, and now he was sweating with the
effort. But he couldn't slow down, it was almost
as if something drove him. The saplings were not
far now.

But what was it? What was behind this dreadful
sense of urgency?

From the start he'd been afraid he'd lost any

skills he'd once had. He'd tried to listen—too hard perhaps—for any signs that they'd survived. And found only emptiness. And yet—last night he'd come close to feeling the intuition that had once been his gift. He'd followed his instincts, not the dictates of others. They'd been certain Harris had died where he'd fallen. They'd been certain that no one in the village could have killed the Colonel. They'd been certain there was no case against Wilton, and he'd found one.

He had his murderer. Didn't he? Then why didn't he feel the satisfaction that ordinarily came with the solution of a vicious crime? Because his evidence was circumstantial, not solid? Or because there was still something he'd overlooked, something that he'd have *seen*, five years ago. Something that—but for his own emotional tensions—he'd have thought of long before this?

He went through the stand of saplings without being aware of them, his feet guiding him without conscious volition.

Something was missing. Or someone? Yes, that was it! He'd spoken to everyone of consequence in his interviews—except one.

He'd never asked *Maggie Sommers* what she'd seen or heard that last morning of Charles Harris's life. He'd assumed she knew nothing. And yet she lived across a stone wall from Mallows land, and Colonel Harris sometimes rode that way—she'd learned to return his wave, shy as she was.

Had Harris passed the cottage that last morning? *Had Maggie seen anyone else!*

Rutledge swore. Impatient with her timidity, he'd treated her—as everyone else did!—as all but witless.

He was in the fields now, heavy with the scent of raw earth and sunlight.

What did she know that no one had thought to ask? She would be the last person to come forward voluntarily. That would have been unbearable agony for her. And yet—now that he was sure the murder had happened somewhere other than the meadow—her evidence could easily be critical. It could damn Wilton to the hangman—or free him, for that matter.

Maggie, he realized, could very well hold the key to this murder, and he'd overlooked it. He glanced toward the distant stone wall, seeing it with new eyes. Maggie, hanging clothes on the line on Monday mornings. Maggie working in her over-grown garden. Maggie, always at home and close enough to Mallows here to hear a horseman in the fields. Or a shotgun going off nearby. Maggie seeing the murderer, for all he knew, waiting among the trees or in the dell or coming over the rise. Maggie, anxious and afraid of strangers, watchful and wary, so that she could hide herself inside the cottage before she herself was seen. And a lurking killer, unaware of a witness he'd never even glimpsed.

And this was the time to speak to her, while Helena was at the funeral. He doubled his pace, as if afraid, now that he'd remembered her, that she might be gone before he got there. Cursing himself for his blindness, for seeing with his eyes and not with that intuitive grasp of people he'd always had.

Ahead he could hear something, unidentifiable at first, a loud, insistent, repetitive—

It was the goose at the Sommers cottage. Something had upset the bird, he could tell from the wild sound, rising and falling without so much as a breath in between.

Rutledge broke into a run, ignoring the neat rows of young crops under his feet, stumbling in the soft earth, keeping his balance with an effort of will, his eyes on the rose-draped wall that separated Mallows from Haldane land and the Sommers cottage.

Helena was coming into town for the services. Maggie was alone—

He could hear screams now, high and wordless, and a man's bellow of pain. He was no longer running, he was covering the ground with great leaps, risking his neck he knew, but unable to think of that as the screams reached a crescendo of something beyond pain.

Reaching the wall, he rested his palms on the edge of it, swung his body over in one movement, paying no heed to the long thorn-laced roses that pulled at his clothes. His feet landed among Maggie's pathetic little flowers on the far side of the wall, trampling them heedlessly.

There was a motorcar in the drive, down by the gate. It was empty, and he ignored it, springing for the cottage.

Seeing him coming, the goose wheeled from her stand near the cottage door and sailed toward him, wings out, neck low, prepared for the attack.

He brushed her roughly aside, and was ten yards from the door when it burst open and a man came reeling out, his face a mask of blood, his shirt torn and soaked to crimson, his trousers slashed and smeared.

It was Royston. Something had laid open his shoulder—Rutledge could see the blue-white sheen of bone there—and he plunged heavily off the steps and into the grass, hardly aware of Rutledge sliding to a halt almost in his path.

Regardless of the pain he was inflicting, Rutledge caught him by his good shoulder and swung him around, anger twisting his face into a grimace as he shouted, "*Damn you!* What have you—"

Inside, the screaming went on.

"Watch her!" Royston cried. "She's got—got an ax—" His knees buckled. "The child—the child—"

Rutledge managed to break his fall, but Royston was losing blood rapidly, his words weaker with every breath. "The child—I killed—"

Without waiting for any more, Rutledge was through the door, eyes seeing nothing after the glare of the sun, but ahead of him was *something*, a figure barely glimpsed. A woman in black, huddled on the floor at the end of the brown sofa, two darknesses blending into one like some distorted parody of humanity, humped and ugly. A primeval dread lifted the hairs along his arms.

Reaching her, he grasped her shoulders, saying, "Are you all right? Has he hurt you? *What has he done to you?*"

She stared up at him, face chalk white, eyes large and wild. In one bloody hand was an ax. His own eyes were adjusting rapidly now. The room was empty except for Maggie and the assorted furnishings of a rented house.

He got her up on the sofa, and she leaned back, eyes closed. "Is he dead?" she asked breathlessly, in the voice of a terrified child.

"No—I don't think so."

She tried to get up, but he pressed her back against the sofa, holding her there, trying to determine how much of the blood was hers, how much Royston's.

"I'll have to get help—I'll find Helena and bring her to you—she's at the church—"

But Maggie was shaking her head, dazed but at least able to understand him. Her eyes turned toward the closed door at the far end of the room. "She's in there," Maggie whispered.

Rutledge felt his blood run cold.

"I'll go—"

"No—leave her! I hope she's dead!"

He mistook her meaning, thinking that she was saying that death was preferable to the cataclysm of rape.

"I saw her kill him," she went on, not taking her eyes from the bedroom door. "I *saw* her! She shot Colonel Harris. And it was for nothing, it wasn't the right man—she'd *thought* it was, but Mavers said—and then that man out there admitted it was true, that he'd killed the child."

"What child?" he asked, thinking only of Lizzie.

"Why, little Helena, of course. Mr. Royston ran over her in his car—in Colonel Harris's car. And the check he sent was in the Colonel's name. So we thought—all these years we thought—but it wasn't the *Colonel*. Helena got it all *wrong*." There was a sudden spark of triumph in her eyes, as if it gave her some obscure pleasure to think that Helena had been wrong. "Aunt Mary and Uncle Martin always said she was better than I was, so pretty, so smart, so fearless—they said they wished the car had killed *me*, not Helena. I was only adopted, you see, I wasn't *theirs*—" There was a lifetime of suffering in her words, a lifelong misery because the wrong child had died in an accident and she had been blamed for living. "They asked for all that money, and it wasn't enough to satisfy them, they wanted her back again. But she was dead. And I was alive."

He wasn't interested in Maggie's childhood; he had a man bleeding to death on his hands, and God knew what behind that closed, silent bedroom door.

"So when Helena discovered that the Colonel lived here, just across the wall—that he was our neighbor—"

Getting up from his knees, his breathing still erratic and harsh, he ignored Maggie and started across the room to the bedroom, forcing himself to face what had to be faced. Hamish had been babbling for the last five minutes, a counterpoint to Maggie's slow, painful confession, but Rutledge shut him out, shut out everything but the long, bright streak of blood down the door panel, on the handle of the knob—

Somehow Maggie was there before him. "No! Leave her alone, I tell you! I won't let you go near her—let her *die*!" And with such swiftness that he couldn't have stopped her if his own life had depended upon it, she was through the door and into the room, turning the key in the lock behind her.

"Maggie!" he shouted, pounding on the door, but he could hear only her sobbing. She'd taken the ax with her. There was nothing to do but try to break the door down with his shoulder or kick it down.

It took him three tries. When it finally swung wide on broken hinges, he was into the room before he could regain his balance.

There was only one bed, narrow, neatly made, now covered in blood. And only Maggie, collapsed across the pretty lemon-colored counterpane like a heap of rags, stained and worn. The ax was on the floor at her feet. He turned wildly, surveying the small room, finding no one else, the window closed, the closet empty. Then he was beside the woman on the bed, leaning over her, lifting her gently. Black lifeblood welled beneath her, thick and pungent. The heavy, ivory-handled knife had plunged too deep. There was nothing he could do.

Her eyes were not able to see him. But she was still alive. Just.

"I had to do it," she said. "I couldn't stand it anymore. *She* knew that. She always knew things before I ever did. But for once she was wrong—

about the Colonel. She'll go to hell, won't she, for killing him? And I'll go to heaven with the angels, won't I? We couldn't *share* anymore. Not with that on her conscience."

"Where did she kill him?" Rutledge asked.

"By the wall. When he came to speak to Maggie. She had the shotgun hidden there, among the roses, where he couldn't see it. And she tried to ask him if he'd been the one driving the car that killed Helena. But he wouldn't listen, he told her not to be a fool, that she was upset and not thinking clearly. So she shot him—she lifted the gun and shot him and his head flew everywhere, and the horse bolted before he'd stopped bleeding, and it was the most *awful* . . ."

Her voice faded. He could see the blood trickling out of her mouth. The way the body lay, graceless and heavy. It would only be a matter of minutes. There was nothing he could do to stop the bleeding, nothing anyone could do to put the torn flesh back together. But he sat there beside her until her eyes told him she was dead. Then he got to his feet and began to search the cottage.

He found the shotgun in a closet. And signs of one breakfast on the table. And only one bedroom occupied, the other with the mattress still rolled up and wrapped in a sheet. Two trunks holding clothes. He went through each cupboard and closet, looked under anything that might hide a body. But there was no one.

He wasn't surprised.

Taking a sheet with him, he hurried out to bind up Royston's bloody shoulder. The goose, smelling the blood, had backed off behind the car in the drive. Royston's car. He'd come to take Helena to church. . . .

Royston was very weak, but alive. Rutledge,

with some experience in war wounds, did what he could to stop the bleeding, and then called his name, trying to rouse him.

Royston opened his eyes, stared at Rutledge with a frown, then groaned with the mounting pain. "In there," he managed hoarsely.

"It's over," Rutledge said curtly.

"I got here a little early. I was talking to Maggie, and she began to ask me about the—accident. All those years ago. Mavers had said something, Helena had told her about it, she said. Then she went into the bedroom to fetch Helena. And Helena came out with the ax. I didn't—there was nothing I could do. If you hadn't come—"

"Stop talking."

"You can't leave Maggie here! Not with that madwoman!"

"Maggie's dead."

"*Gentle God!*"

"And Helena died with her."

"*What?* She killed her cousin?"

"You killed Helena. In Colonel Harris's car. When you were twenty. You told me so yourself."

"I don't understand—"

"There never was a Helena. Only—Maggie, and years of being told that Helena was better and brighter and stronger than she was—until she believed it. And tried to be Helena herself. And couldn't. But somehow she created Helena inside herself." He shivered, thinking of Hamish, wondering if one day in the future, he'd create the man's image in his own flesh and be a divided soul, like Maggie Sommers. "And it was—Helena—who shot Charles Harris."

He got Royston to his feet and somehow to the car. Then he was driving as fast as he could toward

Upper Streetham, watching the man's face, watching the rough breathing.

Someone fetched the doctor from the church, and then Warren threw them all out of his surgery as he worked over Laurence Royston. All except Rutledge, who stood in the doorway watching the gentle, swift hands moving across the savage wounds of the ax. "I don't know how this happened," Warren said over his shoulder. "It will be touch and go, if he lives. But he's got a strong constitution. I think we can save him. I won't give up without a fight—"

The front door opened and Rutledge could hear Wilton's voice, and then Forrest's.

He went out to speak to them, leaving Warren to his work.

Later, he called London. Bowles growled at him, wanting to know what he'd done about Wilton.

"Nothing. He's in the clear. I've found the murderer. She's dead—"

"What do you mean? *She? * What *she?*"

So Rutledge told him. Bowles listened, grunting from time to time. At the end of it, he said, "I don't understand any of this business—"

"I know. But the poor woman lived in such wretchedness that I can't blame her for trying to bring Helena back to life. You'll have to check with the police in Dorset, see what's known about Maggie. It's going to be routine, I think. I don't expect any surprises."

"How can two women live in one *body?*"

Rutledge was silent. How could he explain? Without betraying himself? And oddly enough, he'd liked Helena. . . . Someday, would other

people like Hamish better than Ian Rutledge? It
was a frightening thought. The doctor had told him
he wasn't mad to hear Hamish—because he, Rutledge, knew that Hamish didn't exist. But Maggie
was different. She'd wanted Helena to exist. Not
out of madness but out of a bleak and lonely need
to satisfy two vicious, selfish adults, trying to *become* the daughter they'd lost and mourned, a desperate bid for love by a shy, bewildered child . . .
until she'd made Helena live again. And one day,
coming across Charles Harris in a town far from
home, suddenly Helena wanted vengeance. Maggie
lost control—was in danger of losing herself—and
when Helena attacked Laurence Royston, Maggie
had somehow found the strength to stop it. Once
and for all.

Bowles was saying, "—and I don't really care.
What matters is that I've got the Palace off my back
now. We can close the case, sweep it all under the
rug, clear the Captain's good name—and we're all
back where we started from."

Except for Colonel Harris, Rutledge thought.

And Maggie Sommers . . .

. . . and Lettice.

He felt waves of black depression settling over him,
swamping him.

No! he told himself fiercely.

No, I won't give into it. I'll fight. And by God,
somehow I'll survive! I solved this murder. The
skills are there, I've *touched* them—and I will use
them again! Whatever else I've lost, this one triumph is mine.

"Ye'll no' triumph over me!" Hamish said. "I'm
a scar on your bluidy soul."

"That may be," Rutledge told him harshly. "But

I'll find out before it's finished what we're both made of!"

Afterward, staring at the telephone, Bowles swore savagely. Somehow, against all expectation, Rutledge had pulled it off.

Scotland Yard would be overjoyed with the results, they'd bring the man home as a *hero*, and he, Bowles, would be left to bask in reflected glory once more. That nonsense about the dead woman—she'd probably committed suicide and Rutledge had been smart enough to see his chance. To put the blame on her, not Wilton. And no one in the Yard would dare to question it. Not when so many reputations had been saved . . .

Well. There's always a next time. Beginner's luck, that's what it was. And next time, no convenient scapegoat would spoil the game. . . .

About the Author

CHARLES TODD lives in Greenville, Delaware. He has traveled extensively in England and knows the country well. *A Test of Wills* is the first in a projected series featuring Inspector Ian Rutledge.